from **WHEN M** ... ...

"Lucia," Jack said, his voice reflecting none of the things she had seen for an instant in his eyes. "What are you doing here?"

She lowered the lantern and stepped closer. He took a step back, as if in fear, then caught himself and straightened, looking her square in the eye and raising one black eyebrow. She fought the shiver of awareness his too familiar expression brought her. She might be dead, but she wasn't that dead. She wanted him still, despite everything.

Her gaze skittered over, then away from, a nearby gravestone. She wasn't ready to look at the name on that stone. Not yet. Perhaps not ever. But she had not come here for that. She had come here for Jack.

Lucia pulled the cloak tighter about her neck, the October dawn as chill as her blood. "We have one day to view the wrongs of a lifetime. If you do not wish to carry this cursed lantern about for eternity, we had best be on our way." She placed the lantern at Jack's feet. "Here you will find it waiting for you when midnight comes. If the lantern's light glows, you will live again. If the flame has died, so have you."

Other *Love Spell* and *Leisure* Anthologies:

TRICK OR TREAT

Lark Eden, Lori Handeland, Stobie Piel, Lynda Trent

LOVE SPELL BOOKS  NEW YORK CITY

LOVE SPELL®

October 1997

Published by

Dorchester Publishing Co., Inc.
276 Fifth Avenue
New York, NY 10001

ISBN 0-505-52220-9

Loving Spirits
Lark Eden

For my ever-patient John. Every word for you, Sandie.

*Soul to soul, spirit to spirit—for my Ashanti prince Derek.
Your Osun, Lark.*

Chapter One

"Green, get in here." His editor's voice squawked out through the speaker phone just as Cameron Green was pulling up his story on the latest fortune-telling scheme in the Bronx.

Cameron smiled grimly at the glowing green computer screen. He had put several weeks into this story, and it was satisfying to see the facts match like pieces of a jigsaw puzzle.

"Cameron!"

"Coming." He straightened his silk tie and shrugged into the suit coat he had hung on the back of his chair. He checked for his tiny tape recorder with a practiced pat over his breast pocket. Clipping his silver pen in the pocket of his starched button-down shirt, he turned out of his cubicle and strode down the office corridor.

"Good morning, Julie."

The editor-in-chief of the *Daily Express* pushed her glasses up on her forehead and frowned. "No, Cam, it is not a good morning." Julia Francis Jones sent a frosty gray-eyed glare directly into Cam's heart. "Sit. I told you to go on vacation. Why are you here?"

"Well, I had the fortune-telling scam story working and . . ."

"Garcia could have picked up on that."

Cam leapt out of his chair. "No, he couldn't. It's my story and I'm the one who has to finish it."

Julie held out her hands palms up. "Cam, this is just an example of what I am talking about. Your temper's shot. You have been bordering on the edge of obsession since your father passed on. You have got to back away for awhile and regain your objectivity."

"Objectivity? I'm the best writer you have on staff. I'm as objective as they come, and darn good too. I have that other thing, that Santeria priest business, almost wrapped. And the psychic-network exposé. I can't leave now. There's no one else my sources will trust."

"I see." Julie tapped her pencil on her desk, giving Cam time to regain his composure. "Let's just review this conversation." An increasingly uncomfortable pause stretched out between them.

"As I see it, you have appointed yourself a watchdog for the paranormal. This is not 'The X Files,' Cam. As of now you are off anything you are working on at your desk. You can select who you want to wrap it for you." She snapped the pencil on the desk like a shot, punctuating the tense atmosphere in the office.

"I am sending you—assigning you—ordering you, whatever you want to call it, to go to New Orleans. You will remain there until you are able to produce impartial

8

work again, or until one month, your accrued vacation, passes. Whichever comes first. And then we'll discuss your areas of coverage again.''

Cam started to sputter.

"No. Not a word. You will go and you will enjoy yourself. Now, because I know you won't enjoy yourself unless you are ferreting around for something obscure, I will give you an assignment.''

Cam relaxed somewhat. An assignment . . . well, that was different.

"I want a story about the true meaning of Halloween.''

A horrified expression crept across Cam's face. "The true meaning of Halloween? You mean, like, the true meaning of Christmas? Julie, please, that's demeaning. One of the interns can do that out of the research room.''

"No, one of the interns will not do this from the research banks. You, Cameron J. Green, will go to New Orleans, and a—relax, and b—produce an insightful story in your inimitable style as to what Halloween means in a city full of believers. You think you are the expert on the paranormal; let's see what you can do with this. Remember: impartial and objective.''

She shoved a folder across the desk at him. "Here're two tickets. Take whoever you want. Relax. You're booked into the Marie St. Comte Hotel, in the French Quarter. Keep your receipts, and do the usual expense thing.

"You've been trying to find the false bottom in the magician's hat for quite awhile now. Finish it.''

Cam picked up the folder slowly. "My inimitable style, eh? Guess I can't turn this down either, can I? You're the boss, Julie.''

"Yes. I am the boss." She smiled, just a bit. "And you are one of my best writers. Don't force me to make this a permanent separation."

Even though Cam walked as carefully as possible, his leather shoe soles squeaked on the vinyl hall floor. He tucked the bouquet of flowers under his arm and frowned at the door numbers.

A man with a World War II army jacket draped over his pajamas clopped by, leaning heavily on an aluminium walker. The veteran stopped and peered at the tall reporter with a nearsighted squint. "Looking for your mom?" His voice was an emphysemic gasp.

"Yes—Mrs. Green. Is she in her room?"

The man coughed and pulled in a trembling breath. "Wouldn't happen to have a ciggie, would ya, son?" He patted the pocket of his pajamas. "I guess I left mine in the room."

"No, sir. I don't smoke."

Disappointed in the failure of his ruse, the old man snorted. "Humph. Well, I reckon she's down there in the bingo room. Always got some kinda visitor disturbin' everybody." He turned abruptly and continued his progress down the passageway.

Cam hated this building. The Sunny Acres Retirement Home smelled like cheap disinfectant and stale clothes and hopeless medicine. Even the sparse plastic plants looked discouraged. There was nothing homelike about it to Cam, nothing like the sunny, music-filled house where he had grown up. But his tiny, elegant mother had chosen this dismal place to live after his father died.

She could have afforded much better, but she hoarded her money to bestow on every crackpot who came to the door. She wanted to speak to her husband, Cameron's dead father. And New York was full of people perfectly willing to make the connection, for a fee.

When Hamilton John Green died, it was as if the spark that had illuminated his mother had gone out. At first she grieved to the point of sickness but then emerged from the mourning with a single-minded determination to contact the light of her life, her love, her husband.

Seeing his mother bilked made Cam doggedly resolve to expose these charlatans to the light of day. He saw them all as vultures who preyed on the innocents who believed, as one by one they stole her money and broke her heart. There was no magic. There was no spirit world, waiting to be contacted, yearning to contact those who wait on the shore of this material life. Just mere mortals, with hands out to snatch any penny from the gullible and grieving.

Mrs. Evelyn Anne Green sat near one of the smudged windows in the common room. Another silver-haired woman leaned close, whispering into his mother's ear, holding her hand tightly and patting it now and then. Cam saw his mother nod and slip an envelope from her pocket and press it into the woman's hand. Another vulture. A little more of his mother's money thrown away.

"Mom." Cam knelt at his mother's side and put his arm carefully around her frail shoulders. "How are you today?"

"Cameron, dear. I'm wonderful, just wonderful." She gestured toward her visitor and smiled brightly. "Madame Wopenski is a talented medium. She thinks she can contact your father."

Madame Wopenski's dark eyes looked like little raisins sunk into a round cookie face. "And this is your

11

son?'' The medium extended her puffy hand regally.

"I'd like to speak to my mother alone." Cam did not seize the offered hand. The woman pulled it back slowly and pressed it against her ample bosom.

"I knew that," she said with theatrical dignity. "As I said, Evelyn, I will be back Wednesday afternoon and we will discuss this matter again. Good-bye, sir." She rose and turned away, making an aggrieved exit.

"Mom, these are for you." Cameron laid the sheaf of pink gladiolus on her lap. The vivid spears were her favorite flower, once springing in great profusion around their comfortable suburban house.

Mrs. Green raised the flowers to her face and beamed at Cam through the blossoms. "My son, so important. The writer." His mother patted his cheek proudly, the way she had done when he had brought home an *A* from grade school.

"Not a writer, Mom. A reporter."

"A reporter, a writer. Words on paper. Like Hemingway. But you write true stuff, not made up."

"I have to leave town on an assignment, so I won't be by for a week or two."

"Where are you going? Paris? Oh, God forbid, Bosnia?" Her faded eyes lit in alarm. "Take a coat, take food. Don't fly; the planes, dropping out of the sky like rocks. It's the walking on the moon that does it, you know." She sighed. "Nothing's been the same since they did that."

"No, I'm going to New Orleans. Just to Louisiana."

"Louisiana." She considered. "Take your coat anyway." She pulled at his collar and frowned slightly. "It's damp.

"New Orleans—I read something about New Orleans. . . .Yes, that's it." Mrs. Green ruffled the pile of tabloids stacked beside her chair. "There are people there who can talk to the spirits."

She sat up straighter and clapped her hands. "You can do this for me, Cameron! Find someone for me!"

Cam groaned inwardly. "Mom, I can't do that. You know it can't be done. You can't talk to dead people."

"Of course you can. People do it all the time. I read about it right here." She tapped the stack of *Star*s and *National Enquirer*s. "It's in *print*. It has to be true.

"Besides, if someone can talk to that miserable Elvis Pretzel, they certainly could find a fine person like your father."

She touched his face and stroked his lapels. "Cameron, take me with you. This could be my chance. I can feel it." Cam could feel the trembling tension in her touch. "This trip . . . it's a sign. Please, son."

"Mother, that's not a good idea. I'm going to pay your rent before I leave. Don't worry about anything. I'll call you." Cam started to rise.

"Cameron, take me. Take me. This could be what I'm looking for." She clutched at his hands, the flowers spilling from her lap. "Please, I just want to talk to your father, just this one last time. Please, son."

He covered his mother's hands with his own. How could he refuse his mother? And after all, his assignment did have a connection. Perhaps this would pull her once bright mind back into the present. "All right, Mother." He swept her into his arms for a hug. "Be ready. I'll pick you up at seven tomorrow morning."

A day's worth of sullen storm clouds hung over the New Orleans International Airport. The humidity of early October Louisiana clung to Cam like a soggy, wet wool glove. As much as he hated to, he pulled off his jacket and draped the tweed garment tidily over one arm.

Sweat began to prickle along his spine. Cam and his mother stood at the curbside pickup, two black leather carry-on bags at their feet. A muddy yellow taxi slid to a stop at the curb.

"Taxi, folks?"

Cam yanked open the door and threw in the luggage, then turned to help his mother into the automobile. "The Marie St. Comte Hotel. Address is 935 . . ."

"Rue de Arlette." The driver finished the address from memory as he pulled away from the curb. "Yeah, I know where that is." He swerved to avoid a green-and-white hotel shuttle van. "In the Quarter. I know where everything is down there." The frigid air conditioning in the cab made Cam's sweaty shirt stick to his body like a clammy bathing suit. There seemed to be no intermediate temperature in this place. His mother calmly pulled a sweater from her large handbag and draped it over her shoulders.

The driver's identification card named him Erzulie James Smith, age fifty-two, eyes brown, hair black. Cam registered the hair as mostly gray, but the ID picture behind the yellowed plastic showed a younger Mr. Smith.

"Be staying long?"

"Maybe a week." Surely he could get this wrapped up, wiggle back into Julie's good graces, and have his mother satisfied by then. He needed to be working, not down here in some tropical tourist trap.

"Well, that's a shame. Just a shame." The driver slipped into a faster traffic stream. "Can't see much of

N'awlins in just a week. The food, well now, that's a life's work itself.'' Mr. E. J. Smith chuckled and flashed a glance in the mirror at his passengers. When he said "New Orleans," it was like one slurred word, as if he had a delicious bite of hot, spicy food in his mouth—*N'awlins.* "Ya'll haven't been down here before, have you?''

Was this that damned Southern hospitality everyone nattered about? Talk, talk, talk. "No.''

"Lord, yes, the food . . . you gotta try Café Royal there on Royal Street. Sit on the balcony and watch the world go by. And then there's the Court of Two Sisters. That'd be for late breakfast. The Café du Monde. Best coffee in the world. In the *world.''* Erzulie James Smith made a smooth lane change. "Make your eyes roll plumb back in your head, that coffee.

"Is this pretty lady your mother? Show her the shops down there, and the Garden District.''

The gray-haired man tuned the radio to a soft jazz station. "Yeah, and music. There's the music.'' His thick fingers pressed the steering wheel in syncopation to the lively brass line of melody. "You like jazz, mister?''

"I'm here on business.''

"I see.'' The driver's soft brown eyes looked sad. No time for music, and good food? they seemed to say. "That's a shame.''

"I'll need to take some tours. Can I get a tour, a guide?''

"A guide? What you want to see?''

"Voodoo stuff, witchcraft, you know.'' Cam drummed on his briefcase, then stopped as he realized he was following the beat coming from the radio. He noticed his mother's attention was focused on the driver.

Smith chuckled. "There's voodoo, and then there's voodoo round here, mister." He reached up and tapped a little cloth doll hanging from his rearview mirror. It was covered with tiny shells and shiny charms. "Certain days, there's dancing and what-all down in Congo Square. Get some good pictures."

"I want the real deal, not tourist stuff."

Smith frowned. "Real stuff? Why would you think there would still be the real thing? Working the mojo, putting on the hoo-doo, that's from the old days."

"New Orleans is an old city, isn't it?"

The driver flicked his turn signal and pulled on to Canal Street. "You got that right. N'awlins is about as old as they come. Nothing here new, nothing here old, you know what I mean? Anything you want, you can find down here."

"The eve of All Saint's is at the end of the month. Halloween."

The coffee brown eyes of the driver caught Cam's glance in the mirror. "Umm hmm. All Saint's Eve 'round here can be pretty special, pretty special, if you know the right people."

"That's what I need to know. The right people."

Cam's mother leaned forward, her hand on the seat back in front of her. "This is very important to us, Mr. Smith."

Erzulie James Smith made another right turn, and then a sharp left down a narrow street. The brick paving was heavily shadowed by the lacy iron balconies that stood away from every window. The driver slowed and stopped in front of an elegant, marble-fronted hotel.

Smith turned to look at Cam and his mother, and

rested his brown arm along the seat back. "If you are serious about Halloween, you need to go down to Saint Rita Street and see Miss Willa." He shook his head slowly.

"Yeah, Miss Willa Robinette, she can help you. She can take you 'round the graveyard, show you things. Her people lived down there for years and years. My momma knew her granma. Yeah, man, and all them Robinette women, they got the Gift."

Smith got out of his taxi and opened the rear door. "You tell her E. J. sent you. She can help you."

Cam shoved a handful of bills into the driver's hand. "Thanks. I'll keep that in mind. Robinette on Saint Rita Street. Is that far from here?"

"Mister, you're in the Quarter. Ain't nothing too far from anything, and I guar'ntee you'll enjoy the trip." Erzulie James Smith flashed a smile that lit up the cloudy late afternoon. "Ya'll have a good day, now."

The taxi swung away from the curb, and Cam could hear golden trumpet music trailing away from the cab like the jaunty swing of a tomcat's tail.

Cam glanced at his wristwatch as he stepped under the striped awning that shaded the hotel entrance. If he checked in quickly, and got his mother settled, he would have time to find Saint Rita Street and the woman with the Gift.

Chapter Two

Condemned.

Fluorescent orange letters screamed at Willa Robinette. *This property condemned.* She ripped the sign from her door and tore it in two. The young resident and proprietor of La Empire Celestique shoved the torn paper into her pocket.

"That weasel!" He did this on purpose. Ernest Sanderham. *Nothing too low for a scorned lover. Can't handle the heat, so you want to burn down the kitchen. You weren't man enough to accept me the way I am, so you have to pull in the City Building Inspector, the Rat Patrol, for revenge.* "It'll be a cold day in Hell before I trust another outsider with what I believe." Willa addressed the fat calico cat sniffing the raindrops on the doorstep. The cat sneezed in agreement and licked its nose.

A rectangular wooden sign creaked overhead as it

swung in the rising wind. LA EMPIRE CELESTIQUE. EST.
1796. LA FAMILE DU ROBINETTE was carved there, the
letters spangled with tarnished gilt. On the rain-spattered
glass of the single window a similar sign was printed,
with an additional line in English, SPIRITUAL SUPPLIES.

A thin woman wearing a maid's uniform hurried past,
clutching a full grocery bag and a plastic umbrella.
"Evening, Willa." She greeted the pensive young
woman but didn't stop to chat.

Willa waved and sighed, then turned back into her
doorway. Slowly, she climbed the stairs to her apartment
above the shop.

Cranston skittered up the steps, threading herself between Willa's feet.

Money, money, where would it come from? She had
already tentatively approached the family bank for an
improvement loan but had been refused by the new man-
agement. The building itself was the only collateral she
had. Getting another job would mean closing the shop,
which was why she needed the money in the first place:
to keep the shop open. It was a vicious circle.

October was almost gone and business was slow; just
a few of the regular faithful customers trickled in. Willa
unfolded the condemnation notice from the city; couldn't
ignore that. But could and would forget about Ernest.
What next!

Get the roof, plumbing and wiring updated or else.
"Or else" had a big price tag. She looked at the little
altar near her bed. It would definitely take divine inter-
vention to get her out of this dilemma. Three green ta-
pers burned in rings of fall flowers, steady golden points
of light carrying her prayers, but no monetary help was
in sight. She laid the torn notice on the altar along with

her prayer for help in saving her family home and business. The condemnation meant more than losing just a building; it meant the loss of her family.

The rain had progressed from dribbles to a steady downpour. The purling sound on the cracked slate roof was soothing, almost drowning out the *plink-plunk* of the leaks filling the containers in the attic.

Perhaps this would be the break in the weather that started the coming of fall. There would be a change in the light, and somehow, even though the temperature had not changed, it would be autumn. Bunches of yellow and purple chrysanthemums would appear in tin buckets down in the French Market, and piles of rotund orange pumpkins and dusty striped gourds would ramble across the pavement.

October was always a testy month in Louisiana, hanging at the ragged edge of the brilliant, heat-sodden summer. The end of the month signaled the passage to the dark side of the year, rest and renewal.

Thunder muttered and the electricity flickered and dimmed. There would be little business this evening; it would be a good time to construct a spell. Willa sat at her desk, deep in thought. She needed help from a higher power. She would put her prayers and offerings out to the Universe and wait for the answers.

The young woman leaned her chin on her hand and ruffled the stack of bills, delaying. Her hand brushed her favorite Tarot deck and the rectangles of cardboard slid out of the desk cubbyhole. The painted cards fanned over the letters and bills.

The chubby cat leapt onto the desktop and scattered the mail further. Cranston pawed playfully over the envelopes and cards, shuffling the paper as if looking for her own message. She picked one card out of the mess and shook it in her fangs like a mouse she had just caught.

"Let me have that, Crannie." Willa took the card from the cat's grasp. Losing interest in the paper, Cranston stepped down into Willa's lap and curled up for a nap, paws over nose.

It was the Tower card. Naturally. Every good witch knew it was the worst card in the deck. A crumbling castle—her shop?—people leaping from the flames of invaders to escape the destruction—herself, her family? But this card could also mean the darkest moment before the dawn, the end of a cycle, transformation after death. "Could it get any worse?" she said to the dozing cat.

Willa flinched, startled as a drop of cold water hit her on the top of her head. The attic leaks needed immediate attention. Before she tackled the spell, she'd have to run up to the attic and empty the buckets. She moved a teacup over to catch any more drops before they hit her desktop.

The stairway to the dark attic was a narrow, almost vertical climb. Even for someone as slender as Willa, it was a tight fit. Cranston followed her. She loved the attic. It was usually good for a plump mousie snack or two.

A long, long time ago a servant girl had lived up here. "What a dreary life that must have been," Willa addressed her feline companion and brushed down a damp cobweb. Two glass-paned French doors let a little light into the gloomy space. Willa pulled up on the corroded doorknob, attempting to free the swollen wood. The wood frame was permanently warped from the humidity, but the hinges swung out with a creak.

Willa dragged the first bucket out through the door

21

and emptied the water over the balcony rail. In this rain there would be no passersby, and in the deluge another gush was hardly noticeable. She replaced the empty bucket and the drops began a heavy, rapid *tunk-tunk* into the five-gallon container. It wouldn't take long to be full again.

Willa swung the second bucket over the rail and emptied the contents with a flourish. This time there was a shout from below.

"Hey! Look out!"

Willa leaned out over the iron rail into the rain drops. Cranston hurried over and placed her paws on the edge to look, too. There was a very wet, very angry man standing at the door of the shop, sputtering up at them.

"Oh, dear!" Willa dropped the bucket and covered her mouth with her hands, then grasped the balcony rail. "Please, I'll be right down." She whirled, slammed shut the French doors and hurried down the attic stairway. As she ran past her desk, the breeze of her passing caused the mail to spill to the floor. From the corner of her eye, she caught sight of the Tower card tumbling to rest face up on the pile of scattered papers. Snatching up a clean towel from the stack near the bath door, she bounded down the stairs two at a time.

Willa ran to the shopfront. "I am so sorry. Please come in." She offered her bath towel. "Here, dry off."

A tall man filled her doorway, fashionable Brooks Brothers raincoat dripping puddles onto the stone floor. His dark hair was plastered to his head. He scrubbed his face and hair with the dry towel and looked accusingly at Willa.

"Some way to get customers." He draped the towel around his neck.

Willa rubbed her hands together. "I'm really sorry. I wasn't expecting anyone to be out in this weather." His broad frame blocked the little light that could squeeze in from the outside. Willa fumbled in the nearby drawer and brought out a packet of matches. She grabbed a red candle from the shelf.

Tall, broad, wet; a jangle of first impressions danced over her senses. There was the elusive pine aroma of a man's cologne. An instant hit of male pheromone rocketed straight to the primitive part of her brain. Something deep inside her body uncoiled a bit, stretched languidly and woke, as if looking for the light.

The devilish exhalation of sulfur bit her nose with the strike of the match. She raised her gaze to meet his. A tiny spark tingled within her left palm where she grasped the taper. *Don't be silly, Willa. It's probably just the candle. You did grab red, after all. Red for passion.* The soft light cast a dim illumination but seemed to make the stranger's face even more obscure.

"No electricity?" The man pulled a handkerchief from under the sodden coat and mopped his face. "That for atmosphere?"

"Oh, there's electricity." High voltage was standing right in front of her. "The building is old, the wires are old and the weather is bad." Willa shrugged. "Sometimes, I like candlelight." There was no denying the fire glow was making this man take on a shine of his own. Tiny reflections of the candle flame danced in his dark eyes.

"Never mind." The man turned away and scanned the racks of colorful candles and books with an expression of distaste.

"I was told that I could book a graveyard tour at this

shop. Is there a Miss Willa here? An old lady, I suppose.'' He faced her and spread both hands on the glass-topped counter.

''I give tours sometimes.'' She looked down at his hands. Long, slender fingers, neat but not scarred, as if he made his living with his wit, rather than his muscle. There was music in the strong stretch of the tendons and the span from the thumb to the small finger. Guitar, or perhaps piano? The dormant sense within Willa that had stirred with Cameron Green's scent warmed further.

''I don't want you. I want Miss Willa. A taxi driver, E. J., said to see her.''

A crease appeared between Willa's eyebrows. She impatiently pulled her hair back from her face and gathered it at her neck. ''I am Willa Robinette.''

There was a flash of lightning and for a moment the silhouette of the visitor was outlined against the rain-silvered window. The candle guttered and went out. In the pause, as the thin smoke rose, the man extended his hand.

''Cameron John Green.'' The smoke swirled lazily, separating and sifting through his fingers. Willa reached forward and touched his hand hesitantly, then gripped it firmly. His palm was damp from the rain but warm and strong. Willa looked hard into his eyes. What did this man really want? Not a tourist nor the usual customer; her intuition was getting mixed signals.

With one smooth gesture, he released her right hand and pulled the red taper from her hold.

''Allow me.'' Cam firmly pressed its length into the crevice of a peach-shaped candleholder, one of several displayed on thc counter. He picked up the match pack and, with a quick flick of his wrist, the flame was ignited.

"Willa." She repeated, "My name is Willa."

She relaxed and let the full impression of the man sweep over her. Dark eyes, sensual as rich chocolate, dangerous as a stormy delta night. Wet hair, slick as a seal, otter brown. An expression that would scorch paint at twenty paces. Lips that could be interesting if they weren't compressed and grim. Meticulous clothes, expensive fabric now wet through, the upside-down sheep on the Brooks Brothers buttons shiny.

"I want a tour of the graveyards. Now."

The effect his physical inventory was having on Willa was suddenly lost in his impatient manner. Willa pointed past the would-be customer and out the front door. "It's raining. Now." *Hardheaded,* she thought, *pushy. You can catch more flies with honey than vinegar, Mr. Green.*

"Listen, I just got in from New York and I need to make the most of my time here." He folded the handkerchief and jammed it into his coat pocket. "How much?"

"I'm sorry, but this is not a good time to be touring the graveyards. It's getting dark and the evening can be dangerous in that area. Perhaps tomorrow." From New York; that made sense. Those people were always in a hurry, even on a vacation.

"What's your fee?" He pulled out a leather wallet.

"That's not the point. It's not a good time." Willa trailed off as the man pulled out a hundred-dollar bill and slapped it on the counter.

"I'm not afraid of some Southern bubba-boogie men. You were recommended. I want a private tour, and I want it now." He slapped out another bill and obviously gave his best shot at a boyish smile. The smile didn't

25

work, but Willa was willing to concede it might, in different circumstances.

That much cash would be a good start to mending the roof. Two hundred dollars was worth getting wet for. It was tempting. So was the smile. His lips curled at the sides as if he knew a secret. Maybe the secret of honey.

"I'm not from New York, but I have enough sense to stay out of the rain and street gang territory at night. Perhaps you do things differently in New York. I'll take you, but . . ."

"That's what I thought." He cut her off. "You mystics, so esoteric, but the bottom line is the green stuff, isn't it?"

"I beg your pardon?" Willa blinked. *What did he say?*

"I'm sorry, nothing." He waved his hand and reached to pluck a book from the shelf.

"As I was trying to say, I'll take you, but only for my regular fee. Twenty dollars. Money doesn't buy everything." The two locked defiant glances, and the reporter dropped his glare first. "We'll go first thing tomorrow morning."

The impatient visitor tossed the book he was holding to the countertop. "Fine." He picked up one of the parchment business cards Willa kept in a basket on the counter. "La Empire Celestique, Spiritual Supplies," he read aloud. With a thoughtful expression, he slipped the card into his shirt pocket.

"So this is your shop. When the taxi driver told me about it, I thought some old crone would be running the place."

Willa folded her arms in front of her chest. "Yes. My shop." If this is what passed for Yankee charm, he wasn't quite making it work. Well, she was used to rude tourists who stumbled off the usual track. She couldn't restrain herself from tapping her foot under the counter.

"A family store, so to speak?" He picked up a brass bell, examining the wooden handle closely.

"Yes, family." She made a real effort to stop her motion.

Cameron Green apparently was trying to coax some information from her; didn't take a psychic to figure that one out. He tinkled the bell and Cranston jumped up on the counter. Willa grabbed the cat in an effort to calm herself, but Cranston wiggled away to rub her whiskers against the inquisitive customer.

"Your father's shop?"

"No." Willa could feel herself starting to grind her teeth. "My mother's." Tapping and grinding. Not a good sign.

"Grandfather's?"

"No. My grandmother's. And my great-grandmother's. Where is this going, Mr. Green? I really do have work I could be doing."

The man seemed to force a smile. "I'm sorry. I want to buy something. How about this?" He put a candle on the counter. "And this, and this." He grabbed a packet of powder and a bar of scented soap. "And this, what is this?" Cam held a thin, gnarled object up to the pale light of the window.

"That, Mr. Green is a chicken foot. Which I don't think you need. And I don't think you need that candle, which is for safe childbirth, unless there is something about you that's not obvious. The Love-drawing Soap and the Fast-Break Hex Lifting Powder . . . well, maybe you could use that. I'm not sure."

27

Cam dropped the dry chicken foot as if it were on fire. Willa covered her smile with her hand. "Please feel free to look around. If you need me, just ring that bell." She started to turn away.

Cam reached across the counter and grabbed her elbow. "Wait." An involuntary rush of warmth flooded over Willa's body.

"I'm sorry. Look, let's start again." He released her. Willa could still feel his fingers imprinted on her skin.

"Here's my card." Cam scrawled his hotel name on the back. "I have to . . . that is . . ." He hesitated. "I promised my mother that I would do something for her."

Willa blinked and focused on what he was saying.

"I promised her . . . I would learn about Halloween." He amended, "All Saint's Eve."

"About Halloween? That's an interesting promise. Why ask me? Go down to Jackson Square and ask the priest."

"I think you are the source I need. And the taxi driver, E. J., he recommended you. If you give me some time I'll make it worth your while.

"How about a hundred dollars? A tour of the graveyards, and whatever else you consider important." He scanned her face.

"And dinner. We can do dinner too." He seemed to be turning on every ounce of charm he could muster.

"Please. Help me keep my promise." Cam turned on an extra-wattage smile.

The gleaming white teeth of the wolf in "Little Red Riding Hood." Beautiful teeth, beautiful mouth. *Don't trust this.*

"A hundred dollars a day for your expert instruction. A consultant."

The wolf *was* knocking at her door.

"We can work all week or however long it takes."

"I told you this was not an issue of money. Halloween is a week away." He could never build her trust in that length of time.

"I'm sure it wouldn't take seven days for you to learn what you want to know. Talk to Father Albert at the Cathedral. Go to the Cellar Club for a night or two; that's a spooky experience." Willa held up her fingers to tick off the sources. "Get on the Internet. Use the library at Tulane. I'm sure you can find a grad student who would love to help you. There's no reason you need me for this."

"Look, this really means a lot to me. This has to be authentic. Not from books, or the priest. I want to find someone who—well, someone who believes."

"Believes?" Her voice was cautious.

"Yes, someone who believes. In witchcraft. Someone who can talk to the spirits. I want to see a Halloween ritual and talk to the spirits. Halloween is when that happens, isn't it?"

Be careful, a little warning bell went off in Willa's brain. *He's after something; is he some kind of religious nut case? A policeman looking for scams? Some kind of vice squad?* "I can take you on a graveyard tour. I have a city license for that. We'll walk around. I'll show you the tombs and some of the haunted houses around here, if you want. The fee for that is twenty dollars." It was hard to turn down good money. There was nothing unusual this man could read into a simple tour. "After the tour we can talk."

Cameron Green stroked the long-haired cat and ran his hand down her tail. Tiny blue sparks danced from the fur when he pulled his hand away. "Yes, that's it. A tour, then talk." He pulled the towel from his neck and handed it back to Willa.

"Tomorrow morning then." Cam rested his hand on the brass door handle and swung the door wide. He flashed her one last smile over his shoulder and stepped out.

"Tomorrow."

Those white wolf's teeth.

Chapter Three

The evening seemed to become abruptly dark after the intriguing man left the shop. Willa pulled the front door shut and turned the hand-lettered OPEN sign to CLOSED.

Willa scooped the wet towel from the countertop and pressed the damp cotton to her cheek. Would there be any vibrations that might tell her more about Cameron Green? The deep musky smell of a male clung to the cloth, mixed with the tangy pine and citrus of an expensive cologne.

Sincerity. She could feel his sincerity. There was also a sense of pain and betrayal. Yes, he certainly wanted more than just a tour of the graveyard. He wanted to know about the highest of holy days in the Wiccan year, the solemn rite for the dead. Asking to see a ritual; that was curious.

What he was asking for involved trust, and trust could not be bought. Trust came freely from the heart.

31

Willa picked up the business card he had given her. She rubbed her finger over the address on the back. His handwriting was a rightward slanting scrawl, as if he was used to using a keyboard rather than a pen. The printed side—black print on white paper—his name, an address in New York that meant nothing to her, an e-mail signature. Willa slipped the card into her shirt pocket, over her heart.

Carrying Cranston draped bonelessly over her shoulder, she trudged up the stairs to her apartment. "Cranston, I have a funny feeling about this man." She put the cat on the floor and tugged gently on its tail. "What do you think?"

"Yoow." Cranston rolled over and regarded Willa from an upside-down angle. "Yow-ow."

"Oh, you say that about everything."

Willa's home consisted of three long rooms and an attic stacked above one another like a layer cake. Constructed of handmade brick in the early days of New Orleans, the design reflected the practical European manner of shopkeepers living above their working space. At the street level was the stone-floored shop, and next up was Willa's kitchen and living room. A diminutive stairway led up to her bedroom and bath. The structure was topped by a terminally leaky attic.

In the rear of the shop, a single door opened into a miniature courtyard, revealing one of the most distinctive features of New Orleans architecture. The shady, fern-filled square was open to the sky but totally secluded from the view of neighbors and passersby.

Mounted on the soft handmade bricks of the rear wall, a worn stone lion's head trickled water from his mouth into a basin hardly as big as a dishpan. A child-sized angel, her marble robe soft gray with moss and ruffled with delicate pale blue lichens, seemed to be hiding playfully in a thick clump of bromeliads. At one time there had been an ancient oak at the center of the brick pathway, but now it was gone, with only a tablelike stump remaining, wreathed in ivy.

Tourists who ventured down obscure Saint Rita Street loved to photograph La Empire Celestique. Each room had long multipaned French doors, opening onto balconies trimmed with lacy black-painted ironwork. The structure was charming but crumbling, and Willa had the city inspector's documents to prove it.

For all the inconveniences, Willa loved the old place.

The shop had been her mother's, and her grandmother's, and her great-grandmother's home. Still was. Four generations of Robinette women inhabited this space, in one plane or another.

Sometimes the ancestors were more present than others. Willa could go for days without finding Grandmother Belle rearranging the silver in the kitchen, or fondling Willa's small box of jewelry. Grannie Belle had a fascination with shiny and precious things that had lasted into the afterlife.

Mother's apparition enjoyed staying down in the shop, where it was more lively. Occasionally she knocked a book or trinket from the shelf to show her annoyance when a particularly irritating visitor was about. Mother kept up a brisk acquaintance with the family of gossipy plant fairies who lived in the ferns and moss of the courtyard.

Formidable Great-Granddame Sophia Martine reserved her appearances for times of particular crisis, always having been one for high drama—or so Grannie

Belle had informed Willa. Cranston disliked Granddame Sophia for her imperious habit of nudging the cat unceremoniously from the cozy rocking chair.

Tonight none of the elder Robinette spirits seemed to be about. The rocking chair was still and none of the china or silver was moving about. Willa would have liked to discuss the visitor with Granddame Sophia. The wise Frenchwoman had the sharpest grasp of business and of men. Her advice was dispensed in crisp-toned, if rather outdated, French.

The rain had become more steady. Willa took Granddame Sophia Martine's scrying bowl from the mantel and walked to the balcony. She held the shallow bowl out into the raindrops until the container was half full. Maybe the ancient black glass would have something to reveal about the intriguing visitor from the North.

Willa placed the bowl near the candle on her table and gazed into the mirrorlike water, slowing her breathing and relaxing her mind. The perfect reflection of the candle flame trembled before her eyes. A picture began to form. The flame became honey brown eyes; the taper, a lick of silky hair. Strong cheekbones; firm mouth.

She breathed deeply and inclined toward the image. A thin hand appeared and thrust a bony finger into the water, shattering the portrait that had begun to build up.

"That, Great-Granddaughter Willa Alexandria, is not what you need to see."

"Granddame Sophia, I was just wishing to see you."

"*Oui, mon petite*, I observe that it is I whom you wish to see," Granddame intoned in her dry manner. The aristocratic woman continued to swirl her fingers in the rainwater. She flicked drops from her fingertips and let the water still. The picture came again, quickly formed as if a photograph lay beneath the cool water.

Granddame hummed softly. "The eyes, yes, they are a mirror to the soul. But what you need is the revelation of this man's heart. Look more deeply."

Willa stared obediently into the black bowl. The image of Cameron Green's face dimmed, and slowly a scene formed.

"Tell me what you see, Granddaughter."

"A woman in a chair, scattered flowers, Cameron Green on his knees. The woman—her hair is silver. The flowers are pink. Is it a hospital?" Willa paused to watch the action develop. "The woman is showing him some papers, newspapers, I think. Cameron Green looks unhappy, maybe angry."

"You are coming closer to the heart of the matter." Granddame Sophia sunk into the rocking chair.

"There is someone else, a man, standing behind the woman. He cannot speak, but he reaches to her. Oh, he is sad, so sad." Willa felt a sympathetic throb of sorrow close her throat.

The scene dissolved in a shimmer. For moments the water was still and black, then a faint spark glimmered at the rounded bottom.

The minute star darted from side to side, as if it were trying to escape, then stopped near the surface and drifted to the bottom. The ember flashed once and died. The water remained empty.

"What was that? It seemed sad."

"A soul, Willa Alexandria. A soul that searches."

Cam peeled off his sodden clothes. He hung his pants and shirt near the air-conditioner vents, then draped his coat meticulously over a hanger. Wet socks and underwear he flipped over a plastic chair back. This left him nude, unpleasantly clammy, and cold. Nothing to do but have a hot shower before dinner and think over the woman he had met that evening.

Cam fished with two fingers down into his shirt pocket. The card from the shop was damp but not damaged. The golden print was clear and fine, like a feminine signature over the card: LA EMPIRE CELESTIQUE. *Yeah, right: the celestial empire.* He propped the little rectangle of cardboard against the bedside lamp.

A bucket of cold rainwater poured on his head; now there was a propitious start. The woman with the Gift, whatever that was. And what was it *for?* Hocus-pocus; he hated it. Facts were his business; give him hard data.

A shower would clear his head and warm him up. The hotel bathroom was spacious, and generous with the white marble. Cam turned on the water taps and gave the HOT handle an extra twist. In less than a minute the steam rolled out over the shower door. Cam stepped in and let the water pelt the top of his head and cascade down the taunt muscles of his shoulders and back. Seemed like those muscles had knotted the day his dad died and hadn't unkinked since.

He put his hands on the white tile walls and leaned into the hot water, his eyes closed. The heat fell over his body, washing away the day's frustrations.

The conversation with his editor came to mind. Would Julia really fire him? He doubted it, but there was a tickle of apprehension there. The threat was just her way of trying to get his attention. But he would have to get this story, get it good, and get it on time.

The story could be revealing, if he got some decent

sources. Didn't have to be a fluffy trick-or-treat thing.

The image of the woman in the shop formed behind his closed eyes. A blur of light hair had framed her face in the candlelit shop. Something about the eyes . . . Why should a woman her age have such childlike eyes?

What big blue eyes she had. Big, lustrous, fascinating blue eyes. Delphinium blue, deep, new denim blue. His mind began to wander.

Cam turned and let the water strike the small of his back. Something about her eyes; what was it?

With his eyes closed, he began to soap his body, running the lemon-scented hotel soap up and down slowly. The lather felt good and the water continued as hot as before. He flexed his feet, using a trick an old yogi in Calcutta had showed him, loosening the tight muscles in his calves.

That was it. Her eyes were like those of the mystics he had interviewed in India. Not childlike; serene. He turned and let the soap rinse away. Serene. Blue. Sky blue.

He rubbed across his face to get the water out of his eyes. Thinking about those indigo eyes was causing a reaction in his body that had nothing to do with serenity. His body was quickly growing taunt at the thought of her golden hair threaded between his fingers.

Cam flipped the water taps from hot to cold. He gasped as a blast of icy water pelted his chest and ran down his belly. Cold as the bucket of water the blue-eyed woman had heaved out the window onto his head. Let that be a lesson, too. No romantic thoughts. This was business.

He stepped out of the shower and wrapped a towel around his waist and threw another over his head. Another plus for a hotel: plenty of big towels.

The electronic shrill of his portable phone ripped his thoughtful mood. Cam flipped the device open. It had to be the office. "Hello."

"Cameron, this is Julie. How is the vacation going?"

Cam plopped on the edge of the bed and pulled the towel across his shoulders. "It's not a vacation, Julie. I've got a promising lead on this Halloween story. It can be good."

"How good?"

"I think I can get a different slant on the material. I've met someone who will cooperate and give me some inside information." He felt like crossing his fingers for luck when he said that. The gold lettering on the business card winked under the lamplight, and Cam picked up the rectangle of cardboard.

"I'll send down a photographer. Pictures would be really good."

"Not yet, but I'll let you know."

"All right. Just checking on my favorite reporter."

"Yeah. I certainly appreciate your deep concern, Julie." Cam knew he'd be on the street in a heartbeat if this story didn't show some real promise. And pictures to back up the text . . . that might be a sticky one. "I'm off for dinner. I'll get in touch later this week." He hung up and paused, staring at the business card. *Oh, Miss Willa, have you got a gift? A gift for me?*

Cam dressed rapidly and checked his watch. Tonight he planned to take his mother to dinner.

A small restaurant had caught his eye on his walk back to the hotel. The place reminded him of a favorite café he had visited in Paris. There were tables draped in white, with small candles shielded by red glass, all arranged on the cozily roofed balcony above the sidewalk. The handwritten menu was posted by the door and an un-Parisian robust smell of spicy shrimp was drifting seductively out to the sidewalk. The night was warm and his mother would enjoy watching the crowds pass below. Nothing like good food to get someone's mind back into the land of the living.

The early morning light was pale through the rain clouds. Brother Amos carefully leaned the tall cross against the wet brick wall. He scrubbed across his seamed face with a gnarled hand and studied the message displayed at the meeting of the crossbar and the upright. Raindrops dripped from the metal. The red LED lights blinked twice, "Ex . . . us . . . 8," then reverted to an old message, "Buy Bud . . . wei . . ." The batteries sputtered. "Bud . . . thou shalt not . . . Bud.

The rain fell heavier and the red lights gave a sizzle and dimmed. Brother Amos smacked the glass panel with the flat of his hand. The marching lights brightened and the message ran briskly across the panel, "Exodus 22: 18 Thou shalt not suffer a witch to live. Repent. Budweiser. Budweiser . . . shalt not . . ." The lights faltered and went out. Brother Amos smacked the glass again. "Wicked machine!"

"Bud . . . bu . . . b . . ."

"Brother Amos." Willa Robinette flung open her shop door. "Come in out of the rain. You'll catch pneumonia." She tugged at his ragged sleeve.

"Get away, woman." He shrugged away. "I'm on a mission." Amos clutched his beaten aluminum cross. "A mission from God."

"You'll be talking directly to God if you don't get

out of the storm." A flash of lightning made the entire street stand out in stark white. "Come inside."

Amos muttered and clung tighter to the metal cross. He frowned at Willa, and for a moment, the confusion that kept his watery green eyes clouded cleared. "Willa? My friend?"

Willa guided the old man toward the doorway. He was already soaked through his ragged overcoat to the skin. "Yes, Brother Amos. It's Willa. Come in and get dry. I think I have some new batteries for your sign." She coaxed him as he tugged the aluminum cross into her shop doorway. Willa bent and lifted the end with the little skate wheels up and over the stone steps. "There."

"Sit at the table and I'll get you something hot." She pressed his shoulders and he sat obediently. In deference to the ancient preacher, Willa flipped a drape over the pink crystal ball that sat on the middle of the table.

"No coffee! Drink of the devil!" He folded his arms firmly. "Do I smell coffee?"

"No, Brother Amos," she lied. "Hot chocolate and a bowl of soup. How about that? And crackers." Willa's mother had fed him when Willa was a child. Probably her grandmother had, as well. Brother Amos was an ageless fixture of Quarter life. His proudest possession, his only possession, was the blinking LED-adorned cross he had cobbled together from a discarded Mardi Gras beer display. Before building the crucifix, he had worn cardboard signs carefully lettered and pinned to his bulky wool coat.

"Drink of the devil," the elderly man warned Cranston sternly as the cat sniffed at Brother Amos's shoes.

Willa hurried upstairs to warm some food for the street preacher. While the soup heated in the tiny microwave, she pulled a light wool blanket from the linen shelf and shook out the folds. Balancing soup bowl and chocolate mug, she flung the blanket over her shoulder and moved carefully down the narrow wooden stair.

"Nice warm tomato soup." Willa draped the blanket around Amos's stooped shoulders. "And hot chocolate." She stepped back from the steamy smell rising from Amos. He smelled like the New Orleans rain drains in the summer, earthy, oily, with a slight overtone of garbage. Amos eyed the soup and chocolate and folded his hands primly.

"Lord, let us be properly grateful for those gifts we are about to receive." He drew a deep breath to launch into a lengthy list of gifts, needs, and sins committed or about to be. Willa recognized the signs.

"Amen." She pressed the pottery cup of chocolate into his grip. He clutched the mug with both hands and drained the dark rich milk in a gulp.

Willa leaned her elbows on her countertop and watched the rain dripping off the shop's single window. "Let me have your coat and I'll dry it for you."

Brother Amos clutched the lapels in both hands. "You'll steal it. It's mine!"

"Look, it's me, Willa. Let me dry it for you. I'll put your coat right here where you can see it." Willa coaxed the preacher out of his garment. She draped the smelly coat over a chair where there would be some ventilation. "There. See?"

Amos shifted his seat so the coat was in his sight. He curled an arm around his crackers and soup. "OK."

The containers in the leaky attic would be filling. The brusque man from New York was coming for his tour of the graveyard this morning. Wet or dry, she had said

41

she would take him. A hundred dollars a day would go a long way toward fixing the roof. She would call the City offices this afternoon and stall. But she had a feeling all was not what it seemed with Cameron Green. Caution was called for.

The small clock that had been hanging above the shop door since before her grandmother's time chimed nine. Early for New Orleans, late for the rest of the world. Many, like Brother Amos, were just finishing their night. The Northern man who had made his mother a promise would be here soon.

Why would he tell her something like that? And Halloween; why would he be trying to pump her for information about Halloween, of all things? Normally, she would share her information gladly and freely, but this one, this man gave off an air of tension and unhappiness. Perhaps he really did have some dark and unwholesome secret behind his brandy-brown eyes.

Every time she looked at him, bells rung in her head. Her head was telling her one thing, and her heart and body something entirely different. Two to one; who would win?

Maybe she would give him one of her reference books and hope that would satisfy him.

Cranston jumped up on the counter to rub against Willa. The friendly feline bumped her head under Willa's chin and purred. The cat had seemed to take to the male visitor, which was unusual. Cranston's instincts were sound. Another little puzzle piece. Willa stroked Cranston's multicolored fur and continued to muse.

Cameron John Green. The generic name told her nothing.

Dark eyes, thick eyelashes, rather long, almost black

hair. She liked that, long hair. Hair she could run her fingers through, twist like ebony silk ribbons. Braid like lovelocks. Warm, fragrant hair to spread over her eyelids and press to her face after making love.

Willa stroked the cat rather more briskly than Cranston cared for, and the cat pulled away from her touch.

Willa rested her chin on her fist. He was tall, seemed to be well built. The wet clothes had been fairly revealing. Yes, definitely well built. There was no hiding those broad shoulders and slim hips. A chest to bury your face in and arms that could shelter from any harm.

Then there was the scene in the scrying bowl, and the imprisoned spark. A lost soul. His soul? No, Granddame said a soul that is searching.

The thunder thumped and rolled like the Mardi Gras parade drums. Autumn was coming. The end and the beginning of the year. The turn of the wheel of life down to the dark side for rest and renewal. Willa rubbed her eyes and pulled her fingers through her hair. A strange request from Cameron John Green, to learn about All Saint's Eve. Halloween. Samhain.

"Brother Amos, I have to run an errand soon. Will you stay here and watch the shop while I'm gone?"

Brother Amos consulted his inner timetable. "If it is God's will, I will attend your shop." He raised a grimy finger to point to the heavens.

Willa glimpsed the tall stranger as he strode down the street. At the same time, she felt her heart lift, as if it had skipped—or added—a beat. She caught her breath and pressed against the pulse point in her neck.

Raindrops spotted his pressed khaki slacks and blue chambray shirt. He held a hand over a carefully knotted silk tie. Judging by his clothes, it seemed as if it was hard for him to relax.

When he stepped into the shop, the space immediately seemed much smaller and warmer than before.

"I'm ready for the tour." Cam glanced around. "What's that? Smells like a wet dog."

Willa grimaced and held her finger to her lips, rolling her eyes toward Brother Amos.

"Oh. Sorry. Your father?"

"No. Just a friend."

"I'll get my umbrella and we can leave." She clattered up the stairs. Her big umbrella leaned in the corner of her living room, tip poked into a flowerpot full of ivy. Willa snatched up a thin jacket and a package she had prepared the night before.

"Let's go." As she stepped out of the front door and huddled under the protection of the gallery, Willa snapped open the red-and-white-striped umbrella. The raindrops hit the fabric with fat popping sounds. Cam stepped close under the stretched cloth. He took the umbrella handle from her hand, his fingers brushing hers, and they both were sheltered, shoulder to shoulder. It felt almost natural to be so close, so warm, like lovers stealing moments together.

"Shouldn't you lock the door?"

Willa smiled. "No one would steal from a magic shop in New Orleans, Mr. Green. Believe me."

"Bad karma?"

"Perhaps. Besides, when Brother Amos wakes up he doesn't like to have the door closed." Willa pulled on her jacket and pulled her ash blond hair from the collar.

"Skip the touristy fluff. I'm interested in anything to do with the magic and voodoo cults in the area. But specifically Halloween things. Serious facts only.''

"All right. Facts only.''

He pulled out a palm-sized tape recorder. "Do you mind if I record this?''

"Why would I mind?''

"Some people do.'' He shrugged and slipped the device back into his shirt pocket.

There wasn't another person on the street. No carriages with sleepy mules wearing flower-decorated hats. Tourists wouldn't venture out in such an early fall cloudburst. The hotel bars were probably full, even this early in the day. Good business for them.

Willa gestured to the left. "Down to the corner and then to the left again. Before we go to the graveyard, I'll show you a house or two you should see.''

They walked on in the light rain. She looked up into Cam Green's face. His face really wasn't so hard. Strong, but not hard. For a split second, Willa wondered how it would feel to kiss that beautiful mouth.

Willa drew a strong deep breath to clear her thoughts and start into her informative speech. "In the Vieux Carre, there is another world between night and day. Some people have said that the French Quarter shines brighter at night time than in the sunshine. Things aren't quite awake until dusk and not quite ready to give up and go to sleep at dawn. People, animals.''

Cam glanced down at her. "Spirits?'' His reporter's instincts twitched at the scent of his subject.

"Perhaps.'' They paused in front of a white-fronted house. The green shutters were latched, hiding the windows. "This is the Lalaurie House. Actually, it's been rebuilt. Madame Lalaurie abused her slaves in a shocking manner. During a lavish party in 1834, the first mansion burned. The firemen found remains of slaves shackled to the attic walls. It was pitiful.

"They say Madame Lalaurie laughed and danced in the street as the house burned and she heard the slaves screaming."

Cam scanned the white facade. "Looks peaceful now."

"It's not. Even though this house has been rebuilt, some say it's actively haunted."

"Hard on the real-estate market. Ghosts bumping around." He found it hard to keep a sarcastic tone out of his voice.

Willa frowned and touched the cold white stucco. "Too many bad deaths here, too much misery and pain. The souls don't know they can leave. They're confused and injured." They walked slowly on.

"I'm really not interested in this tourist stuff."

Willa faced Cam and touched his arm lightly. "It's not tourist stuff. You want to learn about Halloween; this is part of it. You must understand that some spirits can be bound on earth, and not want to leave, or be able to leave."

Her face was serious, and her forehead wrinkled in concern. She had tied back her butterscotch-colored hair with a ribbon that was the same denim blue as her eyes. The rain was almost over, but Cam continued to hold the umbrella over their heads. He was beginning to enjoy the light contact it gave him with the earnest young guide.

Their shoulders brushed as they walked. She was not as small as she had seemed in the candlelit shop, and her body had an athletic firmness. Her fingers were strong when she grasped his arm to halt him.

"It's said that this is the place where Marie Laveau lived. She was the Queen of Voodoo in New Orleans in the early 1800s."

The small house was unremarkable to Cam's reporter's eyes. Not very pretentious for someone who called herself a queen of anything. They paused to read the small marker. Cam did not comment, and they walked on toward the graveyard.

They passed the whitewashed gate portals and took an indirect path through the cemetery, turning and winding through the narrow passages between walled graves. Willa guided Cam with a touch to the sleeve to turn, right, then left, then right again.

Rather than a rolling lawn with sedate flat markers, this graveyard looked like a miniature city, crowded with elaborate marble and masonry dollhouses. The graves were elevated sarcophagi, embellished with stone and brass vases, wrought metal grills, statues of sorrowing nymphs, and festoons of carved marble or cast cement flowers. Some graves had concrete benches or ornate metal lawn chairs arranged nearby, as if to facilitate a chatty visit with the departed.

"Originally, the tombs were built this way because of the water. The ground was marshy and the coffins would float up out of the ground.

"The graves are like homes, shared by families, paid for for a year and a day. Then the bones are swept to the back and the next coffin can be placed inside." Willa ran her fingers over a crumbling wet brick wall and picked a small piece of the clay.

"Reminds me of the big cemetery in Paris. Landlords still get rent out of you even after you're dead." Cam smiled at Willa.

"You can see bones if you look inside." Willa gestured to a gaping crack in a tumbling brick wall.

Cam stooped slightly to peek inside the neglected tomb. It was dark, but at the very back a glint of lighter objects caught his eye. Old bones? He leaned closer. A furry black spider rushed out of the litter toward Cam's nose. "Whoa!" Cam jerked his head back. "I didn't expect any movement in there."

"In New Orleans you should always expect the unexpected." Willa seemed to be suppressing a giggle. So, his serious guide did have a lighter side, even if only spiders and dry bones brought it out.

They walked on a few graves farther. Here and there, Cam peered into small glass windows set into the metal-bound crypt doors. Sometimes there were withered flowers visible. Others were too grime-obscured for anything to be seen.

It seemed as if they must be in the center, the heart of the necropolis. They stood before a vault built modestly of plain white stone, but marked by scores of small red chalk *X*'s. Bright red carnations, packets of cigarettes, polished pennies and assorted sweets littered the gravesite. Small loaves of bread and baked sweets were stacked against the stone tomb wall. Folded letters, envelopes, and torn bits of paper with scrawled messages were tucked under most of the clutter.

Willa closed the umbrella and leaned it against the neighboring tomb, across the aisle. Cam took a step back to observe the unusual grave and watched as Willa faced the door to the tomb. She set down the paper bag she was carrying and crouched next to the polished brass plaque at the foot of the vault.

Willa rummaged through the sack and pulled out a

fresh coconut, a new comb decorated with yellow silk flowers, and a sweet cinnamon sticky bun, wrapped in red cellophane. After considering the position of the other tokens, she placed her gifts near the newest offerings and petitions for help.

"I must ask you to be respectful of what I do and say until we leave." She looked up at Cam. Cam nodded sincerely.

"One more thing." She pulled out an unopened bottle of dark rum and set it with the other bottles that made a line along a ledge of the grave. Some of the containers had been there so long the labels had faded and slipped to crumple at the bottom of the bottles.

"This is Marie Laveau's resting place. She has a soft spot in her heart for lovers but will help grant any wish if you ask her properly." Willa gestured to the offerings that lay on the ground before them.

"Are these from people who want something?" Cam's voice was a mixture of reverence and the enthusiasm of a child being taught a new game.

"Yes, these are gifts of thanks. Would you like to help me with a wish?" Willa rolled the bit of red brick she had picked up between her fingers.

"Sure." *Thought she'd never ask. One step closer to that ritual.* "What should I do?"

"Follow my lead. Do you have nine pennies in your pocket?"

"Probably." Cam dug deep in his pockets. "I have a nickel and four pennies, will that do?"

"Only since you're a beginner. Put them next to my coconut."

Cam stacked the coins neatly against her offering.

"Scrape your feet three times and knock on the tomb

door three times. Then follow what I do.'' As they made the movements in unison, Willa felt a wave of warmth run down her spine. Not a cold shiver, but a delicious sensation that lingered. Momma Marie was already listening—with interest. Willa could feel Cam's wish before it took form in his mind—or was Madame Marie being a mischievous matchmaker?

"Take this.'' Willa handed Cam a chip of brick from the spider's home.

His brow knit in a questioning expression. Willa gave him a firm tutorial look and began to pace around the tomb. "Follow me. Keep your wish in your mind. Hold a picture of it in your thoughts.'' They circled the grave three times to the right and again three times to the left, then stopped before the mausoleum door.

Cam was grateful the drizzle had kept the tourists away. There was no one near to disturb or observe them.

"Make your wish. Then mark three times, like this.'' Using the red clay chip, Willa made three large crimson *X* marks on the wet wall. She placed her palms to cover the red streaks. Out of the corner of her eye, Willa could see Cam follow suit.

Willa closed her eyes. Instantly wild thoughts of romance, wet kisses and caresses flashed through her mind. She squeezed her eyes tighter and shook her head, trying to dredge prayers of roof repair, money, and good business to the forefront of her mind. The harder she tried to visualize building reconstruction, the more intense was the sensual image, the urge that this rude Northern stranger would press her against the hard wall and kiss her even harder.

She felt strong, warm fingers at the base of her neck. *Don't be silly, Willa. Momma Marie is playing tricks on you.* Plain as day, she could feel the touch, as real as the rough whitewash beneath her palms. The same fingers threaded through her hair, turned and pulled her away from the wall.

Afraid to open her eyes, Willa gave in to the fantasy kiss. Another hand traced a raindrop from her cheek and smoothed a thumb across her lips. She felt the warmth of breath on her cheek. Again, her mouth was captured beneath the power of a man's kiss. It was what she had wished for in her heart and she responded, melting into the slick tangle of new beginnings, of tasting a real man. She felt hot and dry and wet all at the same time.

Sparkles behind her eyelids made her eyelashes flutter. Cam was kissing her, kissing her hard against the wall of the spirit. Willa's eyes flew open.

"How dare you?" She pulled back, but Cam didn't release her, his hands on her shoulders. "You don't kiss like that in church, do you?"

"No, but you did say I'd get my wish. I'd say it was granted in a big way, but I'm sorry if I've offended you or Ms. Laveau." Cam slid his hands down her arms, then stepped away and released her.

Oh, I'm sure she's not offended. Willa shot a glance at the crypt door and could almost hear Momma Marie giggle at her handiwork. *In fact, it's just the offering she probably likes the most.*

"I'm sorry. I just couldn't help it."

No, he couldn't help it and she knew it. Marie Laveau loved a good romance, especially an unlikely one. Madame was only encouraging the deepest wishes that, apparently, they both had expressed.

"Have some respect for the dead." This was not a good idea; she didn't know this man and he was much too curious, too forward and willing to intrude into her business. *Stop it, Madame Marie!* It didn't help that the kiss had felt too good, started such a cascade of unspiritual excitement.

Cam hesitated when he saw the glint of tears—or was it anger—in Willa's eyes. He held up his palms. "I apologize. I can get too intense, I know. Let me it make up to you. Could you show me a good place for dinner?"

"When we get back to my shop, I'll write down an address for you." Willa picked up the umbrella and opened it with a snap, turning away.

"I'm sorry. Really, I meant would you have dinner with me tonight?" He reached a nearby crypt and yanked a plastic rose from the container at the iron-barred door. "Please?" He offered the faded rose. "And call me Cam. Only my mother calls me Cameron."

Willa snatched the bedraggled flower from his hand and thrust it back into the crumbling concrete vase. "Oh, all right. Cam. We can talk more. It's strictly business, though." She tossed her hair back and narrowed her eyes. "I certainly want you to get your money's worth."

They set across the graveyard at a fast clip. Willa's shoes crunched briskly on the wet gravel. They dodged traffic to trot across the four-lane street back into the Quarter. A taxi honked and Cam saw E. J. wave and flash a grin. "Yo! Mizz Willa!" E. J. shouted as the taxi pulled away from the light.

Willa slowed and waved in return, then set down the street at a different tack.

"Where are we going?"

"Back to my shop. This is a shortcut." They cut across a courtyard with a fountain banked with white geraniums, then ducked through a low, wide passageway. Cardboard boxes full of empty green bottles were stacked to one side.

A man wrapped in a stained white apron stepped from a doorway. "Miss Willa! That you?" A smile lit his face.

"Yes, Jean Paul. How are you?"

"Well, just fine, just fine." He wiped his hands down the sides of the apron. "Can I ask a favor?"

"Of course."

"When you see your grandmama, ask her where my gold chain has got to. I can't find it anywhere."

"I'll do that, Jean Paul."

"Thank you, Miss Willa." The man ducked back into the doorway and popped back out with a wrinkled brown bag. "Something for you." He drew back into the opening before Willa could thank him.

"Does everybody know you?" Cam followed Willa through one final cluttered courtyard and stepped out on Saint Rita Street, almost directly in front of her shop.

"Yes." She answered curtly. They entered the shop. Cam noted the musty smell he had noticed earlier was gone. So was the old man at the table. A gray-haired woman was puttering about the herb jars in the rear of the shop. A faint rattle and clink of glass could be heard now and then as she picked up the jars and shook the contents.

"The tour is over."

Cam picked up a red candle and ran his fingers over the cold wax. "Could I look over your shop, ask you some questions as I think of them?"

Willa narrowed her eyes but had to agree. "Of course. We agreed to an interview. Please look around and ask me anything you wish." She had made a bargain and she would have to earn her money. Was it worth a hundred dollars to be burdened with this irritating, incredibly forward man for another interminable period of time?

Cam slipped his portable phone from his pocket. "First, let's make dinner reservations. Where would you recommend?"

The dinner; she had agreed to that in the graveyard. More time with this perplexing person. Willa fluttered her fingers on the counter and seemed to be deep in thought. She glanced back at the woman in the back of the shop. There was a crash as one of the small glass jars slipped from the woman's hands and shattered on the stone floor. One corner of Willa's mouth crept up slightly. "Mother always could express an opinion in few words," she muttered.

"I'd like to have something special tonight." Cam held the phone expectantly.

"Really special?"

"Yes. I understand New Orleans is famous for good food. I'd like to try the best."

"Dial 555–4422. Ask for Claude and tell him you are calling for me. He'll give us a good table." Willa gathered her hair with both hands and let it sift through her fingers. "Make the reservations for nine. That's the best time."

Cam punched out the numbers, spoke briefly, and flipped the phone shut. "It's on."

Chapter Four

Before Willa could answer, a thin woman dressed in a flowered cotton dress shuffled into the shop. "Afternoon, Miss Willa."

"Hello, Mrs. Thibedeax."

Mrs. Thibedeax pulled a wrinkled envelope from her pocket. She narrowed her eyes at Cam, then shielded the paper from the man's possible glance. "Looka here, I got a list. Can you help me?"

Willa took the paper from her hand. "Of course, Mrs. Thibedeux. Let's see what we can do." She ran her finger down the penciled list. "Famous Luck candle, Money-Come-To-Me Powder, Everlasting Prosperity Oil, a Saint Michael medallion and a half-ounce pack of High John the Conqueror root. I'm sure we have everything except the High John root. That's been really popular lately." As she spoke, she placed the items in a shopping bag. "I should have some fresh coming in next week, though."

She totalled the amount owed. "That will be twenty-two dollars and seventy-five cents."

"Can you put it on my bill, darlin'? I bought two extra lottery tickets this week and the check hasn't come in yet this month." Mrs. Thibedeux scooped up the bag and held it tightly, as if Willa would take it back. She gave an extra fierce glare at Cameron Green.

Willa sighed. Mrs. Thibedeux's check never quite seemed to come in, but Willa's bills always arrived right on time. All the more reason to be nice to Cam Green and his checkbook. "Of course I will. You just remember me in your prayers, now."

The woman patted Willa's hand and whispered loudly, "Tell your Grandmama Marie that I found that silver teaspoon. It was just where she said. I'll say an extra Hail Mary for her this Sunday, I will." She left the shop, stepping wide of Cam and hugging her parcel to her chest.

Willa noticed Cam had slipped his recorder from his shirt pocket again.

"What did you sell that old woman?"

Willa pulled the identical items from the shelves. She stacked them in front of Cam. "Look. You can see them yourself." She held up the candle. "Famous Luck" was printed at the top of the glass in ornate gold letters. The candle was dark green with streaks of gold glitter. The wax had been poured into a cylindrical glass holder with a picture of a saint on the glass.

Cam took the candle and turned it in his hands. He didn't recognize the saint, who looked less than prosperous or lucky to him, as the saint was pierced by a number of spears and apparently on his last breath. On the back of the glass there was a prayer.

"This is the Everlasting Prosperity Oil." Willa handed him a pint-sized plastic bottle. Cam unscrewed the top and took a whiff of the contents. The oil was a faint green color, like second-pressing olive oil.

"Smells like mint." He took another sniff. "And cinnamon?"

"And the Money-Come-To-Me Powder. I always know when the lottery is really big. The Money Powder sales go crazy." Willa tore a corner off the small packet and sprinkled what looked and felt like green cornstarch into Cam's palm.

"What shall I do with it?"

"Rub it on your hands and put it in your pockets. Put it where you want the money to come." Willa folded the corner shut. "Here. It's on the house."

Cam rubbed the dust between his fingers. *What a crock,* he thought. "And you believe that this will bring you money?"

"No."

"Then why do you sell it?"

"Mr. Green, the power is not in the item, it is in the mind of the person who makes the wish. The visualization of the need is important. If you concentrate your mental power—and keep an open mind—an opportunity for creating what you want is formed. These things, these candles and oils, are just aids."

Willa looked into Cam's dark eyes and saw an emotion rise and, as quickly, become cloaked. What had it been? Anger? The expression intrigued her more than she cared to acknowledge. What was he after? There was definitely something she hadn't put her finger on.

"Concentration is what does it. Magic or whatever?"

"Concentration of desire, concentration of emotion. You must agree that strong emotions like love and hate can produce a physical effect on people and their surroundings." Willa moved to the rear of the shop. "Would you like a cup of coffee, Mr. Green?"

"Please call me Cam, and yes, coffee would be fine."

Willa took two mugs from a small shelf. She kept a pot of thick chicory coffee there on a hot plate, steaming slowly for most of the day. She poured two cups and added sugar to hers. "Sugar?"

"No, black." He cradled the mug in his hands. "Let's sit here and talk." They sat opposite each other at the round table where Brother Amos had sipped his soup and chocolate. Willa uncovered her pink crystal ball and Cranston jumped up to settle by the coffee cups.

"Cam, I don't know what your experience in life has been, but I feel that you are an observant person."

Cam sipped the bitter coffee. The tiny tape recorder reels were turning slowly. "Yes, you could say that."

"I showed you the Lalaurie House. What kind of emotions do you think could produce such a person as Madame Lalaurie? She starved and tortured her slaves—other human beings—chained them in the attic and laughed when they burned. She was deeply disturbed and filled with hate. Is it any wonder that place is said to be haunted?"

Willa watched Cam's face, looking for a hint of the expression that had crossed it in the unguarded moment before, but she saw nothing. He stroked the calico cat as he listened, but there was no shade of any emotion other than interest.

"On the other hand, love can attach a spirit and keep

it bound in a place where it should not be." Willa was interested to see a flicker pass across Cam's face. Was there someone he loved who had died? Was that the key to his interest in Halloween? She paused, hoping he would ask a question that would reveal something to her intuition.

"Where should a spirit be?"

"Spirits should return to the source of all souls to be refreshed and nurtured. Maybe to be reborn and learn new lessons. Most of all, to maintain the emotional balance."

Cam snorted into his coffee. "So the stuff you sell is just fake."

"It's not the ritual or the candle or the powder that creates good or evil, but the intent that is within a person's heart. The emotions are like a powerful radio transmitter beaming into the atmosphere." Willa leaned forward and gazed into Cam's eyes. What was hidden behind that grave amber stare?

"After all, if a chicken foot was magic, do you think so many of the birds would end up at KFC?" She smiled, but he did not return the expression.

Cam put down his coffee and laid his hands over the crystal ball. The long-fingered hands wrapped around the cool crystal so no part of the pink rock showed.

"I want to know about Halloween."

"Halloween is a time when the border between the spirit world and this world is thin. The time between the seasons is like a portal. If you reach out, sometimes you are able to touch the essence of someone who is connected to you by time and love."

Willa saw his hands tighten on the crystal, his knuckles white.

"You are saying you can talk to the spirits?"

A quartet of tourists burst into the shop, laughing loudly. Cranston leapt from the table, upsetting Willa's coffee cup. Willa grabbed a handful of paper towels from over the sink and dabbed at the tablecloth. The mood of confidence shattered as surely as a mashed potato chip.

"Hey! I want some of this love potion. Maybe I'll get lucky tonight." The sweaty man in the purple T-shirt waved a bottle of oil at Willa. The woman with him just rolled her eyes and took a drag from her cigarette.

"How 'bout you, honey?" He leered over the counter.

"I don't think so." Willa found it difficult to hold to Southern hospitality faced with this approach. "That will be five dollars and ninety-eight cents."

"Looky there, Orvus. A crystal ball." All four vacationers turned to stare like hypnotized turkeys.

"Hey, missy, tonight we're going to the Casino down to the river. How 'bout looking up a little luck for us? Some numbers or something?" Orvus opened his bottle of love oil and dabbed a drop behind each hairy ear.

"I'm sorry, it doesn't work that way."

"What, you mean you can't get that channel?" Orvus and his friends brayed with laughter.

Ms. Orvus tugged at her man. "Aw, come on, Orvus, let's go down to the bar and get one of those hurricane drinks. You get to take the glass with you. This spooky old stuff makes me nervous. What would Brother Jerry Bob say if he knew we were in a witchcraft place?"

Orvus patted her on her rotund behind. "Anything you want, little darlin'. A drink sounds like a good idea."

The cluster of tourists bumbled out the door and down

the street. Willa tucked the money in her pocket.

Two young women strolled in and began to pull books from the shelves, discussing the titles in low voices.

Cam saw the mood had been lost. "You have customers. Suppose we meet tonight at Antoine's. You can tell me more then."

"Yes, at nine." Willa stood at the door and watched as Cam strode down the street. She saw him pause before he turned the corner and look back. An impulse to wave almost reached her fingers before she resolutely shoved her right hand into her pocket.

There was a crash from the herb shelves and the smell of rosemary swept across the room. Willa whirled. "Mother! What are you doing back there?"

"Listening to you make a fool out of that man. A special dinner? He'll have a special dinner all right, at the most expensive place in the Quarter.

"I know that phone number; hasn't changed since I was a girl. It's Antoine's." Her mother laughed. "What's that poor Yankee ever done to deserve that?"

Willa twisted a hank of her hair in her fingers. "He thinks he is taking advantage of me. I just thought I'd turn the tables a little.

"Mother . . ." Willa walked to the herb shelves, but her mother had delivered her comment for the day and departed.

There was the sharp sound of someone rapping on the counter for attention. "Hello? Anyone here?"

Willa turned away from the herbs and answered, "Yes, just a moment." She saw a messenger waiting, holding a long, official-looking envelope.

He shifted his gum from one side to the other. "I'm supposed to hand deliver this to the owner of this place.

That you?'' At Willa's nod, he shoved a green slip of paper at her. "Sign here."

Willa stuck her finger under the flap and pulled out the letter slowly. The large letters at the top said it all: FINAL NOTICE OF CONDEMNATION OF PROPERTY.

Chapter Five

Willa wrapped a light shawl around her shoulders. A few of the cat's white and orange hairs floated over the black cashmere. Willa caught them between thumb and forefinger. She wasn't in the mood for being nice to Cam Green. He had annoyed her in the graveyard and she was sure he would have the same effect over dinner. The kiss hadn't exactly been an annoyance, she amended to herself, but it had been . . . something. Forward, disturbing, whatever. Something she wasn't ready to consider. She flicked away the cat hair and pulled the shawl tighter around her shoulders.

Disturbing; yes, that was the sensation.

This letter from the City Offices was a worry bigger than the leaks in the attic and the bad manners of any good-looking visitor. But she had made the bargain.

And a dinner at Antoine's was not to be turned down. A bottle of good wine and a fine dish of *Coquilles Saint*

Jacques à la Creole, topped with a bit of *Le Marquis au Chocolat* would make the world seem a better place, at least temporarily.

Standing in front of the mahogany-framed cheval mirror near her bed, she whirled once to see the skirt of her black jersey dress flare. As she faced the mirror again, her mother's face appeared in the glass.

"Have a good time, dear, and tell Claude hello." The apparition faded. The clock downstairs chimed nine.

The condemnation letter lay on the desktop. She touched the paper and frowned, but no solution came to her.

She latched the door and stepped down the brick street. No rain tonight, but the moon was veiled by scudding clouds. It was a short walk to Antoines's, with the life of the Quarter pulsing around her.

"Hi, Miss Willa. How you?" The musician sitting on a crate at the corner of Saint Rita Street greeted her. An open instrument case with three wrinkled dollar bills planted "for seed" rested at his feet. "This one's for you, darlin'." He began a series of quavery golden notes on his battered trumpet.

Willa blew him a kiss and kept walking. "Thanks, Howie. You take care, now." She stepped off the curb and crossed the street.

At nine o'clock in the evening the Vieux Carre, the French Quarter, was just coming alive, stretching like a sleepy woman on satin sheets. The scents of bourbon, late blooming flowers, and fine food mixed in a rich smell like none other. Musicians tuned guitars as they settled on street corners. Lithe youngsters jammed bottle caps into the toes of their sneakers to tap for coins to the music of boom boxes. The foot traffic on Bourbon

Street was body-to-body, too thick to stir with a stick. Tourists peeked into the dark doorways to see the famous dancers, willowy men more graceful and beautiful than the fantasy women they impersonated.

At Antoine's Cam stood in the vestibule, near the fountain. He looked reluctantly relieved as he stepped forward to greet her. "I thought maybe you wouldn't come."

Willa threw the corner of her shawl over her shoulder. She lifted her chin and met his eyes. "We have a bargain. I keep my bargains."

"Mademoiselle Willa. How glad I am to see you." The maître d' rushed forward. His tidy gray mustache twitched over a genuinely happy smile. "It has been much too long."

Willa held out her hands for his welcoming clasp. "Thank you, Monsieur Claude. You are looking well."

Monsieur Claude lifted her right hand and bowed his head over her fingers. "For you, your special place, *non?*"

"That would be wonderful. Claude, this is Cameron Green." She lowered her hand and gestured to include Cam in the conversation.

The restauranteur's eyes narrowed slightly. "How good to meet a friend of Mademoiselle Willa." Plainly, Cam was being measured for suitability. "Welcome to Antoine's, Monsieur Green."

Claude set off, threading his way through the ranks of less desirable tables until they reached a quiet alcove. A round candlelit table waited, elaborately draped in starchy linens. Places for two were set with a battery of gleaming silver on either side of the service plates. The intimate area was partitioned from the common room with a tall carved screen. "I remember, when you were a child, you loved the little fireplace so."

"It's beautiful, as always."

"Your grandmother fancied this place also, and then your lovely mother." Claude gave another appraising look at Cam. "The Robinette women, unforgettable."

He lowered his voice and turned slightly away from Cam. "After dinner, perhaps I might have a word with you, mademoiselle."

"Of course."

The distinguished host offered menus to each diner. Willa saw Cam blink as he scanned the offerings. Two unchangeable traditions of Antoine's were that the menus were handwritten entirely in French and no prices were listed.

Claude discreetly pinched the top of Willa's menu. "Mademoiselle, if you will permit?"

"That will be excellent, Claude." She turned to Cam. "Cam, Claude has always provided the best. If you wish, he will make the selections tonight."

Cam nodded in agreement. "Fine."

All business now, the host spun on his heel and snapped his fingers. A server with a napkin-wrapped bottle appeared. He poured the perfectly chilled wine and withdrew.

Cam picked up his glass and twirled it, watching the light liquid coat the inside of the crystal. "You certainly seem to be a star around here."

"My family has lived here for four generations. In this place we value that." She lifted her wine flute and reached forward to touch the rim to Cam's crystal. "What shall we drink to?"

"Family?"

It seemed an odd toast for a virtual stranger, but it must mean something to him, Willa mused. She touched his goblet with hers, and the crystal sang. "To family." They drank. The wine was superb, round and mellow, with a promising, impertinent effervescence.

This dining alcove was as private as if they were in a secluded castle tower. The fireplace cast a dancing orange glow, making Willa's light hair take a tawny tint. The low conversation of other diners behind the plants and screen was an oceanlike murmur. Soft piano and flute music cast a gentle layer of sound that seemed to grow from the stone walls. Everything about the restaurant invited romantic intimacy.

"This is a beautiful place." Cam slid his goblet on the white damask. "Very French. Very romantic."

Willa chuckled. "You mean very expensive, don't you?"

"Not at all. It suits you."

She was surprised to see a rather wistful expression cross his face. "Tell me about yourself, Cam."

He settled back in his chair and Willa saw a curtain drop in front of his eyes again. "I live in New York. I'm on a vacation."

"A vacation?"

Cam shifted. The movement was a bodily gesture Willa had learned often meant a reluctance to tell a lie.

"I'm working, too. I told you, I have to do some research on Halloween."

"Yes, the research. For your mother." Willa took another sip of her wine. "For a book? I don't believe you told me."

"No, it's more personal, but I will write about what I learn."

"Interesting." Why did he seem to be evading the truth? Willa placed her hands on her lap as the first course was placed silently before her. "So you're on vacation but you are working, and this is personal but you will write about it."

Cam took up his salad fork and pointed it defensively. "This isn't about me. I'm not here to have fun. Do you celebrate Halloween or not?"

"Yes, I do."

"So can I watch?"

"No, you cannot." Willa took a bite of lettuce.

Cam ripped a roll in two. "Look, I told you I am willing to pay."

Willa pushed back her chair and stood. She threw her napkin down. "This is a celebration of a holy day. Why don't you go down to the Cathedral and offer to pay Father Andrew for watching him celebrate All Saints? Do you think his reaction would be any less outraged than mine? What is your point here?"

Cam rose and they faced across the table, furious whispers flying over the lettuce and bread. "I want to see it, to be there."

"No."

"Why?"

"It's private."

"Oh, I see; it's secret."

"I didn't say secret, I said private. I keep the holiday with my ancestors privately. I'm not going to be dancing around a bonfire naked, waving a chicken foot and sacrificing a cat, if that's what you want to know." Willa glared across the narrow space separating them. "Are you disappointed?"

She saw the smallest hint of a smile creep into Cam's

eyes. "Maybe. About the naked part, anyway." He stepped around the table and pulled out her chair to urge her to be seated. "I'm sorry. I seem to be approaching this is in the wrong manner."

He picked up her fallen napkin. "Look; a white flag." He flourished the linen and draped the cloth over her lap, bending near enough for his breath to brush Willa's cheek. She turned her head and was startled to meet his glance.

For a frozen second they stared. Willa saw the amber sparks in his dark eyes. A flush flamed its way across her cheeks and she looked away hurriedly. If a man's soul was revealed in his glance, what had she just seen? Her heart gave an alarming flip, as it had the time she had taken the wrong stop on the streetcar line. She thought she was lost, but . . . She closed her eyes.

"Willa?" Cam touched her hand gently. She felt his breath stir her hair. She must open her eyes. When she did, he had taken his seat near her.

"The soup, miss," the waiter murmured and set a shallow soup bowl in front of her. Willa was glad for the interruption and looked down to fiddle with the steaming cream soup. "Crab and asparagus bisque, with sherry." A second bowl was placed before Cam.

"Smells delicious." He stirred the green-flecked golden soup and lifted a spoonful to his lips.

"It will be. Everything here is very special." Her voice sounded faint, even to herself.

Cam looked into her eyes again. "Yes," he said, "I think it must be."

They finished their soup without further comment, and the empty bowls were whisked away.

"So what do you wish to ask me? You should get

your money's worth.'' Willa sat very straight in her chair, ready to be interrogated between courses.

"This morning you talked about the haunted house and how some spirits stay where they are not wanted. Do they ever stay because they want to?''

"Yes, they do.''

Cam seemed to be waiting for further details, and an awkward silence grew. "And ... ?'' he primed.

"Sometimes it is a good thing that they stay. They can help or guide us. Sometimes it is not so good for them to stay. The spirits can be unhappy and confused and create a chaotic atmosphere.'' Willa's expression darkened. "They can be dangerous then, to people who are not protected.''

Cam snorted derisively. "Protected? By what? Garlic and a crucifix?''

"No, Cam. By their inner faith.''

"I see. Faith.''

The waiter appeared with the main course, interrupting the barely underway discussion. For Willa, there were succulent scallops, carefully arranged in a large shell, drizzled with a piquant red sauce. "*Coquilles Saint Jacque à la Creole*,'' the waiter announced as he settled the plate.

"*Carbonnade provencale,*'' the waiter pronounced as he placed a steaming dish before Cam. The beef looked tender enough to float off the plate, only held to earth by the rounds of carefully browned potatoes.

Cam cut a bite from the beef and chewed thoughtfully. His expression took on a look of appreciation. "This is wonderful.''

Willa nodded in affirmation.

"Can you cook like this?''

"Yes. My grandmother taught me." She touched her lips with her napkin. "My family is French. We respect good food."

"Is this the grandmother who finds gold chains and silver teaspoons?"

"Yes, that is her gift. Beside good cooking, that is." Willa smiled. *Mother and Grandmother rattling the pots in the kitchen with rapid-fire French and battling wooden spoons. Mother's gift was not good cooking.* Mother had developed the deep relationship with Claude that was now presenting her daughter with such a delectable dinner.

"Her gift? How does that work? The taxi driver said you had a gift." Cam took a deep swallow of wine. "Actually, he said you had *the* gift. Is *the* gift different from *a* gift?"

Claude stood at Cam's elbow, beaming at Willa. Once again they were interrupted just as Cam felt himself closing in on an important point. Damn all this good service anyway. Couldn't they just throw them the food, snarl, and disappear, the way they did in New York?

"And did you enjoy, Mademoiselle Willa? I remembered, the coquilles, they were your mother's favorite, and yours, too."

"It was perfect."

Claude stepped closer. "For you, a gift. It is my pleasure to give this to you tonight."

Willa frowned. "Claude, you are my friend, but I cannot accept such a costly gift."

The dignified man held his leather-bound menus tightly. "I wish to ask something of you. For me, this is difficult, but you are the only one I can ask. It will be a more than equal trade, I assure.'' He glanced in Cam's direction.

''All right, Claude. Tell me how I can help you.''

Claude took a deep breath. ''I have purchased a house, on the edge of the Quarter. Now, not so fashionable, you know,'' he raised his hand and cocked his head in the Parisian manner, ''but soon it will change. The building is very old, very old, *mai non,* and will be perfect for,'' he lowered his voice even softer and glanced around furtively, ''my own café, *oui?* But there is a problem. The previous owner, how shall I say, he does not wish to leave.''

Willa lowered her glance, long eyelashes shadowing her expression. ''I understand.''

''*Oui,* I knew you would.''

Cam looked mystified, watching first the man's face, then Willa's.

''The time, before All Saints, is a good time for this, is it not? When the Other World approaches closely and the veil between, it is thin. It will be a blessing for the owner and for me also.'' The maître d' rapped a nervous, silent tattoo on the back of the menus.

''I will be glad to do this for you, Claude.''

Claude grabbed Willa's hands and her wine goblet crashed to the floor. ''Mademoiselle Willa! Thank you, me and my family, always we will be in your debt.''

Cam could not be a passive bystander for another second. ''What is it? What are you going to do for him?''

Willa smiled serenely. ''Set a spirit free.''

Willa and Cam walked briskly down the street. That is, Cam walked and Willa stomped. Late-night revelers pulled aside as if they could sense the annoyance radiating from the couple. Willa clutched her woolen wrap tightly around her shoulders, her arms held close to her chest. "No. I said no, and I meant no." She stopped and yanked the shawl even tighter. "What is it about *n-o* that you don't understand?"

"Let me watch this." Cam stepped in front of her. "Let me watch this spirit-freeing business and I won't bother you about the Halloween thing."

"I don't have to make any bargain with you to watch anything. This is not part of any deal." Willa brushed past him.

"OK, OK. How about I pay? Five hundred dollars."

Willa stopped again. Her eyes looked menacing, and Cam took a step back. *Wrong move there, Green. Big wrong move.*

"You just don't get it, do you? Money does not make any difference. If I have to spell this out, you won't ever understand, either."

"That's it." The answer dawned in Cam's brain. "That's your gift. *The* gift. You can talk to the spirits." He reached out and enveloped her in a huge hug, waltzing her across the wet cobblestones.

"You're the woman with the Gift." He let go of her and placed his hands on each side of her face. When he looked at her like that, so close, so vital, he could almost believe it. Her gift. He felt as if he was falling into the blue shadows of her eyes.

Willa pulled away from him. "Yes, I can talk to the spirits. But you don't believe that, so what difference does it make to you?" She pushed him away. "I can find my way home, thank you. Good night."

* * *

Cam wasn't a good reporter for nothing. He knew how to find out what he needed to know. He looked at the business card he had picked up at Antoine's the night before. Claude du'Lac.

He pulled the thick city phone book from under the nightstand and looked up the City Records office number. "Yes. A Mr. Claude du'Lac purchased some property on, ummm," he fumbled with the small map on the back of the phone book. Stabbing with a finger, he picked out a street name at the edge of the Quarter. "Rue de Pommes Street, is that right?" He held the receiver with his shoulder as he scribbled with his hand. "Oh, *not* Rue de Pommes. It's Saint Rita Street." Interesting, indeed; that was Willa's street.

All this Southern helpfulness could pay off, after all. "And what's that number? I see. Six thirty-seven. Uptown. Thank you so much."

The loquacious clerk at the office was not yet finished with her generous information. Cam flipped his pencil between his fingers as she continued with her helpful speech.

"I see. The whole neighborhood. A national treasure. Umm, hmm." He doodled a lightning bolt striking a telephone receiver. "Can't change anything. Yes, I see. Yes, a restoration medallion. How wonderful." A second lightning bolt struck a stick figure with a large mouth. "Thank you so much." He was still being gracious as he firmly pressed down the phone button with his forefinger.

God, these people loved to talk. Well, he amended, *most of them. It was like pulling teeth to get Willa Robinette to tell him anything.* He'd show her; he could find out what he wanted with or without her help.

Cam hung up the phone and flicked the paper where he had written the address. Now around the corner to the camera shop and he was on his way.

There was a tapping at his door, then the door opened. His mother bustled in, a small stack of books in her arms.

"Cameron, dear, this trip was a wonderful idea. There are the most amazing shops here. Look at all these books I found. Look at the bindings, all leather, so lovely." She offered one volume, gold-tipped pages lovingly worn, impressed leather cover thick and rich.

Cam remembered how she had collected old books in their home when he was a boy. He hadn't seen her this animated since before his father's death. Surely this was a good sign that she was moving away from her obsession with his ghostly father.

His mother laid out the books one by one on the desktop. "No one makes real books like these anymore," she said wistfully, running her fingers over the kidskin. "Your father would love them."

She spotted the doodlings and scribbled information Cam had scrawled across an envelope back. "Saint Rita Street. I was there today. You know, the taxi driver said to find Miss Robinette on Saint Rita Street."

Cam frowned. "You went to the shop there?"

"Yes, I found it, but the door was closed. And Cameron, there was a condemnation sign tacked there. What a shame; such an interesting building. We'll have to hurry if we are going to find Miss Robinette and talk to your father."

75

Chapter Six

Cam arrived as evening darkened into opaque, sinister black shades at 637 Saint Rita Street. Claude had been astute in his choice; this end of Saint Rita was one of those fringe areas that was just short of decay, but with care would blossom into carefully restored fashion.

Six thirty-seven looked much as Willa's shop did, but it was larger and moldering on an even grander scale. The house was closely shuttered under the drooping balconies, paint was scaling in the damp, and the iron work had gaps here and there like neglected teeth. Cam went to the side of the house, looking for a passage to the inevitable courtyard at the rear.

He squeezed through the alleyway, jumping once when something large scuttled over his foot. The thing was heavy and seemed to be furry, but he was pretty sure it wasn't a cat.

At the rear of the house two of the shutters had been

pried away, and the French doors hung ajar. Leaves at their base drifted inside the empty rooms. Cam pulled the small flashlight from his bag and flicked on the light as he stepped into the room.

It seemed colder inside than outside, and the air pressed against him like inquisitive and not too friendly hands. He flashed the beam of light across the walls and floor, as if that would keep the feeling of menace at bay. There was a broken marble fireplace at the end of the long room, and the corroded remnants of a mirror still tilted crazily above the mantel.

Cam groped in the bag and pulled out the tiny tape recorder and a fist-sized video camera. He loved electronic gadgets and this was a gem. State-of-the-art Japanese made, night vision, self-adjusting. If anything could be recorded, this little machine could do it.

The entire ground floor had been gutted and was one long room. Shining his flashlight up, Cam saw several holes in the ceiling. Perfect. If he went up there, he could see everything that happened down here. As he started up the stairs, he heard a car door slam and then a key rattle in the front door lock. He hurried to get into position before Willa came in.

Willa walked in slowly, carrying a purple cloth bag, a pet carrier cage, and a flash light. Cam could hear her sigh as she opened the cat carrier and Cranston emerged, eyes saucer-wide in the dim light. The cat sniffed to the right and left. Willa knelt to prop the flashlight to the side and untied the drawstring and pulled open the bag.

Moving stealthily, Cam positioned the video camera and began the visual recording. The tape recorder was voice-activated, so it would catch any sound in the room below. Now all he had to do was wait and watch. He stretched out on his stomach, chin on folded hands, watching through a small hole in the plaster.

Willa stood and took off her jacket. Her breath was clear as puffs of white on the air. Was it Cam's imagination or was it getting colder? Willa pulled her fingers through her hair and took out the combs that had held it back.

Cam recalled his impression in the candlelit restaurant: ethereal. Her eyes had reflected the gentle and graceful, ephemeral beauty of another world. She was now preparing to do battle with that other world. An unbidden swell of admiration swept through Cam. Her actions showed she was stubborn and strong in her convictions.

He was glad he had kissed her in the graveyard, even though the impulse had seized him in an uncharacteristicly straightforward manner. A smile crossed his lips at the thought of doing it again. Yeah, the trip was business, but Julia had insisted on pleasure, too. Maybe that wasn't such a bad idea.

Willa and he just kept getting off on the wrong foot. He would make it up to her after this "house-cleaning" thing. How long could it take to clear a house of some raggedy ghost?

The serious young woman took a fat white candle out of the bag, lifting it with both hands. Rising, she stood and turned in a circle, as if to determine the exact center of the room. The flashlight made her shadow slide across the wall like a thin, skeletal thing. For the first time, Cam felt an uncertainty in his non-belief.

"Here," she said aloud. She settled the candle on the floor. She stroked Cranston, who crouched beside the candle like an alert sphinx. "Good girl. The spirit is old,

Crannie, but it doesn't feel evil. I sense melancholy, and loss.''

''Yow-yow.'' The cat yawned and displayed her fangs, then stretched her paws and unsheathed her claws. Fang and claw flashed bone white in the unnatural illumination. Cranston seemed ready for anything that could materialize.

Willa pulled out two quart glass jars of clear liquid and set them aside. She retrieved a white-handled knife, blade wrapped in a twist of red silk fabric, from the very bottom of the bag.

''This is sea water, a natural combination of water and salt, perfect purifiers and cleansers.'' Willa talked to the cat as if to keep her mind focused, Cam thought. Her voice was steady and clear, perfect for triggering the tape recorder. He glanced at the video cam and tape recorder. Both were operating smoothly.

A gust of wind pushed a branch across the roof to scratch like a caged animal. Upstairs a door slammed explosively, making them both jump. Cam cursed silently as he saw Willa glance up to the place where he was hiding. Perhaps she had heard or sensed his start at the unexpected sound. It seemed impossible, but the room below was growing darker by the minute.

Willa picked up her knife and unwrapped it with an air of reverence. The blade flashed silver star-sparks and the darkness seemed slightly less dense. The young woman began to circle the room, arm outstretched, knife pointing down to the foundation of the house.

''Darksome night and shining moon, Hearken to this witch's rune. East, then South, West, then North. Hear and come. I call thee forth.''

Cam could not supress a shudder as he heard her call

below him. But it seemed a lot of theatrical hocus-pocus for the benefit of no audience but the cat. Nevertheless, another nervous spasm tickled its way down his arms and back.

She paced the circumference of the room, then returned to the center, stretched down with the knife and then reached up, drawing the sacred star in the air, left then right, then left. Pressing the steel to her lips, she kissed it and lowered the blade. "It is done."

A rumble like thunder but was not thunder started from the corners of the room, deep and ominous. Cam felt the vibration deep in his body, like a close-passing train. Willa slipped the dagger between her belt and jeans, caught at her hip.

With open hands held high, arms spread wide, she made her offering. "Hear me now, spirit. I command you to leave this place and return to the healing of the powers of light."

Heart-wrenching weeping began, growing and resonating from the walls. Cam froze, then turned his head slowly to peer from corner to corner, looking for the source. A soft scent of violets, faded blue vapor, rose from every dry crack. Cam felt a droplet of moisture splatter on his hand. A chill swept his body. Did ghosts cry real tears?

How did she do that? It had to be a trick. What an effect!

"Leave? How can I?" A woman's voice trembled, softly accented in Creole French. "My love has not returned from the War." A weary voice, so real and alive it shocked Cam as it called out an answer. "He will never find me if I leave this place, our home. I promised I would wait."

80

"Let me help you, sister. Your husband passed over with honor and now awaits you in the higher plane. You must release this place and know that he will be there to greet you and welcome you into the next world." Willa spoke with compassion.

The fragile voice trembled with emotion. "You've come to help me?"

"Will you accept my help?" She paused for an answer. "I must have your permission."

"Yes, yes . . . anything for my Sidney, to see him again."

Willa acted with calm composure. She lifted the jar of seawater and dipped in her fingers. Walking in the same circle she had traced with the knife, she flicked the water right and left.

> "Waters of the sea and ocean,
> Hear this spell put to motion,
> As the tides ebb and flow,
> Return the spirit, send it home."

Where the water met the walls and floor, the moisture sizzled and disappeared in tiny wisps of steam, as if it had been dropped on a hot skillet. The strange blue vapor flowed hurriedly away in eager retreat. It billowed in a low cloud, formed into an amorphous, graceful embrace. Willa whirled, flinging water generously.

> "Soundless, boundless, bitter sea,
> Return this spirit. So mote it be."

The vapor lifted and faded to a faint spinning haze at the boundaries of the releasing spell. Cam was enthralled, puzzled, and totally engrossed all at the same time. How was she doing this? Why was she doing this?

Willa continued around the circle, shaking the droplets from her fingers. The haze looked like lilacs, smelled like lilacs. Cam pressed his mouth against the back of his hand in amazement. This thing was getting much too real.

A peal of eager laughter burst from the air. "Sidney! Sidney, are you waiting for me? I'm coming, darling!"

The steam and sweet smell of faded lilacs ceased, replaced by a peaceful calm. Cam saw Willa shiver, then resolutely stand tall.

"Spirits of love and light, reclaim this lost soul." She kissed the hilt of her knife and pressed it to her heart, breathing as if she had been running a race. "Return her to her soulmate."

The image of a tall man, pale to the point of dust, but with eyes that burned like candle flames materialized in the tarnished gilt mirror above the crumbling fireplace. His body was lean, clad in faded gray with epaulets of gold.

Cam was too fascinated to check his camera. He stared down into the room as if it were a stage.

"Estelle, come to me. Step through the mirror." The man in the mirror opened his arms wide. Steam gathered and poured into the heart of the looking glass. The mirror exploded, flying shards of silvered glass showering about Willa. A jagged sliver sliced across Willa's cheek and a trickle of blood raced down, dripping to stain her shirt.

"I regret the pain you feel, but know this is the only sacrifice you must make for your own true love's return." Willa heard the dignified male voice pronounce.

"It is in our gratitude, we can give this favor to you."

Above, Cam clenched his fists and reminded himself that Willa needed no defense; this was illusion, all illusion.

The cat stood and arched her back. The feline hissed and yowled, adding her own note. Cranston kept her tail bent almost flat against her back and puffed as big as a brush. She lifted one forepaw and bared her claws.

Willa knelt beside the protective cat. She grabbed the lighter and struck the flint rapidly. She held the flame to the wick. "As I light this candle, I ask that the powers of light be with me." She drew a breath. "May the light protect myself and all who are within these walls. Benevolent powers that live in the light, aid the spirit of Estelle to rejoin her beloved husband."

Silence. No smells. No noise. For a moment, it all seemed normal. Except for the drip of blood from her cheek down the front of Willa's blouse, Cam could imagine nothing had happened here.

The candle flame sunk and fluttered, then grew to a handspan tall, then taller: a foot, a yard high. Willa peered into the growing pool of wax around the flame. The pure white began to pink, as the energy transformed sadness to a loving essence.

Cranston sneezed, and jumped on top of her carrier. The cat crouched and watched the candle as if it were prey.

The wick danced and the flame grew, releasing a thin black stream of soot into the air. The wax pool was growing.

Willa began to chant softly. "By the power of light and love, I release thee, spirit. Return and find peace."

At her words, the entire candle liquified, gurgling like

an overflowing teapot. Willa scrambled backward. Cranston hissed and clawed. The wax spilled and boiled on the floor, gathering life. The substance spread rapidly, oozing toward Willa, growing in size as it came. Willa jumped to her feet.

The liquid wax began to form a circle of script around Willa. Flowing letters spelled out, "Soul to soul, spirit to spirit, thank you."

Willa smiled. "You may visit your home whenever you like, but know it will now be a place of joy, happiness, and celebration of love."

A faint "Goodbye" murmured on the wind.

It was quiet.

Cam could hear the normal faint traffic noises from the nearby streets, and the thump of a passing boom-box in a car. He glanced at the video cam; the small red eye still blinked to signal "recording."

Willa buried her face in Cranston's fur. "She's gone," Cam heard her whisper. Even to Cam, it was apparent that something was different. The house was empty.

Willa pulled the scrap of silk from her pocket and wrapped her knife before returning it to her belt. Weariness was etched into her every movement.

"Come, Cranston, come Crannie, love. In your box." The cat stepped in calmly and began to groom herself.

Above her, the plastic reels of the recorder still spun slowly.

Cam waited until he heard the click of the key in the lock before he sat up and looked around. What had happened here? Something undeniably had. There was no reason for this sound-and-light—not to mention smell—show. It was an obviously sincere performance on Willa Robinette's part. She had done what had been requested of her.

Chapter Seven

Cam hurried into his hotel room, shucking out of his jacket and digging out the video camera at the same time. He squatted in front of the television and inserted the tape into the VCR. There was a burst of electrical sputters, and he reduced the volume hurriedly. It was late, and he presumed his mother, in her room nearby, was sleeping.

This ghost-busting was on tape; what a story. It could change the entire course of his investigations. And beside that, the recording would be his source for satisfying his mother. Both his pressing assignments wrapped up into one ball.

The static and gray blur continued. The tape looked as if it had been run through a powerful magnetic field; exposed, but no picture to be seen. Cam swore colorfully and fast-forwarded the film. A blur of dancing black flecks was all that could be seen. Suddenly, at the very end, with perhaps one minute remaining, a picture appeared. A perfectly clear scene of Willa and her cat shaped on the screen. Cam saw Willa put the cat in the carrier, look around the room, turn, and leave. The tape showed the empty, dark room for some seconds, then ended.

Cam slapped the top of the television. "That can't be it. Where's all the action?" He sputtered and grabbed the camera. Poking the knobs and buttons, he could see the device was functioning perfectly.

He rubbed his hand across his face and resisted the impulse to throw the camera across the room. He had the tape recorder for backup. That was what backup was all about.

Cam took the tape recorder from the bag and sat it carefully on the desktop. *Gadget, don't fail me now.* He punched the play button. A whistle and hum shrieked out of the tiny speaker, then settled into an unintelligible electronic chatter. At the very end, there was silence and a click that might have been the door lock as Willa left the house.

"What?" Cam stared at the little gray machine incredulously. "What?" The recorder had never failed him before; why now?

He knew what he had seen, what he had heard. The video should have been spectacular—*my God, talk about lights, and action—steam, colors, hissing cats.* And tears—he had felt them. Cam rubbed his hand where the drop had splashed. No; he could not possibly have been hallucinating or hypnotized. Willa hadn't even known he was there; there was no way she could have influenced him. In his heart he knew it. But this video. Blank. Well, almost blank.

What did it mean? And not even a peep on the voice-activated tape recorder. There had been plenty of voices and noise, and he had checked for reel movement several times.

Now what?

Willa measured the chicory coffee into the pot and added water. How many more peaceful days might she have in her home to do such sweet, regular tasks? She had come downstairs to find another condemnation notice tacked on her door. She pulled the cardboard down, but that would scarcely solve her problem, or even buy any time. It did, however, make her feel better when she ripped the paper into little shreds.

She rubbed the spot between her eyes where the headaches started whenever she thought about her problem. It seemed like every avenue she had approached was blocked, as if by an invisible hand. The banks refused to take on a condemned building as collateral for a remodeling loan. She had nothing to pawn or sell. Even the stock of the shop, taken in all, was not worth more than a few hundred dollars. There had to be a way. A dilemma like this had to be an opportunity in disguise; it had to.

She felt like a mouse in a maze; she had to keep trying doors until one would open and give her the cheese-reward.

Granddame seemed unconcerned that there was a problem. Grannie Belle refused to even think about the situation—if ghosts think, that is. At any rate, Grannie was not troubled. Mother made a few cryptic comments that it would work out and disappeared into her favorite maidenhair ferns in the courtyard. The solution was obviously squarely in Willa's jurisdiction.

Jurisdiction. The word made her think of Ernest, the scorned lover. Him with all his connections at City Hall. He could pull her out of this quandary. *Don't even think like that; he's the one who got you into the whole mess.* Willa shook her now painful head. *Getting pretty desperate to even consider Ernest.*

Maybe she should just set a big juicy price and do a Halloween ritual to beat all for Cameron Green. That thought made her look up at the clock. The persistent man should be here any minute, ready to pry away. He was not one to take no for an answer. Tomorrow was Halloween and the pressure was really on.

She had to smile. Actually, she was enjoying her daily battle of wits with the reporter, or writer, or whatever he was. It helped that he was certainly good to look at. When Cam wasn't on his quest to persuade her to let him see her perform a ritual, he could be charming, and entertainingly intellectual. The other night at dinner, it had been satisfying and exciting to have someone so handsome and polished to match banter with.

And attractive. Definitely attractive. The unexpected kiss at the graveyard had set off lingering sparks she didn't even want to consider. *Momma Marie, still matching lovers.* The spirits always seemed to be moving around and with Willa.

Claude the maître d' had never approved of Ernest. Yes, Ernest was a dim bulb compared to the attractive flame of Cam Green.

Willa filled her favorite blue mug with bitter black coffee and stirred in a large splash of hot milk. The dark brew made her think of Cam's dark hair and then, with cream stirred in, the caramel brown of the northerner's eyes.

Cranston stood by Willa's chair and put her forepaws on her mistress's thigh. "Mee-yuup."

"Come up, Crannie. Are you all recovered from last night, love?" Willa scratched under the cat's chin and over her ears. "Pretty big job, huh? Poor lonely ghost."

Cranston responded with a purr and a roll of the head. She stretched out her orange paws and prepared to settle into a nap on Willa's lap.

Willa gave a start that made the cat leap away when Cam came slamming into the shop.

"Have you got a VCR?" he demanded.

"Upstairs, in my living room. And good morning to you, too."

"Can we go up there? I want to show you something." He brandished a tape cassette.

Cam loped up the stairs, two steps at a time. Willa followed as quickly as possible into her small living room. She had a television, but the set was buried under a stack of books and papers. Cam fidgeted while she removed the litter. "There. Sorry, I don't use it much."

Cam grabbed the remote control and punched in the correct channel, then shoved the tape into the VCR. "Look at this."

A smear of gray and black spread over the screen and danced there.

"So? What's to see?"

"That's just it. Last night I saw you, you and the cat. There was smoke, and fire and . . . and Sidney and Estelle. I saw it. But there's nothing here."

Willa clenched her fists. "You followed me? You *watched* me? You *videotaped* me?" Her voice was rising. "What kind of a person are you? I told you this was a private thing. Are you some kind of spy?" She poked Cam in the chest with a finger. "Out. Out, out, out."

Cam grabbed her hands and held them tight. "Willa, listen to me. I saw it all. Yes, I admit I shouldn't have hidden and spied like that."

Willa jerked her hands, but Cam wouldn't let go. "It's important to me, Willa. The tape's not for the story. The recording would have proved it to me. Just me. Pictures, sounds would have been hard evidence. But listen: I saw it and I have to believe you."

"I don't care if you believe or not." She tagged at his grip again. "Let go."

"It's what my mother has been searching for. Can you help her? Will you help her?" Cam pulled Willa closer and looked into her face. "Can you help me? Let us come to your Halloween ritual."

Willa wrenched away. She clutched the back of her chair and kept the seat between them like a barrier. "Cameron Green, get out of my house. How dare you spy on me to get your story, then come wheedling around when it didn't work. And the audacity to use your mother as an excuse. You're a rat." She stalked over to the television and ripped the tape out of the VCR. "Here, take your wretched tape. Now get out." She flung the cassette at Cam.

Cam caught the flying tape in one hand. He hesitated a second, then tossed the tape into a nearby wastebasket. "OK. I'm leaving." He spun on his heel and clattered down the stairs and out of the shop.

Willa scrubbed across her face and was not surprised to feel tears burning in her eyes.

"Shameful."

The voice came from behind her. She turned to see Grannie Belle shaking her head.

"Yes, it is. Spying on me, and then such a spineless ploy to get into my good graces again. His mother! Really." Willa plopped down onto her sofa and clutched a pillow to her chest.

"No, dear. It's your performance that is shameful. Look into your heart. Don't deny this request. This is your duty, and it will become your pleasure. I can see it."

Willa bent and buried her face in the down pillow. "No, no. I am too angry about this. Grannie Belle, I can't be wrong. I have the Gift, too. He's not the one who I would ever leap over the Samhain fire with. He makes me crazy!"

Grannie Belle stroked Willa's hair. "Raise your head, love, and don't mumble."

"Yes, *mon cher,* most unattractive." The voice of Granddame Sophia chimed in, with a definite note of disapproval. "Gather yourself; this disarray is altogether too common. *Zut alors,* straighten your spine."

Granddame offered a spectral lace-edged handkerchief. "Attend to the repairs," she commanded.

Willa obediently sat up straighter and dabbed her eyes with the filmy linen square. Would anyone in this family ever understand that she only cried when she was angry? And her great-grandmother and Grannie Belle scolding *her.* Cam Green was the one in the wrong; why were they taking his side? This was too unfair.

"Willa, I know that expression. We are not taking the wrong side in this problem. You have not thought this through."

"Mother, not you, too. Of all people, you should understand. He deceived me."

"Look to your heart and see why he is here. It's not for himself, but for his family. He is here for the same reason as you. To gather his family together. For love. For you."

"Let him in, Willa. You know the rules. No arguing or fighting on Hallowmas." Grannie Belle added her persuasion.

Granddame Sophia swished her black taffeta skirts imperiously. "He will come to the circle in sincerity. This I know. No longer is he seeking merely a story."

"Let him in, Willa. Everyone has a gift, and his is the gift for you that none of us can offer. The gift you have been waiting for."

"But what can he offer me?" Willa looked at the three loved faces that had surrounded and advised her all her life.

"*Mon cher,* he offers you the love and strength you deserve." Granddame stood before the fireplace in a regal pose. "It is the next step in the circle of your life."

Willa's practical mother levitated the telephone from the table to hover in front of her daughter. "Pick up this phone, girl, and give him a call. Time's wasting. Take our word for it."

No arguing, no disagreeing, those were the edicts of the day. Honor the ancestors. Grannie Belle pressed Cam's business card into Willa's hand. Willa turned it over to see where Cam had scrawled his hotel phone number.

"All right, but only for you all," she said to her family as she dialed the number. The ghosts drew closer and crowded about Willa as the phone made small electric noises.

Willa covered the mouthpiece with her palm. "Could I have some privacy here, please?"

The three glanced at each other in satisfaction, then disappeared. Granddame's scent of violets lingered in the air as a piquant reminder of duty and good posture.

"Green here."

Indeed, Willa felt the warmth of forgiveness start to melt her heart at the sound of his deep voice. Perhaps the ancestors were right. They usually were. "Cameron, this is Willa Robinette." Willa forced calmness into her voice. "I have reconsidered letting you and your mother attend tomorrow's Halloween ritual."

She heard an intake of surprised breath and continued before he could comment or interrupt. "There are a few conditions you must abide by."

"Anything you say, Willa." He *did* sound sincere. "First, bring a bottle of red wine. Second, mind my instructions. And you may not write about anything you see or experience. Can you agree to this?"

"Yes. No stories, nothing written on paper. Just the experience."

"The ritual starts at midnight."

Chapter Eight

The moon, a perfect silver orb, hung full and heavy above the secluded courtyard. Moonlight spilled into the private garden that had been Willa's sanctuary since childhood.

Willa paced about the edge of the courtyard sprinkling aromatic Solomon's Seal as an offering to the elemental spirits. The heady, sweet scent hung on the evening air. As the herbal powder slipped through her fingers, she recalled tea parties she had held here in the shadows, a child with imaginary friends. Willa had taken her first vows here, standing in a circle cast around the oaken stump, as had her mother and grandmother. Her great-grandmother had stood on these paving slates, new stone then, and the stump had been a young, vigorous tree. The magic had began for Willa here in this house, in this garden. Would it end here as well?

Crisp and clear, the weather was perfect. Willa drew

a deep draught of the cool night air. Preparations for tonight's ritual were almost complete. Representing death as an integral part of the wheel of life, the oak stump served as an altar. Four candles stood in a semi-circle on the back of the wide wooden surface; one candle of black, one of red, and two of pure white. A silver-lined ram's horn filled with deep blood-red Beaujolais would serve as a chalice. A thin white cloth was draped over the mouth of the horn. A small copper statue of a shapely fairy held up a crystal dish, offering incense to the element of air.

"Cranston, where is Grandmere's silver bowl with the salt?" Willow laid her athame on the stump and addressed her familiar.

"Meeeow!" Cranston jumped up to the stump top, playfully pawed a pomegranate to the ground, then turned and disappeared into the house as if her tail had been set on fire.

"You're not being much help tonight," Willa scolded and plucked the pomegranate from the dry grass at her feet. She set it back on the altar between an apple and the round loaf of pumpernickel. Turning, she surveyed all the prerequisite offerings and ritual tools for the evening's celebration.

"Pumpkins, apples, gourds, walnuts, acorns, oak leaves, and branches. Bread, honey, salt, water, knife." Several yards in front of the altar a low pile of dry oak wood stood ready to be lit. "Matches."

"Another year I wouldn't be leaping the bonfire with my true love." Willa spoke aloud, as she kindled the fire, touching the dry wood here and there with the match. The oak splints caught as if they were eager for the night's actions to begin. Small tendrils of smoke rose and danced, with a mellow autumnal scent.

Tonight should be a time of happiness, but Willa felt a finger of sadness touch her heart. This would be another year ending without her finding her own true love. Would no daughter of Willa's own ever look into a Samhain fire and think of her face, remember her touch, think of her laughter?

Tonight Willa must focus on Samhain, the day the new year and the old swing on the same hinge. Tonight she would forget all else and honor her ancestors. The Old Ones would cross through the veil and meet her to celebrate the turning of the wheel. Endings and beginnings must be celebrated to remember that there is no death, only the never-ending cycle of transformation.

The celebration would remind her that true love never dies. That was, after all, why Mrs. Green wanted to be here tonight. To be sure her husband would always be there for her. How could Willa stand in the way of real everlasting love?

"Not to be so apprehensive, *ma petite*. This visitor will come to the circle in sincerity, I am certain." Granddame Sophia Martine murmured from the drifting smoke that caressed Willa's hair. "He has a gift for you that none of us can give. Something we can only wish and pray for."

The sharp smell of burning wood drifted through the night air. Cam and his mother stood at the edge of the courtyard. The pebbled walk crunched as Cam shifted from foot to foot. Willa smiled at the sight of the green bottle cradled in the crook of Cam's arm. So far so good. He remembered. She listened to their anxious whispers.

"Cameron, do you think I look all right for Daddy?"

Mrs. Green patted a few stray hairs back from her forehead. "I'm wearing his favorite color."

"You look wonderful, Mom. He'll be thrilled to see you, I'm sure." Cam reassured his mother, nervously giving her a quick hug.

"We're about to begin, Mrs. Green. Do you have any questions?" Willa attempted to sooth any apprehensions.

"No, dear. I just want to hear it from him—I mean my husband—that we will be together always."

"Cam?"

"No."

"There's no need to be afraid. Nothing you see will harm you. These are people who have loved us and are coming back to help us. They would not hurt us in this life and won't harm us from the other. You are protected by those who love you." Willa squeezed Evelyn's hand, then stepped back into the center of the courtyard.

"Willa," Cam spoke. He held out the green wine bottle. "Thank you."

Willa turned to face him. She accepted the bottle and placed it on the altar. Her thin silk robe swirled and lifted gently around her bare ankles.

Facing north before her altar, she closed her eyes and sent a silent prayer to the universe. *Am I doing the right thing?* Never before had she allowed anyone or anything to participate in such a sacred circle. But somehow, something deep inside felt at peace with letting Cam and his family in. Was this what love and real trust truly felt like? She felt her answer as the wind wrapped an embrace around her. She opened her eyes and stepped back to Cam and his mother.

Willa reached for Mrs. Green's hands to escort her before the altar. The old woman's once cloudy eyes sparkled. In the moonlight, she seemed younger, more vibrant, and her expectancy of seeing her love radiated from her like a beacon. Her gnarled hands felt warm and strong in Willow's grasp.

"Merry meet, Evelyn. Welcome to the never-ending circle of life." Opening with the traditional Wiccan greeting, Willa kissed the woman's cheek. Mrs. Green kissed the younger woman on the forehead.

"Merry meet, my child. Is that right? Thank you." The elderly woman responded as if she'd been here before. Willa positioned the woman to her left.

This was it. She truly was standing on the edge between life and death. If she let Cam in, there was no turning back. Willa held her breath for a moment, then reached out with both hands and took Cam's hands into her's. A shock like an electric current ran up her arms as she touched his palms. "Merry meet, Cam. Welcome to the never-ending circle of life." She grazed both of his cheeks lightly with her own. Without thought, she suddenly felt her mouth pressing to his full lips in the traditional welcome of a mate. A heady full scent of male filled her senses. She drew away and spun him to the right of her.

Starting at the northern quarter, Willa pointed her white-handled knife out. An electric blue flame appeared to leap from the ground and trail the point of her knife. Mrs. Green shot a wide-eyed glance at Cam and clasped her hands under her chin in quiet excitement.

"I conjure and create thee, circle of power." Willa intoned the ancient words as she paced around the altar. "Be thou a boundary between the world of men and the realm of the Mighty Ones, a sphere of protection to preserve and contain all power raised within. Let now this circle be a place of peace, love, and power. As I do will, so mote it be.'' With a final slash of her athame, the circle was sealed. The blue flame, brilliant and hard as a sapphire, flared and trembled around the sacred space; no ending, no beginning.

"Cam, read this.'' Willa handed him the heavy leather-bound grimore and pointed to the verse.

"For as above, so below, so the universe, so the soul. As without, as within, let our rite now begin. So mote it be.'' Cam read with notes of curiosity and reverence in his voice.

As Cam read the words she knew by heart, Willa lit the candles on the altar. Willa gestured to hand the book to his mother. She stood by the woman, shoulders brushing, to steady and comfort her. Willa could feel the tremor of excitement sweeping through Mrs. Green's body. "Don't be afraid,'' Willa whispered. "Open the book and read.''

Mrs. Green slid her fingers between the pages where the marker stuck out. "Here?'' she whispered back to Willa, and pointed at the passage underlined faintly in blue ink. Willa nodded, and Cam's mother balanced the book on both palms and read, "We are gathered tonight to pay homage to our ancestors. To release all negative thoughts and vibrations which might hinder the growth and progress of our goals in this life.'' Mrs. Green shut the book, handed it back to Willa, and looked about with an expectant expression.

Willa stretched tall and held up her arms in the ancient gesture of entreaty. "Hear me, my ancestors, and those of the family Green. I do summon, stir and call thee forth to celebrate the love we cherish and share with you.''

A star winked. Another shot across the sky and disappeared. Wind began to braid the smoke and the candle flames twisted.

"Are they coming?" Mrs. Green could contain her enthusiasm no longer.

"Yes, look toward the fountain. My grandmere loves the water. She will be here first."

Within the water, the shape of a woman formed. She stepped from the cascade and stood beside the fountain's bowl. Tonight, Granddame Sophia chose to robe in her most lovely ball gown, assembled of stellar sparkle and spun moonlight-on-the-ocean. Silver sea foam twined at her feet and pearls draped and shimmered from chin to knee.

"The circle looks lovely, great-granddaughter. Welcome." Granddame raised her hand graciously as a queen toward Cam and his mother.

"Thank you, Granddame. This is Evelyn Green and her son, Cameron."

Impatiently, a trail of shimmering lights swirled, circled the humans twice, then formed into a filmy column. The dancing starshine began to take a womanly shape, clothed in rainbow gems. The multicolor reflections cast darting lights across the walls of the courtyard, like the mirrored balls hung above a dance floor.

"Grandmother Belle, always so brilliant and dramatic," Willa whispered, leaning close to Mrs. Green's ear. "She loves anything that sparkles."

"I just couldn't wait to meet Cameron and Evelyn." Grannie Belle extended a bejeweled hand to Cam.

Automatically, he took her hand and gave Willa a shocked look.

"Didn't expect someone old and dead to have such a firm grip, did you?"

He blinked and shook his head, speechless. Cam's mother giggled. She was clearly enjoying the events, all fears subsiding.

"Welcome, welcome, Evelyn." Grannie Belle pressed a kiss to Evelyn's cheek. "I'm such a sucker for romance," she murmured in a conspiratorial tone.

A rustle came from a far corner in the fern bed. "Thank you for inviting me to such a nice party." A derriere poked out from the fronds, "but, I really must go visit my daughter now. Yes, yes, a previous engagement. Ta ta."

A lithe woman dressed in plain blue turned to face Willa and her guests, covered dish in hand. "Just saying thank you to the fairies for such a nice party. They always have the best food, you know. They sent you some." She set the crock on the oak stump.

"Momma, this is . . ."

"I know, I know. Nice to meet you both. Are you enjoying New Orleans?"

"Yes, ma'am." Cam nodded still uncertain about ghost etiquette.

"We know of your request, Mrs. Green. Are you prepared?" Great-grandmother Sophia Martine asked, in order to pull the proceedings into some order.

"Yes, yes, is my sweet Hamilton here?"

Cam saw his mother's eyes alight with emotion and anticipation.

"My little dove." The fire dipped, then flared with a puff of fragrant smoke. The smoke laid to a haze on the paving stones but left a column that firmed into a thin, handsome, elderly man.

"Hamilton! Hamilton, it is you!" Evelyn threw her arms about the man and started to weep.

102

"Now, now, pumpkin. There is no need to be sad. No tears." He wiped a thumb across her cheek. "I know how hard you've been trying to reach me. We just haven't had the right connection. Rather like trying to reach me on a tin can and string when you really need to use the phone. You needed someone who has the gift of a heart full of love, ready to be given without price."

With one arm still about his wife, Hamilton reached out to Cameron and clasped his son's shoulder. "Good to see you, son. I'm proud of you, you know. Thank you for bringing your mother and me together. This couldn't have happened without you and Willa. Thank you, Miss Willa."

Willa inclined her head in assent. "I can give you the hours between now and first light of dawn. You may walk and talk, but when the moon sets and the sunlight begins, you must say good-bye." She reached out and touched first Evelyn, then Hamilton, on the shoulder. "It is a time to settle problems and tell truths. Then you must say good-bye. Can you do this?"

The man and woman looked at each other and then at Willa. "Until dawn. And we can talk until then? And see each other? And touch?"

"Yes. Walk to the river and be near the power of the water. But remember, at dawn you must say good-bye. But now you know it is not good-bye forever."

Evelyn offered her hand and her husband took it. They smiled over their shoulders at Cam and Willa, but it was plain that their thoughts were on the proof of deathless love and not anyone or anything else. The maternal ghosts gave a shimmer and disappeared, their business done, having set the wheels of love in motion. "Farewell.'' The voices of the trio blended and faded on the air.

The fire burned low. The courtyard seemed both empty and very crowded. Willa and Cam faced each other over the smoldering wood.

''Thank you.'' Cam peered across the flickering embers. ''I've been wrong. I can admit that.''

His voice made Willa shiver unexpectedly.

''You've showed me it's blind faith that makes magic and miracles happen.'' He looked across the blaze. The fire crackled and leapt, bathing his face in a golden glow, as if encouraging him. The power of the flame seemed to fill him. ''Thank you for your help. I've been a jerk.''

Willa raised her hand slightly, in gracious denial. ''I know you've been persistent for your family's sake, for the love of your parents. It was a good reason.''

''I've seen your beliefs are unbreakable. I'm sorry I handled them so roughly. Harm none, isn't that how it goes?'' He jammed his hands into his pockets. Feeling the miscellaneous coins and papers hidden there made the scene he was involved in feel even more strange.

''No harm done.''

''Willa, there's something I have to tell you. I hope this doesn't embarrass or upset you.'' Cam tested the waters, sticking one toe in first. Willa gave him a look that read, tread carefully. ''Mom saw the notice that your home, your shop, was condemned.'' He paused for a moment to see whether he should continue. ''At first I thought I'd look into it to see if I could use it for leverage to get you to show me your ritual.'' He swept his fingers through his hair.

''Yes, I know . . . pretty sleazy of me. I'm sorry. But then I thought it over. I know it's very private and probably none of my business, but I realize that you may lose your family home, your business. And of course, this special place." He gestured to include all: the ferns, the fire, the wine chalice.

Reality flooded back to Willa and lodged in her heart. Tears shimmered in her eyes, making the fire blur into a smear of gold and red. Nothing had changed. Her home was still in jeopardy. Her chest felt tight, grasped by a fist of reality.

"I couldn't let that happen to you," Cam rushed on. "When I was trying to find the house to tape the house-cleaning ritual, I discovered your house is in the same district—a historical preservation district."

Willa looked stunned. She had thought of that, but Ernest had shown her bogus property lines and told her she was ineligible for any historic refurbishment grants. He must have paid off the clerks before she checked; they had told her the same lie. Ernest had wanted her out of that house and at his mercy.

Cam continued eagerly, "I did a piece on historic restoration not long ago. There are all sorts of grants you can apply for. And I can help."

"I don't know what to say." A breeze fanned her hair around her face, and she swept it out of her eyes with the back of her hand. "It's a prayer answered."

"Hell . . . oops, sorry. Willa, after you called and said we could attend your ceremony even though I'd been such a jackass," Cam kicked at the ground with the toe of his boot, sending a spatter of dust into the fire, "I just wanted to do something nice for you. Say yes, Willa. Say you'll let me help you."

He was imbedding himself in her heart. Immovable

and irresistible. A tiny voice in her head whispered, *Let go*. Willa felt her mind and heart connect.

"Will you come to me?" Willa extended her hand above the heat. "To step over the flames on this night means a commitment of the heart. Can you do that?"

Without hesitation, Cam grasped her hand and leaped through the flames. Death had left the circle and now life and love would replace it, to fill the void Willa had so long felt.

"There should be nothing hidden, no single thing to come between us."

Cam's eyes locked on hers. Willa felt the spiral guarding her heart release as emotion uncoiled throughout her body. The shadows and firelight caressed his face.

Cam boldly tugged at the tie of Willa's robe, pulling her to him. He slid his hand around her waist, to the small of her back. Cam pressed the length of his body to hers. There was no denying he was all man and wanted her completely. They stood face-to-face in the shimmering moonlight. Willa felt her mind join her heart in letting go completely.

He cradled her face in his palm. "You're beautiful. You stop me in my tracks." He kissed her as lightly as summer rain, slow, drugging kisses.

Hypnotized by the love swirling between them, Willa murmured the ancient words, "As the lance is to the male."

"The chalice is to the female," Cam broke in, threading his fingers through her hair. He had studied the book he'd bought from her. The sacred words had stuck in his mind the first time he read them, presenting themselves ready for use at the proper opportunity.

"Cojoined they become one," she continued.

"One in truth, power, and wisdom," Cam finished.

Cam brought his mouth to hers and kissed her hard. His embrace encompassed her to the point of punishing pleasure. Willa's body ached for the raw act of possession and yielding submission. She knew, as he seemed to, instinctively, this was a union of soul-to-soul, spirit reuniting with spirit. This was a bliss beyond flesh pleasing flesh.

Velvet chains of emotions bound her to him. He had crossed the threshold of fire for her. She buried her face in the hard wall of his chest and drank in his deep masculine scent.

"This past week I've seen what my life is lacking. I've witnessed your kindness, your compassion, your beliefs, your genuine love. My life is lacking you, Willa. I love you." Willa looked up at Cam. She could see her reflection in his eyes. The love that she'd been searching for, the soul that had been searching in the scrying bowl was staring back into her eyes.

"You are a shining example of what every woman should be. You deserve all those qualities in return and more. I'd like to be a part of your life, Willa Robinette."

"Seal your promise with a kiss." Like a desert to rain she absorbed the vital essence of his energy. She felt the healing elixir fill her, the magic of eternal life, eternal love, the true meaning of Halloween.

When Midnight Comes

Lori Handeland

For Anna Baier,
one of the last with class,
thank you for your friendship and guidance.

Chapter One

New York City, 1869

Jack Keegan wandered the streets of his youth. He had come a long way from his boyhood days in this immigrant ghetto of New York City. He'd come even farther from the land of his birth.

Ireland. He remembered her well. A land of beauty so deep and mystical the memory made him ache. A land of ugliness so stark and painful he could still hear the howls of the hungry and the tears of the dying. Especially here, on this dark street where children starved in a land of plenty.

How long since he had said good-bye to this place? To his past? To her?

A lifetime. Where was she now? Was she well? Was she happy? Had she forgotten him? Despite his angry words and desperate need, he had never forgotten her.

Despite his wealth and power and position, he was still a child of this place, a child of Ireland.

The mouth of a long, dark alley gaped before him. Jack took a deep breath, welcoming the burn of midnight air into his chest, then stepped into his past. The smell remained the same—dirt, damp, death, and decay. In the depths of the darkness he heard scuffles and shuffles.

Rats. Dogs. People. Hiding from the unknown. For a moment he saw himself as they must see him, out of place here. A swell ripe for the picking.

A scrape from behind made Jack pause, then slowly turn. A boy, or perhaps a young man, small for his age most likely, growth stunted by starvation and depravation. The silver hint of a moon revealed the hopeless glint to the boy's eyes and Jack tensed. He had been hopeless once and knew how desperate one became. This child could have been him twenty years ago, except for the knife. Jack had never relied on a knife to get what he wanted. He had cheated and he had stolen, but his wits had been his weapon.

"No need fer that, son. I'll give ye what I've got."

The brogue Jack had fought so long and so hard to erase from his voice returned without warning. The boy's eyes narrowed with suspicion and his fingers tightened on the knife.

"Here, boy." Jack reached into his pocket. Without ever making a sound the child sprang forward, plunging the knife into Jack's chest.

As Jack fell, he heard someone screaming his name from a very long way away. Jack recognized the voice—a voice that had haunted him for the past ten years.

"Lucia," he whispered.

And then he died.

112

When Midnight Comes

*   *   *

"Jack!"

Lucia Casale clutched her chest, feeling the slice of the knife deep into her own heart. They had been one person, one heart and one soul. Jack had turned away from her, but she had never turned away from him. Even in this purgatory where she existed, paying penance for sins she refused to acknowledge, she was still one with the man she had always, would always, love.

Once he had saved her from certain death, had kept her safe and warm and given her life. She must now try to do the same for him.

Her world was a gray place without substance. Lost and lonely souls haunted the murky mist, and she ran by each one without a word. She ran until her aching heart threatened to burst, and then she ran some more. At last she reached the place where the one who had power over them all could be found.

"Buon giorno!" she called. "Hello?"

The gray mist separated and he appeared, a tall, gentle-eyed man who reminded Lucia of her long-dead father.

"Lucia." He sighed. "What is it now?"

"Jack. He's dying."

"He's already dead, and on his way to . . ." He stopped, looked downward. Lucia winced. "Why would you want to help a man like him? A man who turned his back on your love? A man without faith, or hope, or charity. A selfish man who cares nothing for what is important and everything for what is not."

Lucia ignored his assessment of Jack. She understood Jack better than anyone. She knew his soul, and it was not as black as it appeared. Desperate, she tried again. "You have to do something."

He was shaking his head even before she finished her plea. "You know I can do nothing."

"You're a saint and yet you can do nothing?"

St. Peter's lips tightened at her borderline blasphemy, but he was used to her irreverence. During her lifetime she had been one of the faithful. But she had lost her faith and with it her chance to enter the realm beyond the gate he guarded.

"You know what I can do, and what you must do."

"Then you will help him?"

St. Peter's warm brown eyes saddened. "Not me." He held out his hand. From his fingers dangled a worn, beaded necklace.

Lucia reached out and took the offering. With a deep sigh she fell to her knees and did what she had sworn never to do again. Her fingers trembled as they touched her forehead, her heart, shoulder to shoulder before she began: "I believe in God, the Father Almighty, Creator of heaven and earth . . ."

Her voice echoed throughout the realm of purgatory. Her plea reached toward heaven and was heard.

Blasting heat, the stench of sulfur, crying, screaming, moaning.

Jack awakened into the darkest darkness he had ever known. Not a speck of light penetrated the cloak of black surrounding him. He reached out and felt nothing. He stood, but the absence of sight made him stumble and sway.

Where was he? What had happened?

He remembered walking away from his office in Man-

hattan, all the way to the ghetto of his youth. And
then . . .

The alley. The child. The knife.

Lucia's voice.

"Well, hell," he muttered.

"Got it on the first try, boyo."

Jack started and bumped into the owner of the voice,
who stood directly behind him. The scalding heat of the
unknown being's flesh made him back away. He did not
want to touch that person again, nor be touched by him.

"Who's there?"

"Who d' ye think, Jackie, me boy?"

Horror flooded Jack. He had thought never to hear that
voice again in his lifetime. But then, his lifetime seemed
to be over. "Da?"

"I never said ye weren't a smart lad."

"Wh-what are ye doin' here?" Jack winced at his
stutter, a certain sign of fear, and the return of his
brogue, which made him again the child this man had
terrorized.

"And did ye think I'd be anywhere else?"

*True. If anyone belongs in Hell, that someone is Pat-
rick Keegan.*

"I didn't know ye were dead."

"And why would ye, runnin' away from mother Ireland as ye did. And ye but nine years old. I thank the
good Lord yer mother went t' heaven long before ye
left. It would have broken her heart t' find ye gone, yer
bein' the only one of our eight t' live."

Jack refused to give voice to the grief and the guilt
his father's words brought him. He had loved his mother,
but her devotion to the drunken, mean-spirited bastard
she'd married had killed his respect for her long before

she'd died, the year before he'd run off. She had always adored Jack, lavishing all her love on the one child who had managed to survive and thrive in their miserable world.

Beaten down by his father's scorn and his fists, Jack had been lifted up by his mother's love. He had begged her to leave Patrick, but she had clung to her stubborn belief in the sanctity of marriage. Her son's refusal to honor his father and pray for the man's soul had put a wall between them that could not be breached. She had died giving birth to her eighth child, the seventh to die, before Jack had been able to make things right between them. He'd lasted a year working alongside Patrick on their tenant farm, and then he had run to the land of promise—America.

Jack had not prayed since childhood. Throughout his life he had refused to believe in his mother's version of Heaven and Hell, reward and damnation, but from where he stood now, his mother had been right.

"Ye always despised me fer killin' yer sainted mother with me base lust. Ye never understood what makes a man, but then ye were just a boy at the time. And what did I always tell ye, Jackie?"

"That I'd be just like you in the end. But I'm not," Jack said, with the same belligerent denial he had always used when talking to his father.

"Yer not? I see ye in the same place as me. And this is the end of the line, boyo."

He was not like his father. He was a successful, rich, respected man. He had not married young and driven the woman he loved to an early grave.

A flash of Lucia's face the last time he'd seen her entered his mind—sad eyes, angry mouth—he had lost

116

her, but at least he had not killed her. He had much to regret in his life, but staying away from Lucia was not one of those things. He had, at that one point in time, acted selflessly.

"So, I'll be tellin' ye how Hell works, Jackie. It's you and me, forever. Right here in this room. Explorin' father and son joys, as it were. Joys we didn't get t' share on the earth."

Panic flared in Jack's mind. Eternity with his father? Had he been as bad as all that?

"Wait," he blurted, grasping at anything to keep his father at bay. "What about Satan, the devil, hellfire, and brimstone? Where's that?"

"A myth, me boy. Just a myth. Hell is eternity with the one who frightens ye the most."

"Wait," Jack said again. "I doubt yer frightened of me. So why are ye here?"

Patrick laughed. "The miracle of Hell, boyo. I can be here, with you, forever. But me soul, the part of me that fears and loves and hates, is with the one I fear the most. Me own dear father." Patrick clapped his hands, then laughed like a fiend. "Enough talkin', let's get started."

Before Jack's father could touch him a scuffle and the wet, sucking slide of a footfall nearby froze them both. Jack tensed as fierce heat slid across his face.

"What's that?" Jack whispered.

His father sighed. "The boss."

"Jack Keegan."

The voice made Jack shiver, though the heat intensified until sweat ran into his eyes. He didn't want to answer that voice, but when a hand shot out of the blackness and cuffed him along the ear so hard reality wavered, he croaked, "Aye."

"You can't stay here."

"Now wait a minute, sir," Patrick said. "He's here; I'm here. I've been waitin' a long time fer this. Don't be tellin' me there's a mistake."

"He doesn't belong here. Or at least he doesn't yet. We have rules. Standards. Only truly black souls, like yourself, Pat, are gifted with eternal damnation. Jack has done wicked things, but he did not do them with evil intent. He did them to survive."

"So?"

An angry sigh hissed through the room, and flames lit the air for just a moment. But that moment was enough for Jack to see into the eyes of "the boss," and he knew he had to get out of there any way he could.

"Someone is praying for him. And if someone's praying for him, he isn't all bad. They want to see him upstairs."

The moist, sucking sound came again, and Jack fought not to cringe from the sizzling, acrid scent that burned the inside of his nostrils and made his eyes water. "But if you fail in the quest they give you, Jack Keegan, remember this place. Remember me."

A large, rough, pain-giving hand grabbed Jack by the chin and held him still. Sour, whiskey-pickled breath hit him in the face. "And me," said the voice of his father.

Just as quickly as he had been in the darkest of dark places, Jack suddenly blinked in the lightest of light. A breeze the temperature of springtime brushed his face; he smelled flowers and freshly baked bread. He heard singing, laughter, and bells.

When his vision cleared, he looked up, up, up the heights of the tallest gates he'd ever seen. He couldn't see the top, which disappeared into white clouds that matched the sheen of the gates. When he brought his gaze back down, his eyes widened at the sight of a man standing in front of him. Tall, thin, with long brown hair and mild brown eyes, his face was unlined, but his gaze held the wisdom of centuries.

"Jack Keegan."

Though the words were not a question, Jack felt a need to answer. "Yes." He was glad to hear his accent had disappeared along with some of his terror.

"I am called Peter."

"Of course you are. That would be St. Peter? At the gates of heaven?"

Peter smiled. "Yes."

"Are you going to let me in?"

The smile faded. "I'm afraid not."

"Then why am I here?"

Peter glanced upward, as if listening to a voice Jack could not hear. Then his gaze returned to Jack's face. "We have rules. Standards."

"I heard that—ah—down there."

Peter's mouth twisted into a grimace, as if he'd just tasted a very sour lemon. "Yes. I suppose you did. Let me explain. You aren't bad enough to stay there, nor good enough to enter here."

"Send me back to my life."

"Death doesn't work that way."

"I never heard it worked this way either."

"And have you heard from many how it works?"

Jack stared at the saint for a long moment. Peter had a point. "I suppose I haven't at that."

Peter acknowledged Jack's words with a slight bow of his head. "Allow me to continue. Someone has prayed for you. Prayed you be allowed a second chance.''

Relief flowed through Jack. ''Wonderful. If I get back soon enough, I can be in my office before anyone even notices I'm gone.''

Peter's sigh was long and aggrieved. ''Second chances do not come so easily. You cannot just return to your life and go on being the way you've been. You must repent. You must learn right from wrong. You must change.''

''There's nothing wrong with me.'' The belligerent tone returned against Jack's will as he recalled all the times his father had labeled him worthless through and through.

Peter raised one dark eyebrow. ''Isn't there?''

''No. I'm rich. I'm respected. I'm happy.''

''Are you?''

''Yes.''

''And do you recall how you came to be who and what you are?''

''I worked for it.''

''At the expense of others.''

Jack couldn't look Peter in the eye any longer, so he looked away. ''What are you saying?''

''A human being is the sum of the choices he makes. Some good, some bad, some right, some wrong. You will be given the chance to view three wrongs you have done to others in your lifetime. A chance to learn how your choices affected others and yourself. A chance to save your soul.''

''How?''

''All Hallows Eve is tonight.''

Jack glanced back at the saint and frowned. ''What

does All Hallows Eve have to do with anything?''

"On All Hallows Eve, the line between the living and the dead is at its thinnest. When midnight comes, return to the place I will send you. If you have learned wrong from right and come to understand what is truly of value, you will be given a second chance on earth.''

"And if I don't?'' Jack held his breath.

"You will wander the earth, alone, with but a lantern for company until you beg to be allowed the release of Hell.''

His pent-up breath came out in a rush as Jack recalled the wet, sliding step of "the boss'' and the heated touch of his father's fingers on his face. He swallowed the sizzling lump at the base of his throat. "I don't think I'll ever beg for that.''

Peter merely raised his eyebrows and did not comment.

"God be with you, Jack Keegan,'' he said, and with a wave of his hand the gates of Heaven disappeared, and Jack stood in the midst of a graveyard at dawn.

He looked down at himself. He wore the same clothes of the night before, black frock coat, trousers, black shoes shined to a gloss, and black tie still tied about his neck. But the similarities did not astound him so much as the differences. His crisp, white shirt was as white as it had been when he dressed for the office the previous morning. No sign of a stab wound or the blood that must have flowed. His watch and chain were gone, as were his cuff links, tie pin, and hat.

Had he suffered some kind of memory loss, then been robbed while unconscious? Could he have dreamed all that happened to him during the night?

Jack let out a sigh of relief. His father's touch and

"the boss" had been but a nightmare. He would visit his personal physician before going into the office this morning and make sure he suffered no ill affects from spending a night in the open.

Glancing around, Jack saw he stood in a graveyard attached to one of the Catholic churches in the Italian ghetto. From here he knew his way home.

Shoving his hands into his pockets to warm them, Jack started toward the gate and almost immediately paused.

Where had the fog come from? The pink hint of dawn stretched across the eastern horizon, but in the graveyard the sun's rays did not penetrate the damp gloom. The gray mist swirled about the gravestones and rolled across the dew-sprinkled grass in his direction. Jack glanced down at his feet as the murky vapor washed over them. He shivered with sudden cold and glanced up just as a shrouded figure stepped from the dense fog and lifted a lantern.

The words of St. Peter came back to haunt him. "You will wander forever with but a lantern for company."

Jack shook his head. That had been a dream, a nightmare, nothing more. Then the figure raised its free hand to push back the hood of the cloak.

"*Buon giorno,* Jack," Lucia said.

He forgot everything but the flood of memories her presence brought to mind.

Chapter Two

Lucia watched the shift of emotions cross Jack's face. Surprise, happiness, wariness, anger, then the blank, cold mask she had learned to despise. Ten years had passed, but he was still the same man she had loved and left.

Why had she hoped he would be any different? If he had been less selfish, less obsessed with wealth and power, if he had at last come to understand, somehow, the value of love above all else, there would be no need for what she had been sent here to do.

"Lucia," he said, his voice reflecting none of the things she had seen for an instant in his eyes. "What are you doing here?"

She lowered the lantern and stepped closer. He took a step back, as if in fear, then caught himself and straightened, looking her square in the eye and raising one black eyebrow. She fought the shiver of awareness his too familiar expression brought her. She might be dead, but she wasn't that dead. She wanted him still, despite everything.

Her gaze skittered over, then away from a nearby gravestone. She wasn't ready to look at the name on that stone. Not yet. Perhaps not ever. But she had not come here for that. She had come here for Jack.

Lucia pulled the cloak tighter about her neck, the October dawn as chill as her blood. "We have one day to view the wrongs of a lifetime. If you do not wish to carry this cursed lantern about for eternity, we had best be on our way." She placed the lantern at Jack's feet. "Here you will find it waiting for you when midnight comes. If the lantern's light glows, you will live again. If the flame has died, so have you." She turned to go.

Jack's fingers dug into her arm, and he yanked her about. Unused to her earthly body, she stumbled into him, her palms coming up to rest upon his chest. Against her will, her fingertips pressed into the bright white of his shirt, aching to touch the skin beneath and allow some of his warmth to warm her. Lucia swayed toward him, desperate to hold, to touch, to feel once more the arms that had held her close and soothed away the tears and the fears of her lifetime. Then she remembered why she could feel him at all, and she tore herself away.

His face gleamed as white as the fading stars against the midnight black of his hair. Those blue eyes she had envied for their beauty were clouded with shock. "Wh-what are ye talkin' about, Lucia?"

She'd never heard Jack stutter before. He had taken great pains to erase the lilt of Ireland from his speech, despite her love of that lilt. When she'd begged him not to deny the land of his birth, and in doing so deny a part of himself, he'd snarled that he would not "be talkin' like a damned Paddy forevermore.'' The fact that his cursed brogue was back now revealed Jack's agitation as nothing else could.

''I have come to help you. To guide you. I have been asked to lead you to the place where your wrongs occurred. There you will see them again, learn how the decisions you made affected yourself and others, and you will be given the opportunity to understand what you did wrong.''

She had not believed it possible, but Jack's face whitened more and his eyes widened further. ''I thought that was but a dream,'' he whispered.

''No, Jack, not a dream.'' She took a step forward in her earnestness, her hands clasped before her breasts. ''You have been given a wonderful gift. A second chance. This does not happen every day.''

His gaze narrowed on her face, and Lucia had to fight not to look away. ''And how did ye become enlisted into this venture? Did ye hear a voice from above, Lucia, me dear?''

''You might say that,'' she answered, too quickly. He had to believe her still of this world and not the other. If he suspected her the ghost she was, he would never be able to achieve that which he must to survive. Luckily Jack did not seem to notice the desperation beneath her words.

''Hearing voices and ye didn't think ye were daft?'' He raised one finger. ''Ahh, but I ferget. Yer one of the faithful.''

He sneered the last word, as he had always done when speaking of such things. Jack had told her once of his mother's endless faith, and how he had lost his own when she had died because of her refusal to deny the beliefs she held so dear. Since then he had not prayed and had always scorned her need for such comfort. What did he think now, after a visit both to Hell and the gates of Heaven? He could no longer deny their existence.

His voice, still heavy with the brogue, broke into her musings. "But ye would not deny a voice from above. When God speaks, ye answer, don't ye now?"

Lucia refused to be drawn into his sarcasm. She understood him better than anyone, knew he resorted to sarcasm when uncertain, and his brogue thickened when afraid. If she wasn't equally afraid of what might happen to them both, she would take him in her arms and soothe away his fears the way he had once soothed hers.

"And when God told ye t' be helpin' me, why didn't ye refuse? The last time I saw ye, ye wished me t' Hell and gone."

"I never said such a thing."

"Perhaps not t' me face, but I'm sure later ye wished me there often enough."

Lucia winced. She had wished him there more than once, but nine years in purgatory had made her regret those words, if nothing else. She would atone for them now.

"We are wasting time, Jack. Time you do not have."

"One question first. Where have ye been all these years?"

Her face froze; her tongue went thick with fear. She did not know what to say, but she had to say something. "Why would you care?"

He ignored her question. "Ye didn't marry that damned Paddy. He came lookin' fer ye often enough."

Her lips pursed at his insult. "I would be careful who

I called a Paddy if I were one, too. And no, I did not marry him.''

''Then where have ye been?''

''Nowhere,'' she answered in truth. ''This is not about me, so, please, let me do what I have to do. It is your only chance.''

Jack's lips thinned, those beautiful soft and full lips she had once kissed and would have endured another nine years in purgatory to kiss again. Then he gave a short nod, and looked away for a long moment, struggling to get himself under control. When he spoke, all traces of his brogue had fled. ''All right. Let's get this over with. I need to get back to the office.''

Lucia merely raised her eyebrows at that. Jack had no idea what was in store for him this day.

The sun rose, burning away the lingering mist. As they stepped out of the graveyard and onto the street, the city came alive. People walked by them, some nodded, others smiled, proving both Lucia and Jack did exist upon the earth—for the moment.

When a fruit-and-vegetable carter rolled by shouting, ''*Frutto! Verdura!*'' Lucia inhaled the scent of ripe tomatoes, the tang of apples, and sighed with pleasure. She had missed the sounds and smells and colors of the earth.

''Where are we going?'' Jack asked.

''You shall see.''

''Why do I have to go to the place? Why couldn't St. Peter just show me my past?''

''Places have memories. The memory of what happened to you lives in the place where it happened. Together we will watch your past. You never had anyone to teach you right from wrong, Jack. God does not blame you for your mistakes, but you must learn from them now. Or pay the price.''

Lucia stopped at the narrow opening between two storefronts. Glancing up, she saw the names of the stores had changed. Twenty years did that to a place. On one side of the alley stood a dressmaker, on the other a baker. Heat and the scent of fresh bread wafted from a window, at war with the stench of garbage rotting in the alley.

"Why here?" Jack's breath brushed the back of her neck.

Lucia fought the urge to lean against the broad strength of his chest. Instead she held herself rigid so she would not touch him again. Touching him, even by accident, made her want to do so much more. "You do not remember?"

"Should I?"

She closed her eyes against the unexpected pain his question caused. She would never forget this place, for it was to her, despite the ugliness, a special place.

"You will." Turning, she motioned him closer, and they watched their shared past.

The year was 1849, and Jack had been in America only a few months, but he was a clever boy. He had landed on his feet, despite landing on the shores near penniless. One of the youngest runners at ten, he was also the best. Already he made enough money to rent his own room. He no longer slept on the streets as so many others did.

Jack allowed himself a small smile. He was on the road to success. No more would his father be able to say Jack was a no-good mama's boy, nose forever stuck in a useless book. Mrs. Keegan's insistence that her only child learn to read and write and cipher had not gone unused in the New World. But Jack had to admit, no matter how much he despised his father, the old man's viciousness had molded him into a streetwise boy. Without that edge, Jack would have been dead within a week of arriving in America.

His youth was an asset in his line of work, as were his blue eyes and glib tongue. All combined, he could make anyone believe him honest. Especially the Irish immigrants, fresh off the boat, looking for a place to stay and a friendly Irish voice. They found both in Jack Keegan, who led them to Mr. Kerry's rooming house, where they were overcharged for room and board and Jack was paid for every trusting soul he delivered to the Kerry doorstep. At this rate, starving in Ireland would be a memory before he reached twelve. By the time he was fifteen he planned to have his own rooming house and his own string of runners.

A ship had come in that morn, and Jack raced south toward the tip of Manhattan. Each ghetto he ran through became more poverty-stricken, the wealthier immigrants living as far north of the near destitute southern sections as they were able.

He jogged through the small Italian region where there lived, for the most part, political refugees come to the United States to escape one revolution or another. The Italians were no good to him. Most had enough money to make their way in this world. Jack's prey was the needy.

As he passed a tiny opening between two buildings, Jack heard a soft, distressed cry. He had places to go, people to cheat, but the tone of that cry stopped him dead. Peering into the dimly lit aperture, Jack heard the sound again. A movement deep within drew him forward.

"Hello?" he called. "Who's cryin'?"

He wrinkled his nose with distaste at the odor of rotting food, then began to move back toward the sunshine, but the sight of a tiny face, peeking about a pile of garbage, made Jack stop. He had never seen such large, brown, sad eyes in his life. The child's face was dirty, streaked with tears, her black hair a puff of tangles and her clothes torn and wet. Still, she was the prettiest thing he'd ever seen.

Jack went down on one knee and held out his hand. "Come here, then."

Amazingly she crept toward him, her eyes on his all the while. Jack nodded his approval. She might be only five or six years old, but she'd been on the streets long enough to know trouble flared first in an enemy's eyes.

She stopped, far enough away so he could not grab her. Jack smiled. "What are ye cryin' fer, miss? Are ye all alone?"

She nodded, all solemn eyes and unsmiling face.

"Are ye hungry?"

Again, the same nod.

Jack sighed. He had to go. Why he had turned into this alley he'd never know. He'd heard cries before, seen much worse than this a thousand times. But for some reason this little girl touched his callous heart—and that he could not allow. To survive in New York he must be the toughest, to thrive he must be the coldest, to succeed he must be the most devious. Soft feelings for an orphan Italian girl were out of the question.

"Here." Jack reached for his pocket, and the child

skittered backward, frightened by the sudden movement. "No, I won't hurt ye," he said, using his most practiced, most soothing tone. "Take this and get yerself somethin' t' eat." He held out a few coins. She stared at them but did not move.

Jack placed the money on the ground. "After ye eat, go t' St. Mary's. Right down this street. The sisters will take ye in. D' ye understand what I'm sayin'?"

She gave him another solemn nod.

"What's yer name?" he asked.

She didn't answer, just stared at him with those so sad, too adult eyes. Perhaps she didn't understand English after all, but he knew no Italian. Jack sighed. He'd done what he could and he had to go. Jack turned away, but just before he left the gray alley and emerged into the bright light of day, he heard a whisper.

"Lucia Casale."

Jack smiled and continued on, whistling all the way to the docks. It wasn't until later in the day, after he'd done his cheating and lying and returned to his small room in the Irish section of town, that Jack realized the happiness he'd felt after helping Lucia had disappeared once he went to work. Even though today had been one of his best days, and his pocket hung heavy with payoffs, he could not recapture his earlier desire to whistle.

Jack threw himself down on his rough bed and stared at the stained ceiling. What ailed him? He couldn't afford to get soft now. He had to make his way in this city. He must become someone. Otherwise his father's taunts of Jack never being more than his father before him would come true. And that Jack could not bear.

A scratching at the door made him bolt upright. Had someone come to steal the money he had sold his soul to make? Jack slid a knife from beneath the bed. He couldn't allow such a thing to happen.

Weapon at the ready, he stalked across the room and yanked open the door, tensing in expectation of an attack. Instead Lucia Casale stared, transfixed, at the knife. Then, slowly, she raised her dark, silent gaze to his. Though she never spoke, never changed expression, he felt chastised just the same. Without a word she walked past him, climbed onto his bed, popped her thumb into her mouth, and closed her eyes.

"Wait just a minute," Jack began, but when she fought to open her eyes and lost the battle, curling her knees up to her chest and sighing around her thumb, he didn't have the heart to wake her. The poor thing probably hadn't had a decent night's sleep since her parents left, or died, or whatever had happened. He could just as easily take her to the sisters in the morning as now.

Jack crossed the room and stared down at the sleeping child. She must have been following him around all day. How else would she have found his room? Small wonder she was tired. He had been back and forth from the ship to the boardinghouses lining the dingy side streets near the docks at least five times. He was exhausted.

Jack hid the knife high in a cupboard, then spread a blanket on the floor and took his rest. When he awoke in the morning, he found Lucia cuddled against his chest, one of her hands holding one of his. Her soft, trusting breath tickled his chin, and her cheek pressed against his neck. When she awoke, she yawned, opened her big, brown eyes, and smiled into his face with such adoration his heart thudded hard and heavy.

Jack never took her to the sisters. Not that day, nor any other.

When Midnight Comes

* * *

The scene faded, and Jack stood again at the mouth of the alley, Lucia just behind him. People passed on the street, but no one paid them any mind. Jack fought to get himself under control. The memory, or vision, or whatever the hell it had been had disturbed him more than he cared to admit. Things had been so different then. He had been different. Or had he?

Wasn't that desperate child still within him, driving him to succeed, to make more and more money even though he had enough now for several lifetimes?

Jack turned and met the gaze that had haunted him for so many years. The adoration had died long ago, killed by the realization that he could not give her what she needed the most. Even though she had given him everything she had. Now those brown, beautiful eyes studied him too closely, as if he were some interesting specimen brought out for her perusal. She could still unnerve him with her quiet, contemplative gaze and her too-still face.

"And whom did I wrong there, Lucia? You? Should I have taken you to the sisters? Let them bring you up instead of me? I don't think I did too badly, considering I was as much a child as you."

Her smile was sad as she turned away and began to walk down the street. He fell into step beside her. "You were never a child, Jack. At least not as long as I knew you. But no, this is not about me. You saved my life, and I will always be grateful."

The temper he had held in check, snapped. "I don't want yer blasted gratitude!"

She turned her annoyingly calm face to his. "I know."

133

"Then what?" He shouted the words, causing several early-morning vendors to frown and cast concerned glances at Lucia. He swore and walked on. "Where are ye takin' me now?"

"You shall see."

They continued, passing the offices of Keegan Company, one of several buildings Jack owned in the city. He had made his fortune through hard work and perseverance, but he also had an intuition about business few could match. He had seen long before the War Between the States erupted that a war would come, and he had convinced a wealthy man to begin a munitions factory. Jack had invested all he had and served as the supervisor. Instead of fighting on the front, Jack had fought from the rear, and his foresight saved many lives. He'd been lauded as a hero by President Lincoln himself, and by the time the war ended Jack had become a very wealthy man.

The munitions factory went the way of the peace, but these days Jack had his fingers in many pies, and he oversaw each one from his private office overlooking the streets where he had once lived.

Jack pointed out the building to Lucia. She smiled with her mouth and not her eyes, then shook her head at him as though he were a little lost lamb. Jack gritted his teeth and followed her onward. It wasn't until he smelled the sea that Jack realized they were heading south. Once there, Lucia stopped and stared out at the endless water.

Jack waited, but when she was not forthcoming, his impatience got the best of him. "What did I do wrong that day?" he demanded. "Or am I supposed to guess and guess until I hit on it myself?"

She continued to stare out to sea, running her thumb along her lower lip, a remnant from her thumb-sucking days. When she did that, Lucia was quite distressed.

"No, I will tell you what you did wrong. It is up to you to discover the lesson." She turned and the sunlight caught gray strands threading her black hair. Twenty-six and life had marked her already. Where had she been? What had she done? How had she lived since he'd last seen her face? Before he could ask again the question she had never answered, Lucia continued. "You lied and cheated for money."

Jack gave a snort of laughter. "That day and countless others. What of it?"

"You hurt people, Jack."

"If it hadn't been me, it would have been someone else."

"That doesn't make what you did right. Do you remember how you felt after you helped me? How you whistled for hours after you'd given for no other reason than just to give? Then later, when you'd spent a day taking and taking and taking, you could no longer whistle, though you could not understand why?"

Jack contemplated her with narrowed eyes. She knew what he'd been thinking, feeling, during the replay of his past. The thought made him uncomfortable, but what could he do? She was in charge of this day. "Yes, I remember. What of it?"

"You knew in your heart right from wrong. But that knowledge faded year by year."

"What can I do now?"

"Nothing. That is the tragedy of the decisions you have made."

She nodded behind him. Jack turned, then blinked in

shock. Davey Delaney stood right in front of him. Davey Delaney was long dead. Caught the pox in '59 and went to see "the boss" years before Jack.

"You had a chance that day, Jack," Lucia said softly. "A chance to change your life, to stop hurting others, and you made the wrong decision. Watch and try to learn."

Jack ran down the dock, skidding to a stop just before he knocked Davey into the drink.

"Jacko, my friend!" Davey clapped him on the back. "Things'll be changin' now. I swear the damned Irish are gettin' dumber and dumber with every boat that comes across." He slid a glance at Jack. "No offense."

Jack shrugged. Delaney insulted his own ancestry as well as Jack's, and for the money Delaney paid him, Jack could care less what the man said about the Irish.

"We'll be chargin' 'em double what we have been. And I want ye t' start stealin' their baggage, too. Tell 'em you'll bring their things t' the boardin' house. They'll believe anything ye say, boy." He laughed and grabbed Jack's chin in his grimy, meaty hand. "Ye must be the prettiest damned thing I've ever seen, and with them Irish eyes and that sweet, bonny lilt, ah Jacko, yer a prince. A prince of thieves, that is."

Davey laughed so hard he had to bend over and cough. His considerable belly shook with his mirth, and his face reddened until Jack thought he might die right there. Instead, he hauled in a deep, hacking breath and straightened. "Run along now, Jacko, and do the deed."

Jack had run along, and he had stolen more and cheated more and profited to higher heights than he had ever imagined. Until this moment he had forgotten what happened right after Davey encouraged him to "do the deed."

An older man, with a cart and a horse, hailed Jack as he ran toward the newly arrived ship.

"Boy, be ye needin' a good honest job? I could use a strong lad like you. Just lost me last one t' the likes of Davey Delaney. All ye'd need do is drive the horse and cart from me ships t' me warehouse. No liftin', no loadin', just drivin'. An honest day's wage fer an honest day's work.

The scene in front of Jack froze. A sea breeze wafted across his face. Instead of fish and salt, he smelled flames and sulfur. Instead of the caw of seagulls, he heard the whisper of his father's voice and the approach of a sucking, sliding footfall.

He took a step back, bumped into Lucia, whirled to face her.

"What?" he shouted. "What do you want me to learn?"

She didn't even lift a brow at his loss of composure. "You could have taken an honest job that day."

"And made a piddling bit of money for it too. I would have never gotten anywhere working for that man."

"Was it so bad, the way we were? I was happy then. Weren't you?"

"No. I'm happy now."

"How can you be happy knowing your decisions have hurt others?"

"I don't know anything of the kind."

"That is the trouble. Not only do you not know, but you do not care. How can you repent if you do not care about anyone but yourself? Every decision you made, every single thing you did changed someone's life. People starved because of you. They lived in hellholes. They died alone and crying. Because of you, Jack. Think about that and then tell me you were right to live the way you lived.''

She turned on her heel and walked away. He followed, wrestling with decisions long ago made and realities he had never considered.

Chapter Three

Lucia cast a furtive glance back at Jack. He was lost in thought. She took a deep, soothing breath. Good. There was so much he needed to learn, and very little time to learn it. If he refused to see the truth, all would be lost.

Her part in Jack's task was going to be much harder than she had thought. Lucia had believed that while her love for Jack had not died with her nine years ago, her adoration of him had. That while her heart cried out for him, her mind despised him. She was finding her beliefs less true with every moment she spent in his presence.

Selfish, greedy, manipulative, he did not understand what was truly important on this earth. But he was her Jack. The hero of her childhood, the prince of her adolescence, the bane of her womanhood. She had lived with him for longer than she'd lived with her parents, having lost both of them to ship fever on the trip from Italy to America. She had reached the shores of the New

World alone, her single asset an understanding of the language drilled into her by her mother in the months before they escaped the political unrest of their homeland. She had been alone until Jack found her. No matter what he had done, she would always owe him her life, and so much more. She believed there existed an innate goodness in Jack that all of his machinations could not kill. It was that goodness she had to uncover in order to save his soul.

But first she had to find a way to stop the treacherous need within her to touch him, just once, with love. Jack had always needed her love, even when they were children. Though he was the sharpest, toughest runner on the streets, when they were together he had been the gentlest of boys. They had often slept holding hands, and when she had a nightmare, he had allowed her to crawl in to bed next to him, and he had held her until the dawn. She had never been cold or frightened once Jack came into her life. After she left him, she had been nothing but.

"Where now?" he asked.

Lucia started and tore herself free of her memories to find Jack had torn free of his. She stopped and waited for him to catch up to her. For a long moment she relished her chance to just look at him once again.

The years had changed him little. Stronger and taller, his midnight blue eyes still held a soul-deep hunger that would never die. His face, always beautiful to her, had matured, making him beautiful, no doubt, to many women. She frowned at the stab of jealousy. Such emotions were not for her any longer.

"Lucia? Are you all right?"

"Fine," she said, a bit too sharply. "It is getting on to mid-day. We must continue."

The location of his second wrong was not very far away. They had lived their youth in the Irish section of the city. Lucia had always felt out of place there and had wandered often to the Italian section just to hear the language of her parents. But she had been out of place there, too—an Italian girl raised by an Irish boy who remembered the language of home but little else.

The only place she'd ever belonged was with Jack, and she had left him of her own free will. He had not come for her, though she'd hoped he might until the day she died. She had been too stubborn, too proud, to go back to him after their last encounter. She still loved him, but she could not forgive him for taking from her all she had to give and never looking back.

Lucia stopped and gestured to the road, dotted with all manner of refuse. Since the city fathers had banned the pigs that used to wander the streets eating the garbage, the mess had gotten out of hand.

Lucia glanced at Jack. His nose wrinkled with distaste. He had obviously not been on these streets lately, but then, why would he be? He lived now in a luxurious house to the north. He only worked near the ghetto, and even then, she was sure, he never ventured outside. Except last night, to be robbed and killed. The very fact that he had allowed himself to die in such a way showed the changes in Jack. Once he would have seen the lad's intention well before the act.

"Remember?" she asked, sweeping out her hand to indicate the filthy gutter before them.

Jack took a step back, as though afraid that if he touched the filth he might return to the days when he had not even noticed it there. His face revealed his confusion even before he spoke. "Should I?"

Lucia sighed. How could he forget such momentous occurrences? But then, most people did not realize at the time of such happenings their significance in the grand scheme of their lives.

"Watch," she said, and like the last time, the past came alive before their eyes.

Jack, now sixteen and lean with growth, ran for home. He had worked from dawn until the sun had long set. Lucia would be waiting, done with her day's sewing of piecework for the ready-made clothing manufacturer who employed her. He wished she did not have to toil so long and so hard for so little. But she insisted on making her way so she would not be a complete burden to him. As if she could ever be that. Lucia's adoration and unconditional love were his only warmth in a world that constantly tried to drag him back into poverty.

Jack slipped his hand into his jacket, curling his fingers about the money he carried.

Payday.

Soon he would have enough money to finance his dream of owning his own boardinghouse, employing his own set of runners. He could not exist forever in the ghetto. He'd rather be dead than poor for the rest of his life.

A scuffle, a cry, and a thump from around the corner just ahead made Jack pause, then approach cautiously. He peered about the building just in time to see a young man, about his own age, raise a knife and plunge the weapon into his victim, who lay half in the street. Surprise made Jack shout, "Hey, what d'ye think yer doin'!"

The youth spun about, fear ripe in eyes that stared from a gaunt, desperate face. One look at Jack and he ran for his life. Jack hurried over to the injured man, who still breathed, but not for long. He knelt, and the man grasped his arm in a surprisingly strong grip for the dying. Blood soaked Jack's sleeve, and he pulled back, repelled.

"I'll get the police," he said, but the man shook his head and motioned Jack closer. He tried to speak, but nothing came from his mouth but a pink spray of spittle. The man sank back, patting his pocket, his hands as frantic as the expression in his eyes. Then he tried to struggle upward again but failed, slumping into the garbage lining the street. His eyes stared sightless at the moon.

Jack reached into the pocket the man had been so concerned about and pulled out a wad of bills so thick his heart turned over in shock. A movement from a nearby storefront and the distant but approaching whistle of the police brought Jack to his senses. He had a dead man at his feet, a wad of money in his hands, and blood all over his jacket. With a last look into the dead man's face, Jack shoved the cash into his coat and ran away.

The past disappeared, and Jack stood next to Lucia at the place where the unknown man had died. The afternoon had darkened, and Jack threw a quick glance at the sky, half afraid he had been lost in his past for too long and midnight approached too soon. But instead of encroaching night, he saw encroaching storm clouds and heard the distant bellow of thunder. The earlier chill of the fog-shrouded morning had disappeared with the advent of sunlight, but now, with the loss of that light, the chill returned and settled deep in Jack's bones. He shivered and tugged his coat closed.

He had been scared that night, more scared than he could ever recall being. At least on this earth.

So many things could have happened. He could have arrived a few minutes earlier and been the one with the knife in his chest. He could have arrived a few minutes later and lost the money that had helped bring him the success he now enjoyed. He could have waited too long and been hung for a murder he had not committed. But what had he done wrong?

Jack looked at Lucia. "I tried to help him."

Lucia still stared at the gutter where the man had died nearly fourteen years ago. "Thou shalt not steal, Jack," was all she said.

Jack shook his head, confused. "He was dead. He pointed me to that money. He wanted me to have it. For helping him."

"You always could find an excuse for your behavior. That does not change what you did."

"What was I supposed to do? He was dead. The money was there. I used that money to buy my first boardinghouse."

"Where you proceeded to lie and cheat and steal from your countrymen at an even greater rate than Davey Delaney."

"You benefitted from it, too, Lucia. You didn't have to work your fingers raw sewing for someone else's gain."

She flinched and hunched her shoulders, the dark cloak shifting forward to swirl about her ankles. Taking a deep breath—for patience or strength, he didn't know which—she turned and stared at the storefront behind them. The storefront where he'd heard a sound that night.

Jack reached for her shoulder, amazed to see that his fingers trembled with the need to touch her. Before he could, she turned. Her gaze fell to his hand, then shifted to his eyes. What he saw there made Jack lower his arm slowly back to his side. When had she begun to fear him?

He tucked his treacherous hands, which ached to take her in his arms and soothe away her fear, into his pockets, then he rocked back on his heels and stared at the now abandoned storefront. "So what did I do wrong?"

"The man had a son. A little boy who hid right there." She pointed to the storefront. "He wanted you to use the money to help the child. When you ran away, so did the child. He lived on the streets, almost starved, and eventually became a murderer and a thief just like the man who killed his father, just like you, Jack."

"I'm not a murderer."

"But you are a thief, despite the expensive clothes and the society parties."

Jack closed his eyes against the unaccustomed shame that washed over him. He had always done what he had to do to survive and to thrive. He had not paused to feel guilt or regret. Lucia had never before said a word of recrimination to him about the way he made his living. She'd known what he did and how he did it. Still she had adored him. Somehow her adoration had made everything he'd done all right in Jack's mind.

"I'll find the boy," he offered. "I'll give back what

I took and then some. Will that make everything all right again?''

Lucia sighed, long and aggrieved, and looked at him as if he were muck upon her shoe. ''You cannot change what he's endured by giving him money.'' She spat the last word from her mouth like a sour pill. ''*You* have to change, Jack. You have to learn what is important in life. God will not give you the precious gift of a second chance to have you waste it as you wasted the first one.'' Her fingers crept up, pushing aside the heavy cloak to reveal a gray, shapeless dress decorated only by the rosary about her neck.

She had always worn that rosary, he recalled. It had been her mother's. Jack's gaze strayed to her hand as she worked the beads, the elegant, slim fingers moving in a rhythm he no longer remembered. Lucia only fingered the beads when she wanted something desperately.

''You will wander like the jack of the lantern in the legends of old,'' she said, the cool, quiet tone of her voice warmed by the cadence of her native language. ''With but a lantern for company, alone, lonely, never finding warmth or love on this earth.'' She stared into his face, searching, and his anger turned to dismay at the heartbreak in her eyes. ''Until the end of time you will wander, or until you beg for Hell, whichever comes first. And believe me, Jack, you will want to die. You will do anything to get free of this earth, because being alone and unloved is the worst punishment any of us could ever dream of.''

He reached out and grabbed her wrist before she could move away. Her hand worked on the beads, making the fine bones beneath his fingers twist and shift. Her eyes widened and her lips parted. Fascinated, he watched her breath quicken, coming in little puffs of steam, warm and moist against the cool approach of the storm, faster and faster, through open, russet lips.

"You sound as if you know of what you speak, Lucia. Tell me, what happened to you after you left me? Did you wander this earth alone and unloved until you wished for death? You had but to knock on my door and I'd have taken you back in. You were a part of me. Since we were children we were together. How could ye leave me when I needed ye so much?"

For a moment her eyes softened, and he glimpsed the girl he had always known behind the impassive face and eerie, calm voice. She tugged on the wrist he still held imprisoned, and he released her. Her fingertips scraped against the stubble on his jaw. She had always touched him thus, right before they kissed. Jack began to lower his lips to hers, bringing his face close enough for her to—

Crack!

Her palm connected with his cheek, bringing tears to his eyes. Jack straightened, putting his fingers to his burning face as he stared at her. Her dark eyes snapped fury such as he had never seen in them before.

"It is always about you, is it not? What you need. When you need it." She turned, the ankle-length black material of her cloak billowing out like a thunder cloud behind her. The sky rumbled, giving sound to the illusion. She stamped past the few amazed onlookers, who had stopped in their midday rush when the pretty Italian girl had slapped the Irish swell, without a second glance. When she realized he wasn't beside her, she stopped, put her hands on her hips, and turned to glare. ''Come along now, Jack Keegan, and I will show you your final wrong. Then you can see why what you need does not matter to me any longer.''

Chapter Four

The anger felt good. Much better than the pain and the longing. Anger was hot and warmed the chill Lucia couldn't seem to dispel from her blood. But then why should she be able to? She was dead, after all; her earthly body but a loan until midnight came. Then her spirit would return to purgatory and her body, as they said, ashes to ashes, dust to dust.

Lucia didn't turn about to see if Jack followed her toward the location of his final wrong. She couldn't bear to look at him right now, to see again the need in his eyes that matched the need she hid in her heart. What was to come would be painful—for both of them.

Night approached—early, she thought, but winter approached as well, strangling daylight more and more with each passing day. The storm didn't help, darkening the sky faster than the sun's fading light.

Before they reached their destination, the storm came

upon them with fury, the wind whipping Lucia's cloak, sending cold shafts of air up her skirt and ending the momentary warmth she'd treasured. Icy rain drenched her hair; thunder and lightning made her flinch and hurry along. This was how it had all begun so long ago. There had been a storm that night, too.

Jack appeared beside her, yanking the hood of her cloak up to shield her head, then placing a warm, helping hand at the small of her back. When Lucia would have pulled away, he grasped her elbow and held her firmly to his side.

"Don't be stubborn, Lucia, there is time enough to see what else I've done wrong. Let's get out of the storm."

"It doesn't matter," she said. "The place is right here."

Lucia ducked beneath the awning of an ancient brick building and opened the door. Heated air, ripe with the smell of last night's potatoes and cabbage, hit her in the face.

She smiled. Home at last.

Water dripped from her cloak onto the floor, the *plunk, plunk, plunk* thunderous in the silence that greeted them. Lucia turned to find Jack standing out in the rain. Droplets ran down his stark, white face, catching on his black eyelashes, hanging for a long second, then dripping onto his already soaked coat.

Lucia beckoned him inside. He backed away, shaking his head. "Not here," he whispered.

She had no time for soothing words or gentle persuasion. If Jack bolted now, all would be lost. So Lucia grabbed his hand and yanked with all her strength. Caught unaware, he stumbled into the rooming house.

The wind caught the door and slammed it shut behind him. Startled, he gasped and nearly yanked his hand from hers. She gentled her grasp, folding her fingers between his, reveling for a moment in the simple pleasure of palm meeting palm, but they did not have time to linger in the dark, dank entryway holding hands like two young lovers with their lives before them. Neither of them could lay claim to that any longer.

"Come along, Jack." Her voice was sharper than she'd meant, but Jack did not notice. He stared upward, his gaze fastened on the gloom and murk that obscured the upper levels of the stairway. Shadows danced an evening waltz with the minute bit of light creeping in through a hole in the roof.

When she tugged on his hand, he looked up at her and gave a slight nod. He was ready, as was she. Together they climbed the stairs to the third floor, the warped wood creaking beneath their feet, the sound almost drowned out by the shriek of the wind through the cracks about the windows and the doors. One particularly high-pitched screech, sounding nearly human, brought a memory, unbidden, to Lucia's mind. Once she had screamed like that—in pain, in fear, in despair.

She pushed the sob that threatened back into her heart with all the others, then forced herself not to shake and shiver as she continued to climb the stairs at the side of the man who had brought her both the most joy and the most pain she had ever known.

The building had not changed much in ten years, becoming older and more run down, as buildings and people were wont to do. Immigrants able to afford a room of their own for their family still resided here, better off than many who lived six or more families to a cellar in

151

the depths of the city. Families, making their way the best they could. Once she and Jack had been family, and here they had lived.

Without a word between them, they stopped outside the room that had been theirs. Lucia let go of Jack's hand to turn the doorknob. The door swung open to reveal an empty room.

Jack took a deep breath. "Is this necessary, Lucia?"

"You know it is."

He let out the breath he'd held in wait for her answer, then stepped closer to her and slid his hand beneath her wet hair to curl about her neck. The familiarity of the gesture made tears well in her eyes. What she wouldn't give for one more chance to love him.

"I'll tell ye right now, I don't regret what happened in this room." His fingers tightened on her neck, and he shook her just once. "None of it, d' ye hear?"

Before she could answer by word or gesture, he released her and turned to view another episode of his past.

Jack ran through the streets of the city, joy filling his heart. He had at last earned enough money to buy a second rooming house. Little by little he was making his way in this world. Someday Jack Keegan would be the richest man in Manhattan. Then no one would dare call him an Irish nobody again. He had but to work hard and never veer from his course. That was the wonder of America. Hard work was rewarded. Those who knew what was important prospered. And Jack knew what was important in life—money, position, success. He would have them all one day soon.

He burst into the boardinghouse and pounded up the stairs, then let himself into the small room he shared with Lucia, surprised not to find her at home. Though he had returned earlier than usual, he had never known her to venture out this late in the day.

Jack removed his coat, frowning at the distant rumble of thunder. Where was she? Perhaps he should go searching before the storm hit.

Quiet voices from the other side of the door caught his attention. Wasn't that Lucia's voice? And the voice of a man? The joy in Jack's heart began to fade, though he could not put his finger on why. Who was she talking to? Where had she been?

Jack strode across the room and opened the door—just in time to see Timothy Monihan kiss Lucia full on the lips.

Jack froze. He could not breathe, could not think for the fury coursing through him. How dare Monihan touch her? She was a child. A child who was Jack's responsibility.

"Just what the hell d' ye think yer doin', Monihan?" he growled.

The two sprang apart, guilt plain upon their faces. Lucia would not look at him, staring instead at the hem of her blue gown, which peeked from beneath her ankle-length cloak. Monihan was not so shy. After the initial flush of embarrassment across his cheeks, he raised his chin, grabbed Lucia's hand, and looked Jack right in the eye.

"I'm doin' nothin' I should be ashamed of doin', Keegan. Unlike you."

Jack, who had been staring at their joined hands, a physical show of unity that made him realize this was not the first time they had met, nor likely the first time they had kissed, returned his gaze to Monihan's. Lucia made a soft sound of distress, which she silenced when Monihan pulled her closer to his side.

"And what might I have t' be ashamed of?"

"Keepin' her here with you. Ruinin' her reputation by livin' in sin."

Jack's mouth fell open. He had never heard such insanity in his life. Before he could answer, Monihan continued. "She swears yer not but brother and sister. Still, no one believes her but me." He glanced at Lucia, and some of the anger in his face faded as love took its place. "I love the girl and I believe whatever she says. T' tell ye true, I do not care if she's known ye. I do not care if she loves ye. Ye don't have it in ye t' love her back. Not in the way she needs."

Jack glanced at Lucia but could only see the top of her head as she continued to study her boots. She'd always been quiet, but never had she been this quiet, and especially when she was being discussed as if she weren't present to hear.

"Loves me? What are ye blatherin' about, Monihan?"

The young man made a disgusted sound deep in his throat. "Are ye so blind ye cannot see she cares fer ye? Are ye so caught up in yer cursed ambition ye don't know a girl of sixteen should not be livin' with a man of twenty? Not unless she's his mistress. But she will hear none of it. She continues t' insist she cannot leave ye. Ye need her. But I think ye need no one but yerself and yer money. The time has come t' make her honest or leave her go."

Jack was having a hard time following the conversation. His mind kept floundering at the idea of Lucia with another man, any man. Lucia having grown into a woman, loving him, as a woman loved a man, it seemed, and he had not noticed.

As Lucia turned her attention from the rapt contemplation of her boots toward her suitor, Jack took the opportunity to study her. She had always been small, her bones fine, her hands slim and elegant. Her face had matured, but the huge dark eyes, the high, exotic cheekbones, looked the same as on the day he had first found her. Beneath her coat, perhaps, lay the body of a woman, but Jack had to admit, he had never looked at her in such a way.

"I've asked her t' marry me," Monihan said.

Panic flashed through Jack's mind. Marriage? He would lose her forever. "Now just a minute, she is but a child. Ye cannot marry her. I forbid it."

Monihan dropped Lucia's hand and turned to Jack with fists clenched. "Who are ye t' forbid her a life of her own? Yer not her father, nor her brother. She says yer not her lover, but ye've not the guts t' make her yer wife. Ye have no rights t' Lucia; she's mine."

Anger drowned Jack's confusion. "She is not yers, nor mine, Monihan. She is her own. This'll be her decision, and I'll not have ye forcin' her into anything." Jack put his hand on Lucia's shoulder. She started but did not look at him even then. "Is this what ye want, Lucia?" he asked gently, even though he wanted to shout and pound his fists against something, or someone, at the thought of losing her.

She took a deep breath, her shoulder rising and lowering beneath Jack's fingers, and he tightened them for a moment, in support or supplication he knew not which. At last she looked at him, and in her eyes he saw the truth. She was a woman, and she loved him.

Well, hell, he thought, *what am I t' do now?*

"Tell him, Lucia," Tim urged. "Tell him ye will not stay here with him anymore. Come away with me now and I'll marry ye tonight. The priest will waive the bans if I tell him what ye've been through."

Lucia didn't spare her suitor a glance. Instead she stared into Jack's eyes, waiting, hope alight in her face. Jack didn't know what to say, what to do. He didn't want her to go, but could he ask her to stay?

Jack turned away from what he saw in her face, turned his back on her need and her love. "Do what is best fer yerself, Lucia. All I want is fer ye t' be happy." He clattered down the stairs and out into the street, but not before he heard Lucia's sob, a sound that broke the heart he did not want to have.

Jack wandered the streets, alone, lonely. He would have to get used to feeling thus. Soon his rooming house, his runners, and his ambition would be all he had. They should be enough. They would be enough.

The storm that had threatened hovered and rumbled but did not break. The air, unnaturally hot for October, seemed to pulse with warmth, electricity, and expectation. The tension within Jack mirrored the pressure of the waiting storm. He wanted to scream and run and do violence to anything in his path. Instead he walked and walked as the thunder rumbled and heat lightning flared over the ocean but did not drift toward the shore.

When he could no longer bear the presence of the storm, which seemed to mock him with its inability to explode, he returned to his room. Stepping inside, the quiet and the darkness gave voice to the state of his life. He would have to become accustomed to her absence.

Shunning a candle, he made his way to the narrow

bed behind the curtain on his side of the room, stripped off his clothes, and lay down to stare at the night, which pulsed so loudly with silence he thought he might run mad.

And then he heard it, the steady cadence of her breathing. Jack jerked his head to the side but could not see her bed through the combination of darkness and the wall of his curtain and hers. But he did not need to see her to know the truth.

She had not left him! Joy filled his heart, and some of the mind-numbing tension faded. He relaxed and, listening to the soothing sound of her breath moving past her lips, he slept.

In the morning she smiled at him as she did every morning. Or was her smile different now? And if so, was it a change in him, in her, or in the nature of their relationship?

"I thought ye'd be gone," he said.

Her smile froze, and he cursed himself for bringing up yesterday's scene. "No," she whispered, ducking her head, avoiding his gaze, "I could not leave you. We need each other."

He considered the top of her head for a moment. He did need her, but was he being selfish, as Monihan said, to allow her to stay with him? He could not marry her. If he married Lucia, children would follow, each one dragging him further into the bog of poverty never to climb out. He could not bear to live like that, nor could he bear to sentence her to such a life. He wanted things to continue just as they were.

"Well, I'll be going to work then," he said, and with her nod he convinced himself things were just as they had been for so long.

But over the days that followed, as the storm continued to threaten but never broke and time moved from mid-October toward All Hallows Eve, Jack learned that nothing would ever be the same between them again. Jack learned what it was like to burn for something he could never have.

For every time he looked at her, he saw a woman where he had once seen a girl. Her smile made his breath catch in his throat; her scent made his arms trill with gooseflesh; her laugh made his chest ache. He didn't even want to think about the sleep he lost every night, listening to her breathe and sigh a few feet away from him.

Then one night, when he had just fallen asleep, he heard her cry out, as she often did with nightmares. Before he came fully awake and realized what he was doing, he had yanked on his pants and crossed the room to stand beside her bed.

"Mi madre, mi padre," she mumbled and shifted, then sighed a sigh of intense pain.

Jack swallowed the lump that sprang to his throat. Despite the lack of light, he could see tears tracking across her cheeks. She dreamt again of her parents.

Gently he put his hand to her shoulder. "Lucia, wake up. It's but a dream."

She came awake with a gasp, sitting up and taking his hand, pressing it between hers against her chest, partially bared by her shift. Her eyes, wide and wet, found his. Their gazes held.

Her hair, damp with sweat, clung to her forehead. He dropped to his knees, reaching out to push the loose, tangled strands from her face. Jack couldn't seem to speak, to move, to do anything but stare into her face and feel the desire spreading through his body, clouding his mind, making him want to bury his fingers in her hair, plunder her mouth with kisses, press her back onto the bed and make her his forever.

The thought broke the spell and he cursed, yanking his hand from hers and backing away, as if terrified of the sight of her.

"Jack?"

"Dammit, Lucia, can't ye see what's happening here? Monihan's right. I'm a selfish bastard t' keep ye with me." He turned and stumbled back to his side of the room, pulling on the first shirt he found, shoving his feet into his shoes and heading for the door.

"Where are you going?"

He stopped with his fingers on the doorknob. "Out," he snapped. "Before I do something we'll both regret. I cannot be what ye want, Lucia, what ye need. Fer yer own good, go before I get back. Go t' Monihan. He'll love ye. I cannot."

Before she could argue he jerked open the door and ran from the room, down the stairs, bursting out onto the silent street. The air still throbbed with the storm, just as his blood throbbed with Lucia. Jack ran until sweat filled his eyes, and still he ran some more. The streets were deserted, unusually so.

Then he remembered. Tonight was All Hallows Eve. The dead walked this night, or so they said. The immigrants who graced these streets, a superstitious lot, would stay inside to be safe, but he would rather be alone with the dead than alone with Lucia.

At last the storm hit the city, bringing relief from the heat and the strain of the waiting. Icy rain pelted Jack's cheeks, froze his hair, soaked through his shirt, and ran down his collar. Yet still he wandered on. He would give Lucia time to gather her things, time to leave him forever. If he saw her again, he just might give in to his sudden and amazing desire to kiss her. To kiss her and so much more.

What ailed him? He had held Lucia in his arms, as one might hold a sister, yet now his treacherous mind had begun to think of her as something else entirely. Had he noticed in some secret part of his mind that Lucia had become a woman? Had he given her any indication that there might be a chance for a future between them as man and wife? Jack didn't think so, but then how had she come to hope for such a thing?

When the night reached its darkest and the storm its most furious, Jack climbed the stairs. His steps were heavy, defeated, his body cold, wet, and bone-deep weary, yet the thought of entering their room and seeing it half empty almost made Jack return to the storm-scented night. As he reached the top of the second flight of stairs, the glow from beneath his doorway drew him forward. Shadows danced with the light, and he stared transfixed as they played upon the floor in front of his feet. Quietly, cautiously he crept forward, placed his hand on the knob, and opened the door.

Lucia stood at the washbasin, in her shift and nothing else. Her skin glistened with water; the golden droplets mirrored the flickering candlelight. When she turned and saw him in the doorway, her startled gasp sliced through the silence that hung heavy in the room. Jack's breath caught in his throat at what she revealed when she turned his way.

Her breasts, high and firm and full, strained at the too-tight material of her shift. Captivated, he stared at them, watching as they rose and fell with every breath she took. He could see the outline of her nipples, round and red, enticing despite the white cotton that covered them. Unable to stop himself, Jack's gaze wandered downward. The lamplight shone through the thin material, outlining her waist, her hips, her thighs, all rounded and soft, just as a woman's should be.

His own breathing quickened, and the chill that had invaded his blood while he walked through the storm dissipated. The heat of his skin beneath his wet clothes seemed to cause steam to waft into his face.

"Jack?"

Her voice, familiar as his own, but unsure, a little frightened, brought him to his senses. What was he doing staring at her as if she were a whore purchased for his pleasure?

Jack nearly groaned, then cursed beneath his breath. He didn't even know himself anymore. When had his protective urges for Lucia changed to the urges of a man for a woman? He slammed the door behind him, making Lucia jump and grab for her robe, clutching the garment to her chin.

"I told ye t' be gone," he snarled, stalking across the room to hide behind the curtain that shielded his bed from hers. He yanked off his soaked shirt and grabbed a towel to dry himself.

"N-no." Her voice came from the other side of the cloth partition. Jack spun around and saw her silhouette, stark against the threadbare curtain. "I-I could not go," she said.

He could smell her on the steamy air, a combination of soap and a particular scent that was Lucia—summer-warmed earth and wild flowers. Jack pressed his face into the towel to stop the temptation from possessing his mind, praying his body would stop reacting to her in this new and unacceptable way.

Had the God he denied for so long decided to punish him at last? Or was Satan rewarding him for his selfishness and greed? He was no virgin, should know by now how to control his urges, yet the flare in his blood and the ache in his loins reminded him of the first time he had been with a woman.

Jack made the futile wish that he had never seen Lucia and Monihan kiss, never heard Monihan's accusations or looked at Lucia with the eyes of a man. Though he had hoped, he knew now they could never return to the way things had been.

"Jack?" Lucia said again, and the sound of her voice sent gooseflesh sliding down his arms.

He lowered the towel and briskly rubbed the chill away. "Aye?"

"We must talk. I do not want to marry Tim. I want to stay here." She took a deep breath, the shadow of her breasts rising, thrusting, begging him with their perfection just as her voice begged him with words. Her hand raised to her mouth, and she stroked her bottom lip with her thumb to relieve some of her distress. "I want to stay here with you."

He sat down on his bed, closed his eyes against all enticements, and said the words he knew must be said. "Ye cannot and well ye know it, girl. Monihan is right about one thing, I'm doin' ye harm by allowin' ye t' stay here. I had not realized, and I'm sorry fer it."

Before he knew what she was about, she drew aside the curtain. Jack's eyes snapped open at the sound, then widened at the sight. She stood too close and too unclothed, her breasts level with the top of his head. He stared at the golden shade of her flesh peaking through a small hole in the fabric near her rib cage, his mouth, even with her belly, eased forward—

Jack bit back a curse and put his hand to his head. "Lucia, go away. Run away. Are ye crazy t' come t' me half-naked? I'm but a man, and I can see very well yer a woman now. Ye should not be here."

"I belong nowhere but with you. Since the day you saved my life, took me in, raised me, I have belonged to you."

"Don't say that!" His voice was too loud, too ragged, too desperate, and Jack forced himself to take a calming breath and speak more quietly. "I told Monihan and I'll tell ye, too—ye belong t' no one but yerself, Lucia."

"You said you wished me to go. But I cannot believe you would be so heartless. You wish for me to marry Tim and never see you again? Because he will not let me see you, Jack. Never. If I leave, everything we have shared, everything we have done, everything we have worked and lived for will be over. I will be Tim's wife and you will be alone."

Jack clenched his jaw to stop his treacherous tongue from begging her to stay. He had not realized until she said it how much he feared being alone in the world. His work and his ambition had kept him from making friends. He and Lucia had had only each other for most of their lives, and that had been enough. Jack hated to think of what his life would be like without her. Dark, lonely, joyless. Exactly what his life had been in Ireland before he escaped.

Her fingers touched his hair, smoothed back the ragged tresses he never seemed to remember to cut. Then she stepped forward, and the heat of her skin beneath the snow-white cotton warmed his cold lips. A fold of her chemise brushed his cheek and he was lost.

He pressed his lips to her belly. She gasped, and her fingers clenched in his hair, bringing him closer, holding him to her. He should have stopped right then. Could have, would have, if she hadn't suddenly framed his face with her hands and tilted his head back so her dark, grave eyes peered down into his. "Ah, Jack, please do not send me away. You are all I have. All I have ever had. All I will ever want on this earth."

Before he could think or reply, she leaned forward and pressed her mouth to his. Jack froze as the lust he'd held at bay ignited within him, sudden and impossible to resist, though he tried with the last vestige of decency he owned.

He stood, trying to hold her away, but she struggled to remain, sliding closer, pressing her barely covered breasts to his naked chest, twining her fingers in his hair and stroking his lips with her tongue. Not untutored in the art of kissing, her mouth moved against his with a skill that made his body harden and strain for release.

Then suddenly they were on his bed, mouth to mouth, chest to chest, hip to hip. She rained kisses across his face, and he reveled in the gentle urgency of her touch. They had loved each other so long, sweetly, innocently, wasn't it natural their love had matured along with their bodies, their hearts, and their minds? He had not realized how very much he needed the touch of someone who loved him until he felt Lucia's touch all the way to his wildly beating heart.

He tried very hard to be gentle, to go slow. But the passion they had hidden even from themselves soared out of control. She was a different person tonight from the sweet and solemn girl he had raised. A woman now, her instincts outweighed her innocence.

Her fingers fluttered over the naked length of his back, then around to his chest. He watched her explore him, learning the texture and the taste of his skin, and the seriousness of her expression, the concentration that creased her forehead, made him smile. In some ways she was very much the same.

Having known him all her life, she possessed no shyness in touching him. Her knuckles brushed the hardness beneath his trousers and he tensed. Her dark gaze shot up to his, gauging his reaction. Then, with a smile that was all woman, she curled her fingers about him and pressed her palm to his fullness, flexing and cupping in a rhythm she should not know.

He gritted his teeth and grasped her wrist, but she made a sound of denial and struggled to touch him again, pressing her mouth against his and using her tongue to drive him to distraction.

All his good intentions fled, and he tore her chemise in his desire to feel her firm, soft flesh in his hands. She sighed deep in her throat when his palms cupped and lifted her breasts and his thumbs stroked her nipples. He pulled his mouth from hers and leaned back to see if he had frightened her with his need. But her face reflected pleasure, her lips, red and swollen, mouthed his name, and when he lowered his mouth to her breasts her gasp of delight and the firm stroke of her fingers along his shaft showed she did not fear him.

He learned her taste as she had learned his. He memorized the softness of her skin with the tips of his fingers. He made them both mad with desire, and when she begged him for what she did not understand, his trousers joined her chemise on the floor as he lifted himself above her.

They were both damp with sweat and breathless with the wonder of each other. He probed at her moist entrance, hesitant to hurt her, but her eyes opened, dazed, glazed, and she rose to meet him, breaking the barrier of her innocence herself, then pulling him all the way into her body.

He heard not a whisper of pain from her mouth, only his name and Italian endearments met his ears before he lost all sense of anything but the two of them. He slid in and out of her body in the rhythm as old as eternity. He had never felt so complete in his life. He who had always striven for the next mountain, to have more, more, more than what he already had, at last knew what it was like to possess for an instant all that was important in the world.

He held back his release while she tightened around him. Her breath caught in surprise and wonder as he sank himself into her welcoming warmth one last time and rode the waves of her pleasure. Despite his loss of control in taking her innocence, a portion of his mind warned him before it was too late, and he pulled free of her body to shudder his release alone. He would not risk giving her a child and dooming them all to Hell on earth.

When they both lay spent and exhausted, Lucia cupped his head with her hands and lifted his face so she could stare into his eyes. She smiled a new smile— one that erased the ever-present sadness in her eyes.

''Ah, Jack, I knew I could not love you this much and be all alone in my love. I promise I will make you happy. Perhaps we can go west and work a farm. I have always loved the land. We can do anything together. I know we can. You will never regret marrying me, this I swear."

Jack, who had been floating on a warm cloud of fulfillment and happiness, went cold with dread. A farm? He swallowed a sudden sickness at the back of his throat. He had farmed himself nearly to death in Ireland. He despised farming. And love? Marriage? He had but to remember his mother, her life and her death, to feel sick all over again at the prospect of either.

Lucia saw the truth in his face and the sadness returned. "You are not going to marry me." She did not question, she knew. She had always known him better than anyone.

Her gaze slid from his. She shoved at him, and Jack shifted so she could scramble free. The loss of her warmth made him shiver. Would he ever feel such warmth again?

Lucia picked up her shift and found it ruined. She stood there for a moment staring at the garment, transfixed. Her hair hung about her face, the black strands emphasizing the sudden paleness of her skin, her usual healthy, golden tinge replaced by a deathlike pallor. She cast the shift to the ground and began to laugh, a sound without mirth that caused Jack to sit up, alarmed.

"Lucia?" He did not know what else to say. He dare not ask her what was wrong. He knew all too well.

She told him anyway, standing naked with naught but her hair to cover the breasts he had so recently worshipped. "I am a fool. But then, you knew that. Most likely took advantage of that fact, just as Tim said you would. I defended you. I always have."

Jack's shame turned slowly to anger. He had not

meant for this to happen. He had told her to go. Twice. Yet she had remained.

"I am only thinkin' of you. Yer too young t' be a wife. T' be a mother. I'll ruin ye."

Her eyes narrowed. "You already have."

Her quiet pronouncement fell between them, and Jack drowned shame with more anger. "Will ye be sayin' I seduced ye, then? Ye know that is not the case. Just because I cannot love ye nor marry ye does not mean I do not have feelings fer ye. I'll take care of ye just as I always have. I swear."

She started to laugh again, and he resisted the urge to shake her until she stopped. That laugh grated on his ears, scraped along the tender thread of guilt within him. "I am sure you will always take care of me. But, I think, not as you always have." She glanced pointedly at the bed, then took a deep breath, closed her eyes, and reached for the rosary that usually hung about her neck. The necklace was absent, most likely lying by the wash-basin, and her hand fell back to her side as her eyes opened and stared into his. "I will be leaving you, Jack. If you decide to listen to your heart instead of the lure of your ambition and greed, I would be willing to see you again. If not, please do not come after me. I cannot bear to look at you and know you have so little respect for love and honor."

"Dammit, Lucia, how can ye walk away from what we just shared? This was more than a mere tumble and well ye know it."

"Yes, I do know it. But you, it seems, do not." She turned and walked to her side of the room, dressing quickly and throwing some clothes into a bag. Then she moved to the washbasin, picked up the rosary, and dropped the necklace over her head. The beads clicked together, sounding loud and hollow in the tense silence between them. She stopped with her hand on the door.

"Good-bye, Jack," she whispered without looking about.

The way she said good-bye, the finality, the despair, infuriated Jack. He needed her; he had always needed her. Just as his mother had needed his father, and she had died, old before her time, mourning the loss of yet another child, dirt poor and starving despite all the love and the need and the honor.

He could still hear his mother's voice begging her husband to stay, telling of her need and her love. Later, when Patrick had gone out to drink, Jack would hear her praying, begging God for the same thing. He could still feel the shame that had enveloped him every time she had begged, his disgust for her weakness at war with his love for her. Over her grave he had sworn never to beg for love, never to need anyone, and never to pray again.

"Go then," he spat, tearing himself from the memories. "I'll not stop ye. But don't expect me t' beg ye t' come back. If ye want me, then ye'll have t' take me on my terms, and ye'll have t' come back t' me."

His only answer was the closing of the door.

Chapter Five

The past receded, and Lucia braced herself for what the future would bring. She stood just inside the doorway, remembering, watching the rain mix with the dirt upon the windows, then trace a leisurely path downward. So much remained the same, so much did not. She had walked through the rain that night to Saint Mary's. They had taken her in, and she had never left there. Alive, at any rate.

The room hovered between dusk and night, difficult to distinguish because of the gray, storm-clouded sky, but the dwindling light combined with the intense urge to finish this and return to the graveyard made Lucia think night fast approached. On the heels of eve, midnight would come.

Even though the scene had disappeared, Jack remained next to the bed, staring down at the worn mattress with intense concentration. That night had been both the most wonderful and the most horrible of Lucia's life. She had experienced the fulfillment of her heart's desire only to have joy snatched from her grasping fingers. The wrong that had occurred here, on that bed and afterward, had been as much hers as Jack's. That was one reason she had been allowed to return to earth as his guide. He might have three wrongs to learn, but she had one—and hers had contributed to his. She must admit her wrong now.

Lucia crossed the room and stood behind Jack, close enough to touch if she gave in to the need. Instead, she allowed herself a moment to feel his warmth caressing her chill. Drawing in a deep breath, she committed the scent of rain and earth and man to memory. She hoped the essence of Jack would remain with her when she returned to the Hell that was hers.

He spun around before she could speak. Fury contorted the beauty of his face, and Lucia stepped back, for a brief second afraid, even though he could do nothing to hurt her anymore.

"I will not repent what happened on this bed. Say I seduced ye. I took yer innocence. Say what ye will. Perhaps I was wrong t' make love t' ye, but it is the only fine memory I have, and I cannot regret it."

His eyes were wild, his hair damp and tousled about his face. How she loved him, despite everything. She wanted nothing more than to take him in her arms, pull him onto the bed that concerned them both so much, and invite him back into her body one final time. But she had one last thing she must do.

"I have not the power to make you repent anything." She gave a slight smile, hoping the calm of her expression, false though it was, would tame some of his fury.

He blinked, as if seeing something in her for the first time, then reached out and cupped her cheek in his hand. Though she longed to turn her mouth and touch her lips to the center of his palm with a flare that seared her soul, she resisted and took his hand from her face to hold it captive between them.

"I was wrong, too, Jack."

"No. You could never do any wrong."

"I did not mean to, but I could not help myself. You were my hero, my savior, both the brother I always wanted and the man I came to dream of." She paused and he squeezed her fingers, comforting her without thought as he always had. She took what solace she could and moved on. "I loved you too much. I never said a word when you lied and you cheated and you stole. I knew you could not bear to be criticized. I knew your burning desire to succeed, to be a rich and respected man, though I did not know why you had so deep a need for something so shallow. I prayed you would stop, that my love would be enough for you. That someday you would see what was important just by looking in my eyes. And on our last night, I begged with all my soul that when you were inside my body you would feel the magic and give up your obsession. I hoped, and I prayed, and I begged, but I never *said* a thing to you, Jack, and there lay my mistake."

He frowned. "I don't understand."

"I should have *told* you you were wrong. That you were hurting people, hurting me. I knew wrong from right, and I should have tried to make you see it, too. And if you did not listen, I should have left you long before the night we made love on this bed."

"You think I would have listened to you?"

"I do not know, but at least I would have tried. Perhaps you did not love enough, but I loved too much, and sometimes that can be just as bad."

Jack yanked his hand from hers and stepped away from the bed, away from her. "And what should I do to right this wrong I did to you, Lucia?"

"Again I must tell you, you cannot change the hurt you caused. You have to learn what is important. What is right. This is all about you. Your life and your death. Each wrong you committed, you committed because of a lack in you."

His eyes darkened along with his expression. Instead of backing away he stepped toward her. "Ye say my wrong came about from a lack in me. Well, as I recall, Monihan told me I could not love ye the way ye needed me to. So if I love ye now, will I have learned the lesson I was set t' learn?"

Fascinated with the fury and the passion in his eyes, Lucia could only stare at him, unable to speak. Before she could answer, deny him or agree, his mouth crushed down upon hers, and she was lost in the tempest between them.

She opened her mouth beneath his onslaught, meeting his desperate kiss with a desperation of her own. She didn't care if she was cast into Hell for this, she would love him one last time.

They fell onto the ancient cot, tearing at each others' clothes, hands frantic, mouths nipping, tasting, soothing. No words were spoken; all that needed to be said right now would be said with their bodies alone.

He pushed inside her with a mumbled curse, and she shattered immediately. Then his mouth gentled and his body slowed. As frantic as they'd joined, they moved toward mutual fulfillment at a more tranquil pace. This time, instead of leaving her empty and alone when he found his release, he held her closer, then lifted his head from her shoulder. Their gazes held as they went over the edge together.

How wonderful their joining felt. So right. So complete. But different than the last time, and that difference she must question even though she wanted nothing more than to hold him in silence for as long as she was able.

Hesitant, unsure, Lucia reached up and traced her knuckles along his cheekbone. "Why did you stay within me this time?"

His gaze skittered away from hers. "I couldn't risk a child ten years ago."

"Why?"

His eyes came back to hers, and in them she saw the pain he'd always kept to himself. "My father killed my mother by marrying her. He killed her with his love and his lust. She died birthing his babe, the eighth she'd lost. If they'd been any more than dirt farmers, and if she'd not been half starved, she might have survived. But she loved him. She would not leave him. And he would not leave her be."

"What does that have to do with us?"

"I swore I'd never be like him."

"You are not him."

"But if I'd given you a child back then, when we were poor and had nothing but each other, I would have been exactly like him. And I would never have become what I am."

Lucia closed her eyes against the unyielding pain about her heart. "And now?"

"I love you, Lucia," he whispered, his breath brushing her cheek. Her eyes snapped open and stared into his, searching. "I always have. I was mistaken to run from your love. I was afraid and I was wrong." He lowered his forehead to hers, and his hair slid against her temples, causing a shiver of awareness to chill her bare flesh. "I truly believed you were better off without me. I did not want to hurt you anymore than I already had."

"Or was not hurting me a convenient excuse for keeping to your ambitious course?"

His shoulders rose, then released on a sigh. "You've always known me better than I know myself. I'm sorry for the past, but I want to make things right. Will you marry me? Tonight?"

Lucia tensed and tears filled her eyes. She was thankful he kept his forehead pressed to hers so he could not see her pain. There would be no life with Jack for her. Hell was not to come; Hell was here and now—when everything she'd ever dreamed of or wanted was offered, and she could not have it. Ever.

He lifted his head, and in his urgency to convince her to agree, he did not notice the too-bright sheen to her eyes. "I can give you everything you've ever dreamed of. I'm rich now, Lucia. Richer than I ever believed possible."

Lucia winced. Jack saw and frowned. "What is it? Are you married? Dear God, Lucia, don't tell me you belong to someone else."

She shook her head, helpless, her voice deserting her. He had not learned a single thing.

"Let me up," she whispered, and the fierceness beneath the words made him move aside. She dressed, not looking at him, her mind frantically searching for the way to make him see his life would be better for the changes he could make.

When she turned to look at him, he'd put on his trousers but nothing more. The sight of his bare chest, the light dusting of black hair at the center trailing down to disappear at the waistband, made her swallow against the earthly lust that still possessed her. Her shoulders slumped in defeat and she glanced out the window. The storm had fled, and a full moon shone, bright and silver, despite the muddy windowpane. "Midnight comes. You must return to the graveyard."

He blinked. "Why? I've learned my mistake. I admitted my love for you."

Lucia sighed. Love was not the problem, had never been the problem. Just because he had not said he loved her all those years ago had not meant he did not love her. His wrong had been something else.

"Still you must return, when midnight comes. That is what I was told. That is what you were told. The lantern awaits to tell you your fate. If you have learned what you must, you will live. If not . . . Well, you know better than I what will happen. I will give you one last piece of advice, Jack Keegan: look around when you return to the graveyard. Look around for the truth of your past. Then you will know the answer to every question you ask."

She began to turn away toward the door, but he sprang from the bed and caught her before she could move a step. "Ye aren't coming with me?"

His eyes were frightened, the eyes of the little boy he'd never been, and she could not say good-bye as she should. He was her weakness still: he always would be. Instead, she reached up and kissed him with her whole heart and soul. He clung to her as she'd once clung to him, proving again, if his words had not already, that he did love her the best he knew how.

"I cannot come with you. You must meet your fate alone."

"Y-ye won't leave me again?"

She shook her head. "I will never leave you. Always, I will be right here." She put her palm against the left side of his chest, memorizing the strength and the warmth of Jack. "Even when you cannot see me or touch me."

He placed his hand over hers, holding her to him. Her words must have given him the comfort he needed, for when he spoke again, the accent she loved so much had fled. "Where can I find you if I've gained my second chance?"

With reluctance she tugged her hand from beneath his. "Have no fear. If you look around and see, you will find me."

Then Lucia turned and ran from the room before he could touch her again. As soon as the door closed behind her, she disappeared as if she had never walked the earth.

Chapter Six

Jack stood in the middle of the room staring at the closed door. With the loss of her presence the air took on a damp chill that made him shiver and reach absently for his discarded shirt. He shoved his arms into the sleeves as he crossed the room in three long strides and yanked open the door.

"Lucia—" Jack stopped and stared. Gone, though he could still smell her scent, earth and wildflowers, upon the air. He stepped into the hall but saw no sign of her. How had she left so quickly?

Jack dressed and hurried through the silver-tinged streets, alert to any shrouded movements from the alleyways. He did not need to be murdered twice. But he seemed to lead as charmed a life this night as he'd led a doomed one on the last.

Through the ghetto of his youth Jack ran, past the children who still slept in the doorways, through the Irish section and many others until he reached the Italian part of town. Just as he gained the street where St. Mary's stood, the cathedral clock began to toll midnight.

He burst through the cemetery gate as the clock struck a second time. He could see the lantern in the midst of the headstones, still burning, and he caught his breath. He would live, it seemed.

Jack picked his way through the tombstones, which shone bright white in the light of the silver moon. Just as he reached the lantern, an icy breeze swept the graveyard, tossing his hair into his eyes, then out again in time for him to see the glow flicker and threaten to die.

"No!" he shouted, as if the flame could hear him, and fell to his knees to shade the fire from the wind.

Still the flame sputtered. A result of the storm or a message from above? The clock continued to toll—five, six.

Through his panic a sense of calm penetrated as he remembered Lucia's words. She would always be with him, even when he could not see her. He took a deep breath and did as she'd bid him. He looked around—and he saw.

In front of his face two gravestones emerged from the earth—one large, one small. He squinted against the darkness, and the flickering shadows of the lantern threw their dying light upon the names inscribed there.

Lucia Casale.

Angelia Giovanna Casale.

Jack stared, blinked, swallowed. The date beneath Lucia's name was eight months after she had left him ten years ago. The date beneath the name he did not know was the same. Only one date on the tiny tombstone—date of birth and date of death.

Jack had learned enough Italian during the years he'd lived with Lucia to interpret the name. Angelia meant angel. Giovanna meant John—his real name, though he had always gone by the nickname Jack. The child was his, and she was dead, just as Lucia was dead.

But how? He had made love to her not more than an hour ago. She had been a woman—warm, responsive, breathing. Alive as he was. The thought made Jack pause and consider. He had been murdered last eve, died and gone to Hell, then Heaven. Was he alive? Or somewhere in between? And if he could exist on this earth in such a state, then Lucia could do the same.

Jack dropped his hands from the lantern, no longer caring if the flame went out. All those years he had spent trying to make money, to show his father he would amount to something, that he was different from the old man in every way, but he was the same, despite all his struggles. He had killed the woman he loved with his lust.

He couldn't even say he was the same as his father; he was worse. For his da had never left his mother. Pat had been there when she died. Because of Jack's pride and his ambition and his hell-bent selfishness, Lucia had died alone along with their child.

Jack lifted his head and stared at the still flickering lamp. What was the blasted thing trying to tell him?

The ninth strike of the clock sounded. Panic flared.

"All right," he shouted. "Take me, then. I'll gladly go t' Hell if ye let her live."

Psst. Psst.

The flame sputtered as if in anger. The clock struck ten.

"What? What haven't I done? What haven't I

learned? I'll do anything. Nothing matters but her.''

The wind came again, harder than before, but this time Jack had no care for the flame. A strange rattle came from Lucia's grave. He crawled toward the sound and saw something hanging over the edge of the stone.

Her rosary. He dived for the beads as if they were a lifeline. His fingers closed about them, and he searched for the words from his childhood. But he had denied them for so long, they denied him now. So instead of the litany, he spoke from his breaking heart.

"Dear God, she did not deserve t' die. I did. I do. I was ever selfish, ambitious, prideful, stubborn, and despite the chance ye tried t' give me, I did not learn a thing. The money, the position means nothing without her. Take it, take me. Do with me what ye will. I do not deserve a second chance, she does. I beg of ye. Please. Please. Please.''

The final three words he spoke in tandem with the final strikes of the clock. Storm clouds drifted over the moon, and midnight descended upon him.

He could not raise his head for fear of what he'd see. So he knelt there on Lucia's grave, fingering her rosary, whispering her name as tears soaked his face.

The wind blew again, this time not cold but warm, scented with flowers birthed in sun-warmed earth. He looked up and there she was. Beautiful, ethereal. A ghost, or an angel.

"What did you learn, Jack?''

He glanced at the lantern where a tiny flame burned against the darkest of night. Jack thought back on all he'd seen and all she'd said that day, trying to understand what he had been unable to understand all his life.

181

He no longer lied or cheated or stole. He had admitted loving her, he had thrown his wealth and power to the winds, yet still it wasn't enough. Then he remembered something Lucia had said—that it wasn't the lying or the cheating as much as not caring about what happened to those he'd wronged. He might no longer be a thief in deed, but he was a thief at heart.

He returned his gaze to Lucia, who waited, hope alight upon her face. "I have to change myself. I cannot go back to the same life I've lived. I have to start again. I have to look at my decisions and make them based on what is best for everyone and not just me. To take my second chance and use it in the same way I did my first is wasting my life."

She smiled. "Yes."

He hurried on, afraid she would fade before he said all he needed to say. "But I don't want my second chance. I want to be with you. And . . ." He glanced at the tiny headstone and his eyes burned. "And her. Why didn't you come to me when you learned of the child?"

"And make your nightmare come true? I could not do that to you, Jack. I loved you too much."

"I let you go so a child would not happen." He shook his head at the irony of it all.

"A child is something we do not control."

His groan was heavy with despair, frustration, and pain. "I'm sorry. I was stupid and stubborn, and you paid for my mistakes. If I could do it over again, I'd change everything."

"How would you change it?"

"I would not change making love to you, Lucia. As I said, that memory is worth a thousand nights with my father. But I would marry you, immediately, and raise our girl away from here. I would see where true riches lie, in the love of the heart, the wealth of the soul, and the memories we make together. You and me and our children would be all I would ever need.''

Incredibly, she laughed, a bright, happy sound in direct contrast to the darkness and sadness of the place that surrounded them. Suddenly she knelt next to him on her own grave, no longer ethereal but solid and warm and alive. She threw herself into his arms and held him to her.

''I hope you do not live to regret your vow, Jack Keegan. Because you have been given your second chance.''

He turned his head to look at the flame, though he kept his arms about her, frightened she would disappear if he let her go for even an instant. But the sight of the lantern, burning high and bright and full, caused his fears to recede. He glanced back at her with a frown.

''What about you?''

''I existed in purgatory for nine years, Jack. My wrong was loving you too much. Forgiving you everything. Even when I died along with our daughter, I did not blame you, I blamed God. And you, who did not know I had died, could not pray for my soul, even if you would have. But tonight you did, and you set me free.''

Jack stood and helped her to her feet. He put his arm about her and held her close to his side. Then he turned to look at the graves, but they were gone, the grass at their feet unmarred by death and its symbols.

''What happened?''

''You said if you could change things you would. You

would marry me, immediately, and take me away from here.''

''Aye, and I will.''

She bent to pick up the lantern and held it aloft. The now merry glow lighted her face, and Jack's heart tightened with love and the promise of their future. ''Then let's be about the rest of our lives.''

He hesitated. ''What about the child?''

''The wonderful thing about miracles is how miraculous they are.'' She took his hand and placed his palm to her stomach. Her smile lit her face brighter than the lantern's light, and the sadness that had always lurked in her eyes had been replaced by delight and wonder. ''She is right here, awaiting her second chance.''

Joy spread through Jack, warming the chill that lingered from the despair and the fear and the night. He looked down into her face and knew he had at last found all the wealth the world had to offer. Lowering his head, he kissed her, his hand protecting the miracle returned to them.

When the kiss ended, he looked into her eyes. ''I never want to spend another day apart from you.''

The corners of Lucia's lips turned upward in a smile full of sensual promise. ''What about the nights?''

''I swear when every midnight comes, I'll be in your arms from now until the end of time.''

Author's Note

The idea for *When Midnight Comes* came about when I was reading a children's book about Halloween traditions and stumbled upon the old Irish story of the jack o' lantern. It seems an old man named Jack was mean, stingy, and tricky. He died while eating a turnip. Too mean to go to heaven, he went to the devil. The devil threw him a piece of burning coal to put inside his turnip. Jack still walks the earth with his turnip lantern, looking for a place to stay. The thousands of Irish immigrants brought this tale to America. Once here the turnip, common in Ireland, became a pumpkin, common in America, and that is how we came to carve jack o' lanterns.

When Midnight Comes is one of those special stories that comes to a writer as a gift. I felt I knew Jack and Lucia from the moment I began to write their tale. I hope you enjoyed your time with them as much as I did.

Lori Handeland

My next Love Spell novel will be a retelling of the tale of Romeo and Juliet for the Legendary Lovers series. Look for *By Any Other Name* in Spring 1998.

I love to hear from readers. Please write to me at: P.O. Box 736, Thiensville, WI 53092. SASE is appreciated for reply. Or look me up on the World Wide Web: http://www.eclectics.com/lorihandeland/.

The Shadow King

King

Stobie Piel

To Yvonne Murphy, with thanks both for your insightful writing advice and your generous friendship. I am very fortunate to know you!

Heartily know,
When the half-gods go,
The gods arrive.

—*Give All to Love,* Ralph Waldo Emerson

Chapter One

She was searching for a dinosaur in Ireland. Cara Reid threw down her backpack and collapsed onto a large rock. *Dinosaurs.* Cara stared out over the cove, watching the early morning mist tremble over the dark water of Lough Leane.

Malcolm Reid had a head cold, so he sent his daughter out to watch the lake. Again. Cara folded her hands over her unopened notebook. Her father would expect a report. He had stacks of notebooks already. *"Thursday morning . . . Ripple in left center, but no Verified Sighting."*

Cara closed her eyes, allowing the monster a chance to surface in private. She loved her father. Despite his peculiar career, Malcolm Reid was a brilliant scientist. He had been top of his class at Yale, then a respected professor of natural biology at Dartmouth College in Vermont. Until his wife died.

Even at nine, Cara knew her father left Vermont and took up hunting mysterious creatures because of his loss. When he went after the Congo Dinosaur, she understood. For a nine-year-old, it was an exciting adventure. At first. When the pygmies chuckled, then told him he "just missed" the dinosaur, she realized it might be an embarrassing adventure as well.

Cara stuck with her father because she loved him. Because he needed her. She went to college in Edinburgh, because he was in Scotland staking out the Loch Ness Monster. Like her father, she graduated at the top of her class in zoology.

She turned down a position at the university to become her father's assistant. Not because she believed in monsters. But because she believed in Malcolm Reid. Her life hadn't been easy, and her choice made relationships awkward, if not impossible.

Cara yawned and stretched her legs. Her khakis were damp from the morning mist, her hiking boots were soaked. She hated getting up early. But the legends said the loch monsters prefer dawn. "Why couldn't you be late risers?"

Cara got up and walked along the lake. It was a beautiful, peaceful morning. Early autumn in Ireland. That counted for something. It was preferable to winter in Nepal, anyway. They had "just missed" the Yeti, too.

The Yeti hunt first attracted the attention of an American tabloid, *The Searcher*. Since then, the paper's most annoying reporter had followed Malcolm Reid's trail. Lucas Sprague never let up. Malcolm was his favorite madman.

Lucas used vile tactics to gain Malcolm's confidence. He professed understanding and interest in Malcolm's projects. He took a job as Malcolm's assistant, and Cara had considered him a friend and confidante. Until his briefcase fell open, revealing notes he'd taken for the notorious tabloid.

Lucas had seemed so . . . normal.

Cara knew Lucas was in Ireland. He'd find them soon. She cast a final glance over the still lake, then looked for the trail back to the secluded inn. Cara hesitated. She couldn't arrive at the inn before ten, because her father would know she hadn't given the monster enough time. She eyed a fork in the path, then sighed.

"I might as well get some exercise." She stuffed her notebook into her backpack, then started down the path.

The path disappeared after a few turns, but the branches seemed to bend back, allowing her passage. A cool thrill sped along her nerves, but she kept going. The path led up a small incline to an overgrown knoll. Cara guessed it was one of the many Celtic burial mounds that dotted both England and Ireland. A few rocks remained on its crest, though it had caved in ages ago.

Cara wondered who was buried there. Some ancient Celtic prince, perhaps. Maybe an aged, venerable Irish king. The sites of antiquity never failed to stir her heart, to reach her on a deep, emotional level. They lived, ages ago, fought, and died. They loved, and dreamed.

And sometimes, those dreams died young.

The cairn made a stirring sight for a picture. Cara took out her camera and focused on the mystic setting. Something flickered just beyond a large tree.

Cara lowered her camera and studied the area ahead. Nothing. She lifted the camera, but the figure moved again. She squinted her eyes. "Is someone there?"

No answer. Cara's pulse quickened. "Hello?" Maybe Lucas Sprague had found her, after all. It wasn't beyond him to accost her in private. "Lucas, if that's you, I still have a restraining order. I'm willing and able to use it!" Cara held her breath, but nothing happened. She heard nothing. The air was still, the branches motionless. Strange, because they had moved when she walked up the path.

Cara drew a deep breath, then started to turn away. From the corner of her eye, she caught movement. She whirled around, but she saw nothing. Cara blinked and shook her head. She'd gotten up too early. Her eyes were playing tricks in revenge. "There's nothing there." Cara steeled her nerves, then took a step forward.

A transparent figure emerged from the trees and Cara froze in shock. A young man with golden hair stood before her. He wore a white tunic with a gold-stitched hem around the collar and sleeves. A red cloak pinned with a brooch hung from his broad shoulders. His boots were laced with thongs over leggings, reminiscent of a Viking's attire.

Everything was transparent. The clothes, the boots, and the man.

He looked real. His sweet, noble face revealed deep emotion. He smiled and held out his hand.

Cara felt dizzy. Her heart raced. "It can't be."

The apparition took a step toward her, and Cara choked back a scream. She spun around and raced back down the forest path. Branches slapped her face, she stumbled, but Cara didn't stop until she reached the main path to the lake.

She caught her breath, then hurried to her car.

*   *   *

"There are no such thing as ghosts, Caroline." Malcolm Reid didn't look up from his desk.

"I saw him, Dad." Cara had driven like a madman to reach her father, and now he dismissed her experience without a second thought.

Malcolm glanced up at her, plainly skeptical. "Girl, you saw a tendril of fog, or maybe your eyes need to be checked."

"He was dressed like a Viking, or a Saxon, maybe. He wore a large brooch on his shoulder."

"Sounds like a Saxon."

"I didn't imagine it, Dad. He was there, by an old cairn. And he was holding out his hand."

Malcolm flipped through her notebook. "No notes? Nothing? You're supposed to write down the water conditions, Caroline."

"There weren't 'conditions,' Dad. It was calm as glass and misty."

"Those are conditions."

"What about the ghost?"

Malcolm fixed his gaze on Cara's face. "I'm not a crackpot chasing ghosts, daughter. I'm a scientist in search of heretofore undiscovered species with which to broaden our understanding of our world."

"I know that, Dad. But I saw something out there by the lake, and it wasn't a monster."

Malcolm sneezed into a handkerchief, then sat back in his seat, assessing his daughter. "You must learn how to distinguish actual sightings of phenomena from flights of fancy. There are no such things as ghosts."

Cara spent the day typing her father's notes, but she couldn't forget the ghost. As the day passed and her shock faded, she began to believe Malcolm's assessment. Maybe she imagined a swirl of fog to be a handsome young man. She'd eaten a peculiar Irish version of mutton pizza. That could make anyone see ghosts.

As credulous as Malcolm Reid had been, Cara was the opposite. She researched her father's mad ventures with calm cynicism, never allowing her skeptical nature to interfere with his enthusiasm. Practicality was her shield. From her earliest childhood, Cara guarded herself well.

Malcolm popped his head into her room. "Aren't we forgetting something, girl? *Someone?*"

"Who?"

Malcolm sighed. "The monster. While you're sitting here, he, or she, might be basking in the afternoon sun."

Sometimes, Cara feared her father was crazy. Yet the sight of his bright eyes never failed to touch her heart. He looked so hopeful, as if something grand and mystical might appear at any moment. So why didn't he see the ghost?

"Yes, Dad. I'm on my way."

Cara went to the lake. It was calm and still and monsterless. As much as she knew she'd never see a monster, or anything magical in any way, Cara kept looking. She wanted to believe, yet faith came hard. She had never known why.

Cara eyed the overgrown path that led to the secret cairn. The branches bowed and swayed, as if to make way for her passage. Her blood tingled, her feet and fingers went numb. She rose slowly and followed. Cara's heart pounded as she came out into the open and looked up the slope.

Nothing. The evening light filtered through the ancient trees, slanting over the cairn. The rocks had tumbled from its crest, the entrance had caved partially inward. Its condition was worse than most Celtic cairns, as if in its own time the burial mound had been hastily laid.

Birds chirped in evening chorus, fluttering from branch to branch. Cara couldn't help a tug of disappointment as she turned away to resume her monster watch.

"I knew you'd come."

Cara froze, her heart in her throat. She turned around. He stood at the top of the mound, still wearing his Viking clothes. Still transparent. Still holding out his hand.

Her shock reached a plateau, then gave way to logic. *There are no such things as ghosts.* Rather than fear, Cara felt anger. Someone was playing a joke on her. And she had a fair idea who.

"Very funny." Cara walked toward the beautiful apparition. "I suppose you're the Prince of Elves?"

The apparition looked surprised. He lowered his hand. Cara wondered how someone programmed a projector image for accurate responses. She turned and looked around. "You can turn it off now, Lucas. I'm not impressed."

"I am not 'Lucas.' "

The apparition spoke with a deep British accent, and he sounded indignant. Cara looked back at him. Obviously, some actor had agreed to play a hoax. A good-looking actor. "Knock it off, pal."

He folded his arms across his wide chest. "This isn't exactly the way I expected you to react."

"No kidding." Cara rolled her eyes and turned away, heading for the path to the lake. "You can tell Lucas

I'm not interested in making a fool of myself tonight. Sorry.''

''Elfgiva, geman.'' His voice came as a deep, sonorous chant, words she didn't understand. Cara turned back to him, compelled on an unfathomable level.

"What do you want?''

The apparition held out his hand again. "Come here.''

She was trembling, her heart ached as if with a deep, sorrowful memory. A memory as acute as love. "Who are you?''

His brow raised. "Your husband.''

The spell shattered. Cara's emotion was raw, painful. She made a fist, then marched toward him. Whatever he had been hired to do couldn't match the violence of her intentions.

Cara walked up to the shadowy man. He didn't move. She could see through him, but images beyond were distorted. She walked in a circle around him. He was dimensional, like a real man, but transparent throughout. He cast no shadow.

Cara returned to his front, contemplating an explanation for his presence. Close to him, she felt a warm energy that seemed to emanate from his transparent body. It didn't make sense.

She looked above his head, but there was no sign of any projector. Nothing explained his presence.

"You're not real.'' She paused. "What are you?'' Cara didn't let him answer. "Why am I asking this thing?''

"Good question. You and I have better things to do.''

Cara frowned. "Such as what?''

He smiled. "Such as this . . .'' Before she realized his intentions, he bent to kiss her. He didn't feel like a real man. He felt like energy and warmth, pure emotion. But she felt his lips. She felt the passion of his kiss.

More than a kiss. He seemed to blend inside her, become part of her. Every nerve stirred, then leapt to fire. Cara shuddered with fierce desire. A desire she had never felt before. She felt him inside her, everywhere. Like a lover.

Cara jerked out of his arms and slapped his face. Her hand swept through his head, spinning her around.

"Oh, God, I'm slapping a ghost!" Cara sank down on the grass and bowed her head. "I have lost my mind."

He sat down beside her. She peeked at him from one eye. "You can sit?" He nodded.

"I'm sorry, my love. I shouldn't have thus accosted you, considering what you've been through. But to have you here, looking at me . . ."

"How do you know what I've 'been through'?"

"With that ne'er-do-well Sprague following you."

Her mouth firmed into an angry ball. "I knew it!" She struggled to her feet, glaring down at him. He just looked up at her, pale eyes wide and innocent.

"Lucas put you up to this, didn't he?"

"You think this man enlisted a ghost to scare you?" He was teasing her. That sweet, full mouth was curved in a gentle, heart-piercing smile. His translucent eyes twinkled.

"You're not a ghost."

His smile deepened as he rose to his feet and faced her. "What do you think I am?"

"A joke."

"I shall prove otherwise. Touch me."

"I will not." She hesitated. "Why?"

"Just do it."

Cara raised her hand tentatively, then placed it on his chest.

"What do you feel?"

"Nothing." Cara was shaking. She felt something. Something unexplainable. Warmth. "You're warm."

"It is the essence of life you feel. It is strong here, in this place." He gestured around the cairn.

"Why?"

"I was slain here."

Cara gulped. Her heart took a strange, unsteady beat. Her blood ran cold. "Who are you?"

"In life, I was called Edwy."

"Edwy." A peculiar surge of emotion churned inside Cara. She didn't know why. "I see. A ghost named Edwy. And I'm talking to you."

"You're the only one who can."

"Why? Oh, of course. Because I'm your wife."

He nodded. "We are bound by the soul."

"I'm not married."

"Not now. But in another lifetime, ages ago."

"What year did you die?"

"In the year of Our Lord 959."

"You have an answer for everything, don't you?"

Edwy smiled. "There is an answer for everything, Cara Reid."

"So I'm your reincarnated wife, and you're my dead husband. Is that it?"

"In essence, yes."

Cara flopped back onto the grass and stared up at the sky. The fog lifted, and the sun rose. She looked over at Edwy. He looked down at her. She could see the sun through him. "Shouldn't you be disappearing?"

"Why?"

"Don't ghosts disappear in the sun?"

"I see no reason why they should."

Cara looked at him for a moment longer. He was so beautiful that it almost hurt to look at him. She turned her gaze back to the sky. "I don't believe any of this, of course. I've seen enough to know a hoax when I see one."

"That much is certain. The abominable snowman, the African dinosaur . . ." Edwy was shaking his head.

"You know a lot for a ghost." Her voice radiated scorn. "Almost as if you've been thoroughly briefed by, oh, say, Lucas Sprague, maybe?"

Edwy reached over and touched her cheek. Again, she felt his strange energy, his warmth. Cara shuddered, but she couldn't push his hand away.

"I know, Cara Reid, because I have been with you . . . always."

"Have you? How comforting!"

"Someone had to watch over you." Edwy sounded serious. He looked guileless, as if he couldn't lie.

"You seem like a nice enough person." He was certainly a good-looking person. "Maybe you think this is funny, but . . ."

"I was with you when your mother died."

The blood drained from her face. He wasn't quitting. He was crueler than he looked. "This is vicious."

"When you were alone in your little room, and praying it wasn't so, and that she would come back to life, I was there."

Cara gulped. Her eyes filled with tears, her throat clenched. "You bastard."

"I am the legitimate son of Edmund . . ."

199

"I meant that you're cruel."

Cara saw sympathy on his face. A kind face, capable of infinite tenderness. But also capable of quick anger, rash decision, boundless pride. Cara wondered how she knew these things about him.

"I would never hurt you, Cara. But the world is filled with people who will, if you let them. I have protected you, of course, but the time of my wraithdom is near its end. Should I fail . . ." Edwy's voice trailed. His transparent jaw firmed. "I will not fail."

"What are you talking about? How have you protected me?"

"You are a virgin."

Cara's cheeks flamed. She closed her eyes to regain her composure. "How do you know? And it's none of your business."

"You're my wife. It was unacceptable to me that any other man know you in the biblical sense." Edwy paused, looking pleased with himself. "So I have learned to infect your would-be suitors with dreams, whereupon I threaten their lives and those bits they intend to utilize in your defilement."

"Is that why no one asks me for a second date?"

He nodded, unashamed. "Yes."

I'm almost believing him. "I suppose Lucas is filming you right now, so that your reactions are correct."

"Why do you feel me when we touch, if what you suspect is true?"

"It's probably my imagination. As we know, I have always been gullible."

"Close your eyes."

"Why?"

"Just do it."

Cara sighed and closed her eyes.

"Now, tell me . . . Where am I touching you?"

This seemed a reasonable test. At first, she felt nothing. Then a soft, tingling feeling ran across her cheek, then over her lower lip. The touch ran down her neck, over her collarbone, to her breast. . . .

Cara's eyes popped open. "Stop that!"

Edwy laughed, his eyes shining. He moved his hand in the pattern she had sensed before. "Is this what you felt?"

"Yes."

Edwy let his hand fall, but his eyes lingered on her lips. "It would please me to kiss you again, flesh to flesh."

Cara gulped. "You don't have flesh, remember?"

"Ah, my love, but I can . . . if you'll help me."

Her suspicions returned and soared. "What do you want?"

"There is a way for me to restore the form of my life. Near this place lies a golden circlet. I buried it in the hours before my death."

"Why?"

Edwy hesitated. "That tale is long. I would wait on the telling."

"I'm not surprised. Anyway, what do you want with this circlet?"

"Bring it, and you will see." His pale eyes sparkled. "If I should turn from ghost to man before your eyes, you would believe me, would you not?"

"I suppose so."

"Good. Then do as I ask you, and you will know. You wish to learn the truth of things, don't you, my love? That makes you more noble than most in this day and age.''

Cara rose to her feet, but Edwy remained sitting. ''Where will I find it?''

''At the foot of this barrow, facing the lake, you will find an ancient boulder. A thousand years ago, the lake reached to that point. Dig on the lakeside of the rock and you will find the circlet.''

Cara shrugged. ''OK. I'll look for it. I don't expect to find anything, but I'll look.'' She sighed. ''I'll probably wake up in a few minutes and discover this is just a dream.''

Cara's gaze lingered on Edwy for a moment longer. If he was a dream, she wanted to remember him. Then again, if he was helping Lucas Sprague perpetuate a hoax, she wanted to feed him to the wolves.

''You'll need a shovel.''

''I've got one in the car.'' Cara eyed Edwy as he sat back against the tree, looking comfortable. ''I don't suppose you're capable of helping me.''

''Mustering such energy takes a period of time, and is accomplished only with great effort.''

''Did you have something to do with Sprague's briefcase popping open, even though it was locked? I always wondered about that. It seemed too good to be true.''

Edwy's expression turned triumphant. ''I did, of course. I helped it to the floor and broke it open, so that you would see the notes he'd taken on your father.''

Cara started to object, then realized what might have befallen her father if not for Edwy's interference. ''Thank you.'' She paused. ''Why haven't you shown yourself before now?''

"You've never come to the sight of my death before."

"What difference does that make?"

"I can only materialize here, on the spot where I was slain. In spirit form, I can go anywhere."

"Naturally. You haven't seen the Congo dinosaur on any of your travels, have you?"

Edwy smiled. "I wasn't looking."

Cara retrieved her shovel, then followed Edwy's instructions to the boulder. As he indicated, the lake must at one time have reached the boulder but had fallen back to its present position over time.

"Coincidence." Cara felt foolish. She felt disoriented. She was digging up a golden circlet because a "ghost" told her to. Even as she jabbed the shovel into the hard earth, she realized it could be part of an elaborate scheme to convince her she had found a real ghost.

Well, no man could materialize from a projection into a flesh-and-blood person. She would prove him a fake, then leave him fumbling for an explanation.

Cara dug for a long while. Evening darkened over Ireland, and she began to feel nervous. She expected the circlet to be easier to find, considering it was probably planted. Her arms ached and her palms were blistering. Cara straightened, resting on her shovel.

One tall blade of grass swayed in contrast to the stillness of the others. Cara felt an odd tingling on her arm. The same feeling she had experienced when Edwy touched her. He meant for her to dig there, closer to the boulder.

Her stomach knotted, but Cara resumed digging. She went through layers of soil. Her brow was damp from effort. The shovel touched metal beneath the ground. Cara's breath caught at the sight of dull gold.

She knelt and scraped through the dirt. The golden object was deeply imbedded in the ground. Roots were twisted around it. Cara picked them away, but they were old roots, long in possession of the golden object.

It made no sense. This couldn't be recently planted, not entangled in roots this way. Cara freed the object. It was a golden circle, like a large ring.

Her hands shook as she lifted the circlet. It looked like an ancient crown, the kind the Saxons and Norsemen wore. She brushed it off and discovered runes engraved on its surface. Runes of Old English.

Cara carried the circlet back to the barrow. She half-expected Edwy to be gone, but as she emerged from the wood path, she saw him, lounging against the tree, waiting. He smiled when he saw the circlet, an eager light in his pale eyes.

"You found it! Good."

"I found something." Cara held it up to the fading light. "What is it?"

"It is my Circlet of Power, as I told you."

"Is it magical?"

"Gold."

"Ah. Now what?"

"Now . . ." Edwy was enjoying the moment. "We will see if an ancient spell, or curse if you prefer, still works."

He knelt before her, his head bowed. Cara hesitated. "You want me to put this on your head?"

He nodded impatiently. "Do so."

"What makes you think it will stay? You're not exactly solid."

"Try."

Cara shrugged, then placed the circlet on Edwy's head. She expected it to fall through him, but it didn't. It fit like a crown, and it glowed. Cara stepped back. The circlet sparkled, emanating a fiery light.

As the glow increased, the transparency of Edwy's body faded, leaving instead a man.

The glow disappeared, and Edwy rose to his feet. In the flesh he was taller than Cara had realized. He ran his hand over his chest, stretched, then clenched his fingers. The color of his eyes as they met Cara's changed to the blue of a stormy sea.

He held out his hand. *"Elfgiva, geman."*

Cara trembled with shock, her arms clasped around her body. "This can't be . . . You can't be real."

Edwy stepped toward her. "Why do you doubt? You have seen with your eyes. Now see me as I am, and remember."

She backed away. "Remember what?" Her voice sounded shrill.

"Remember me, remember yourself. Remember who you were when we loved."

"I don't understand. I don't remember anything."

"You have taken a new form, my love, but you are the same. Like a tree that grows a new ring for each year."

"What are you talking about?"

"It is the way of things." Edwy seemed impatient with her lack of knowledge concerning spiritual matters. "You live, you grow, and you die. But it doesn't end there. You grow and take a new form. Over and over. I don't know why, but that is the way of things."

"You mean reincarnation. But why are . . . were you a ghost?"

Edwy moved closer, touching her. This time, he felt like a real man. His hands trembled, as if he restrained himself. "I have a brief while in this form, but I am still a ghost." He gestured at the ground. "Do you see? My form casts no shadow."

Cara looked down. Her shadow stretched before her, cast by the afternoon sun. Though Edwy stood beside her, there was no shadow anywhere. "How can that be?" It had to be some kind of trick, but what it was eluded her.

"The circlet allows me to take my ancient form to complete my task, but my life is not yet whole, or lasting."

Cara looked from the ground back to his face. She saw eagerness in his bright eyes, and restrained desire. "What task?"

"I have three tasks to accomplish before sunset on All Hallow's Eve in order to regain my full life." Edwy paused. "When is All Hallow's Eve?"

"Well, if you mean Halloween, it's in ten days."

"That is sufficient." Edwy's gaze whisked from her face to her chest. His lips curved slightly, as if the sight pleased him. "I must regain what I lost, then settle things with my enemy."

"What did you lose?"

His gaze held hers. "You."

Cara bit her lip. Something about this man attracted her, on a level she'd never experienced before. His mouth looked tender, kissable. She averted her eyes from his face and saw his hands. They looked gentle, but strong. She cleared her throat.

206

"Why did I get to reincarnate, if you're still a ghost?"

"You accepted your death, my love. I didn't."

I want you. The thought came before she could stop it. *It's a setup, or worse, and I'm falling for it.* Cara sank to her knees, her face in her hands as tears flooded her vision. "I have lost my mind."

Edwy knelt beside her. He slid his arm around her, settling her back against his strong body. She felt . . . at home. "There are many mysteries, Cara. You must know that, from the life you've led with your father."

"We've never proven any of those." Cara sniffed and dried her eyes. "You said you had to 'settle things' with someone. Who?"

"Dunstan." The change in Edwy's voice was astounding. It radiated controlled, cold anger.

"Who is Dunstan?"

"He was the abbot of Glastonbury."

"Glastonbury? The town in England?"

Edwy nodded.

"What did he do to you?"

"He was responsible for my death, and yours, yet in later years he was made a saint. When I have sought him out, and found vengeance, I will reclaim what is mine by right and by birth."

Cara hesitated. "What is that?"

"The throne of England."

Chapter Two

"The throne of England . . ." Cara drew a long, strained breath, then struggled to her feet. "The throne of England! Just out of curiosity, why would that be your 'right'?"

Edwy hesitated. Cara had endured a great shock, he knew. But he needed her with him to fulfill his quest. "Because I am king."

Cara groaned, then spun around in a circle, waving her arms. "I should have guessed. King!"

"You know this in your heart."

"Of course! I'm queen!" Cara seized her backpack and headed down the slope toward the path.

"Where are you going?"

She stopped, looked back, and pointed her finger at him. "You . . . you're a loon, that's what you are! I don't know how you've done all this, but you're nuts and I'm going home."

"You need time to think."

"You can say that again."

Edwy studied Cara Reid for a long while. The Irish breeze fluttered through her dark brown hair, sifting soft tendrils over her face. He had seen her this way a thousand times. He knew her. He remembered her as she had been, a thousand years ago. Elfgiva, his wife.

He had watched her grow, again and again, into life. From the moment of her birth as Malcolm Reid's daughter, he had known she was his again. He had watched her search, disbelieving in the monsters her father pursued, in the love young men offered. Disbelieving hope.

Edwy knew why. Ages past, he had offered her hope. He had promised her love, and life, and a world built together. He had failed, bitterly. When he came to her, it was too late.

"We must return to the site where I last saw you . . ." He didn't tell her the full story. When he last saw her, she was dead. Cara recoiled as if she guessed what he concealed.

"I'm not going anywhere with you."

Edwy's jaw firmed. "Once, you obeyed my every word."

She rolled her eyes. "Ha! I obey only my own conscience."

"That is sick and twisted." Edwy considered her defiance. "But you are wise to protect yourself. Still, I have returned to you, and you must accept your place."

"My place? As what?"

"My wife and queen, which means you will bow to me in all matters."

She eyed him as if she couldn't believe he was serious. "I will do you great honor, Cara." Edwy studied her body. Firm and fit, with long legs, even encased in man's leggings. "Henceforward, you will wear gowns that reveal more of your flesh to my eyes."

She huffed. "I don't think so." Her eyes narrowed suspiciously. "I thought men of the past kept their women covered."

"Such is not my preference."

"Is that so? Maybe you'd rather your 'queen' wore a bikini?"

"What is that?"

"A small bit of cloth worn swimming, which covers . . ." Cara indicated the space over her breasts and a small line across her hips. A visual image flooded Edwy's mind. His loins tightened.

"That would please me." His voice came husky and raw. They had been so young, their marriage so new. They hadn't had time to learn new arts, to practice love-making in its fullest. Their lives together were spent fighting to survive, to stay together.

Edwy swallowed hard. "We will find new ways of pleasuring each other." What if he failed in his quest? Then they only had ten days. "We must make the most of our hours together."

She dampened her lips, as if the same imaginings filled her mind. She shook her head as if to clear her senses. "You're crazy. Maybe I'm crazy. No. It has to be something I ate. That mutton pizza . . ."

"Cara, the time is right. In a thousand years, you have taken forms, lived lives. But in this life, you have returned to the form of Elfgiva . . . my wife."

"What form is that?"

"A beautiful form. Your brown eyes, your midnight hair. The shape of your little nose and your soft lips . . ."

Edwy stepped toward her, but she backed away from him. He longed to touch her again. He had hovered near her, protecting her, loving her, for ages. He wanted more, and he wanted it now. He wanted to prove to her, and to himself, that love never died.

"If you're the King of England, what are you doing in Ireland? I don't recall the Saxons conquering Ireland at any point in history."

"Only because my reign was cut short. I escaped to Ireland when my brother seized my throne. I planned to raise an army among the Irish—they're good, crazy warriors, you know. But the evil monk Dunstan guessed my plans, and sent a pursuit." Edwy stopped, remembering. "At twilight on October first they found me."

Edwy watched as Cara fought believing him. She didn't want to remember. The past was bitter. Yet its sweetness had haunted him for a thousand years.

"Why did you bury your crown?"

Edwy moved closer to her. She tensed, but she didn't back away. He needed to regain her trust, but there was so little time. "In the hours before my death, I enlisted the aid of an old Irishman who considered himself a Druid. Crazy old man, but it was he who took pity on me and fed me in my exile. He taught me the method of defying my own death, and leaving this symbol . . ." Edwy paused and touched the circlet. "This symbol of resurrection, so that one day, when the circumstances were right, I would fulfill my destiny."

"You can't expect me to believe you."

Elfgiva was more stubborn than he remembered. "I say it, so it is so. A woman does not question a man's judgment. Especially when he is king . . ."

She issued a long groan, disbelieving both him and perhaps herself.

"Why do you doubt me?"

Cara threw up her hands again, dislodging her backpack. "Oh, I don't know. . . . I meet a ghost who says I'm his dead wife and thinks he's the King of England. Who wouldn't be thrilled?"

Edwy smiled. "You always had a way with words. It pleased me then. Though perhaps you are sharper now. Maybe that comes with reincarnation."

"Maybe."

"Your beauty, too, is richer." Edwy assessed her slender body carefully. The desire that had been part of his whole energy seemed focused now. Right where it belonged. "You will make a pleasing queen."

Cara groaned. "Will I? What about Queen Elizabeth?"

"Who is that?"

"The queen, the real queen, of England!"

"My usurper is female?" Edwy paused, considering this. "It makes no difference. I shall supplant her."

"I'm getting out of here."

Edwy watched as Cara shouldered her backpack and darted into the dark woods. She disappeared, but Edwy stood a while gazing over the cairn. For a thousand years, his soul had lingered in this spot, waiting. He had lost his throne, his love, and his life. He refused to accept the utter defeat and go on, though he knew Elfgiva had chosen otherwise.

Instead, Edwy remained behind, waiting. He knew she would come back to him. He knew the cycle of life moved in waves. If Elfgiva had returned, Dunstan would walk the earth also. Souls, like trees, grew outward, spreading. Some trees gave sweet fruit. Some brought poison.

Cara found her father in his room, still perusing his notes. She didn't speak, but he noticed her and motioned for her to sit beside him. "Not ghosts again, girl?"

"Not exactly. Dad . . ." Cara took the offered seat and collected herself. "You know a lot about English history. Have you ever heard of a King Edwy?"

Malcolm sat back in his seat, pondering the question. "Edwy? No, can't say that I have. Can't have been an important king."

Cara's emotion deflated. "He probably wasn't a king at all."

Malcolm seized a book of English history and thumbed through the index. "Edwy. *Eadwig.*" He turned to the indicated section and read while Cara held her breath.

"He was Alfred the Great's great grandson. Son of Edmund the Magnificent. Known as 'Edwy the Fair.' "

Cara swallowed hard. "That much fits."

"He was young when he became king. Seventeen." Malcolm read farther. "Crowned by Archbishop Oda at Kingston-on-Thames, January, 956. Seems to have gotten into a pickle with a monk, Dunstan. That would be Saint Dunstan, whom you've certainly heard of."

Cara wasn't sure, but she nodded. "Go on."

"The Church had a lot of power then, more than a king. Especially a seventeen-year-old king. For some reason, the Church didn't like his marriage, and they didn't want him to be king. Apparently, they made him divorce his wife . . ."

"He divorced her?" Cara's voice came high and

shocked. Malcolm eyed her doubtfully, and she forced a smile. "I didn't know they did that then."

"You aren't well-versed historically, Caroline." Malcolm clucked his tongue. "Vikings divorced, too. Anyway, as I was saying . . . Edwy had Dunstan exiled. A mistake, it seems. The boy king ruled less than two years. Dunstan came back and replaced Edwy with his brother, Edgar the Peaceable. Edwy died wandering in Ireland, in the year 959."

"Ireland." Her voice was a whisper. "Then it could be true. . . ."

"What?"

Cara bit her lip. "Nothing. I was just wondering."

"Why do you ask about him?"

Cara couldn't think of a good answer. "I'm just learning a bit about English history, that's all." She felt an intense wave of guilt at lying to her father, but she wasn't ready to tell him about Edwy, either.

"It also says the boy was vain and arrogant." Malcolm set the book aside. His brow furrowed, as if another thought had struck him. "But you must remember that history is written by the winners." Cara waited, but Malcolm shook his head and turned back to his notes.

Cara rose from her seat. Her heart felt heavy. Could a young, proud king, murdered by his enemies, really be haunting an ancient barrow? Still yearning for revenge, for her? No, he couldn't. It seemed far more likely that Lucas Sprague had staged an elaborate hoax, for the purpose of a new *Searcher* article. Cara needed to settle the matter now, lest she turn too easily to fantasy.

Outside, rain began drumming on the old windowpanes. Edwy, or whoever he was, might still be waiting. If he was part of a hoax, he would leave. But if he was crazy, he might linger. Cara could help him, get him therapy, find his family . . . She had to try.

"I'm going back to the lake, Dad. I forgot something."

Malcolm looked over his shoulder. "I hope it wasn't your notebook! Not that you've taken any notes . . ."

Malcolm was still muttering as Cara went out the door.

Cara drove back toward the lake, wondering if Edwy was gone now, if he had ever been there at all. The rain fell in a steady mist, and her windshield wipers made squeaking noises as they worked. The headlights of her rented Mini car flashed on someone walking. Someone wearing a red cape and Viking leggings. Edwy.

Cara squealed her brakes, then pulled over to the roadside. She opened her door and he walked to her. He looked as if he expected her. "What are you doing out here?"

"I was on my way to your quarters." Rain dripped over his forehead, down his firm cheeks. His hair hung damp to his shoulders. "Travel is difficult and tedious on foot. I had forgotten."

"I suppose you're used to flying."

"You could call it that. Better described as 'maneuvering.' "

He hadn't changed. He still looked young and beautiful, and utterly sure of himself. He was tall, at least six foot two. "You're tall. Men of the past were small."

Edwy's brow angled. "Who told you that?"

"It's . . . known."

"I am tall, of course. Kings are taller and better in all ways than other men." Edwy scanned her appearance.

His gaze lingered on her breasts. "You are well formed. It pleases me that your breasts don't sag to your waist."

Cara grimaced. "How foul! What am I supposed to do with you?"

"Assist me in my quest, of course. What else?" Edwy paused. "Is it your virginity that troubles you?"

"*What?* No!"

"Because if it is, know that I will be tender and careful. I am well versed at your pleasure."

"Stop right there!" Cara took a quick breath. "I can't take you with me."

His stubborn chin rose, his eyes narrowed. "Then I will follow you. I will ask questions of the local peasants until I find your location."

Cara endured an image of Edwy interrogating "peasants." For the sake of the Irish citizens, she seized Edwy's arm and led him to the car. "You can't go walking around dressed like this. You'll be arrested. Of course, if you talk, you'll be committed."

Edwy's brow rose. "In your company, I have had occasion to learn about modern customs. I'll fit right in."

"Uh-huh. Until you go demanding the English throne, that is."

Edwy straightened, an imperious light in his eyes. "It is my right."

"This should prove interesting."

"It will be a simple matter. I will gather thanes and husbandmen, then lay siege to my usurper . . ."

"Oh, right! You'll fit right in." Cara opened the passenger door and pointed. "Get in. You can worry about besieging Buckingham Palace later."

Edwy seated himself inside the tiny red Mini car.

"This vehicle does not conform to my stature." He paused. "I sense it does not convey . . . importance."

"It was cheap to rent, and I think it's cute. Consider it a little, wee Rolls-Royce. We don't have these in America." Cara took the driver's seat, then started the engine. She pulled back onto the road. "You didn't mention that we're divorced."

Edwy grasped her arm, jerking the car to one side. Cara steadied the vehicle, then drove forward more slowly. "You remembered?" The hopefulness of his tone pierced Cara's heart.

"No, I didn't remember. My father told me."

Edwy's hopeful expression faded. "How does he know?"

"He read it in a book."

"So our divorce was recorded?" Edwy sighed.

"It's true?" Cara was disappointed, despite her better judgment.

"It's true. That Danish bastard, Dunstan, had our union declared uncanonical. He claimed we were too close kin."

"Were we?"

"No. My mother's name was the same as yours. Dunstan used that to claim you were my mother's niece."

"Yuck. Making us cousins!"

"We were not."

"Good."

Cara drummed her fingers on the steering wheel. "So you divorced me . . ."

"I did it to stave off Dunstan's threat to my throne. I intended to restore our union when I had defeated the usurpers."

"Sure."

Edwy didn't speak for a moment. Cara frowned, though she didn't understand her anger.

"You didn't take it well then, either."

"What did this Druid person say you have to do to become human again?"

"He was vague, as Celts usually are. He said I must renew our marriage to what it was in life, and honor you as our souls first vowed. That poses no problem. You will be my wife and queen, and I will honor you nightly."

Cara repressed a smile at Edwy's interpretation of honor. The thought was intriguing. She allowed herself a quick glance at his strong, lean body. Her insides tingled as if in recognition. He noticed her attention and smiled. Cara cleared her throat. "What else?"

"I must restore my crown."

"What does that mean?"

"It means I am to regain my throne, of course. After that is done, the Druid said I would face my enemy, and choose which path leads to victory."

"What did he mean, 'which path'?"

"The method of my vengeance, naturally."

Something seemed askew about Edwy's reasoning, but Cara wasn't sure where to begin to untangle his logic. "Oh. But that's not exactly what the Druid said."

"There can be no other end between enemies. Victory or defeat."

Cara nodded, but she wasn't convinced. "I think you're going to have trouble proving it's your throne, and not Queen Elizabeth's."

"My blood is closer to Woden's than the Usurper Elizabeth. My claim is therefore greater."

"Woden? That's a Saxon god. A pagan god. I thought by your time the Saxons were Christian."

"We were." Edwy paused, as if her comment made no sense. "Christians descended from Woden."

"Perfect sense." Cara paused. She felt disoriented. Nothing seemed real. "I don't believe any of this, you understand."

"How do you explain our encounter, then?"

"I'm not sure. I ate this Irish pizza thing, which could have caused any number of hallucinations. My father isn't entirely normal. It may be a genetic predisposition, and I am now lapsing into some form of insanity."

"What if I'm real?"

Cara's heart took a sharp twist, then raced. "You can't be."

His voice came lower, softer. "What if I'm real?"

She tried to answer. To say something light and cynical, to show she wouldn't fall for his hoax. He had ten days. Ten days to find vengeance on a man who died a thousand years ago. Ten days to become King of England.

Very slowly, Cara looked up into Edwy's gentle, beautiful face. "If you're real, then I'll lose you." She spoke in a whisper, with a pain she didn't know she carried, until now.

Edwy didn't attempt to reassure her. He nodded. "If I fail, we will be parted again." He reached across the car and pried her left hand from the steering wheel, then folded his fingers over hers. "Love isn't measured by time, Cara. You and I, we were little more than children when we loved. Yet that love is forever."

The narrow Irish road curved like a snake before her. Edwy's touch on her hand felt strong, sure. She wanted to believe he was real. But her experience had taught her that anything that seemed too good to be true, *was* too good to be true.

"You doubt me because I failed you."

Cara looked across the car, her gaze fixed on his. She saw no guile, no deceit. She saw his eagerness, his passion, but no treachery. "I doubt you because you can't be a ghost. If ghosts could just show up as they wished, everyone would see them."

Edwy's brow angled. "It takes an incredibly advanced soul, with a regal purpose, to dictate their fate as I did. It takes sacrifice. I could have gone on, as you did. I chose to defy my life's fate, and win the long battle."

"I thought a Druid helped you."

Edwy huffed. "He was a commoner. A Celtic commoner. And he was odd." He waved his hand vaguely at the darkening landscape. "All Celts are odd, of course. He did, however, know of a method to gain my revival, at the final hours of All Hallow's Eve."

"I see. He *helped* you. Commoner or not."

Edwy looked more stubborn than ever. "He was a commoner, who did his duty by a king."

"It's rude to call someone a commoner."

"I am king. All men are beneath me, and thus, equally common to each other."

"Your reasoning is so bizarre."

"Celts are especially common. Oft learned in witchcraft. Dunstan himself was instructed in the black arts by the Celts. From them also he learned the harp. A foul and grating sound, if ever there was one."

"Harp music? Foul?" Cara shook her head. "What kind of music do you like?"

Edwy's eyes narrowed in thought. "I have heard

sweet strains whilst in your company, in my unseen state.''

Cara turned on the radio. Edwy pushed her hand away and began fiddling with the dials. He sneered in disgust at a classical BBS station, winced through static, hesitated over soothing pop, then stopped short at blasting heavy metal.

Cara gaped in horror. ''God, no!''

Edwy adjusted the volume higher, smiled, and sat back. Cara groaned at the cataclysmic discord and screeching guitar sounds emanating from the radio. ''You like that?''

''It is pleasing.'' Edwy spoke loudly to be heard over the music. Cara eased her hand low and turned it down. ''What else did your Druid tell you?''

''He refused to speak directly, offered only vague warnings. A more annoying man never existed than the Druid who enchanted me. He actually implied I was challenged by my own failings rather than my enemies.''

''That sounds reasonable.''

Edwy's brow angled. ''I am king. Which means . . .''

Cara sighed. ''I know. You have no failings.''

''Exactly.''

''How am I supposed to explain you to my father? To anyone?''

''I will handle the introductions. As king, it is my place to do so, with diplomacy and skill. I was well skilled at diplomacy.''

Cara eyed him doubtfully. ''You were ousted.''

''By inferior persons. I will blend with ease into your culture.''

Cara snapped off the radio. She pulled the car to the

roadside and faced Edwy. "What do you want from me? Exactly."

Edwy smiled, and her pulse quickened. "Take me to Gloucester Cathedral."

"We're in Ireland. Gloucester Cathedral is in England. Why do you want to go there?"

"The first part of my task is there."

"What part?"

"That you will see when we arrive. Take me to Gloucester, Cara."

His request bothered her. Cara had no idea why. "I don't want to go there. My father went there once, and I found an excuse not to go. Why?"

Edwy's bright eyes bored into her. "You must trust me. I asked that of you once before, and you gave it without question. I failed you then, Cara. I give you the word of my soul. I will not fail you twice."

"You have ten days to get back the throne of England?"

Edwy nodded. "And to win vengeance, and . . ." He paused. "To restore our marriage."

"What if you fail?"

"Then I will truly die."

You'll leave me. Again. Fear crept through Cara's heart. *No.* Practicality was her shield. She needed it more now than ever. "You were dead before, so you say. You're probably some kind of elaborate joke. But even if you're a ghost, you're odd. And my father needs me here."

Edwy's bright eyes never left her face. "I need you more."

Cara's reason faltered, and her voice sank to a whisper. "I don't know what to do."

"I know. But you must choose, Cara. We have so little time."

Cara chewed her lip. "There's something you're not telling me."

Edwy looked both guilty and annoyed. "Now is not the proper time for disclosures."

"It is if you want a ride to Gloucester. You were pretty specific about two of your 'tasks.' Getting the throne back, and getting vengeance. What about the third? The part involving me. There's something more to it, isn't there?"

Edwy puffed an impatient breath. "A small element which I have not disclosed . . . Nor do I see a need . . ."

"You could always take a ferry, on your own, if getting to Gloucester means that much to you."

When annoyed, Edwy's lips curved into an impatient and sensual frown. Cara wasn't sure how a frown could be sensual, but it was on him. "Start talking, Edwy. What do you want from me?"

"Our relationship must be restored."

"I gathered that. What else?"

He looked uneasy. "To what it was before I lost you."

Cara's eyes wandered to one side. "So?"

"The condition between us must be in the same . . ." He paused, hedging.

"What condition?"

"I had thought to wait, to become reacquainted . . ."

"Now, Edwy."

"When I last saw you, you were . . ." He paused again. "Um."

"Edwy!"

"Fat with child."

223

Cara's mouth dropped open, and stayed open. A small giggle bubbled in her chest, then erupted. "Fat with child? Delicately phrased." She stared at his sweet, innocent face. Once, far in the past of her soul, in its earliest dawn, she had lain with this man. Shared his body. And carried his child. "If I was pregnant then, and the condition must be the same . . ." Cara's mouth opened wider, and a small squeak emerged. "Then . . ."

Edwy winced, then attempted a casual shrug. "My seed must be planted within your womb within ten days."

Cara clamped her hand to her forehead. Then she groaned. "What if I'm not in a fertile mode? No! What if I think you're a screaming lunatic, and decide perhaps to take the next flight back to the States?"

Edwy bowed his head. "Then I will truly die, and my quest will remain forever unfulfilled."

"Well, I'm sorry. There is no chance of you getting me pregnant. None." Cara paused. "How does this involve Gloucester Cathedral?"

"You must be my rightful wife. I promised to come to you there, and . . . Do you find me handsome?"

Cara hesitated, fidgeting. He expected lavish praise, and he deserved it. She'd never seen or imagined a man so beautiful. Or so utterly sure of himself. "You're . . ."

"Yes?" He looked so smug.

"Cute."

Edwy braced into indignation. "Cute?"

"It means . . ."

Edwy's eyes formed imperious slits. He looked like a king. A cute king. "I know what it means! It generally refers to something round and furry." Edwy said the words *round and furry* with such disgust that Cara giggled. "You possessed a rat you called 'cute.' "

"He was a guinea pig, and yes, Edwin was cute, too."

Edwy frowned. "I am to be described as noble of stature. Handsome. But not cute."

Cara enjoyed his reaction. "You were known as Edwy the Fair. Fair means cute. Edwy the Cute." He looked too appalled to answer. Teasing Edwy had its joys. "You also look young."

Edwy sneered, as if he deemed youth insulting. "I was seventeen when I took the throne—well a man."

"Seventeen? How old was I?"

"Sixteen."

"Sixteen? That's disgusting! No wonder women died so young!"

"It's true, you're older now." Edwy assessed Cara's appearance. "Yet despite your advanced age . . ."

"I'm twenty-six!"

Edwy nodded. "Yes. Despite that, age doesn't show on your face. No lines around your eyes, no fat around your jowls."

"I don't have jowls." She'd never felt old before. Jowls, indeed! "How long were you king?"

"I held my rightful position for three years." Edwy's eyes darkened with anger and eternal pride. His hands clenched into fists. "They wanted to control my throne, but I was strong. I would not yield. So they used my weak, frightened brother in my place. They locked you in a nunnery at Gloucester, where they . . ." He paused, as if fearing to say too much.

Cara considered pressing the matter, but Edwy was stubborn. "So you came to Ireland?"

"Aye. They hunted me down and they stole my life. But I will never let them win . . . never."

Cara touched Edwy's strong arm. "Edwy . . ." Her voice came soft, with more emotion than she intended. "They won a thousand years ago."

He looked at her hand, then her face. "You took a lion to husband, Cara. Not a lamb. My battle isn't over, because I am not over. I will regain what I lost, and he who wronged me will suffer my vengeance."

Cara's heart dropped, though she wasn't sure why. Edwy was crazy. Even if he was a ghost, which she couldn't quite believe, he was a crazy ghost. "Do you have special powers?"

"My power is endless."

"I mean, can you get the throne by magic?"

Edwy appeared insulted. "I am not a wizard. I am a king."

Cara shrugged. "So, do kings have special powers?"

Edwy drew himself up, proud. "A king is stronger and better and wiser than other men. As a boy, I won every race, on foot or on horseback. I am a better swordsman, archer, and hunter than anyone. I am smarter at language, in the manipulation of numbers, which is known as 'mathematics.' I was more adept than anyone at writing the lettering Alfred the Great created."

Edwy paused, waiting for Cara to reveal the depth of her admiration. "You are the most conceited man alive. Or dead."

Cara eased the car forward again, back onto the narrow road, then glanced over at him. "What happened to our baby?"

Edwy didn't answer at once, and Cara's pulse moved slow. She started to shake her head. *I don't want to know.* Edwy touched her shoulder. A gentle touch. A husband's touch. "Dunstan feared I would leave an heir.

Despite our divorce, a child between us could have destroyed Dunstan's ambitions, and threatened my brother's heirs."

"I see."

"At Gloucester, I will tell you more. Not here, Cara."

Cara watched Edwy's face. This tale grieved him, too. "Did we truly love each other?" She knew she risked making a fool of herself by asking, by taking him seriously. If he was an actor, he would enjoy a good laugh later at her expense. But for the moment, Edwy looked both sorrowful and honest.

"We did."

"I thought marriages were arranged back then."

"Not for us. I chose you, you chose me. We loved on sight, Cara." Edwy touched her hair, then drew the dark ends to his lips. "You want to know if I love you now." He didn't let her speak. "Cara, you are part of me. I have loved you for centuries, in every form you took. My soul has danced with yours, and held you while you slept. I will not fail you twice."

Cara's eyes blurred with tears. Maybe she had always known. "I don't believe this is real, you know."

"I know."

"Even if it is, I don't think you'll get your throne, or your revenge, or . . . anything."

"I know."

She looked over at him. "I would like to believe, but I don't."

"I know that, too. But it doesn't matter, Cara. You don't need to believe. You will see for yourself, and believe."

Edwy turned back to the road, convinced. Sure. Cara endured a pang of envy, the kind she felt when her father believed a monster waited around the next corner. They turned toward Killarney, and Cara slowed her car. "What do we do now? Where shall I take you?"

Edwy considered the matter, then nodded. "I am feeling peckish."

Cara's face colored. Edwy noticed her embarrassed expression and he chuckled. "Hungry."

She breathed a sigh of relief. "The inn where we're staying doesn't serve dinner." Cara paused, feeling a sense of foreboding. "I could take you to a restaurant if you like."

"Do so."

"Your clothes are weird . . . It's a little early for trick or treat. I can say you're costumed for a play."

Edwy adjusted his gold-hemmed sleeve. "Costumed, indeed."

Cara turned her car down a side street, aiming for a small pub in Killarney. "I'll take you, but please, don't mention the English throne."

Edwy settled back in his seat. "Wise advice. I don't want to alert the peasants to my quest too soon. My usurper must not learn of my intentions until I am upon her. . . ."

Chapter Three

Against her better judgment, Cara brought Edwy to the Sword and Buckler pub. She chose it because it was dark and had a small, secluded dining room. When they got out of the car, Edwy stood on the sidewalk, his hands on his hips, his legs apart. Like a king.

Cara raced around the car and tore off her coat. "Here, put this on." She fumbled with his brooch and removed his red cloak.

"What are you doing, woman? Do you know how long I've worn this mantle? A thousand years . . . And be careful with that brooch! It was passed to me from Alfred the Great."

A half-drunk sailor walked by, hesitated at Edwy's pronouncement, then stopped before entering the pub. "Guess I've had enough for the night." He shook his head and went back up the street.

Cara stuffed Edwy's cloak into her car. Edwy held up

her oversized barn jacket. It was olive green with a beige corduroy collar. "You do not wear garments befitting a queen."

Two women tourists passed by as Edwy spoke.

"Hush!" Cara seized his arm and drew him out of the tourists' way. "I'm not a queen . . ."

The tourists overheard her and glanced doubtfully at each other before entering the pub.

Edwy didn't notice. "You are."

Catching his argumentative expression, Cara held up her hand. "Not here, and not now." She paused while he waited expectantly. "Not *yet*. Now pipe down and put on my coat. It will make you look more . . . normal."

The word resonated through her entire being. *Normal.* Without question, Edwy was the least normal man she'd ever met. It was a strangely comforting feeling.

Edwy put on the coat and Cara stepped back to assess his appearance. With his gold-stitched tunic covered, he fit in adequately.

"That's okay. Let's go." She seized his hand. "But remember, no talk about kings or anything like that. People in this town already think my father and I are crazy."

"I shall correct that assumption. Let us enter this establishment, love. My peckishness surges . . ."

Cara suffered Edwy's choice of words, then opened the door to the pub. It was dark, as she had hoped, and they took a table near the back of the dining room. Thankfully, it was a slow night at the Sword and Buckler.

The tourists sat near the window, looking over their menu, and a tired farmer sat in the corner finishing a bowl of stew. Cara relaxed. Edwy's first physical brush with the modern world would prove uneventful.

The Shadow King

A small, round waitress entered the room. Cara smiled, but Edwy banged on the table.

"Serving wench! Bring hence a roast pig!"

Cara wanted the floor to open and swallow her whole. The farmer spilled his ale, and the tourists whispered. Cara seized Edwy's arm and pinched hard. "Hush!"

She smiled weakly at the waitress. "He's joking. Had a bit too much."

The waitress nodded and approached the table. "Have you decided?"

Cara glanced at the menu. "Fish and chips, please."

Edwy looked blank. Cara tapped his arm. "What would you like to eat?"

"I don't like fish."

"All out of the roast pig tonight, sweetheart." The waitress gestured toward a blackboard indicating the specials of the day. "But we've a very nice shepherd's pie."

"Yes. Bring it hence."

The waitress eyed him doubtfully, then started off for the kitchen. Cara cringed. "Be polite."

"I require mead. Serving wench . . ." A sharp jab at his side cut off Edwy's order.

"Behave yourself. And you can't order mead. It's weird. If you must, have an ale."

The waitress's brow angled. "I don't think it would be wise to get him drunker."

"True. Have milk, Edwy."

Edwy grimaced at the suggestion of milk. He waved his arm at the waitress. "An ale, if you will, good woman."

The tired farmer looked over at Edwy and chuckled. "Pickled to the gills."

231

Edwy smiled and nodded at the farmer. "For this noble fellow, as well."

The farmer's eyes brightened, and the waitress laughed as she produced a tankard of ale for Edwy. "This must be you're lucky day, O'Grady."

Edwy took a drink. Cara chewed her lip. "Maybe you should eat something first."

"Ale is heartening." Edwy drank again, then turned his attention to the pub's collection of swords and shields. " 'Tis a scramasax, that one." He gestured at a short, thick sword. "Such a blade is wielded in close combat with good success, especially in combination with yonder buckler. Of course, my personal collection was better stocked."

Edwy rose from his seat to examine a mail shirt. "Poor quality. One can easily penetrate these rings, here . . ." He indicated a spot beneath the sleeve. "With a sharp thrust, I could sever an opponent's rib entirely."

The tourists grimaced and whispered again. Cara sighed. "Sit down. You're not severing anyone."

Edwy's brow rose. "I am a masterful swordsman. I slew many before falling to my . . ."

Cara hopped up from her chair and yanked Edwy to his seat. "None of that! Just sit down, and have some more ale."

Edwy returned to his ale and the waitress delivered their meals. To Cara's relief, Edwy set aside his drink to attend to his shepherd's pie. He spotted the salt cellar. "What's that?"

"Salt."

Edwy's eyes brightened. "Salt! How rare!" He sprinkled the white crystals over his pie, then seized his fork. "A fork. A pronged instrument for feeding." He stuck the fork in the pie's center, letting the steam spiral upward, then took a large bite of his pie. "Chewing requires more effort of the jaw than I remembered."

The waitress shook her head and Cara smiled sheepishly. "He can be a little eccentric at times."

"There's an understatement." The waitress looked more closely at Cara. "Say, aren't you that mad scientist's daughter?"

Cara's eyes narrowed. "Dr. Malcolm Reid is my father, yes."

The farmer laughed. "Doctor, is he? Doctor of what? Dinosaurs?"

Even the tourists chuckled. They didn't have to be in town long to have heard of Malcolm Reid's dinosaur hunt. An old pain resurfaced in Cara. She had defended her father a hundred times this way.

Edwy touched her hand, then set aside his pie. "Do you call a man crazy because he pursues mysterious beasts?"

The farmer laughed again. "Sure do. Don't you? Or are you drunk enough to be seeing them yourself?"

Edwy smiled. "No. But Dr. Reid seeks to prove the reality, or unreality, of these creatures. Now, if he saw them when no one else could, I'd say he was crazy. If he's saying he'll find out for himself, I'd say he was a wise man."

Edwy settled back in his seat. For an instant, Cara imagined him as a real king. "He might not find much in the lake. But you won't be finding much in that pint, either."

This time, the farmer laughed at himself. "Got a point there, you do." He drew another long draught of ale. "You never know what's around the next corner, do you? Old Malcolm just thinks there'll be something pre-historic.''

The waitress slapped the farmer's shoulder. "If you sit in that chair much longer, Sean O'Grady, you'll turn into something prehistoric. Get moving.''

Cara watched as their attention turned to other matters. She shifted her gaze to Edwy. He smiled, then resumed eating.

"Thank you." Her voice was a whisper.

Edwy nodded, his mouth full.

"If you've been with me all my life, you know my father. Do you think he's crazy?''

Edwy swallowed. "There is a saying, he 'marches to his own drummer.' That doesn't make him crazy. That makes him a man.''

Cara felt better. She tasted her fish and chips, then poured vinegar over the fries. "You were right about my father. He thinks there might be strange animals, but he doesn't claim to have seen them. I guess I'm lucky he's not interested in UFO's.''

"Or ghosts.''

Cara saw his gentle, sensual smile, and her heart skipped a beat. "I think I must be dreaming. I'll wake up and you'll be gone.''

Edwy's smile faded and his gaze returned to his plate. He made no comment, but Cara knew something was wrong.

Edwy finished his meal, then sat back from the table. He looked serious now, grave. "If I fail in my quest, I will be gone, Cara Reid. I must regain what I lost.''

Cara's pulse felt heavy, her breath labored. *My shadow king.* "I have felt this way before.''

Edwy's eyes met hers. "Yes.''

Tears gathered at the rims of her eyes. "I don't want to feel this way again."

"I know."

Cara set her fork aside and stared into the flickering candlelight. "Maybe there's a way to trick this spell of yours. You could play the King of England in a theatrical production."

Edwy looked offended, but he didn't argue. Cara chewed the inside of her lip as she pondered the possibilities. "I don't know about this 'seed' business, but . . ."

Edwy grinned, and Cara blushed. "But what about this Dunstan person? I'm not sure getting vengeance on him in a play would be enough."

"It would not. I must find him, and face him, and choose my path to victory."

"If you're sure he has reincarnated, then why don't you just hunt him up in spirit form? You haunted me, after all."

"I wouldn't call it 'haunting.' I was with you because you and I are bonded in the soul. I have access to you. Dunstan and I are enemies. He has protection against my wrath."

"Then how will you find him?"

Edwy sat back in his seat. "It is this very matter that troubles me most. Restoring my position as king will be simple. I shall return to the site of my coronation at Kingston-on-Thames and reclaim my throne, muster my thanes and husbandmen, and march upon the usurper's castle."

"Hush!" Cara looked over her shoulder, but no one had overheard Edwy's declaration.

"I shall impregnate you . . ."

Two sharp gasps indicated that the tourists had, in fact, overheard this. Cara blushed furiously, but Edwy looked proud. "Simple. It is the final portion of the Druid's spell that concerns me. Dunstan was crafty, learned in witchcraft. A man of vast evil and wiles."

"You said he was a saint."

Edwy's eyes darkened with anger. "An undeserved title. Dunstan will expect my return, and be prepared. I must act swiftly."

Cara sighed heavily and turned back to her fish and chips. "How will you find a man who's been dead over a thousand years?"

"Dunstan will live again, like you. And I will find him. The Druid said the rivers of time would bring the circumstances of my fate together, and I would choose the outcome."

"How will you know this Dunstan when you see him?"

"I'll know him. He had pale blue eyes, thin, light hair. He also played the harp constantly. It irritated me more than I can describe."

Cara rolled her eyes. "He could be a poodle now for all you know."

"If reincarnation were a fair system, he would be a newt. But no matter. I trust that I will know him when the time comes."

Cara finished her chips, then reached for the bill.

"Allow me." Lucas Sprague took the check and grinned.

"What are you doing here?" Cara snatched the check from his hand, but Lucas turned his attention to Edwy.

"I don't believe we've met."

Edwy glared. "Haven't we?" He rose to his feet, and Lucas shrank back.

Lucas eyed the golden circlet on Edwy's head, then looked down with misgivings at the thonged Viking boots. He glanced at Cara. "Who is he?"

"I am Ed . . ."

"*Win!* Edwin . . . King. He's working with us now."

Lucas chuckled. "Well, good luck, Ed."

Edwy's eyes narrowed to blue slits. "Edwin."

Cara looked between them. She wondered how she had ever considered Lucas Sprague even remotely attractive. Next to Edwy, he looked . . . normal. "Lucas . . . Shouldn't you be tormenting a celebrity somewhere?"

"I have a job to do, Cara." His dark gaze whisked over her body. He grabbed her chin and leaned close to her face. "*The Searcher* pays. Give me a few words on your father's 'career.' "

Cara tried to twist away, but Lucas tightened his grip. "Never."

"Unhand her or die."

Lucas laughed. "Noble fellow, here. I'd think twice before fighting for her, Edwin. She looks good, but she's as frigid as a glacier."

Cara didn't see Edwy move, but in a second's flash, he held the scramasax at Lucas's throat. "I warned you. Your doom is at hand."

Cara's breath stopped. Edwy considered himself king, above any law. "Edwy, no. He's not worth it."

Edwy flicked his wrist, severing Lucas's tie. Lucas went white. "You will die slowly, in bitter agony. One rib at a time."

The waitress entered the room and dropped her tray.

The tourists eased toward the door. Cara touched Edwy's arm. "If you do this, I'll lose you."

Edwy glanced at Cara, then turned his burning gaze back to Lucas Sprague. The point of the sword dented Lucas's thin, white neck. "Leave this isle and never return. If you do, your life is forfeit."

Lucas lifted his hands. "Back off, man. I've got no trouble with you."

Edwy lowered the sword. "You do now."

Lucas backed away, rubbing his neck. He nodded at Cara. "You sure know how to pick them, sweetheart. This one may be even crazier than your old man."

Cara felt unexpectedly satisfied with Edwy's performance. "Yes, but Edwin handles a sword much better. Wouldn't you agree?"

The farmer rose unsteadily from his seat. "Got to hand him that. Snatched that blade off the wall like King Arthur himself."

The tourists approached Edwy. "You had us scared for a minute there. But we've guessed your secret."

Cara paled. "You have?"

The younger woman smiled. "He's an actor. I thought I recognized you. Now, what's your name?"

Edwy looked puzzled. "An actor? Do you mean a minstrel?"

Cara cut Edwy off. "This is Edwin King. He's been rehearsing a play. He likes to wear his costume to . . . stay in character."

Before the tourists could ask what play, Cara hurried to the cashier to pay their bill. "Edwin, let's go."

Lucas backed away from the door. "Edwin? Funny, but I could have sworn you called him 'Edwy' a moment ago."

Cara clenched her teeth. "It's his nickname."

Lucas's expression turned mocking. "You learn something every day. Be seeing you, sweetheart."

Lucas left, but Edwy fingered the scramasax. "If he calls you 'sweetheart' again, I will slay him outright."

Cara sank back into her seat and bowed her head. "'Uneventful.' What made me think any moment with you could be uneventful?"

Cara drove Edwy to the inn, but she hesitated before leaving the car. "I'm not quite sure how to explain your presence to my dad."

"There's no need for him to know I'm here."

"You're not exactly inconspicuous."

Edwy touched his circlet. "Ah, but I can be, my love." He lifted his crown and disappeared. The golden circlet dropped to the seat.

Edwy saw her mouth drop, but her surprise faded with a shrug. "I'll assume you're following me. Come on." Cara left the car, and Edwy followed. As always before, his presence centered around her. Where she went, he went also.

Cara entered the inn, leaving time before shutting the door, presumably for Edwy to enter. Her gesture touched him. Doors gave him no trouble in the past. Cara went upstairs, down the hall, and checked her father's door. It was open, so she looked in.

Malcolm Reid sat asleep at his desk. Cara tapped his shoulder, and he jumped. "I'm sorry, Dad. I didn't mean to wake you."

Malcolm rubbed his hand over his eyes. "I'm sorry to announce, my dear child, that our research has reached a standstill."

"Why is that?"

Edwy wanted to interject that the absence of an actual monster might have slowed the investigation, but his ghostly form prevented any response.

"Three Irish priests saw the creature in this very lake. That was over twenty years ago. I'm thinking they may have been mistaken."

"It's possible."

"Sorry to have dragged you into this, Caroline. If you want to abandon the project, you should be able to acquire a reasonable position at any university."

Cara smiled. "I don't want a 'reasonable' position, Dad. I want an interesting one. Working with you may not be the most reasonable thing, but it's certainly interesting."

Malcolm patted his daughter's shoulder. "Don't want to keep you from something better. But if you're sure . . ."

"I'm sure."

"Good." Malcolm turned back to his desk and adjusted his notes. "I've been thinking that we should look for someone to replace Sprague. Maybe you should do the hiring this time. I picked Sprague, and that didn't work very well."

You can say that again. Edwy longed to enter the conversation, to point out that Malcolm's gullibility had caused his daughter endless trouble.

"I was thinking Sprague might have had something to do with the 'ghost' you thought you saw."

"Lucas didn't have anything to do with that. We saw him tonight, and . . ."

"We?"

Cara gulped. "I met a friend at the Sword and Buckler."

"A male friend?" Malcolm looked hopeful.

"Sort of."

"Good, good. I trust you'll be seeing him again."

"I'm fairly certain of it." Cara kissed her father's cheek. "Good night, Dad."

Cara hurried down the hall, unlocked her door, then waited for Edwy to follow. She seemed confused. Edwy waited for her to realize the obvious. "Oh, right!"

Cara pulled his crown from her pack and held it up. Edwy positioned himself beneath it, and felt the power of life surge through his limbs. A bright smile lit Cara's face as he appeared before her.

"You didn't expect me?"

Cara looked up at him, vulnerability obvious in her parted lips, her wide eyes. "I wasn't sure."

"Be sure, Cara. I won't fail you."

Her expression softened, and Edwy bent to kiss her. She turned away and moved to the other side of her bedroom.

"I'm not sure it would be very smart for me to become emotionally attached to you."

Edwy followed her, but he didn't touch her. "You already are."

She looked back at him, her chin raised. Edwy recognized the posture. He had seen it before. Her arms were clasped around her waist. "You know what I mean."

"I know." He took a step closer, then stopped. He knew she wanted him closer. He let the wanting grow. "You just told your father you didn't want a reasonable life."

"I was referring to my career."

"I can see why you don't want to work in a university. Stodgy and boring. But how long can you chase monsters you don't believe in?"

Cara sighed. "My father needs me."

"What do you want?" She looked wistful, and Edwy smiled. "I think I know."

"How would you know what I want? I'm not even sure I know myself."

Edwy closed the space between them and touched her hair gently, fingering the waving tendril. "You studied zoology because you love animals. Real animals. I think you would like to work with them. Maybe in a naturalist-run zoo?"

Cara's mouth dropped. "How do you know? I've never mentioned that to anyone."

"I have been with you all your life. I know you."

"Wonderful! How very relaxing for me!"

"I've done you no harm thus far."

"I didn't know you were there." Cara stopped, her brow furrowed. "You've been with me all the time?" Edwy nodded.

"Did you see my mother?"

"After she died, she was with you. There is a part of her that reaches out to you even now, though it is my belief that she, too, has moved to a new form."

"How is that possible, if she's someone else?"

"I don't know the specifics, my love. But I would say she isn't exactly someone else, just re-formed. The bonds you make in life are forever."

Edwy seized the opportunity to draw her closer into his arms. She resisted, then leaned her head against his shoulder. He ran his fingers through her hair, sifting the dark mass around her shoulders.

Edwy's heart raced, his nerves vibrated. She slid her arms around his waist and sighed. He didn't want to risk this moment, but his desire was strong in this physical form.

Cara was thinking. He hoped she was thinking the right thing. He turned to kiss her, but she drew away and looked up at him. *No, not the right thing.*

"Didn't you ever allow me privacy?"

"I left you alone in the latrine."

Cara drew a strained breath. "Thank you for that." She bit her lip. "No other time?"

"No."

Edwy guessed the direction of her thoughts and he grinned. "On occasion, when you were of age, ripe, I took the opportunity to touch you."

"Ripe?" Her mouth dropped as his meaning became clear. She pulled away, then clasped her hands over her eyes. "Oh, God! What a nightmare!"

"You didn't think so at the time."

Her face turned bright pink. She sank down on the edge of her bed, her eyes squeezed shut. "How embarrassing!"

Edwy seated himself beside her, close. "We are married."

She peeked up at him. "Weak reasoning."

"It was enough for me."

Edwy watched her running over the events of her life. He knew when an embarrassing thought surfaced, because she uttered small moans of misery. He allowed her to continue for a while longer, then took her hand.

"It is my belief that some part of you has always known of my presence. For this reason, you have never loved another."

Cara fiddled with her bedspread. "No, I never have . . ." Her voice faded and her gaze fell to his lips. Edwy's pulse surged. He touched her cheek, then softly kissed her mouth.

She trembled, but she didn't pull away. Edwy deepened the kiss, tasting her lips, her breath mingling with his. His fingers slid into her hair, to the soft skin of her neck. His heart slammed beneath his chest as she answered his kiss. Her arms wrapped around his neck, he felt her surrender.

Cara's door burst open and Malcolm Reid charged into the room. Cara gasped, but Edwy was gone. His golden circlet slipped to the floor and Cara nudged it under the bed.

"Dad!" She drew a quick breath as Malcolm flipped on the overhead light.

"It's intelligent! It's the only explanation."

"What is? The monster?"

Malcolm puffed impatiently. "It is not a 'monster,' Caroline. It is an undiscovered species, probably reptilian."

"I'm sorry. Go on." Cara tried to clear her thoughts, but her heart still raced from her encounter with Edwy. "What makes you think the . . . reptile is intelligent?"

"It knows we're watching for it, girl!" Malcolm rubbed his hands together, then clapped. "It's obvious what we have to do."

"What?"

"Hide, of course! I'll start working on a blind tomorrow. By the way, what about an assistant? Any ideas?"

"Not yet, Dad."

"The sooner we get one, the better. We need to watch

that lake constantly, get out on boats, that sort of thing."

Malcolm started to get up, but his foot bumped Edwy's crown. Cara held her breath as her father picked up the circlet. "What is this?" He held it up to the light. "It's gold!"

"It's nothing, Dad."

"Nothing? Hell! It's old . . . look at these runes." Malcolm eyed her suspiciously. "Why didn't you mention this earlier?"

Cara attempted a casual shrug. "I . . . forgot."

"Caroline, this artifact may be priceless. It belongs in the Natural History Museum in London, not under your bed."

Malcolm took the circlet and started for the door. Cara jumped up from the bed and grabbed her father's arm. "You can't take that!"

"Why not? It would be wrong to keep such an artifact in a private collection, daughter."

"It's not exactly my property. I can't give it away." Cara fumbled for a way to keep the crown, to keep Edwy.

"Then whose is it?"

"It's mine." Edwy appeared beneath the crown, then straightened.

Malcolm lurched backward in shock, his hand over his heart, his eyes like saucers. "What in the name of God . . . ?"

Cara grabbed her father's arm, supporting him. "Dad, I can explain. This is . . ."

Malcolm sank into his armchair. "Don't tell me."

Edwy positioned himself beside Cara. "I am Edwy, King of England." He paused. "Your son-in-law and sovereign."

* * *

"I think he took it rather well." Edwy stood looking down at Malcolm's prostrate form while Cara wiped her father's brow with a damp cloth.

Cara glared up at him. "I thought you were going to be tactful, diplomatic?"

"I introduced myself in the way proper for a king."

Malcolm opened his eyes, saw Edwy, and groaned. His eyes closed, as if deliberately blocking the sight. Edwy frowned. "Slap him."

"I will not!"

Malcolm's eyes popped open. "You be off, boy!"

"You are to refer to me as 'my liege.' "

Cara winced and helped her father into an upright position. "It's all right, Dad. I met Edwy this morning . . ."

Malcolm struggled up from his chair, waving his arms in dramatic agitation. "Girl, you put him back wherever you found him, and we'll pretend this never happened!"

"I can't do that, Dad." Cara helped her father from the chair. "He's our new assistant."

Malcolm eyed Edwy in distaste and suspicion. "What's he wearing? And what did he call himself?"

Cara drew a tight breath. "He calls himself 'Edwy.' " She paused. "He is under the impression that he's some kind of king, from the Saxon period." She lowered her voice. "He could be crazy."

"*Could be?* Girl, that's a given."

Irritation flooded through Edwy's limbs. "You will cease speaking as if I'm not present. Old man, you will abandon your monster hunt and become my first thane."

Malcolm eyed Cara. "What is he talking about?"

"I require thanes, husbandmen, warriors . . ."

"Why?"

Cara shrugged in an attempt at casualness. "He has a few tasks to perform, dad. Nothing you need to worry about."

Malcolm finally looked to Edwy for an explanation. "What tasks?"

Edwy refused to answer, and Cara sighed. "He has to get revenge on the man who killed him, impregnate me, and become King of England—before Halloween."

Malcolm hopped on both feet, while waving his arms in violent circles. Well done for an old man. "*What?* No one, *no one* impregnates my daughter without a good, solid marriage in place first!"

Malcolm's violent agitation had the effect of calming Edwy into a deeper regal grace. Malcolm seemed familiar, though Edwy couldn't place the connection. *Not Dunstan . . .* But still annoying. "Your daughter and I were wed in a prior lifetime."

Malcolm positioned himself between Edwy and Cara, then turned his back to Edwy. "Girl, that's the stupidest New Age line I've ever heard."

Cara hesitated. "You saw him appear and disappear, Dad. He doesn't have a shadow, either."

"That doesn't mean he can just go getting you . . ." Malcolm paused and cleared his throat. "In a family way."

Cara's lips twisted to one side. "That's better than 'fat with child,' as a phrasing."

Edwy looked between them. "My seed must be implanted . . ."

Cara held up her hand. "Never mind that."

Malcolm glared at Edwy. "Ghosts don't have 'seed,' boy."

Edwy raised his chin to an imperious angle. "Fertile

247

in life, fertile always.'' He turned his back to Malcolm. ''The night deepens, woman.'' He studied her face, then her neck. Her chest rose in quick gasps beneath a blue shirt, revealing her small, firm breasts. His fingers twitched with the desire to touch her.

Edwy waved his hand absently at Malcolm. ''Leave us.''

Malcolm shoved him aside. ''I say we drive a stake through his heart and bury him behind the inn.''

Cara puffed an impatient breath. ''That's for vampires, Dad. Edwy is a ghost.''

Edwy grimaced. ''It would still be painful. Your father is an irritant. I shall have him dismembered and thrown to the ravens, once my throne is secure.''

''Stop that, both of you!'' Cara clapped her hand to her forehead. ''Dad, Edwy wants me to take him to Gloucester Cathedral.''

''Tonight?''

Edwy glanced toward Cara's bed. ''Tomorrow morning will suffice.''

''Not a chance, boy!'' Malcolm waved toward Cara's luggage. ''Pack your gear, child. We're leaving Ireland tonight.''

Cara's eyes widened in surprise. ''What about the monster?''

''That monster's not going anywhere, girl. I'll be back.'' Malcolm raised his voice, as if the monster might be within hearing distance.

''It's too late to catch the ferry to Holyhead tonight.''

''Damn. So it is.'' Malcolm glared at Edwy. ''I'm not leaving you at this lunatic's mercy.'' He eyed Edwy's crown. ''Give it here.''

Edwy braced. ''I will not.''

"I'll get you to Gloucester, boy, on one condition: that crown of yours stays in my possession tonight. A ghost can't do much damage without a body. Tomorrow, I'll slap it back on your crazy head. You'll carry our luggage, and we'll head off for the Dublin ferry."

Cara looked a little disappointed, and Edwy smiled. "I agree to your terms. But when your daughter wears my ring, she becomes mine, and you will leave us in peace."

Malcolm hesitated, then nodded. "Agreed."

Cara rolled her eyes. "It's good of you both to decide my fate. Might I have some say in the matter?"

"No." Edwy and Malcolm spoke at once. Malcolm held out his hand.

Edwy touched his crown, cast a final look Cara's way, then removed it from his head. Malcolm was startled at his disappearance, but Cara looked sad. As if she feared their ending, as if she hadn't expected him to stay.

Cara sat on the edge of her bed. She looked around, as if trying to see Edwy. "Do you think he's still here?"

"We're not so lucky as to be rid of your ghost that easily, girl. He's still here."

Edwy nodded in spirit form. Cara adjusted her pillows for two. Edwy's whole being vibrated with affection. "You believe him, don't you? Why?"

Malcolm didn't answer at once. When he spoke, his voice came low and haunting. His faint Scottish burr emerged, reminding Edwy of another crotchety and annoying old man. "The English, they're the most stubborn race on Earth. Once, long, long ago, I saw a boy so stubborn, so proud, as to make all the others pale in his shadow. Once, I saw that boy on his knees. And the thing he cried about was love."

Chapter Four

Having a ghost, a male ghost, in the immediate vicinity offered its share of embarrassments. Cara eyed her nightgown, sure he was standing beside her. She felt shy, but her skin was warm and tingling. He had seen her before.

She took a quick breath, then pulled off her shirt. She removed her khaki trousers, then her underwear. For an instant, she stood naked, knowing she wasn't alone. Knowing that he wanted her. Knowing she wanted him.

A wild desire to tantalize grew inside her. She closed her eyes and saw his sweet face burning with need. She dampened her lips, then crawled into her bed, to the left side. She waited, sure he lay down beside her.

She couldn't see him, but her sensitized nerves felt his presence. Warmth touched her cheek like a soft kiss. It rustled her hair, then trailed along her neck. Her heart slammed beneath her bare breast, her pulse raged.

"You have done this to me before, haven't you?"

He couldn't answer, but she knew. "I have felt you here before."

She felt the warmth along her collarbone, over the swell of her breast. She pulled back the covers, lying exposed on her bed. Alone, but not alone. The sensation circled her breast, then teased the peak until it pebbled.

"If this is madness, let it never stop." Her words trailed into a soft moan as his unseen hand moved lower. She bit her lip hard, and felt the tingling over her soft curls, over her woman's mound. She closed her eyes tight, and it found her small, feminine peak.

Her body quivered, weak to the delicate touch. The sensation deepened, as if she felt his arousal, too. *A ghost can't make love.* Cara opened her eyes. *What do I know about ghosts?* She felt his male energy, knew he blended himself with her.

Her release came as if from a great distance. She couldn't move, lest it be lost in physical pulses. It was as if her very soul endured the rapture, joined with his. Her breath came swift, her body quivered. She felt him inside her, gently. She felt the intangible pulses of his soul, and knew ecstasy gripped him, too.

The passion lingered, then faded. Cara lay alone on the bed, knowing he lay there, too. Her fear abated, her doubts abandoned for the night. She closed her eyes and slept peacefully in invisible arms.

Malcolm stood by the car as Edwy lugged their gear from the side door. Edwy wore Malcolm's dark green jacket over his kingly tunic. He looked . . . British. Cara followed Edwy in and out of the inn, carrying books and notes. She had offered to help with the luggage, but he refused her assistance. He muttered and grumbled the whole way.

"A king is not a servant. A king does not bear burdens."

The old inn door banged shut, catching half the bag. Edwy cursed, yanked it open, and flung the bag toward Malcolm's car. "Watch it there, boy! My vestments are in that bag."

Edwy dropped the other bags to the ground and glared. "Vestments? What do you need with vestments?"

"My spiffiest suit, my polished shoes . . . Young man, we are going to London."

"We're going to Gloucester."

"How long can it take? We'll stop on the way."

Edwy considered the matter. "Very well. London is also my destination."

Cara sighed. "Good. Let's go." She stuffed her notebooks into the trunk, then aimed for the driver's seat.

"Not a chance, girl!" Malcolm eased her aside and took his place at the wheel. Cara sighed again. Her father was a terrible driver. Bad enough in Vermont; in Britain, his skills were life-threatening. Cara suspected that being born Scottish, transferring to American roadways, then returning to England had been too much for him.

"Are you sure, Dad?"

Malcolm started the engine. "In, girl." He eyed Edwy. "What do we do with him?"

Edwy surveyed the car, then pointed to the back. "A king travels behind, the position of honor."

Cara shrugged, and held her seat for him. He crouched and inserted his tall body into the car. Cara climbed into the front as Edwy sputtered his displeasure. "This is cramped. There is no space for my legs."

The car lurched forward, stopping Edwy's complaints. Malcolm wheeled out onto the small road, on the wrong side. "Left, Dad! They drive on the left here." Her voice sounded shrill.

Malcolm whipped the small car to the left, then sped forward. Edwy leaned forward and tapped her shoulder. "You will teach me to operate this cart."

"Car. And you can forget it, Edwy. The thought of you at the wheel is even scarier than my father."

Malcolm leaned to the left as he spun around a tight corner. Edwy gulped. "Is it possible to get my usurper into this seat?"

"No, it isn't."

"Unfortunate." Edwy looked out the window, studying the small farms as they passed. "Halt!"

His harsh command brought a too-quick response from Malcolm. The tires squealed, the car spun, then stopped. Cara bowed her head in defeat. "What is the matter, Edwy?"

"Let me out."

"He's not that bad a driver. I mean, he hasn't killed anyone yet."

Edwy was already extracting himself from the car. Cara let him out, then followed. Edwy stood with his hands on his hips, staring at a small farm with a thatched barn. Sheep grazed in the misty fields beyond. Edwy's gaze fixed on a tractor. "That vehicle has potential for destruction. I shall use it while storming my usurper's castle."

An image of Edwy riding a tractor into Buckingham Palace flooded Cara's mind. A giggle burst from her throat, until he started into the yard. "Edwy! No!"

She bounded forward and seized his arm. "You can't just nab someone's tractor!"

Edwy peered over his shoulder, his expression ripe with disdain. "I can. I am king. All properties used by peasants are subject to the king's confiscation."

Cara struggled for a reason to prevent theft. "It's a tractor. Only farmers use tractors. Commoners."

A low tactic, but it worked. Edwy's eyes narrowed. He stiffened, then nodded. "Then it is beneath me." He turned back to the car. Cara released a long, drawn-out sigh, then hurried after him.

Edwy climbed back into the car, and they started off again. He leaned forward, watching the road. "When I have restored my position, I will have the entire countryside of my realm covered in this firm, black substance."

Cara eyed him doubtfully. "Do you mean you're going to pave all Britain?"

Edwy nodded. "Travel would be swifter." Malcolm increased his speed, as if Edwy's comment was a request.

Cara shook her head. "I would have thought men from the past would appreciate a natural habitat."

Edwy just looked confused. "I see no need . . ."

Malcolm missed a turn, slammed on the brakes, sped backward, and zoomed forward down another road. Cara leaned back against the headrest. She felt Edwy's hand on her hair, gently, as if he missed contact between them.

"If there were more space, you could sit at my side."

Cara glanced back. Her lips curved into a smile. She felt sure they had made love, in some form, last night.

He had been a part of her, he knew her. Yet she didn't feel shy or embarrassed. Probably because they had spent many such nights that way.

Edwy's smile deepened, as if he read her thoughts. "Sit with me."

Cara glanced at her father, who was looking out the side window as water came into view. "Someone has to watch the road."

Edwy groaned. "Someone should."

They reached the ferry docks at ten minutes to nine. Edwy left the car and stood at the railing, watching the sea. Cara stood beside him, watching his face as the sea wind ruffled his hair. *You are so beautiful.*

He took her hand as they left shore. "Today, we return to our land, my love. I return from exile. Do you know how I've longed for this moment?"

Cara smiled, but sorrow filled her heart.

Edwy squeezed her hand. "Tonight, we will lie together." He paused, watching her face. "In flesh. I think you are more than ready."

Now she blushed. No, it wasn't a dream, and she hadn't imagined his lovemaking. A small whimper of embarrassment was all she could muster. Edwy smiled, pleased with himself. "I am better when solid."

"Is that a fact?" Cara was startled at Lucas Sprague's mocking voice.

"No. Lucas . . ."

Lucas leaned against the railing, a camera around his neck. Despite the wind, his dark hair remained . . . manicured, well tended. Edwy's whipped around his face like a young god's. Cara moved closer beside Edwy, and Lucas's eyes darkened to black.

"Something more than an 'assistant,' eh, sweetheart? I guess you only pick the ones crazier than your old man."

Edwy looked down at the waves lapping against the ferry. "It would be no effort to hurtle him overboard. . . ."

Cara considered Edwy's suggestion, then shook her head. "You have more important things to do." She glared at Lucas. "Is there some reason you're following us?"

Lucas shrugged. "Just a hunch."

"A hunch about what?"

Lucas looked slowly from Cara to Edwy. "That you've finally picked someone who makes a better story than Malcolm Reid."

Cara slipped her hand on Edwy's arm. "Let's go back to the car, Edwin. It's getting cold and unpleasant here."

Edwy smiled, a taunting and somewhat mocking smile, then nodded to Lucas. "I look forward to reading your story, Sprague. I'm sure you will soar in the estimation of your readers."

His bright eyes twinkled. Lucas's narrowed to slits. Cara pulled Edwy from the rail. "Why on earth are you baiting him?"

Edwy looked innocent. Too innocent. "I don't know what you mean."

Cara led him back to the car. Three college-age girls whispered as if a celebrity passed in their midst. "He's so gorgeous. . . . He must be an actor. Maybe a rock star. He's got to be someone."

Edwy beamed with pride. "I am . . ."

Cara squeaked. "No one!" She seized Edwy's shoulder and pulled him close. "You don't want to alert your usurper, remember?"

"Ah. True." Edwy smiled at the girls, and walked on. Cara heard them talking as she hauled Edwy toward the car.

"I knew it! He's . . . someone."

Cara sighed. "They have no idea."

They landed in Holyhead and drove across Wales toward Gloucester. Edwy tried counting the homes of his future subjects, but gave up by the border of Anglesey.

"My usurper has amassed a worthy kingdom. I shall do her honor . . . before I have her drawn, quartered, beheaded, and arranged for exhibition."

Malcolm navigated onto the speed lane, then looked over at Cara. "He's likely to land us all in jail, with talk like that."

"True. Quiet, Edwy. Dad, Lucas Sprague is following us."

Malcolm glanced in the rearview mirror. "I know that, Cara. He's the only one driving an American Town Car. It looks like an ocean liner on this road." Malcolm patted the steering wheel of their tiny Mini car. "Wish they had these back in the States."

Malcolm eyed an exit sign fondly. "Maybe I should forget the M5, and take one of those little winding roads to Gloucester. That would throw him off."

Cara weighed the alternatives between Lucas's pursuit and her father driving on England's narrow, twisting roads. "Well, I don't see what damage he's going to do. Stay on the highway."

They reached the M5 at Worcester and drove south. With every mile, Cara's anxiety grew. "I don't see the purpose of going to Gloucester. Buckingham Palace is in London.''

Edwy watched her intently. ''It is necessary.'' He touched her shoulder. ''Trust me, Cara.''

She looked back at him. She couldn't speak, but she nodded. *Why am I so afraid?*

Malcolm seized a map and read it while driving. Cara tensed, ready to grab the wheel. ''It's a long way yet to London. You two stop in at the Cathedral, and I'll call ahead for a hotel reservation in London.'' He glanced at Edwy. ''Maybe make a few arrangements.''

Cara took the map. ''Good idea, Dad.''

Malcolm dodged past a lory, then cut it off. The subsequent blast of an angry horn left no impact on his driving. Edwy turned in his seat and studied the truck. ''Are those vehicles also operated by commoners?''

Cara caught her breath. ''Yes! And so are uzis, stealth bombers, and patriot missiles. It's not your style, Edwy.''

''A shame.'' Edwy faced front, brow furrowed. ''Get hence to Gloucester, old thane. My time grows short.''

Gloucester Cathedral was among the most beautiful in Western Europe. It crowned the city with eternal peace and lasting beauty. Cara felt as if she looked through the gates of hell.

''I don't want to go in there.''

Edwy took her hand and kissed it. ''We must.''

''Why?'' Her voice came sharper than she had intended. ''Why am I afraid?''

Edwy met her gaze and smiled gently. ''All you

wanted, all you dreamed, came to an end here, Cara. Let it be the place of a new beginning.''

Sweet words, yet her heart still throbbed mercilessly. ''How long do we have to stay?''

Edwy hesitated. ''I'm not sure. We're looking for something.''

''What?''

He looked uncomfortable. ''Well . . . you.''

''*Me?* What do you mean, *me?*''

Edwy cringed. ''Your remains, to be exact.''

''Dear God!'' Cara backed away and bumped into Lucas Sprague. ''How much worse can this day get?''

''Looking for something, sweetheart? Your . . . remains, did I overhear?''

''I left my purse.''

Lucas looked at the hobo bag on her arm. ''You've got it.''

Edwy frowned. ''Her other purse.'' He took Cara's hand again, turned his back on Lucas, and led her into the church.

Tourists mulled in the Great Cloister, organ music echoed in the cavernous hall. A group of choir boys listened to the choir master. When he turned his back, one small, blond boy shoved another child.

''Knock it off, Edwin!''

The choir master turned around. ''David, behave.''

Edwin looked angelic, then stuck out his tongue. Cara's eyes filled with tears. She looked up at Edwy, who looked proud. ''If you had a son . . .''

Edwy's smile turned gentle. ''When I have a son . . .''

Lucas Sprague stood watching them. Edwy glanced his way and nodded. Cara considered the gesture challenging. She picked up a brochure and examined it.

"Wait a minute! This place wasn't built when you . . ." She caught herself and gulped. "When you said it was."

"Not this structure, no. It was a monastic house at the time of your . . ." Edwy lowered his voice and checked for onlookers. "Death."

"Stop saying that."

"Your passage."

"Then what are we looking for?"

Edwy waited for a group of German tourists to pass by. "Beneath this structure are catacombs. There, in the floor, we will find . . ."

"Not . . . bones?"

"Your bones are withered, dried, and returned to dust, my love."

"What a comforting thought!"

Edwy examined the brochure. "This way." He started down a corridor, turning the brochure right-side-up, then turned around. "That way."

They headed down another hall and out into the gardens. A wide hedge surrounded the field, and a long row of archways led toward the King's School. Edwy stopped and closed his eyes, his face deep in concentration.

He opened his eyes and pointed. "This way."

"What are we looking for?"

"An object."

"What object? And what makes you think it's still here after a thousand years?"

"It's here."

Edwy led Cara down the arched hall, then through a small doorway. "There's only one way to do this. Take my crown."

Cara looked furtively around, then reached for Edwy's

crown. He bent, she removed it, and he disappeared. "I suppose I wait here?" She stuffed the circlet into her backpack and waited.

Cara stood casually while Edwy did whatever it was he had to do. Lucas Sprague came around a corner. Cara forced a smile. "He's in the men's room."

"I'll wait with you, shall I?"

Cara's jaw set hard. "That's not necessary."

"I've got nothing better to do."

Cara waited a while, wondering what Edwy expected of her, what he was looking for. *I died in this place.* Something touched her cheek. Edwy.

"Excuse me, Lucas." Cara darted into the restroom, held up the crown, and Edwy appeared. An elderly woman walked in, screamed, and fled.

"Did you find whatever you were looking for?"

"With great power, I was able to locate the object and summon it to the surface. We must hasten there swiftly."

Edwy shoved open the bathroom door, and emerged face-to-face with Lucas Sprague. Cara rolled her eyes. "Wrong door. Come on, Edwin."

Edwy led Cara to a uniformed guard. "I believe you're expecting us?"

Cara eyed Edwy. "Is he?"

The guard looked a little dazed, but nodded. "Mr. . . ."

"King. Edwin King. This is Miss Reid. We have permission to examine the lower catacombs."

"Of course." The guard sounded dazed, too. "I seem to remember hearing that. Of course."

He brought them to a barred door, unlocked it, and stood back. "This is restricted, you know."

"We understand." Edwy glanced back to see Lucas Sprague watching them. "You'll be careful not to let anyone follow us."

"I will."

Edwy took Cara's hand and led her through the door. Cara's heart throbbed, her skin felt cold. The door closed and locked behind them. "What did you do to him?"

"A ghostly suggestion." Edwy led her down narrow, dark stairs, and into a lower basement. Old tombs and crypts lined the wall, too delicate to be visited by tourists.

Cara was shaking. "Am I . . . here?"

"Beneath this earth, my Elfgiva lay." Edwy took her shoulders and drew her to face him. "But you, *you*, Cara Reid, are standing before me. The past can't hurt you now."

Edwy brought her to the far end of the catacombs. The musty smell filled her nostrils; the cold, damp air chilled her flesh. Edwy knelt by an old tomb, and chills coursed along Cara's spine.

"Is this . . . mine?"

"This spot is closest to where you lay." Edwy looked up at her. "The past can't hurt you, Cara. Remember. *Geman.*"

Cara closed her eyes to block the dank hallow, but her brain swarmed with images. Herself, kneeling at Edwy's feet, her heart so filled with love that she thought she would die. *I don't care if you're king. We can escape. Together.*

She saw Edwy as he touched her hair, smiling despite tears in his blue eyes. *Never, my love. Wait for me. I will come to you, and all England will be ours again.*

Then, as now, he was too proud, too strong to surrender. Cara's breath mingled with Elfgiva's and caught on a sob. "I don't want England. I want you."

Cara opened her eyes. Tears stained Edwy's cheeks as he watched her. "You spoke those words at our last parting. The last time I saw you alive."

"I know." Cara's chin quivered. She remembered herself as another woman, alone in dark chambers, waiting. "A man came for me in the night." Edwy started to shake his head, as if he couldn't endure the story of her ending.

"I thought it was you. I thought you had come for me."

Edwy rose to his feet and touched her arm. "No . . ."

"It was a monk. He gave me a message. He said you were waiting. I followed him to the gardens. They were much as they are today. And . . ." Her voice cracked. Edwy took her into his arms.

"No."

Cara looked up at him. "You didn't know?"

Edwy pressed his cheek against her head. "I came too late. When I found you, you were laid to rest. They said you died naturally, because of our child."

Cara's breath came in short gasps. "I was looking for you. I was so happy. He came up behind me and wrapped a cloth over my face. I couldn't breathe." She trembled with the memory, her lungs aching as she seized breaths.

Edwy's hands clenched, as if he could still fight the man who murdered her. "Curse him, curse his soul forever."

"I died. I lost you." Cara's voice broke on a sob. She leaned against Edwy's chest, and he stroked her hair.

Gently, he cupped her chin in his hand. He waited

until their eyes met. "Cara, love never dies."

Tears dripped down her cheeks, down his. Cara touched his face. Her fear eased, her pulse moved slower. "I believe you." A smile grew on her face, and on his. "I believe you."

Edwy bent to kiss her. His lips met hers softly, with eternal tenderness. She wrapped her arms around his neck, but he drew away. He knelt again beside the tomb, and held his hand over the cracked, stone floor.

As Cara watched spellbound, a golden object emerged. It looked like his crown, only smaller. Small enough for a finger. Her finger.

Edwy took the ring, then faced her, still kneeling. He held out his hand, and she gave him her hand. "This ring, I once placed on your finger, and all my life I placed at your feet. We married despite the Church, despite all who stood against us. We married for love. Cara, I love you still. Wear it now, again, and be my wife once more."

Cara stared down into his sweet face. Tears glimmered on his face. "I want to be your wife."

He smiled, but his tears still fell. For the first time, Cara saw doubt in his eyes. "If I fail you . . ."

Cara held out her fingers. "Kings never fail."

"How I wish that were true!" Edwy bowed his head, then looked up at her, his face young and vulnerable. "Cara, what if I'm wrong?"

The balance shifted from her disbelief to his. "We'll find a way. You'll get your throne back, if I have to shove Queen Elizabeth off myself."

"I will impregnate you at once."

Cara blushed, but she nodded. "What about your revenge?"

"This troubles me. I must face my enemy."

"Couldn't Lucas Sprague be Dunstan?"

"I considered that. I do not sense any connection with him to our past. He is a weak soul, new to human form. Odd that he should pursue you thus, but he is not part of our past."

Edwy lifted the ring to her finger. "Are you sure, Cara? I could fail, and in failing, leave you truly alone."

"We have ten days."

"Nine."

"I want to be with you."

Edwy smiled and slipped the ring on her finger. "With this ring, I thee wed."

Cara closed her eyes. "For all time." She sank to her knees before him. "Edwy."

Edwy kissed her mouth, and she leaned against him. "You are now my wife. . . ."

Cara looked at him. "I'm not sure it's valid this way."

"Our marriage is valid because I am king, and I pronounce it so."

He ran his hands through her hair, then down her arms. "This is not a good place for a marriage bed. Here, among dried corpses and foul odors." A slow smile curved his sensual mouth. "I want you on a soft mattress, your hair spread across the bed, your eyes on fire."

Cara gulped. She couldn't argue, because she wanted that, too. "Now what?"

Edwy rose to his feet and held out his hand, looking sure and handsome. A king. "We go to London."

Malcolm was waiting outside the Cathedral. He watched suspiciously as Edwy and Cara emerged hand in hand. Edwy saw the old man's eyes flicker at the sight of Cara's wedding ring. "You two married that quickly?"

Edwy nodded, proud. "We did."

Cara looked uncomfortable. "I'm not sure it's exactly legal."

Malcolm's brow furrowed. His bearded chin scrunched into a ball of displeasure. "I suspected as much. Into the car, boy. We've got one stop before we head on to London."

Edwy obeyed, though he disliked the old man's imperious attitude. "You remind me of someone. Someone grating, bossy, and . . ."

"Into the car, boy."

Edwy stuffed himself into the back seat, watching intently as Malcolm navigated Gloucester's busy streets. Malcolm jerked to a stop outside a small white building, got out, and pointed. "In there, both of you."

Cara got out, too. "What is this place, Dad?"

"You'll see. Move, boy."

Edwy extracted himself from the small car, his fists clenched with anger. " 'My liege.' "

Malcolm pretended to ignore him. The door of the small building opened, and a frazzled, scrawny man appeared holding a half-empty bottle. "This them?"

Malcolm shoved Edwy forward. "Do your duty, boy."

Cara examined a small sign over the door. " 'Weddings, quick and cheap.' Dad!"

"In, both of you."

Edwy followed Cara into the front hall of the building. It was stark, unadorned, and unpleasant inside. "This is not the proper setting . . ."

Malcolm poked Edwy's chest. "This fellow is a justice of the peace. He doesn't ask questions. Now's your chance. Are you going to marry my daughter or not?"

"It is done already."

"Now or never, boy."

Edwy eyed the unkempt "justice." He looked drunk. "Old man's got you, kid."

Edwy's hand moved to his side before he remembered he had no weapon. "Curses."

Malcolm tapped his shoulder in warning. "You can marry my daughter here, all legal and straight. Or . . ." His voice trailed away meaningfully.

Edwy looked at Cara. She chewed her lip as if she feared his intentions. Edwy's heart softened. "When first we married, I arranged the greatest pageantry, and we came to grief. If we marry here, in circumstances that are foul beyond belief . . ."

The justice sputtered angrily, but Edwy paid no attention. "Mayhap our lives together will prove eternal."

Tears welled in Cara's soft eyes and she nodded. "Yes."

Edwy faced the justice. "Proceed."

The man took another drink of a noxious liquid, then produced a little red book. He mumbled a few lines that Edwy didn't understand. "Yes or no, kid."

Edwy braced. Malcolm jabbed him in the ribs. "Yes."

The man belched, then turned to Cara. "You?"

Cara straightened. A small smile appeared on her lips. Her eyes misted with feminine joy. She looked up at Edwy, and he saw love. "I do."

The justice of the peace burped again. "Sign here, and move along. I've got . . ." He burped a third time, and

Edwy contemplated striking him. "Work to do."

Edwy eyed the parchment as Cara signed her name. She passed him the pen. He took it gingerly. Cara peered over his shoulder. "Write Edwin King." He braced into indignation. "For now."

"For now." He scrawled Saxon lettering, which the drunken man eyed with misgivings.

"Well, you're married. The papers will be filed in Gloucester." The justice took another swig of liquor. "Not that a marriage this rushed and cheap will ever last."

Edwy went to the door, then turned back. "You're wrong, my friend. It has already lasted a thousand years."

"The site of my coronation wasn't . . . paved." Edwy stood in the center of a parking lot and glared. "This isn't Kingston-on-Thames. Check the map again, old thane."

Malcolm passed the map to Cara. Her brow furrowed as she examined it. "I'm afraid Dad is right, Edwy. This is it. This is where you were crowned. I'm afraid it's just a modern London suburb now. Not even one of the interesting ones."

Edwy looked left, then right, then turned in a circle to view his surroundings. Tall, modern buildings stood on all sides. Fast cars swooped past his position. Some honked when the lights changed color.

He tried to remember the day of his coronation. "There was a hall, here." He pointed toward a blinking light. "It was in this spot that Dunstan and I first came to grief."

Cara moved closer to his side, buttoning her coat

against the chill wind. "Maybe he'll be around some-where."

"He kept me in the banquet hall, forcing me to listen to his views on the Church. He refused to allow your attendance."

Cara's lips puckered angrily. "Why?"

"Your mother opposed Dunstan's Reform movement. He feared by my love for you, I would favor her with power." Edwy couldn't see the landscape—it was lost in the London suburb. Nothing looked the same as he remembered. "I left the banquet and went to your chambers. Dunstan followed me and accused us of carnal behavior. Ridiculous, because your mother was with us. Of course, he accused her of favoring me likewise."

Cara grimaced. "How rude!"

"He hauled me back to the banquet, by the hair . . ." Edwy touched his head, remembering the fury and humiliation, the pain. "I had him exiled the day after my coronation."

"I take it he came back."

"He did, but in secret. I didn't know until too late."

Edwy positioned himself in the center of the parking lot. He knelt along a painted white line. He bent his head in silent prayer. "This England, I will rule, and my heirs after me." He met Cara's eyes. She watched him, shivering. Malcolm looked sympathetic.

"I've gotten us rooms at Brown's Hotel, lad. You'll be needing rest before you go storming Buckingham Palace."

Edwy met Cara's eyes. She fidgeted nervously, but he saw her anticipation. *She must bear my child . . .* Thoughts of impregnating her faded as he saw her, vulnerable and trusting. Maybe it was too soon. Maybe she wasn't ready.

If I fail, she will suffer again.... For a thousand years, he had refused to consider that possibility. Today, it loomed before him as a likelihood. Edwy stood and took her hands in his. "We have time, Cara."

What is wrong with me, that I should doubt this way? Edwy's brow furrowed as he fought doubt. *I must be strong, lest I fail her.* With a cool flash, he realized it wasn't his throne he wanted back. It was his life. His life with the woman he loved.

Something hovered at the brink of his understanding. His pride demanded his throne, his pride demanded vengeance. But his heart longed for Cara.

He would have all, because he had to win to keep what he wanted most. Edwy's jaw set in determination. He lifted his head and looked across the parking lot. "I have restaked my claim. It is time to go."

Chapter Five

Brown's Hotel was dignified, staid, and beautiful, suitable for a king. If the concierge had heard of Malcolm Reid, his good taste forbade any mention. Cara stood with Edwy as Malcolm checked in. Soft music played in the lobby. Edwy looked around in disgust.

"When I have assumed my reign, I will issue a mandate that requires only the sound of fine music."

Cara remembered his taste in music. She pictured a paved England, with blaring Heavy Metal on every radio. "Are you *sure* you have to be king?"

"It is as the Druid commanded."

Lucas Sprague entered as if on cue, and Cara groaned.

"Fancy meeting you here, sweetheart. Edwin."

Edwy smiled. "We've been expecting you."

Lucas didn't like Edwy's response. The corners of his lips twitched. "Care to tell me what you were doing in that parking lot?"

Cara copied Edwy's expression. "Edwin lost a contact lens."

Lucas's brow angled in obvious disbelief. "Hope you found it."

Edwy didn't answer, but his smile deepened. Cara felt sure his posture was intended to provoke Lucas, but she couldn't guess why.

Lucas sauntered to the front desk. The concierge looked him up and down, a faint trace of disdain on his face. "I'm sorry, sir. We've no vacancies tonight."

Lucas's mouth formed a snarl. "You gave them a room."

The concierge remained nonplussed. "The very last two, I'm afraid. Sorry, sir. I am happy to recommend another establishment, if you wish."

Lucas shouldered his camera bag. "I'll find my own place." He headed for the door, then stopped near Edwy. "Still wearing the gold headband, eh, *Edwin?*"

Edwy revealed no discomfort at Lucas's probing question. "I'm sure when your story is told, you'll be able to purchase one for yourself."

Cara placed her hand on Edwy's arm. "I wouldn't recommend it, Lucas. It takes a special man to carry it off."

Lucas noticed Cara's ring. "What . . . ?"

She held up her hand proudly. "Didn't I mention? Edwin and I are married."

"Quick work."

"We've known each other for years."

Lucas frowned. "I've followed you and your old man for years. I've never heard of this . . . person."

"We were childhood sweethearts."

Lucas appeared suspicious, probably because he knew

she hadn't come to England until her college years. Cara turned her back on him and looked up at Edwy. "Shall we go to our room?"

He smiled, but Cara thought he looked a little sad. "Yes, love."

Their room was decorated with fresh flowers. A bottle of champagne waited, chilled, with two glasses. Cara examined the card. "It's from my father." Her eyes filled with tears as she read his message.

" *'Love isn't measured by time, but by the heart. Follow the heart, and all else follows. Follow pride and fear, and all fails.'* " Cara looked at Edwy. "I wonder what he meant by that."

Edwy stared at the note. "I have heard these words before."

"Where?"

Edwy didn't answer. He turned to their window and looked out at the quiet street. "Your father knows much that he doesn't say."

Cara touched Edwy's shoulder. "Is something wrong, Edwy?"

He turned to her and drew her into his arms. "Do you know how long I've waited for this? To hold you, flesh to flesh. To look into your eyes, and know you're seeing me. To know you're mine again."

"A thousand years. Edwy, I have waited for you as long."

Cara realized she was trembling, but not from fear. Two days ago, she had been sitting by an Irish loch, watching for a dinosaur. Tonight, she stood in a bridal chamber with a ghost.

Edwy looked down into her face. He looked vulnerable, even shy. "From the time I first saw you, I meant to give you the world. Instead, I led you into hardship and pain and loss."

Cara placed her hand on his cheek. "I wanted you. I want you now. Edwy, those things we wanted were outside ourselves, things determined by fate. You lived in a violent time. Now this spell says you have to do what seems impossible. But we have now what we had then. We have each other."

"For eight more days. If I fail . . ."

Cara pressed her fingers over his mouth. She felt his warm breath, his tenderness. "You didn't think you could fail in Ireland. Why do you fear now?"

Tears welled in his eyes. "I could lose you again. Maybe forever."

"Not tonight." Cara's voice sank to a whisper, and she rose up on tiptoe to kiss him. "Not tonight."

Edwy seemed unsure, but when her mouth brushed against his, his whole body tightened. His fingers clenched on her shoulders as she pressed closer to him.

She drew back and looked into his eyes. She saw his past in his face—the young king, surrounded by enemies, guarded by pride and skill and heritage, destined to fall. She heard the echoes of battle, of clashing weapons, as he fought not to survive but for honor.

She saw him kneeling by a woman's still body, crying. She knew that woman was herself. Her memory came from her soul. Even in that ancient time, she knew his pride wouldn't let him surrender. He would go on and on, and never give up. So she had only a brief time at his side, as his lover. Then and now.

"Edwy . . ." Cara's eyes grew wide. "I knew it then." He didn't understand, and she couldn't explain.

She stood back and took his hand gently in her own. She led him to the wide bed. "Tonight, we have each other. Tonight, I have you."

He nodded, but he couldn't speak.

She drew off his borrowed coat and dropped it to the floor. A new power surged inside her as she unfastened the leather belt around his tunic. He swallowed, still silent, as she untied the string at his collar. Edwy's hands shook as he pulled it over his head and let it fall.

Cara examined his leggings leisurely, aware of the firm, large bulge outlined beneath the snug cloth. She ran her finger along the waistband, then beneath against his taut skin. Edwy drew a sharp breath, his flesh tightened.

She met his gaze and smiled. "Sit."

He dropped to the bed, wide-eyed with pleasure. She knelt before him and removed his thonged boots. "Stand." He rose unsteadily, and she chuckled.

Still kneeling, Cara fumbled with his leggings, then drew them slowly down over his narrow hips. She closed her eyes, then allowed herself to view his masculine form. He was beautiful, his male organ in perfect proportion, slick and hard and full with desire.

Fierce tremors surged through Cara, demanding. His blue eyes blazed as he recognized her desire. "I said you were ready, love."

She nodded, then drew a quick breath. "I am."

He reached out his hand and she took it. She rose and stood before him. He touched her cheek with one finger, then let it fall. All the while, his smile grew, both teasing and gentle.

He touched the base of her throat, and her pulse throbbed. "I have watched you undress a thousand times, and each time, the desire to assist you grew stronger.'' Edwy's eyes twinkled. ''Now, I will show you what I've learned.''

He slid his hands to her waist, then raised her large, gray sweatshirt. Cara wished she'd worn something more feminine, but it didn't matter. Edwy's eyes darkened to a satisfying shade of deep blue.

The sweatshirt came off, leaving her unremarkable, comfortable cloth bra. *If only I'd invested in one of the push-up styles . . .* But Edwy seemed pleased with the sight. He unfastened her jeans, and she wished she'd worn a skirt. He knelt at her feet and pulled off her hiking boots and heavy wool socks. Cara pictured delicate high-heeled shoes and sheer stockings, and held her breath.

I've waited a thousand years for this man, and I start my wedding night dressed like a lumberjack. . . . Edwy slid down her jeans, but he left her white panties untouched. She picked up one foot, then the other, and he tossed her jeans aside.

Edwy stood up, smiling as if he guessed her discomfort. Cara bit her lip hard. ''I suppose I dressed more like a lady . . . before.''

He studied her thoughtfully, head to toe. ''You dressed like a queen. Yet my memory is unclear on this point. It may require more for reminding.''

He ran his hand along the strap of her bra, then around to the back. *If only I'd worn the clasped variety!* Without warning, he pulled the bra up and over her head. For an instant, she stood with her arms raised, feeling foolish. Edwy's warm murmur eased her embarrassment.

His bright gaze fixed on her exposed breasts, his breath came swift. ''This, I remember.''

276

He ran his hands along her side to her waist, then to the top of her panties. His fingers grazed her bottom as he pulled them off, too. She stepped out of them, her heart pounding. She was naked. He was naked, too.

Without his Saxon tunic, his exotic heritage disappeared. He was a man, young and strong, powerful with desire. Without her clothes, Cara was a woman, neither a hopeful young queen nor a cynical American. Neither was bound to a time, but to each other.

Cara placed her hand over his heart and felt his life beneath his smooth, warm skin. "I love you."

He clasped his hand over hers. "I love you." Their lips met, their arms wrapped around each other. Edwy sank back onto the bed, drawing her down with him. She kissed his face, his neck, his shoulder.

She felt his male length against her body, she felt the urgency of his ageless need. Her own flared with such power that she trembled.

She lay above him, gazing down into his beautiful face. Desperation coiled inside her, to know him, to keep him, to stand against time. The world she knew fell away, and she remembered herself before, young and desperate and so in love that every breath hurt with the fear of its loss.

Edwy looked up at her, and she knew he understood. She hadn't left Elfgiva behind. The young queen lived inside her. She rose up and became Cara. She reached and pulled her husband closer.

Edwy kissed her, soft and teasing, then rolled her onto her back. He sat back, his dark gaze flashing from her face to her body, and back to her face. He touched her collarbone, then ran his hand lightly over her breast. His fingers grazed the sensitive tip, and she caught her breath in anticipation.

He bent and brushed his mouth over the small peak, and Cara caught his hair in her fingers. His lips teased her nipple while his hand slid along her stomach to the nest of soft hair between her thighs. He found the tiny bud within, and drew slow, exquisite circles until her hips twisted with pleasure.

"You have done this to me before." Her voice broke on a moan, and Edwy chuckled.

"Many times. But never so well, or so warm, or so wet."

Cara moaned again. She was slippery and damp, her body aching for him. "I didn't do anything to you."

"Just tortured me with need." He rose up to kiss her mouth, still teasing her moist flesh. Cara met his eyes and smiled.

"There is much I could do." She didn't wait for his approval. She slid her hand down between their bodies and found his thick staff. Her fingers coiled tight around its base, and Edwy shuddered with pleasure.

"You are hot, and I feel your pulse." She squeezed a little tighter and he groaned. "It is strong. I think I would feel it within."

His groan came harsher this time. Cara moved her hand up and down, feeling his length, feeling his skin grow hot to her touch. "I think with you inside me, no one will ever part us again."

He didn't wait. He positioned himself above her, he parted her thighs with his own, and readied himself to enter her. Cara watched his face, and she knew she wore the same expression as her father when he stared hopefully at a monster's hiding place. Wonder, pure and forever. Any magic is possible, there for the taking if you believe.

Edwy hesitated, and she saw doubt. A doubt she had abandoned in favor of hope. "Cara, if we do this, you may bear my child."

"Isn't that the point?"

"It was, but not now. I do this for pleasure, for you and for me, because no matter what happens, I want this now."

Cara nodded vigorously. "Me, too."

He smiled, but his eyes held sorrow. "I may succeed in the planting of my seed, yet fail against Dunstan."

Her heart slammed, her blood raced. "Edwy . . ." She puffed an impatient breath. *Now he doubts.* "I can take care of our child. I want our child. But I want you, too. You will not fail."

He drew faith from hers. Cara watched his face change. "I will not fail." As he spoke, he entered her, slowly. Her body opened for his, welcoming him as if it recognized his presence and had prepared forever for his entrance.

Their gazes held as he sank deeper inside her. Cara felt every pulse. Her feminine shield resisted, then gave way, and he became part of her.

For an instant, neither of them moved. They stared at each other as if seeing a wonder for the first time. He took her hands and held them close to his heart. He began to move, first slowly, then deeper and harder, until her breath came as small gasps. She murmured his name, her fingers clenched around his.

She remembered, yet it was new. He knew her, yet he shuddered with every stroke of their bodies, as if for the first time. Broken Saxon words rolled from his throat, but he called her Cara.

Cara's legs clamped around his. Her body arched beneath him. He drove deeper, and her senses shattered, rolling and striving toward the endless stars, toward heaven. Edwy's body quivered and spasmed, and he joined her there.

For an eternal moment, they quaked together. She felt him inside her, the perfect joining. The fierce currents subsided, his body stilled, and she wrapped her arms tight around his shoulders.

Cara kissed his forehead twice. "Edwy, I've missed you."

"This is my usurper? The woman in the peculiar headgear?"

Edwy sat with one leg crossed over the other, staring at the television in disbelief. Queen Elizabeth nodded politely, and moved down a line of well-wishers. The announcer's voice was superimposed over the screen images.

"... the second of the Queen's museum visits, as she dedicates new wings, and examines noteworthy new acquisitions. Museum directors hope the Queen's support may garner new donations. The Queen's edict allows for a monetary reward ..."

Edwy uncrossed his legs and sat forward, elbows on his knees as he stared at his usurper. "Where are her armaments? Why is there no king?"

"That's Prince Philip behind her. Isn't he handsome?"

Edwy looked disgusted. "He is unarmed. No mail, no scabbard. What if someone hungers for her throne?"

Cara smiled. "Do you mean besides you?"

"I do not 'hunger,' Cara. It is my right." He shook his head in dismay. "It will be no effort at all to supplant her." Edwy sat back in his chair. "A shame. I harkened to the challenge."

Cara adjusted her robe, then sat on his lap. "The Royals now are basically figureheads." Cara glanced at the screen. The news story flashed to coverage of royal scandals, and the Queen's stoic endurance. She snapped off the TV before Edwy could learn that his arrival might not be entirely unwelcome.

Edwy wrapped his arms around her waist, drawing her closer. "We have known bliss, you and I. I wish it to last."

"Yes." Cara kissed his cheek, close to his ear.

"It is clear that I'll have no trouble regaining my throne." He paused, and Cara didn't argue. "But if I do so now, immediately, Dunstan will have the chance to interfere. I must find him first, then relieve that small woman from power."

"So in the meantime, you and I can work on this impregnating business?"

Edwy grinned. "Every morning, every night, and once at noon."

"Good." Cara leaned her head against his shoulder. Someone knocked on their door. She passed Edwy the Brown's Hotel hospitality robe, and he put it on.

"Room Service."

A waiter appeared with a cart of food and wine. Edwy watched the man intently, as if searching his identity. Cara reached for the check, but the waiter smiled. "Signed for by Mr. Reid. Enjoy yourselves." He left, and Cara seated herself to eat.

Edwy drew up his chair. "How did your father know we were finished?"

"He was young once. I suppose he remembers."

Cara's appetite surged, and she devoured a crusty roll. Edwy seemed preoccupied. Cara set aside her wine. "What's the matter?"

"I must find my enemy. But how?"

"The Druid said time would bring you together, right?"

"Yes. I hoped that servant . . ." He gestured at their door. "But, no."

"You thought the waiter was Dunstan?"

"He could be anyone." Edwy rose from the cart and looked out the window. "He's out there, somewhere. And I must find him if this bliss is to last."

Edwy fell silent, staring into the night. Cara didn't know what to say, so she waited. Edwy turned back, determined, but not as sure as when she first saw him. "Tomorrow, we begin the hunt. We will walk these streets, search these buildings, and interrogate every peasant until we find him. Our love depends on my vengeance."

They walked until Cara's feet blistered. Edwy decided his Saxon outfit was too conspicuous, so Cara purchased a pair of jeans, black sneakers, and a white shirt for his use. He looked perfect. Women stopped to stare as he walked by.

Lucas Sprague was never far behind. Cara noticed him questioning people Edwy had spoken to, but obviously his story wasn't going well. He lingered across the street, still watching. Edwy paid him no heed. He just kept looking for his enemy.

They stopped to rest in Piccadilly Circus. Cara leaned against Nelson's statue, but Edwy watched every passerby. If a blond, pale-skinned man came near, Edwy asked if they'd met. One barrister had already threatened a lawsuit for harassment.

"Edwy, this isn't working. I don't think Dunstan is a lawyer."

"Dunstan was shrewd, deceitful, and manipulative."

"Then again, it's a place to start." Cara rubbed her ankle. "There's a woman with a Welsh Corgi. Maybe that's him."

Edwy glared. "Dunstan is not a pet. And he wasn't Welsh."

Malcolm came toward them, wielding a walking stick. He looked dapper and handsome, less odd than usual. His beard had been trimmed, too. "Still searching for the enemy, are you, lad?"

Edwy nodded, too bitter and depressed to answer.

Malcolm and Cara exchanged a knowing glance. "What are you going to do if you find him?"

Edwy rubbed his chin thoughtfully. "I could slay him outright. But after a thousand years, it seems insufficient for his crimes, and the grief he has caused me. No, I think I will have him slowly dismembered, then put up for display."

Malcolm laid his hand on Edwy's shoulder. "Boy, there are countless roads, some marked and clear, some hidden. You choose. Sometimes the right path is the one you don't see."

Malcolm didn't wait for an answer. He nodded to a middle-aged woman, then continued on his walk. Cara stared after him. "My father has always been odd. But I've never heard him talk like that."

Edwy glared at Malcolm's back. "I have."

*   *   *

They stalked Dunstan for five more days. Halloween came, but Edwy's hope was gone. He had failed. Without Dunstan, there would be no reason to claim his throne. He hadn't slept, he couldn't eat. He made love to Cara as if each time were the last. This morning, with the warm shower pouring down on their faces as their bodied entwined, he feared it truly was.

Cara dressed silently, but she gave no indication that this would be their last day together. Their eyes met, but neither spoke.

They went to the door together, and Edwy took her hand. "Today is the last." The words hurt, but Edwy knew they must be spoken. Cara shook her head, but he touched her lips, silencing her. "My quest is over. Yes, I will again await my enemy, but there is no point regaining my throne without first finding vengeance. Cara, my love, I will be gone. But know, this thousand years of fruitless waiting has brought more than I ever dreamed. These days with you have been bliss. A man can want for no more."

"Edwy, no . . ." Tears dripped to her cheeks, but she stopped her words. She took his hand and kissed it. "For me, also."

She swallowed hard, cleared her expression, and smiled. "This day isn't over yet."

Lucas Sprague followed them into Hyde Park. The English didn't celebrate Halloween the way Americans did—no trick or treating, few parties. A few shops displayed pumpkins and spiderwebs, but since the more festive celebration of Guy Fawkes Day occurred five days hence, October 31 passed uneventfully in England.

The Shadow King

All Hallow's Eve had been a sacred time for the Druids, however, but nothing outward indicated the momentous occasion Edwy now faced.

Edwy and Cara sat on a bench together, quiet, holding hands. The reporter took a few pictures. Edwy wished he'd found Dunstan in the persistent reporter, but vanquishing even a lesser enemy might bring satisfaction.

"That man will give you no peace. If I disappear, he will hound you forever. I do not like leaving you knowing what grief he caused your father."

Cara glanced toward Sprague and sighed. "He is annoying, true. But it means nothing, Edwy. You're all that matters now."

"Shall we give him the story of his dreams, love?"

Cara didn't understand, but Edwy's plan formed and congealed. He stood up, then motioned to Sprague. Cara tugged at his shirt. "I'd rather be with you alone."

"Just a momentary lapse, my love."

Edwy waited as Sprague approached. The reporter looked wary. Edwy's smile deepened to a kingly challenge. "Sprague."

"Edwin."

"You wanted a story."

"There's one here. Not sure what it is yet, but I'd imagine the *Searcher's* gullible readers will fall for it. Might even sell it to one of the Brit tabloids."

Edwy nodded, sincere. "My story is one I fear I cannot tell." Sprague's lip curled in potential sarcasm, but Edwy held up his hand. "It is a sight that must be seen to be believed."

Cara fidgeted on the bench. "Edwin . . ."

"Edwy, my dear. We can't fool a reporter of Master Sprague's quality forever. Why try?"

Cara hopped to her feet. *"What?"*

"Remove my crown."

"No!"

Edwy turned to her. "Defiant to the end. My sweet, remove my crown."

Cara glanced at Sprague, then back at Edwy. "I hope you know what you're doing."

"I am king, Cara. I know what I'm doing."

Sprague coughed. *"King?* King of what?"

"King of England, Sprague."

Sprague's laugh was cut short when Cara pulled off Edwy's crown. He gasped, he choked, he stumbled backward. "What the hell . . . ? How did you do that?"

Edwy watched the scene with rising pleasure. Cara looked casual, even bored. "Edwy is a ghost, Lucas. If you hadn't guessed . . . He was King of England in the year 959. I was his wife. We were both murdered."

"Very funny."

Cara held up the crown, and Edwy positioned himself under it. He stood tall, towering over Sprague. It felt good. Sprague went white. "That's . . . impossible."

"No more impossible than loch monsters, the Congo Dinosaur, or the Himalayan Yeti, Lucas. Now we've given you your story. I'm afraid you'll have to leave."

Sprague shook, his eyes looking white with small, black dots in the center. He backed away, his breath swift. He lifted his camera, then let it drop back to his chest. "I've got calls to make. I want an interview."

Edwy smiled and nodded, his most gracious, kingly demeanor in place. "Of course. You will find me at the Natural History Museum at six o'clock, sharp."

"Why?"

"I thought I'd lay claim to the English throne." Edwy

paused, bemused by Sprague's lack of understanding. "It is my right, you know. And with all the trouble with Charles . . ."

Sprague's round eyes darted back and forth. He wet his lips, then turned away. He ran across the park, dove into a black cab, and sped away. Edwy watched him go, then sat back beside Cara.

"Are we really going to the museum at six?"

"We are."

"Why?"

"Since this is my last day, there is one thing I must do for my country."

"What?"

"You'll see when we get there."

Lucas Sprague was waiting. He'd hired several cameramen, each with elaborate video and sound equipment. Cara felt sick. The sun was lowering over London. According to Edwy's Druid, the spell ceased at sunset on Halloween.

They made love for the last time, several times. In their room, before, then after lunch. They made love before dressing for this last event. Malcolm had met them at their door, as if he knew the importance of this last evening together.

They hadn't told him much, but he seemed to understand. He stood on the museum steps, cheerfully answering the cameramen's teasing questions about the Loch monsters. "Never did see him, but he's a crafty one, to be sure."

"How do you know it's a *he?*"

Malcolm clucked his tongue. "Boy, you don't know anything about women. I had a camera. How many pretty girls do you know who can resist a camera?''

The cameramen all laughed, but Sprague stood staring at Edwy. Cara leaned closer to Edwy. "What are you going to do when he announces you're a ghost?"

Edwy took her hand. "A golden ring, a symbol of eternal love. Would you let me borrow it, love?"

Cara started to remove her ring. She closed her eyes tight. *With this ring, I thee wed.* "Will you still be mine?"

"Always, Cara. Always, forever."

Cara met his sweet gaze, then pulled the ring from her finger. He took it and slipped it on the tip of his left pinky. "Thank you."

"Whatever you wish, but how . . . ?"

Several more reporters showed up, hurrying as if they feared to miss a big story. They gathered around Lucas, who looked smug. "I've got a story for you. But remember, the rights are mine."

"Where's the subject?"

Lucas pointed at Edwy, who smiled and nodded. "Get pictures now, before it's too late."

"Too late? This better be good, Sprague."

"The best Halloween story the world has ever witnessed!"

The cameramen glanced at each other and sighed. "Americans."

Edwy stepped forward, holding Cara's hand. "I am flattered by your attention, gentlemen. You are philanthropists, I see."

Sprague's eyes narrowed. "You won't get around it, Edwy. I know your secret."

Cara didn't listen. She stared at the horizon, as the sun sank beyond the highest buildings. *So little time . . .*

Malcolm came up beside her and touched her shoulder gently.

"My dear child, choice takes only a second. One second, and the world turns on its ends."

"Dad . . ."

"Watch."

The museum curator appeared on the steps. "Mr. Sprague has told me you have an announcement to make, young man." He hesitated, looking uncomfortable. "Yet something scandalous enough to appear in the tabloids may not be quite in the Museum's interest."

Edwy looked bemused. "I, too, was surprised by Mr. Sprague's attention."

Lucas stepped up beside Edwy. "Take off the crown! Let everyone see Edwy, the Shadow King of England!" Edwy looked at him as if Lucas were joking. Cara held her breath.

A final ray of sunset pierced through the tall buildings, glancing off the museum wall onto Edwy's face. His beauty caused a soft ripple through the crowd, as if every person there beheld a true king, a man who traced his ancestry to the gods, and beyond.

Edwy looked back at her, his blue eyes shining with eternal love. He touched the ring on his finger and smiled. Then, very slowly, so slowly that Cara hurt, Edwy bent forward and removed his crown.

All time held, Cara shook as one second formed two. And Edwy remained, solid and strong. Visible. Malcolm exhaled a long, shuddering breath. "Well done, lad."

Cara trembled, tears flooding her eyes. "But . . ."

"Wait, lass. He's got one more to go."

"One more what?"

Edwy knelt and passed the crown to the curator. Cara

heard his whisper, soft and poignant. "For my England . . ."

The curator studied the golden circlet. "It looks authentic. My God, where did you find such a precious item?"

"I am a student of the past . . ."

"An archaeologist?"

Edwy shrugged. "You could say that. Dr. Reid and his daughter came upon an interesting site in Ireland. There, we unearthed an ancient burial cairn. I believe when studied, you will find it is the grave of King Edwy, great-grandson of Alfred the Great."

Lucas growled. "You're King Edwy!"

The cameramen groaned and swore. "It's a nice little story and all, Sprague. Finding some beat-up old crown. But to drag us all out here?"

A British reporter took out his notepad. "The real story here is how Lucas Sprague turned from investigating loonies to becoming one himself. How about it, old fellow? Give us a few words? Yank reporter sees ghosts on Halloween!"

Edwy turned with guileless sincerity to Lucas. "Do you gentlemen know, this peculiar person has followed us all over Britain? I can't imagine that people take his stories about Dr. Reid seriously."

The British reporter sighed and shook his head. "From now on, they won't."

The curator sent his assistant into the Museum. "Young man, your find may be priceless, but the Queen's edict is clear. Ten thousand pounds upon donations of such magnitude."

Cara watched as the assistant appeared carrying a

package of cash. "You're giving him cash? Here, now?"

Edwy cast her a warning glance. "The Queen's edict, my dear. You're not questioning the curator's knowledge of priceless artifacts, are you?"

The curator huffed. "I know a genuine artifact when I see one."

Edwy smiled. "It's genuine. And it belongs to England." He took his cash doubtfully, as if wondering what use it would be when only minutes remained in his life.

Edwy reached for Cara's hand as the crowd dispersed. The reporters were following Sprague now, and the cameramen took a few parting shots of the fallen reporter before packing their gear.

Malcolm watched them leave, a grin on his face. "I'll almost miss the young fellow. Almost."

Tears dripped down Cara's cheeks. She kissed Edwy's hand. "You are a brave man, and a great king. And I love you now, and for all time."

"As I love you." Edwy kissed her hand. "Let us walk, shall we? Through the park, perhaps."

The sun reached its lowest level, casting a final, cold light across London. Edwy and Cara started toward Hyde Park, but Malcolm stood watching.

An old beggar shuffled toward Edwy. Cara bit her lip impatiently. They didn't have time to talk. She fished around in her pocket for money to silence him, to spend just one more moment at Edwy's side.

Edwy noticed the old man, and he stopped. For a long moment, the old man held Edwy's shocked gaze. His held out his trembling hand. He wore tattered gloves, with his bent fingers exposed. His voice came cracked and broken, the product of a long and bitter life: "Forgive . . . and forget."

Chills vibrated through Cara's being, resonating through her soul. Edwy recoiled; his breath came short. All hatred, and all anger, and all loss glittered in his blue eyes. From the corner of her eye, Cara saw Malcolm waiting, expectant. As if he knew.

The souls of the past rose up into the present as the last sunlight faded into All Hallow's Eve. Spirits, Cara knew, did not dwell outside the living, but within.

Time held for Edwy's choice. Cara felt the dawning awareness in him. Slowly, as if he disbelieved his own action, Edwy placed the packet of money in the beggar's hand.

The beggar's pale blue eyes brightened, a crooked but genuine smile grew on his parched lips as his fingers closed tight around the money. "Thank you."

Edwy said nothing. He stared, wide-eyed, as the old beggar walked away. Cara touched Edwy's arm. "What is it? Who was that man?"

Edwy's shock faded, and his blue eyes burned with new wisdom. "I found Dunstan, after all."

"Dunstan . . ." Cara looked down at Edwy's feet, and saw a full shadow. A man's shadow. She gasped in shock. "Edwy, you have a shadow!"

Edwy saw his shadow and closed his eyes in silent prayer. "Thank you." He drew her ring from his finger, and he didn't disappear. He placed it back on her finger, and kissed her forehead. "Elfgiva, your husband has returned."

Malcolm joined them. "The most stubborn, proud Saxon boy who ever lived . . ."

Cara's understanding dawned. "Dad . . . You were the Druid!"

Malcolm nodded, and for the first time, Cara understood her father's deep wisdom, his eternal curiosity. "Never witnessed a fairer ending. The crown restored, not by ambition and pride, but by sacrifice. The way to victory, paved not by vengeance, but by forgiveness."

Edwy turned to Cara. "And love restored for its own sake, to what it was when I first saw your face."

Cara brushed away her tears. "Does that mean I'm pregnant?"

"If you're not, you will be." Edwy kissed her hand. "This time, love, we follow your dreams."

They flew first class from England, thanks to the Natural History Museum. Edwy's donation drew attention to Cara's qualifications, and her desire to form a naturalist habitat had finally come true. Edwy had accepted an offer to speak on early Saxon archaeology, a vocation he relished, since he could correct history's misconceptions.

They were happy. They were together, and life moved forward. Cara ate her last peanut and gazed at Edwy as he surveyed a map. "This portion is called 'New England.' Why is that?"

"Well, before the American Revolution, the United States was a British colony."

Edwy sat forward in his seat, indignant. "Revolution? What revolution?"

Suddenly, Cara wished she'd kept this facet of American history to herself. "Oh, it's nothing, really. The Americans didn't like British rule, so they declared their independence."

"Oh, did they?" Edwy huffed, then faced forward, his expression determined, sure. "We'll just see about that."

Cara started to argue, then stopped. With Edwy, life would never be dull again.

The mist settled over Lough Leane as twilight faded to night. Word had traveled across the Secret World: Malcolm Reid was in London writing his memoirs.

The Loch Ness Monster allowed just the tip of her head out of the water, opened one eye, and looked furtively around. No one in sight. She drew a deep breath of the sweet clean air, and sighed.

Alone at last.

Cat Magic
Lynda Trent

For Blue Lion and fond memories.

Chapter One

"So you see, it's a perfect solution if Rhiannon will come to live with us," Amaryllis Griffith said as she folded her hands in her lap.

"Perfect," her twin sister echoed. Even though the twins were now in their late seventies, Amethyst still dressed exactly like her sister. Even people who had known them all their lives confused them from time to time.

Shadow Dancer settled more comfortably on the sofa and gazed from one woman to the other. This was the best idea they had come up with in months.

"Wouldn't it be nice to have a young person about the house, sister?" Amethyst said with a pleased smile. "Especially Rhiannon. She's always been my favorite niece."

"Great-niece," Amaryllis corrected. "She's so like her grandmother. Now *there* was a talent."

"I do miss her," Amethyst said with a sigh. "Having Rhiannon around will be like having our dear sister back, almost."

"Do you suppose she will agree to come? She's only been out of college a short while."

"Yes, but she and that young man have ended their engagement. I wager she will be glad of a change of scenery. You know how she's always loved visiting here at Hallowmoon."

A small frown puckered Amaryllis's forehead. "I wonder if she's come to terms with her talent yet."

"All the more reason for her to come here. We can teach her to use it. It's nothing to fear if one knows how to handle it. She reminds me of our own grandmother, the other Rhiannon." Her blue eyes grew dreamy. "I sometimes wonder if she could be Granny reincarnated. That would explain so many things, like the way things have moved around her. Remember when she was five? My teapot flew across the room almost every morning. I became very skilled at intercepting it."

"I remember. Her papa told her it was on wires or some such nonsense. Imagine thinking that Rhiannon would be afraid of her talent."

"It's not poor Arthur's fault. He only inherited the tiniest bit of the gift." She turned back to Shadow Dancer. "If you would give us a little help on this, we would appreciate it."

Shadow Dancer blinked his golden eyes and stood, stretched, and jumped off the couch. Sunlight from the window glistened in his black hair. He walked purposefully across the room, nudged his way out the screen door, and went onto the porch.

"Will he do it, do you think?" Amaryllis asked as

she watched the cat jump effortlessly onto one of the pedestals that flanked the front steps.

"He seemed to be considering it. Such a pity we haven't been able to learn his language or he ours. Still, he so rarely lets us down. He's always liked Rhiannon. I'm sure he will help bring her here. We should write a letter, too, and invite her."

"Of course. That would be the polite thing to do." Amaryllis got carefully to her feet. With winter approaching, her knees were creaky at times. "I'll go fetch the stationery."

"Thank you, sister. I'll find a pen and we'll write her right away. The sooner done, the better."

The elderly sisters soon sat with their gray heads together over the writing desk and composed a letter inviting their great-niece, Rhiannon Griffith, for an extended visit. They made it clear that if she liked, she could move in with them permanently and make Hallowmoon her home.

Rhiannon got the letter, read it, then read it again more slowly. Somehow her aunts had gotten word of her breaking her engagement with Rick Morris. She shook her head in amused tolerance. The way news spread in her family was amazing. She didn't remember having told any of them that her wedding was off.

The invitation couldn't have come at a better time. Every street in Longview, Texas, reminded her of happier days. She and Rick had planned to live here forever. He taught at the high school just as her parents had and they had been interested in a house not far from the neighborhood where she had lived all her life. Longview wasn't a small town, but she seemed to run into Rick and his new girlfriend everywhere she went. All her friends still saw him as well, and she knew they felt awkward with the situation. Getting away for a while would be a welcome change.

Since getting her master's degree in anthropology, Rhiannon hadn't yet begun to work. Her grandmother and her parents had left her a sizable fortune, and she didn't need the money. After she and Rick were married, she had intended to stay home and raise their children before embarking on her own career. Now all that was over. She sat down and answered her aunts' letter, accepting their invitation and saying she could come right away.

Thinking of Hallowmoon with its acres of woodlands and grassy meadows and huge oak trees dripping with moss was like a balm to her soul. Her relatives had always lived in the small town of Cypress, Louisiana. Hallowmoon had been built by the first of the Griffith clan and was a lovely plantation-style house, though there was no record in the family of it ever having been an actual plantation, since there were no fields to work and there had been no slaves. Then as now, the family fortune seemed to materialize of its own accord. The Griffiths had always been lucky in both love and money.

As she packed and made the necessary arrangements to leave her apartment for an extended period of time, she had her first doubts about going to Hallowmoon. Although she loved her aunts, they were hinting that she should move in with them permanently. She wasn't so sure she wanted to do that. No, she corrected herself, she was positive of it. She no longer knew anyone in Cypress except them and she didn't want to live their reclusive life forever. No, this was only to be a visit. Not a permanent move.

She arrived by noon on the day she had promised to be there. When she rolled to a stop in the curving drive, she saw her aunts waiting for her on the porch. Rhiannon glanced back down the drive. The road was hidden by the thick trees but somehow at every visit the sisters were waiting on the porch before the car arrived.

"There you are, right on time," Amaryllis said as she came down the steps. "How good to see you, dear."

"My goodness, you're more beautiful than ever," Amethyst said, her voice perfectly matching her sister's. "What lovely dark hair you have! Doesn't she, sister? It's the image of Granny's. She has the family's blue eyes, too."

Amaryllis nodded happily. "You could pass for her twin."

Rhiannon smiled. "Then I guess it's a good thing I was named for her and not someone else."

"Oh, no, dear. That was no accident." Amethyst took her hand and drew her toward the house. "Here's Shadow Dancer now, come to welcome you."

Rhiannon bent to pick up the cat and cuddle him close. "I think he's even larger than he was on my last visit." She ruffled her fingers through his thick black hair. "He's such a beautiful cat. I've always loved him." A thought flickered through her mind and she frowned at him. "How old is he, anyway? I don't remember a time when he wasn't here."

Amethyst laughed as if she had said something funny. "I forget. We're all of us old here, I guess."

"That's why we thought you might come here to live.

We're getting on in years, you know. Can't live forever.''

Amethyst frowned at her sister. "Can't you let her get into the house before you spring that on her?"

Amaryllis drew up to her full height which was less than five feet. "I was only making conversation. She knows why we asked her to come."

They went up the porch steps. Rhiannon breathed in the clean aroma of autumn woods. Smoke from the fireplace curled about the house and made her think of jack-o-lanterns and harvest moons. As they crossed the deep porch, she said, "Actually, I don't. I thought this was only a visit." She stroked Shadow Dancer who was purring loudly.

"It is, dear, but you know Hallowmoon will belong to you some day." Amaryllis opened the screen door and they went inside. A swirl of red and gold leaves tried to follow them.

"I don't know what to say. I never considered that you would leave it to me. Not that you will have reason to leave it to anyone for a long time yet," she quickly added.

"Oh?" Amaryllis said with interest. "Have you seen that for certain?"

"I think she's only being polite," Amethyst replied. "The point is, Rhiannon, you're the logical one to leave it to. You have the Gift."

Rhiannon looked from one to the other. Then she laughed. "Please, Aunt Amethyst. You know I don't believe in that."

The twins exchanged a look. "I'm afraid it's real, whether you believe in it or not," Amethyst said.

"We've always encouraged you to develop it," her

sister added. "It's not like it's a new idea to you."

Rhiannon put down the cat, who strolled over to lie on the warm hearth. Flames snapped in the burning logs only inches away. "Isn't he lying awfully close to the fire? Should I put the screen in place?"

"Shadow Dancer is fine," Amaryllis said. "Like us, he enjoys warmth on a chilly day. Don't change the subject, now. It's high time you learned to use the talent you've been given. We're the last of the line who can teach you. None of the others inherited as much of the Gift as you have and they wouldn't know where to start in training you to use it."

"I don't want to use it." Rhiannon had had this argument with her aunts all her life. "I don't believe in psychic phenomenon."

"Why on earth not?" Amethyst asked in astonishment. "Everyone in the family has had at least a smattering of it, even your father, rest his soul."

Amaryllis nodded. "He was able to call money to him, even if he couldn't do anything else."

Rhiannon wasn't sure how to answer. She didn't want to argue with her aunts, especially not within minutes of arriving, but she could see they weren't going to drop the subject. "Dad was good at investing. He and Mom were as down to earth as any couple I've ever seen. I'm positive he didn't believe in the Gift."

"All the same he had it. Everyone in our family does."

"You have to learn to use your talent, because it's so much stronger than usual. It's like a force or an energy. It can be used negatively as well as correctly and it's up to the family elders to impart our knowledge to you young people."

"We worry that you'll put off learning to use it until we're gone and can't teach you," Amaryllis said. "You have certain responsibilities, you know."

"Responsibilities?" Rhiannon asked warily.

"Why, to the town, of course," Amethyst said, as if that was obvious. "We take care of it. Always have."

"I don't understand."

"It's very simple, dear." Amaryllis paused to pour them each a cup of steaming tea from the tray balanced on the marble-topped table. "When the very first Griffith came to Louisiana there was no town. He built Hallow-moon, and Cypress grew up beside it. We're responsible for the welfare of the town."

"You mean you make donations to the charities here. I can do that."

"Oh, no, dear, she means we cast spells on it." Amethyst leaned forward to pass a plate of tea cakes to Rhiannon. "Have one. I made them myself this morning. I believe they may still be warm."

"I think we're going too fast," Amethyst said. "You know how we tend to rush into things. Why, Rhiannon hasn't even brought her bags in from the car and here we are schooling her in Wiccan One-oh-one!" She laughed and lifted the teacup to her lips. "Sorry, dear. I suppose it's because we're so eager to teach you. There's plenty of time to go into all this later." She glanced over at the cat and winked at him.

Rhiannon saw Shadow Dancer wink back before easing closer to the fire. She shook her head as she laughed. "I must be more tired from the trip than I thought. We can talk about this later." She hoped by then her aunts would have forgotten the subject. Although she knew her aunts and many of her cousins practiced what they referred to as the Old Ways, she hadn't been aware that they might expect her to do the same.

Magic, real magic, was a fable in a storybook, not something that one could use in everyday life. The Burning Times, as her family referred to the years when witches were killed along with assorted others accused of heresy, was an unfortunate chapter in history. Psychic phenomena, if they existed at all, had nothing to do with a religion or system of beliefs.

The things that had happened around her all her life had a logical explanation. At times it was difficult to come up with the reason why books slid across tables to her or flowers bloomed out of season if she tended them or why people called when she needed to talk to them, but there was an explanation if she thought about it long enough. And coincidences happened. To everyone.

That night she went to the bedroom she remembered so well from her childhood. The rest of the evening had been perfectly normal and comfortably pleasant, with no talk of spells or inheritances. The sisters had caught her up on all the family gossip and what was going on in Cypress and which of her childhood friends had married whom. Rhiannon had discovered more of her old friends lived in town than she had assumed would still be there.

Her room was still papered in the roses and violets she had chosen one summer as a teenager. She remembered how pleased she had been when her aunts let her pick the wallpaper and the pale lilac paint for the wood trim. The bed even had the lilac chenille spread to snuggle under. It smelled as fresh as the breezes that filled the house in the warmer months. Although she had never lived in Hallowmoon, Rhiannon felt the house was a part of her. This room had been her grandmother's as a girl, and her great-grandmother's before her, reaching back through generations. In many ways Hallowmoon was more her home than the house in which she had grown up back in Longview.

And they said someday it would be her's.

Rhiannon snuggled deeper in the soft mound of sheet and quilts. She refused to think of the inevitable day when her aunts would be gone. As with Hallowmoon, she couldn't imagine them not being in her life.

"I can't tell you how glad we are that you've come to stay with us for a while," Amaryllis said as she painted the handle of her new broom black.

"We've missed you." Amethyst looked up from the door wreath she was decorating with red and gold silk leaves and small black cats. "Aren't these darling? I think they look like Shadow Dancer, don't you?"

Rhiannon leaned closer and nodded. "They even have his golden eyes." To her, all black cats looked pretty much alike, but she knew how fond her aunts were of their pet. She sat at the breakfast table after pouring herself a cup of herb tea. Shadow Dancer jumped into her lap and settled down as if he belonged there.

"I remember when I first felt the 'Charge.' Do you, sister?" Amaryllis stopped painting and gazed dreamily out the window. "We were in the meadow and it was a lovely full moon. After that, I had no doubt of my path in life."

"Of course I remember. I felt it myself less than a week later during the Yule ceremony. I've always loved the Christmas season. All that holly and greenery and candles. I believe people smile more at Yuletide." Amethyst smiled at Rhiannon. "Have you felt it yet?"

306

"No. Not yet. Or if I have, I didn't recognize it." She stroked the cat, and he responded by purring and going completely limp in her lap.

The sisters exchanged a smile. "When it happens, you'll know. It comes to all of us sooner or later." Amaryllis stood the broom in a corner to dry. "We always get a new broom at Samhain—or Halloween, as you probably call it. It's the beginning of our new year, you see. We decorate it early in the month and put it on the porch until Samhain, then we bring it inside and take out the old one and burn it."

"It's a way of beginning anew. When you finish your tea, would you like to help decorate?"

Rhiannon nodded. "I love this time of year, the smell of leaves burning and seeing the woods wearing scarlet and gold. I like the touch of cold in the air."

"We'll carve some pumpkins, too. The market always has some lovely ones. Maybe you'd like to drive into town and pick out several." Amethyst put her head to one side to view the wreath. "It needs something. Maybe some pinecones?"

"I'll gather some for you," Rhiannon volunteered. She knew it was difficult for her aunts to get about in the woods once the cool weather set in.

"Go to the meadow. The best ones are there." Amethyst didn't need to tell her which meadow she meant. They had taken Rhiannon there since she was a toddler.

"I put in a call to the law office," Amaryllis said as she put away the can of paint. "Mr. Hagar wasn't in and Mr. Phillips is out sick. That nice Mr. Rawlson will probably be the one to come out. Did you know they've taken on a new lawyer? Chad Dawson is his name."

"Dawson," Amethyst said thoughtfully. "Is he the Dawson boy whose father has the drugstore?"

"I believe so."

"He's awfully young. I hope Mr. Rawlson comes instead of him. We don't want just anyone doing our legal work."

"Why do you need a lawyer?" Rhiannon asked.

"We want to make out our wills, dear," Amaryllis explained. "We aren't getting any younger, and we want to be certain our things are disposed of properly. It's the reason we invited you here."

"I don't understand."

"Don't you remember last night when you arrived, we told you we have to take care of the town? Of Cypress?" Amethyst snipped the orange ribbon that held the last tiny cat to the wreath.

"As our heir, it's your duty. We could get Cousin Gretchen, of course, but she has her own town to consider, and you're much more talented than she is."

"Gretchen means well, but she's too much like her poor mother. Addle-brained." Amaryllis started taking orange and black candles from the cabinet and fitting them into holders of all sizes and shapes.

"Aunt Amethyst, I don't have the vaguest idea how to cast a spell."

"I know. We're going to teach you."

"I don't believe in spells. It's completely illogical."

Amethyst pursed her lips thoughtfully. "We could prove it to you, I suppose." She took the cat from Rhiannon's lap and held it so their eyes would meet. "What do you think, Shadow Dancer? Should we prove it to her?"

Rhiannon looked on in amusement. Her aunts' slightly

wacky ways were endearing to her. The cat meowed softly. "I'll tell you what. If you can make me fall deeply and truly in love by Halloween, I'll believe in your witchcraft. If not, you have to let the matter drop and we'll just enjoy my visit. Agreed?"

"Well," Amethyst said hesitantly. "What do you think, sister?"

"I suppose we could do that. The one stipulation is that none be harmed, Rhiannon. You can't ask us to put the spell on anyone in particular, like Rick Morris, for instance."

"I don't want Rick back." She looked out the window, where a playful breeze was lifting and tossing leaves over the yard. "But it's because of Rick that I know you won't be able to work a love spell on me. It's going to be a long time before I want to love anyone. I don't have a great deal of faith in love right now."

"Yes," Amethyst said decisively. "In that case, the test is a perfect one. We'll have you in love by Samhain."

Rhiannon felt the too-familiar twist of pain near her heart. "Give it your best shot. I can make it even more challenging." She took a square of notepaper and wrote "Crystal butterfly" on it, then folded it and put it in her pocket without letting her aunts read it. "If a man gives me this object on Halloween, I'll believe you can do what you say you can do."

"All right," Amaryllis said. She washed her hands and said, to her sister, "We had better get right on it. Samhain is only weeks away. Come along, Shadow Dancer. We'll need you for this."

Rhiannon watched in amusement as her aunts, led by the cat, left the kitchen and went upstairs. She loved them dearly but hadn't the slightest belief that they could work magic. In a way she felt guilty for testing a practice that she knew had no chance of working, but she didn't want to hurt their feelings by refusing to learn spells during her visit.

But a part of her—the part that had been too lonely and too unhappy since Rick found someone else—wanted her aunts to succeed.

"I don't want to go out there." Chad frowned at Ed Rawlson. "That house looks as if it comes into its own at Halloween."

Ed shook his head. "I can't go. I'm tied up in court this afternoon and the Griffith sisters don't like to be kept waiting."

"Why can't they come to the office like everyone else? We don't make house calls."

"To them, we do. Hagar has some connection with the family, and there are standing orders that we go to them, not the other way around. They are nice old ladies. If I wasn't busy, I'd go myself. You won't leave hungry, I can promise you that. Sometimes I think they dream up reasons to have us come out just so they can give us cookies and cakes." He smiled at the memory of past visits. "Go ahead. It won't take long to humor them."

Chad looked at his cluttered desk. "I'm knee-deep in work myself." He sighed at the inevitable. "When I was a boy, I was convinced that house was haunted. I remember being amazed when I found out someone lives in it."

"They've been there for as long as any of us can remember. But they've done a lot for this town. While they may be a little nutty, they're generous to a fault. They're expecting you in an hour.''

Chad bit back his grumbling and nodded. ''Okay. I'll go. But it means I'll be behind on the Whittaker case.''

Ed grinned at him. ''Give the sisters my best.''

When Chad arrived at Hallowmoon, he parked in the drive and started for the steps. A huge black cat was waiting for him on the porch and gazing at him intently. Chad had always loved animals, and as he stepped around the cat, he paused to pet him. The cat got up and trotted around the corner of the porch.

He knocked on the door and waited for someone to open it. In spite of his reluctance to come out here, he was curious about the house and the elderly twins who had lived in it all their lives. They were Cypress's leading eccentrics and were fascinating in their own right. Although he had known them by sight for years, he still couldn't tell one from the other.

The door opened and he found himself staring into the silvery blue eyes of the most beautiful woman he had ever seen. For a moment he couldn't speak.

''Yes?'' she prompted.

''I'm Chad Dawson.'' He blinked and tried to recover his equilibrium. ''I'm with Hagar, Phillips and Rawlson.''

''Come in. My aunts are expecting you.'' She opened the screen door and held it for him. Without the haze of the screen between them she was even more beautiful.

Chad tried to stop staring at her and stepped into the Victorian elegance of the entryway. The walls were polished oak and there were several pots of ivy, fern, and other greenery about the room. A graceful stairway curved up the side and back walls. Brilliant colors from

311

a stained-glass window on the landing splashed over the entry.

He followed the woman into the front parlor. Like the entry, it was Victorian, but luxurious rather than fussy. It was easy to tell the furniture was not only antique but of superior quality. The Griffith sisters sat waiting primly, as if they had expected him at that exact moment. Both smiled their identical smiles when he entered the room.

"Hello," he said. "I'm Chad Dawson from the law firm. Ed Rawlson said for me to tell you he's sorry he couldn't come himself but he's tied up in court."

One of the sisters glanced from him to the young woman and back again. "Did you meet our niece, Rhiannon Griffith? She's here to stay with us."

"For a visit," Rhiannon amended. Her eyes met his. "I'm glad to meet you."

"Yes." He couldn't look away from her level gaze. "Glad to meet you."

Amaryllis looked at Amethyst and they exchanged a pleased smile. "Well," Amaryllis said as she got to her feet. "I believe I need some help in the kitchen, sister."

"I'll help you," Rhiannon said quickly.

"No, no, dear. You stay in here and keep Mr. Dawson company. We won't be but a minute." The sisters left the room with their heads together, whispering between themselves.

Rhiannon frowned. They weren't being terribly subtle. She glanced across at Chad. He seemed to be about her age and looked as if he had played football in college, judging by his height and broad shoulders. Intelligence lit his eyes and he looked as if he laughed often. She had no idea what to say to the man.

"You're visiting here? From where?"

"Longview, Texas. My aunts seem to think I'm moving to Cypress, but that's not the case."

"Too bad." He caught himself and added, "It's obvious they care about you a great deal."

"We've always been close." She listened to the grandfather clock tick several beats. "I'll go see what is keeping them." She hurried across the room and out the door.

In the kitchen she found her aunts taking their time about arranging a silver tray of cookies and fried pies. They seemed surprised to see her.

Trying to keep her voice to a whisper, Rhiannon said, "This is dirty pool, inviting a good-looking young man out here on the pretext of drawing up your wills. This is matchmaking, not magic!"

"We didn't plan this," Amaryllis objected. "We haven't seen the Dawson boy in years. We had no way of knowing he'd grown into such a fine young man."

"Handsome, really," Amethyst added. "I think he's very handsome. Don't you, sister?"

"I don't want you to throw me at every eligible man in town just to win our bet. That's not fair."

"We didn't do that," Amaryllis said. "We called the law office before the wager was made. Don't you remember, dear?"

Rhiannon frowned. Now that she thought about it, she did recall her aunts were talking about having a lawyer come out. The subject of spells had come up later.

"Now you go back in there and be nice to him while we finish up in here. It's hardly polite to leave him sitting in there alone."

"All right. But don't be long." She saw the sisters

exchange a conspiratorial glance and smile. They might not have planned it this way, but they weren't above using it to their advantage.

Chad was walking about the parlor, studying the myriad photographs in silver and gold frames that stood everywhere. When she came into the room, he straightened and said, "This is a photo of your aunts with President Carter." He couldn't keep the surprise out of his voice.

"Yes, I know. They don't get around much these days. I don't think they've been to Washington since Reagan was in office."

"Your aunts move in circles I didn't expect."

If only you knew, she thought as she wondered what sort of spell her aunts had worked the other night. "One of my cousins is Senator Olsen. Through him they've met several presidents." Until she explained it to him, she had never questioned how unusual that was for two elderly women who had lived in Cypress, Louisiana, all their lives.

"You have a surprising family," he said, as if he had followed her chain of thought.

"That's not the half of it." She didn't elaborate but moved to his side. "I used to spend hours in this room, looking at the photos and all the memorabilia. My family is made up of pack rats. Over there we have Uncle Harry's collection of sand dollars, that case against the wall holds my cousin Emily's meteorite collection. Grandpa collected St. Cuthbert's beads when he was a boy visiting in England. They're small stones with a natural hole in the center. They wash up on Holy Island," she explained.

"What do you collect?"

She looked up at him and found his hazel eyes mesmerizing. "Nothing. I'm not that interesting."

He shook his head. "I think you may be the most interesting of all."

She opened her mouth to ask what he meant by that and to put him firmly in his place, but he moved away.

"What are these? Dolls?" He was peering in a glass case where a number of small figures were arranged.

"Those are members of my family." The explanation came out before she had time to examine it. "I mean, they represent family members. They're like photos, sort of." She had seen the figures for so long, she had forgotten they were still there.

"I've never seen anything like these."

"No, I don't think you probably have," she admitted. The figures were poppets made by several generations of women, representing their contemporary in the family who possessed the greatest Gift. They were regarded, by those who believed, as protective spirits who still watched over the family. The most recent ones were of her aunts in their youth, when their hair was still glossy black and their skin unwrinkled. They wore identical green dresses trimmed in ivory lace and feathers.

She was glad when Chad moved away from the case to look at the pieces of meteorite collected by her cousin Emily.

"You know," he said when their eyes met over the meteorites, "I have the oddest feeling of knowing you. Yet I'm positive we've never met. I certainly would have remembered you."

"We've never met. I guess I just resemble someone you know." But as she gazed into his eyes, she had the same strange sensation. It was as if she could almost recall his name and it wasn't the one he had now. She shook her head to pull her thoughts back in line. "I would have remembered you." Then she recalled that he had just said that about her.

She was relieved when her aunts returned to the room and started serving cookies and fried pies and herbal tea to Chad. Rhiannon could watch him unobserved while he discussed legal business with her aunts. She thought he was unaware of her interest until he stopped in mid-sentence and looked at her.

"What did you say?" he asked.

"Nothing. I didn't say a word."

He frowned slightly. "Funny. I could have sworn you did."

She tried to keep her attention on the cranberry-pink tea in her cup. She was far too aware of every move he made. His voice was a pitch that warmed something deep inside her. She could all too easily imagine that voice murmuring words of love in her ear. His large, capable hands would know exactly how to touch her.

Embarrassed, she put her teacup on the table. Where had those thoughts come from? It wasn't her style to have fantasies about men she had just met. Not even ones who were as sexy as Chad Dawson. She found herself staring at him and forced herself to look away.

All too soon the meeting was over. She walked him to the door while her aunts cleared away the tea tray. At the door he turned and their bodies almost touched. Rhiannon felt it all the way through her and her lips parted in surprise. It was almost as if he had caressed her. Yet he hadn't so much as touched her hand.

He hesitated, as if he was as reluctant to leave as she was to see him go. "Is it all right if I call you?"

"Sure," she heard herself saying. "Call me."

His eyes gazed deep into hers and her world altered. She heard seagulls calling as if in a dream and had the sense of being on a high cliff overlooking a storm-tossed sea. There was an urgent poignancy about the moment, as if they were lovers who knew they might never meet again. Then the image faded and she was herself again, standing on a porch in Cypress, Louisiana. "Good-bye," she said.

"Good-bye. I'll call you." And he was gone.

Chapter Two

Behind Hallowmoon was a log cabin that had always been a favorite place for Rhiannon. It had been built as a temporary residence by the first Griffith to come to Louisiana and had been lived in until the grand house could be built. Since then the cabin had been used as a workshop for the generation of the family currently in residence. Amaryllis and Amethyst used it to concoct their potions and amulets. Rhiannon used it as a place to make her divas and angels.

Since she was a child, Rhiannon had been making the small figures and dressing them in snippets of cloth. Her hobby fit perfectly with her field of anthropology. The figures looked as if they would be at home in an ancient civilization. Her aunts called them her poppets and encouraged her to make them, even if she had always insisted they contained no magic at all. The aunts kept a quantity of feathers, dried herbs, and swatches of cloth on hand for her visits, and she had always done her best work in the cabin.

Her aunts attributed it to the fact that her family was filled with Wiccans, shamans and soothsayers who had made poppets along with amulets, talismans, and dozens of other items to work their magic. Rhiannon let them believe as they chose.

Recently she had started selling the figures through a store owned by a friend in Longview, simply because her apartment was filling to the brim with the little people. Their success had been amazing and she had been approached by a national company to sell them through their chain. She considered herself lucky to be able to earn money from something she found so enjoyable.

She was hard at work when she looked up to find Amaryllis beside her. "Oh! I didn't hear you come in," she exclaimed.

"I'm sorry to startle you, dear. I thought you heard me call your name."

"You called me?" Rhiannon frowned. While she often lost herself in concentration, she hadn't been aware that her attention could be so focused as to exclude someone calling to her.

"Sister and I were wondering if you would do us a favor. Shadow Dancer seems to be lost. Would you mind searching for him?"

"Lost?" Rhiannon put aside the poppet and stood. "How could he get lost? He's lived at Hallowmoon all his life."

"I know, but we can't find him anywhere and he isn't coming to our call. Would you look for him?"

Rhiannon smiled down at her aunt. "Of course I will."

319

Amaryllis's face lit up with a smile. "You're a good girl. You always have been. Just look in the woods. I'm certain you'll find him."

Rhiannon left the cabin and headed for the back of the property. Soon the forest completely surrounded her. She knew the woods well, having played in them since she was a child, but it had been years since she was alone there. The acres surrounding the house were hilly, with an abundance of trees and bushes. Over the years the family had planted trees, shrubbery, and bulbs that weren't indigenous to the area in celebration of weddings, births, and other important events, so a walk through Hallowmoon's woods was full of surprises.

As she walked, she called to Shadow Dancer but didn't see the cat anywhere. Like a dog, he always came when his name was called, and she was mystified as to where he could be. She only hoped he hadn't met with an unfortunate end. Her aunts were devoted to the cat and his loss would be a blow to them.

Back at the house, Chad was arriving. Although they hadn't set a date, he had felt compelled to see Rhiannon again. "I'm sorry to drop in without calling," he said to the sisters, "but I happened to be driving this way and . . . well, I turned into your drive. If this is an inconvenient time, I can come back another day."

"No, no," Amethyst said as she patted his arm. "We thought you might come by today. Rhiannon will be glad to see you, I'm sure."

"She's in the woods," Amaryllis added. "Looking for Shadow Dancer."

"Who? Is that the cat?"

"He seems to have misplaced himself," Amethyst said. "He does that from time to time."

Cat Magic

"You can help her look." Amaryllis led him through the house to the back door. "Just go across the yard there and into the trees. Keep going and I'm positive you'll find her. And the cat."

Chad was ushered onto the back porch and heard the door click behind him before he had a chance to suggest that he wait for her to return. He couldn't help but chuckle at the lack of subtlety in the aunts' ploy to get him alone with Rhiannon. He had owned pets all his life and he had never heard of a cat getting lost on its own property. At least, he thought, he had changed from his suit to jeans before coming out.

The woods were beautiful. Although they weren't landscaped, the grounds seemed to have been mowed to keep vines and brambles from taking over the underbrush. The woods were in a semi-wild state, but walking through them was easy.

He came to a stream and paused on the mossy bridge to look down into the water. His reflection gazed back at him, blue and green in the wavering water. The trees over his head were filled with calling birds. He couldn't remember when he had heard so many of them singing at once, especially in autumn. In the trees beyond the bridge, he saw a deer. It stared back at him, then trotted away, but it didn't seem the least afraid of him.

Chad crossed the bridge and walked farther into the woods. He was no expert on horticulture, but many of the bushes beneath the trees were the sort that were usually found on lawns, not deep in the forest. Several crimson trees with delicately fingered leaves looked Oriental, and he saw a number of others he couldn't identify at all.

He found Rhiannon in a clearing thick with knee-high

scarlet flowers his mother called skyrocket lilies because of the shape of their blooms. He called to her and she turned to look at him as a breeze billowed her long black hair about her shoulders to her waist. She smiled and he felt his world spin.

"I didn't know you were coming out today. My aunts must have forgotten to mention it."

"I dropped by." He came nearer. She was taller than he remembered and the sunlight put russet highlights in her hair. Her skin seemed to glow with health. "To see you," he added without realizing he was going to say it aloud.

She looked pleased but didn't comment. "I'm looking for Shadow Dancer. Will you help me?"

"I never heard of a cat getting lost before."

"Neither have I. And it's not like he's new to the area. My aunts have had him forever, it seems to me. He must be ancient in cat years."

"I thought that was just an excuse to let us talk together."

"That sounds like something they would do, but Aunt Amaryllis sent me out to look for him before you came. We'll have to give them the benefit of the doubt this time." She turned and whistled. "Shadow Dancer! Come here!" To Chad she said, "I've called until I'm blue in the face and there's no sign of him."

"Since when does a cat come when you whistle and call his name?"

"Shadow Dancer does. He's not an ordinary cat." The admission made her frown slightly.

Chad walked through the scarlet flowers and called to the cat. "There's a path over here."

"Let's follow it. Maybe he went that way."

They went back in the coolness of the trees and down the sloping path to where another stream trickled over amber dirt. A series of flat stones made a convenient walkway. On the other side the ground rolled up toward a patch of sunlight. Chad reached the meadow first.

It was almost perfectly round and the grasses were gold and silky in the autumn breezes. In the center of the meadow was a stone circle that held the remains of old fires.

Chad went to the circle and looked at it, then stared around. "Why would anyone come way out here to build a fire?"

Rhiannon hesitated, then exclaimed, "There you are, you naughty cat! What do you mean giving everyone a scare like that?"

Shadow Dancer trotted up to her and let her pick him up.

"Rhiannon? Why would anyone build a fire here?" Chad repeated.

"Wiener roast?" she asked, watching him carefully.

"This far from the house?"

"My family has always been eccentric."

"Did you know it was here?"

"Of course. I know every inch of these woods. My aunts and cousins used to come here often. Especially my aunts." She cuddled the cat under her chin and went to Chad. "On moonlit summer nights, the moon rises between those large magnolias over there." She smiled at the memory of the happy summer solstices spent in this place.

She knelt in the grasses. "Those of us who were children used to sit here while the moon rose high above us and the fire snapped and sang and the grown-ups told us stories about fairies and wood sprites. On the way back to the house, all of us pretended to see them hiding behind the bushes and trees.'' Her smile was soft at the memory.

"That sounds like a nice way to spend the evening. We had bonfires, too, but only on cold nights.''

"My family has fires in every season.'' She wasn't about to explain to him that the fires were a part of an ancient celebration.

"I wish I had known you as a child. It's surprising we didn't meet, since Cypress isn't that large.''

"I often spent the summer here, but there was so much to do at Hallowmoon I seldom went into town. I loved riding the horses my aunts used to keep and playing in the barn with my cousins. There always seemed to be at least two or three visiting here whenever I came. My family has always been close, even though we don't all live near here.''

"I envy you. I was an only child. I have a few cousins, but I barely know them. My parents still live here.''

"I lost mine a few years ago. Mom died in a car wreck, and it was as if Dad just gave up. A few months later he had a heart attack and died. Aunt Amaryllis said it was because they were soul mates and each couldn't bear to be without the other.''

"Do you believe in that? In soul mates?''

"I don't know. My parents didn't. Not the way my aunt meant it. But they were in love and I couldn't imagine one of them without the other. They always seemed to be together and to prefer it that way. I was grown and away at college, so it wasn't as if Dad needed to stay around for me. I think he's happier now.''

Chad studied her face, then sat down in the grass be-

324

side her. He stroked the cat in her lap. When their fingers touched, Rhiannon felt the sensation tingle up her arm.

"Do you believe in soul mates? In two people who are meant to be together, come what may?" she asked.

"I don't know. My parents aren't, though they will never divorce. I'm not sure I've ever seen any couple who was that happy together." The sunlight was golden in his hair and lit amber flecks in his eyes.

"It's why my aunts never married. I've been told the story all my life. They had more than their share of suitors, but none of them was their soul mate. Rather than risk having unhappy marriages, they decided to remain single. It must not have been an easy decision back in their day."

"Do you intend to stay single?" His voice was caressing, though he hadn't moved any closer.

"I don't know. I was engaged. I loved him and I thought he loved me, but he found someone else. Aunt Amethyst says that's proof he wasn't meant for me. She said my soul mate is out there somewhere and he will be as true to me as the sunrise." She shook her head. "I'm not sure I believe it. These days life is more complicated than it was when they were young. And there are a lot more people in the world. Even if there is one man meant for me, I might never find him."

"You have a good point." He smiled, his eyes on her lips.

"Aunt Amaryllis would say I couldn't help but find him, that it's set up that way."

"Maybe it is."

She gazed into his eyes, and the breeze urged her to lean toward him. Chad met her halfway and they kissed. His lips were warm on hers and her heart skipped a beat.

Rhiannon's breath caught in her throat. Instead of pulling back, she leaned closer.

Chad's arms went about her and she embraced him in return. The meadow seemed to dip and spin beneath her, and fire rushed through her veins. No kiss had ever affected her like this. She was dizzy and languorous, yet at the same time she wanted more. So much more.

As if both suddenly realized what they were doing, they sat back. Rhiannon opened her eyes to see Shadow Dancer sitting in her lap and regarding her thoughtfully. She couldn't look at Chad. "I'm sorry," she stammered. "I don't usually kiss people in meadows."

"I'm glad you made an exception in my case."

"You don't understand. I just broke up with my fiancé a few weeks ago. The last thing I want is another relationship. Not now. Maybe not ever."

"I feel the same way. I don't have an ex-fiancée hiding in the closet, but I'm just getting started on my career. I have to spend too many nights working to have a relationship with anyone. On the other hand, you're only visiting here. You won't be here forever. We couldn't have a relationship, even if we wanted one."

"That's right. We couldn't," she said firmly, as if she was trying to convince them both. "Besides, I'm an anthropologist. I intend to go on a dig next summer. I'm being financed by a Dallas museum and will be living in a tent on the upper Nile in a few months. I don't have time for anything permanent."

"You had a fiancé," he reminded her.

"But it was a mistake. No, I'm not looking for a commitment. Not at all."

"Neither am I. We seem perfect for each other."

Rhiannon looked at him. Amusement was sparkling

in his eyes and the breeze ruffled his hair. In his fisherman knit sweater and jeans he looked more relaxed and even sexier than he had in the suit he wore when she first met him. She had never seen any man who was more desirable.

He lifted his hand and stroked her long hair back from her face. She knew she should get to her feet and break the golden web of intimacy that was spinning between them, but she couldn't force herself to move. His hand laced in her hair and was warm against her cheek. He cupped her face before leaning over to kiss her again. This time Shadow Dancer jumped from her lap.

Chad lay her back in the soft grass. When he lifted his head, she looked at his face against the blue of the sky. Again she had the sensation that she had known him before in other circumstances and in another place. Was it a trick of the sunlight, or did his hair seem longer and more golden for a moment, and was his sweater replaced for an instant with chain mail?

Chad kissed her again, this time with more passion. Rhiannon found herself unable to think of anything but loving him. Of giving herself up to his love in return. Loving? She stirred against him and he pulled away.

She sat up, confused and breathless. "I . . . I can't . . ." She couldn't finish the sentence. She shouldn't say she couldn't love him when the word had never been spoken. If she stayed where she was, more might happen than either of them intended.

Across from her, Shadow Dancer sat on the ring of stones, watching them. Rhiannon got to her feet and picked him up. He meowed in protest.

Chad stood and looked around as if he, too, was surprised at what had almost happened between them. "I guess we had better get back to the house. Your aunts are worried about the cat. They should know we found him.''

"Yes. I was about to suggest that.'' She refused to look at him. Shadow Dancer made a rumbling sound that wasn't exactly a growl but told her of his displeasure. Rhiannon told herself it was foolish to think a cat could care if she stopped kissing someone or not.

"This place has an odd affect on me,'' Chad said, almost as if to himself. ''I don't understand it.''

"It's magic,'' she said in a tight voice.

"Right,'' he said with a laugh. ''That must be it.'' He stepped closer to her and again tangled his hands in her hair. ''It must be magic.''

Shadow Dancer purred and patted playfully at her hair. Rhiannon regarded him without humor. No, she told herself, it wasn't possible. Whatever her aunts might think about him, he was only a cat. She led the way back into the woods and away from the meadow.

Sunset was beginning to color the western sky when they reached the house. Amaryllis and Amethyst were sitting on the porch, matching crocheted shawls about their shoulders.

"Look, sister,'' Amethyst said as they approached. ''They've found Shadow Dancer.''

Amaryllis took the cat from Rhiannon. ''You naughty rascal, running away like that.'' The cat blinked at her. ''Oh?'' She glanced at her sister with an I-told-you-so look. ''Well, let's go inside and let the young people talk, sister.''

Amethyst braced her palms on the arms of the wicker rocker and pushed herself to her feet. ''I do believe I'm tired. Perhaps we should call it a night.''

Rhiannon gave them an exasperated look. "We haven't had supper yet. Remember?"

"Oh, my stars and garters, you're right." Amethyst laughed at her forgetfulness. "That's what we'll do then. We'll put supper on the table. You'll stay with us, won't you, Mr. Dawson?"

"Please, call me Chad. No, I can't stay this time."

"Next time then." The sisters exchanged a smug smile and went indoors.

When the door shut, Rhiannon said, "They're outdoing themselves in matchmaking."

"I like that in an aunt," he replied with a smile.

"And they're so subtle," she added wryly. "I'm sorry, Chad. They've got it in their heads to throw us together. I know it must be embarrassing for you."

"No, on the contrary, I appreciate their efforts."

"I don't think that cat was really lost. It was just one of their ploys."

"But you were searching for him when I dropped by. How could they have planned that?"

Rhiannon didn't answer.

"You have an unusual name. I've never heard it before."

"I'm named for my grandmother, as well as for my great-great grandmother. In my family, when a baby is born, the elders of the family get together and decide who the baby reminds them of, and that's the name the baby is given. They say I'm the image of my grandmother. She died before I was born, of course."

"Why 'of course'? Both my grandmothers are still alive."

"That's the other part of the naming ceremony. The person you're named for has to be dead." She didn't point out that the elders chose the name through meditation and that the baby was assumed to be the reincarnation of the ancestor. "My parents didn't go along with the idea, but Dad loved his mother and when my aunts suggested I be named for her, he and Mom agreed."

"I never heard of a family where babies are named by anyone other than the parents."

"I suspect we're the only one. As I said, my family is unusually close. My cousins are like brothers and sisters to me. We visit as often as we can. I never felt like an only child."

"That's unusual in this day and age. Most families don't see that much of each other."

"I don't come from an ordinary family," she said with some misgiving. Because she hadn't taken an active part in the Wicca religion, she sometimes felt left out, even with all the closeness. Her parents had valued logic and reasoning, but she had seen how happy the others were with their celebrations and dancing and singing under the moon. More than once she had been tempted to toss logic aside and fit into the niche waiting for her.

Overhead the sky was turning to gold and scarlet. Purple clouds trailed like fingers across the vivid colors. To the east, the sky was a deep blue shading into the darker hues of night. Soon the moon would rise. "I love this time of day," she said as she leaned against the porch railing. "If I had my way, I'd live outside."

"You'd get pretty cold before morning."

"But it would be wonderful to sleep with the trees whispering overhead and wake up to dawn and bird's song. Unless it's freezing, I sleep with my window open so I can be as close to nature as I can."

"There's a strong pagan streak in you," he observed

with a smile as he came closer and put his arms around her.

"What?" she said sharply. "What did you say?"

"You love nature. I can picture you dancing under the moon, barefoot in the moonlight."

"I should go in and help my aunts." His image was too close for comfort. She was one of the few people in her family who didn't do just that.

"I have to go." He sounded reluctant to leave. "When can I see you again?"

"Do you work on Saturday? You could come out then."

"That's several days away." He drew her into an embrace and rested his cheek on her hair. "I'm not sure I can stay away from you that long."

"We're going too fast. I'm not ready for this. Didn't we agree in the meadow that neither of us is looking for a relationship right now?"

"Yes, but I'm not sure I was entirely accurate when I said that. Right now, all I can think of is seeing you again." He lifted her chin so he could look into her eyes. "You've bewitched me."

"Don't say that!" She pulled away.

"Did I say something wrong? I'm not trying to railroad you into something you don't want. Say the word and I'll leave you alone."

"No." She wrapped her arms about her body and stared moodily into the deepening evening. "I don't want you to leave me alone. I just have to sort out my thoughts. That's all."

He came to her and put his arms around her, pulling her back against his chest. "We'll take it as slow as you like. Maybe I was wrong to say anything about it. After all, I do have a load of work following me around most of the time. I'm going back to the office when I leave here and put in some extra hours."

"Are you a workaholic?"

"No, I just like to keep my head above water." He turned her to face him. "You set the pace, Rhiannon. Neither of us wants a permanent relationship, but I don't see anything wrong in us sharing company for as long as you're here. I like you. You fascinate me, in fact. There's something about you that mystifies me."

Behind them the rattan chair moved forward several inches.

"What was that noise?" Chad looked around and saw they were still alone.

"Nothing. I didn't hear anything." Rhiannon frowned at the chair. This one was going to be hard to explain.

"Wasn't that chair against the wall a minute ago?"

"I guess it must not have been or it would still be there. Right?" She could usually explain away her involuntary psychokinesis by logic. People were willing to accept any explanation.

"But I'm sure . . ."

"I have to go in. And you have work to do."

"I'll see you Saturday." He bent and kissed her.

Rhiannon found her arms about him and she kissed him in full measure. As in the meadow, she had the curious sensation of their souls melding and hints that she had kissed him often before—and much more besides.

When he was gone, she went into the house and helped her aunts put a bowl of tossed salad, cheeses, and several varieties of crackers on the kitchen table, along with a bottle of wine. At night they seldom ate a large meal, and since they were vegetarian, simple foods suited them.

"When is that nice young man coming back?" Amethyst asked as she put three plates on the table.

"Saturday." Rhiannon glanced at them as she put wineglasses beside the plates. "I want to call off our bet."

The sisters exchanged a look. Too innocently, Amaryllis said, "What bet is that, dear?"

"You know exactly what I'm talking about. Call off your spell."

"I thought you didn't believe in the Old Ways," Amethyst said mildly. "Have you changed your mind?"

"No. Of course not."

"Then what is there to call off?"

"Besides," Amaryllis said as she placed cloth napkins beside each plate. "It's too late."

"Yes, we've already cast that spell. I must say, it worked remarkably fast, didn't it, sister? We quite outdid ourselves." They put their gray heads together and exchanged girlish smiles.

"No. I don't believe in this. But even if I did, I don't want to fall in love with someone because he was slipped a love potion or something. I want the normal, old-fashioned kind that happens for no reason."

"Oh, there's always a reason, dear. And we never thought of giving him a love potion. That would be against the rules."

"Yes," Amaryllis seconded with a nod of her head. "You must never cast that sort of spell because that would be interfering with another person's destiny. Manipulation is harmful."

"You know the rule, dear. 'And none be harmed.' We would never go against that."

Rhiannon had heard this rule all her life. It was the reason most of her family were vegetarians. The rule protected every life form—from people to rain forests.

"But you told me you've placed spells on all of Cypress. You can't go around doing things like that. If there were such a thing," she added.

"We work prosperity and health and happiness spells for the town," Amaryllis explained. "That's why the divorce rate is so low here and we don't have any people who are really poor. The ones who need to experience that in their lives simply move to another place."

"Cypress's state of affairs is well documented. We've even made the national news," Amethyst said with pride. "We have a lower crime rate than any other town in America. That's why it's so important for you to learn to keep the spells updated after we're gone. We love this town and the people in it, and it worries us that they might fall on hard times someday."

"The spells wear off, you see," Amaryllis said. "They have to be renewed from time to time."

"It's also why our family has always been so wealthy. We draw wealth to us. That way, we can make donations to charities and build hospitals in other cities. We use it to found hospices and to fund medical research and all sorts of things."

"Yes, but I don't believe in magic," Rhiannon protested. What her aunts were telling her was unfortunately familiar. All her family was wealthy and they did make donations, most of them anonymously and in cities other than their home towns, in order to preserve their real identities. And a documentary had been filmed in Cypress about the low crime and divorce rates and how the people here were generally healthier than anywhere else. Her parents had said it was a coincidence. Rhiannon was beginning to question that. "I have to think about all this."

"All right, dear, but don't take too long. There's so much we have to teach you." Amaryllis put the silverware on the table and sat down.

"But I don't want Chad to love me because he's under a spell," Rhiannon protested.

"Haven't you been listening?" Amethyst asked. "We only cast a spell to bring your soul mate to you. We had no idea he was right here in Cypress. I guess we put too much English on it. Overdid it, so to speak."

Rhiannon sat down and automatically put salad on her plate. "I have a lot to think about," she repeated.

Chapter Three

Chad sat opposite the elderly sisters and waited for them to read the will. "If everything is the way you intended, I'll have the final draft typed up."

"There's one other thing," Amaryllis said. "We want to leave Shadow Dancer to Rhiannon."

"There's really no reason to list him," Chad explained. "Your cat, along with your other belongings, will go to Rhiannon."

"Oh, I don't think he would like to be listed as a 'belonging,' " Amaryllis said with a small frown.

"No, indeed," Amethyst agreed. "It would put him in a snit, I'm sure. We don't own him, you see. He only lives with us."

Chad smiled. "Most cat owners feel that way. It's no problem. I'll add his name in a separate paragraph, if that will make you happier." In his few visits to Hallowmoon, he had come to view the sisters as everyone else in Cypress did—they were eccentric, but somehow that made them all the more lovable. "Is Rhiannon here?" he asked with studied casualness.

The sisters exchanged one of their looks. "She's in the cabin," Amethyst said.

"Working on her poppets," Amaryllis added. "Just go on out back, if we're through here. You'll stay for lunch, won't you?"

"No, thank you. I can't today. I have an appointment at one, and I have some papers to look over before they come." He put the papers in his briefcase and snapped it shut. "I do have time to speak to Rhiannon, however." He would take the time to do it, even if it made him late to the meeting.

He went out to his car to put away his briefcase before circling the house to the log cabin behind it. In the days he had known Rhiannon, she had become a part of his every waking moment. She also figured largely in his dreams, and the dreams were the most vivid and erotic he could ever remember having. He couldn't get her out of his mind, and he dreaded the day when she would leave Cypress and return to her ordinary life. In spite of all logic, he was falling in love with her.

The idea scared him half to death.

At the cabin he tapped lightly on the door and it swung open. Rhiannon sat across the room beside a fire in the fireplace. She wore a long skirt and blouse that looked homespun. Her black hair was loose and flowed about her shoulders. For a moment he could have sworn she was from another century.

Then she smiled. "Come in. I was hoping to see you before you went back to town."

He went to the worktable. "What are you making?"

"It's an angel." She nodded toward several finished angels and divas she had made since coming to Hallowmoon. "I find I think best when my hands are busy."

He picked up a poppet and studied it. "These are quite good. I can see how you were able to find a market for them."

She tied a silver and fawn feather in the angel's wing. "If I didn't sell them, I would have run out of space in my apartment by now. They all have different chores," she explained. "I've written it on the hem of their dresses."

He turned the diva upside down and read aloud, "Elfwen helps in matters of love."

"Some balance checkbooks, some help find lost articles, some paint sunsets. I let them tell me what chore they want and I write it as a finishing touch."

"They tell you?" he asked teasingly.

"It's only a figure of speech," she said quickly, looking back at the angel in progress.

He picked up several of the others. They had intriguing little faces, some wrinkled and merry with age, others young and beautiful, but all had innate wisdom in their eyes. "I don't see how you got so much expression in them. It's as if they could come alive."

"I make the faces first, then I design clothing from feathers and mosses and fake fur or leather. I never use real animal skin."

He looked at her curiously. "Not even the food animals that would be killed anyway?"

"Killed is killed, as my aunts say. I find myself becoming a vegetarian, too. Lately the thought of eating meat disturbs me."

Chad put down the two angels he was holding and

again picked up the diva that had drawn him first. "I like this one. Can I buy it from you?"

"Take it as a gift. As I said, I only sell them because I have to part with them somehow." She laughed. "For some reason, people in stores are suspicious if I try to give them away for free. I tried that at first and no one would give me shelf space."

Chad laughed with her. "People are peculiar." He looked into the calm face of the diva dressed in soft feathers and suede cloth. "They are almost magical, aren't they?"

"No," Rhiannon said firmly. "No matter what my aunts told you, they aren't."

He looked at her with interest.

"I mean, some of them are based on ancient cultures and I've used that culture's symbols for magic, but it's only decoration as far as I'm concerned." She frowned at the diva he held. She knew she was talking too much. "Don't mind me. Being around my aunts has this effect on me. So does the cabin." She glanced around the familiar walls. For generations the women and men of her family had practiced their Craft here, and the resultant mood of the cabin was mellow and inherently magical.

She glanced back at the closed door. "Will you open the door? Shadow Dancer wants in."

"He does?" Chad went to the door and opened it. The cat strolled in and lay down on the warm bricks of the hearth. "How did you know . . . That reminds me. Your aunts want me to mention him in the will. You're to have him."

"I am?" she asked in surprise. "I get Shadow Dancer?"

"Who else? I told them it wasn't necessary to write

it down, but they insisted." Chad bent to stroke the cat. "He may not outlast them, you know."

"I think he will." Rhiannon studied the cat. She really couldn't remember a time when he wasn't living at Hallowmoon. Of course, it was possible that her aunts simply got a black cat to replace the one that had died and gave it the same name, but Shadow Dancer had a distinct personality, and Rhiannon couldn't remember it ever changing. "You're right, of course. He must be awfully old by now."

"He doesn't seem old to me. I'd say he's in the prime of life." He straightened and came to sit in the chair beside her. "Since you will eventually inherit Hallowmoon, will you come here to live?"

"I hope I don't inherit it anytime in the near future," she retorted. Then, after thinking a moment, she added, "Yes, I suppose I will." It troubled her that she was considering it a foregone conclusion. If she took Hallowmoon, it was implied that she would also take over the care and tending of Cypress. "I don't know. I haven't decided yet."

"I hope you do." He took her hand and enclosed it in his. "I don't want you to drive out of my life and never return."

"Naturally I'll return. This is my real home." The words surprised her. "I mean, this place is like the roots of my family. If I don't live here, one of my cousins will. I'll certainly never sell it. None of us would do that." Even as she considered which of her cousins would be her aunts' second choice as resident witch, she found herself aching at the thought of parting with the house. She, more than any of the others, identified with the family home.

"I don't think any of your cousins would have the same appeal to me," he said softly. His thumb traced lazy circles on her hand and sent fire up her arm to her heart.

"You haven't met them," she murmured as she found herself becoming lost in the hazel depths of his eyes. "Your eyes—they're the color of pines reflected in the pond in the woods. The exact same color. I never noticed that before."

"Rhiannon, don't go back to Longview. I want you to stay here. Forever."

"Don't say that." She tried to pull away but not very hard. Holding hands with Chad was delightful. His touch worked all sorts of magic with her libido. "We barely know each other."

"I know. It's crazy for me to feel this way, but I swear I'm not feeding you a line."

"I know you're not. That's what scares me." Across the cabin a rocker began moving rhythmically. Rhiannon ignored it and hoped it was out of his field of vision. "It's too soon for us to feel this way."

"Then you're feeling it too?" His eyes searched her face.

She was afraid to give in to the love she felt growing within her. If it was only some trick conjured up by her aunts, it might not last. She couldn't bear to let herself love Chad only to lose him. After Rick, she had ample reason to know her love wasn't enough to hold anyone if it wasn't shared. "It may not last."

"Then again, it might. Haven't you heard of love at first sight?"

"Yes, but I don't believe in it. To love someone, you have to know them completely—their habits, what they like or dislike. Their background. How could a person know that at first sight?''

"I don't know. I never believed in it either. Believe it or not, I'm usually as logical and level-headed as they come."

"So am I. That's why I can't let my hormones make this decision for me." She pulled her hand out of his. A glance told her the rocker was behaving properly again. "You don't know anything about me."

"I want to learn." Chad removed the angel from her hands and took both of them in his to turn her toward him. "Rhiannon, I've never felt anything like this before. Tell me you aren't leaving anytime soon."

"I don't know," she replied honestly. "I should go home."

"This is your home. You've said so yourself."

"I have commitments. Next spring I'm scheduled to go on a dig. Remember?"

"This is only October. You have lots of time to pack."

"I have a life there. People who would worry if I don't come back."

"Don't leave me. Not yet. Not until we see what this might grow to be between us." He leaned toward her.

Rhiannon felt as if fate were pulling her into his arms. She wanted to fight it out of sheer stubbornness, but not badly enough to pull away. Their lips met and she couldn't remember why she was fighting not to love him. She went willingly into his embrace.

Love magic. It was a term she had heard all her life. Until now she had thought it referred only to sex. Now she knew it was so much more. Her cousins had tried to explain it to her, but she had never been in love at the time and she hadn't understood when they referred to it as the most magical of times. As her soul melted into Chad's and their hearts beat in rhythm together, she understood. If she allowed herself to love Chad—if she had a choice—she wouldn't lose any of herself, as she felt she had with Rick. With Chad, she was more than she had been before. Her spirit soared along with his.

With sheer force of will, she pulled away. "We can't. I can't."

He looked as stricken as she felt, to be physically apart from her. "I know. We have things we have to do. Places we have to go." His words lacked conviction. "Rhiannon, I don't know what's happening to us, but I don't want it to stop. Do you?"

"I don't know," she whispered. "It frightens me." She gazed into his eyes and saw he understood.

"I'm falling in . . ."

She stopped his words with her fingertips. "No. Don't say it. Not yet. You may regret it later." She couldn't explain to him that he was only under a spell. Even to herself it sounded ludicrous. "Give me a few days. Don't call or come by. I have to think."

There was pain was in his eyes, but he nodded. "If that's what you want. I don't understand it, but I'll give you space."

"Thank you," she murmured. She wanted to take the words back. To ask him to stay with her forever.

Chad stood and walked to the door. He paused and looked back. "You can call me when you're ready."

She nodded, trying not to look at him.

"Will you call me?" he asked. "Are you telling me you don't want me in your life?"

"No. I don't mean that." She held on to the worktable

343

to keep from rushing to him. One of the shutters unlatched itself and banged against the window.

Chad glanced at the shutter and back at her. "I'll call you in a few days if you haven't called me. I'm not going to give this up unless you tell me to leave you alone." When she didn't answer, he turned and left.

Rhiannon leaned her head on her folded arms on the table, pushing her work aside. She ached for him. Her lips still felt the imprint of his kiss and she wanted more. Was she being a fool to risk losing him? She was falling in love and perhaps their love was too new and tender to withstand a test. Or maybe it was only a spell and their absence from one another would render it void.

She didn't want her love to go away. It was too right, too all encompassing.

Rhiannon lifted her head and looked around. When had she begun believing in spells? She didn't. Magic was only for fairy tales. Both her parents had told her that the family was too ready to confuse religion with facts. She had always agreed with them, even when she had just come from a family reunion at Hallowmoon and had seen things she couldn't explain with logic.

The box of feathers slid across the table toward her. Rhiannon caught it before it landed in her lap. What would Chad say if he realized how often things moved around her? When her emotions were running high it was more pronounced than ever. Worse, she couldn't stop it. Her aunts used this as proof that she was gifted and had a responsibility to the world, or at least to Cypress and those less fortunate than she was. But they couldn't be right. All Rhiannon's logic rebelled against what that would mean.

Shadow Dancer jumped onto the table, causing Rhiannon to start. She laughed at her nervousness. "I forgot you were in here." As she stroked his silky fur, she found herself gazing into his golden eyes. "I wish you could talk and tell me if I'm wrong about how old you are. Chad is right, you certainly don't look or act like an old cat." Beneath her fingers his muscles were strong and supple, his fur soft with health.

Shadow Dancer meowed as if in answer and blinked.

"What do you think, fellow? Have I gone nuts to think there might be some magic in the spell my aunts created? What if Chad and I are really falling in love and I mess it all up by not talking to him?"

The cat watched her intently.

"What if I go along with the rest of the family and become Wiccan? What would happen if I sent you to get Chad for me? Could I keep him under a spell forever, be content to have him love me whether it was by his own volition or not?"

Shadow Dancer tensed, as if he were about to jump off the table.

"I must be losing my mind. I don't believe in spells. And if there *is* such a thing, I want the old-fashioned kind of love, not the conjured kind."

Shadow Dancer gave her a look of disdain and left the table to go back to the warmth of the hearth. After a few moments, Rhiannon picked up the angel and resumed weaving feathers into its wings.

Rhiannon's plans to avoid Chad weren't entirely successful. He lived up to his word about not calling her, but that didn't remove him from her mind. When she left the house, she frequently saw him from a distance or passed his office on her way to run an errand for her aunts. Often she found herself dialing his number instead of the one she had intended to dial. Each time she forced herself to hang up before he could answer, but she was becoming more and more convinced that her aunts were the cause of it all.

On an errand to buy a bottle of rose essential oil for one of her aunts, she ran into Chad on her way out of the store. "Sorry," he said automatically before seeing who had plowed into him. "Rhiannon?"

"I'm sorry. I wasn't watching where I was going."

"I miss you. It's been a week. How much longer do you have to think about this?"

She drew in a deep breath and said, before she could change her mind, "I can't see you again. Not ever."

Chad's face mirrored his pain. "Why not? You owe me that much. Am I so far from what you want that you won't even give yourself a chance?"

"No! No, not at all." She searched for words as he walked with her toward the small park near downtown, where she had left her car. "You don't feel for me what you think you do."

"Now you're going to have to explain that. Are you saying you know better than I do what I'm feeling? With all due respect, that's bull."

"You don't understand. It's my aunts' fault."

"What do your aunts have to do with me falling in love with you?"

"Everything!" As they stepped beneath the bare trees, she turned to him. "It's all their fault for putting a spell on us."

Chad laughed and stared at her. "What? A spell?"

"I know it sounds far-fetched, but it's true. We made a foolish bet. I told them I would believe what they were

346

trying to teach me if they could make me fall in love by Halloween.''

"Are you saying in a roundabout way that you love me, too?''

"I don't know! How should I know what either of us would be feeling if it wasn't for their magic?''

He was silent for a minute. "You can't possibly believe what you're saying. Nobody puts someone under a spell. Your aunts aren't into voodoo.''

"No, of course not,'' she said with exasperation. "But they *are* witches, and you only care for me because of whatever it was that they did. We might not even like each other, for all we know.''

"That's crazy. If you don't want to see me again, just say so. It's going to hurt like hell, but at least you'll have been honest.''

"I am being honest! I never believed in the things they say they can do either, but how else can you explain what's happening to us?''

"It's not that mysterious. We met and are falling in love. There's nothing complicated about that.''

"We both expressly said that neither of us wanted a relationship at this time. Don't you remember saying that to me in the meadow?''

"Yes, but that was before I admitted to myself that I felt this way about you. This took me by surprise, too.''

"There! You see? I want nothing more than to be with you, but if it's a spell, it may wear off someday. I couldn't bear to be the cause of you being hurt. It's better if we never start than to find out months from now that it's all been a fabrication.''

"I'm not fabricating anything. And neither are your aunts. Rhiannon, it's nonsense to think they have any part in this. I love you. Whether you love me or not and whether you want to be with me or not, I already love you.''

''No,'' she said as she backed away from him. ''You should never have said that to me. I have to go!'' She turned and ran to her car, leaving him staring after her.

Chad didn't know what to think. Until now Rhiannon had seemed as logical a person as himself. Talk of witches and spells made no sense. But when he thought about it, the whole matter had happened terribly fast. When he counted up the times they had been together, he could do it on the fingers of one hand. Yet here he was wanting to spend the rest of his life with her.

He kept his thoughts to himself until Saturday, when he could contain them no longer. He went to Hallowmoon in search of Rhiannon. The aunts directed him to the path that led to the meadow.

She was there gathering dried grasses, bark, and moss in a large woven basket she carried on her arm. When she felt his presence, she turned and looked at him.

''We have to talk,'' he said. ''I don't believe in love spells and I'm positive that what I feel for you is real. What do you feel for me?''

Her lips parted, as if she were struggling to find the right words. ''I was going to call you when I went back to the house. I miss you so much.'' She was gripping the basket handle so tightly, her fingers were white at the knuckles.

''I miss you, too.'' He went to her and took her in his arms. Her arms went around him and he sighed with pent-up emotion. Eyes closed to keep his feelings in check, he said, ''It feels so good to hold you. All week it's been as if part of me were missing.''

"I know. I've felt the same way."

"Why did we put each other through such torment? I don't know how long you'll be here. I don't want to waste a single moment that we could be together."

"I'm leaving right after Halloween. It's a special holiday for my aunts and I promised I'd spend it with them."

"Please don't start that again. How can you call such sweet old women witches?"

"It's not a derogatory term," she said tersely. "I'm sorry. I didn't mean to jump down your throat. They follow the religion of Wicca. Technically that makes them witches, or Wiccan."

"You're serious?" He held her close, trying to assimilate what she was telling him. "Black magic and things like that?"

"Never black magic. They wouldn't do anything to harm anyone. It's just that I doubt they would see a love spell as being harmful. In some ways they're so innocent. They think love is the beginning and end of all things. They don't understand that it can be damned inconvenient at times."

"You're not an inconvenience to me. Am I to you?"

"I didn't want to fall in love with anyone. I'm supposed to be on the rebound for a while, then gradually get my feet under me and get on with my life. I don't even live in this state! I have plans for spring and most of the summer."

"I'm not the sort to expect a woman to be tied down and not set foot out of the house. I suspect there are other anthropologists who have managed to combine marriage and work."

"Please, whatever you do, don't you dare ask me to

marry you," she groaned as she held to him tightly. "Not now. Not when it feels so good just to be in your arms."

"If that makes sense, I fail to see it, but okay. I can wait. But I should tell you, I don't fall in love easily and it's not something I do often. In fact, I'm not entirely certain that I've ever been in love before. Nothing has ever hit me the way this has. If you go back to Longview, I may follow you."

"Your license is with the Louisiana bar," she protested.

He laughed. "My work is the last thing I'm thinking of right now." More seriously, he looked down at her and tilted her face until their eyes met. "I can't let you go. Especially not now that I know you love me."

"You don't know for certain that either of us do, really!" She pulled away and went to stand beside the stone circle. She frowned at the ashes, as if she were wrestling with some monumental problem.

"I'll go ask your aunts point-blank and see what they say."

"You can't do that! I'm not supposed to tell outsiders about their . . . interests."

"Then what do you suggest? That we go our separate ways and never see each other again? No, Rhiannon, I'm not willing to do that. I love you and I want to be with you."

She looked back at him, and he could see the misery in her eyes. "I know you think you do. I believe I love you, too."

He sighed in exasperation. "You're enough to try the patience of a saint. Do you know that?"

"Just give me a little more time. It can't last forever.

Spells don't. At least I don't think they do.''

"Okay, have it your way. We're bewitched. So what if it never wears off? What if we live happily ever after? Is that so bad?''

Rhiannon came to him and put her arms around him. ''If I thought that was a possibility, nothing would keep me from you. But what if I'm wrong? What if I return to Longview, and as soon as there is distance between us we both return to our senses and realize we've made a terrible mistake?''

"If I believed in voodoo, I would give that some consideration. But I don't.'' He bent and kissed her. Rhiannon's breath was sweet and warm in his mouth. Her body molded perfectly to his. ''We fit together as if we were made for each other.''

In answer, she drew him back down for another kiss. Heat pounded in his veins and it was all he could do not to lay her on the billowing grasses and make love to her beneath the sky. There was a quality about Rhiannon that encouraged him to do wilder acts than he had ever considered before.

She held him as if she would never let him go. ''Chad,'' she whispered in his ear, ''I hope you're right and I'm wrong.''

"If I can't ask your aunts, you can. See what they say. But whatever it is, I'm not going to walk away from you willingly. You'll have to send me away.''

"But what about all the things you don't know about me?''

"We'll have all the time in the world to learn them. Maybe we'll disagree on some things. What couple doesn't? It won't mean anything. All that matters is our love.''

"I wish you'd stop saying that. You're too persuasive."

"Good," he said as he nuzzled her mane of hair. "I want to persuade you. I'm warning you, I'm going to do all I can to poke holes in your screwball theory until you see there's nothing to it."

"Can I wish you luck?" she breathed as she kissed him again.

Chad lifted her and stood for a moment with her cradled in his arms before he lay her on the ground. Her hair circled around her head like a nimbus of night, her eyes dark with passion. He lay down beside her.

She traced her finger along his face as if she were memorizing it. "I'll never forget this day," she whispered.

"No, you won't. And if you do, I'll be there to remind you."

"I have trouble thinking clearly around you." She laced her fingers behind his neck and drew him down.

Chad kissed her until he thought his desire would override his good sense. She was having doubts, and this was no time to do anything she might later see as coercion. "I want to see you in the morning when you first wake up," he said softly as he looked deep into her eyes. "I want to fall asleep with your hair across my pillow and to feel you warm and soft beside me."

Her eyes were soft and liquid and a smile lifted her lips. "I want that, too."

"I want us to have children who are just like you." To his surprise, he saw the wariness come back into her face. "What did I say wrong?"

"You don't know me. Not really."

He looked up to see the trees around the clearing bend

as if in a great wind, but there wasn't so much as a breeze. Over them the white clouds stood still. As he watched, the trees bounced back upright, swayed a bit, then were still. When he looked at Rhiannon, she was looking at them, too, and her eyes were filled with unhappiness.

"You don't know me," she repeated.

"I can learn. You can teach me."

She met his eyes. "It might be more than you expect. What if I tell you all about me, what I think and what I can do, and you discover that you don't want that in your life?"

"You let me worry about that. I can't think of a single thing that you could say that would drive me away. Even if you said you don't really love me, it wouldn't matter. I have enough love for both of us."

For a long time she was silent. Then, never taking her eyes from his, she said, "I have to go. My aunts are worrying about me."

He looked up and found Shadow Dancer sitting on the stone circle only inches away. Chad had no idea when he had arrived or how he'd gotten there without him noticing. He moved away and Rhiannon sat up. She used her fingers to comb the grass from her hair, then got to her feet. Chad continued to stare at the cat and wonder.

Chapter Four

"I'm curious," Rhiannon said to her aunts over their morning tea. "How did you cast that love spell?"

Amethyst smiled first at her sister, then at Rhiannon. "I was wondering when you'd get around to asking."

"We're so happy you're starting to show interest in your Gift. You'll be so good at it," Amaryllis said happily.

"I'm not saying that I believe in it. I'm only curious about what you did." She didn't want her aunts to assume that she was a convert to their way of thinking, but she had to know whether there really was a spell and, if so, how to undo it.

"We made poppets," Amaryllis explained. "One for you and one for your intended."

"You've seen us cast circles for years," Amethyst added. "We used the back room. These days it's often difficult for us to go all the way to the meadow. Our old joints ache in the cold weather."

"But the back room has been dedicated, so it works just as well as the meadow," Amaryllis put in quickly. "We wouldn't go halfway on a spell for you. We love you too much."

"You made poppets?" Rhiannon prompted. "What do they look like?"

"Not like yours, dear. Ours were quite plain. Sister cut them out of white cloth. They look rather like the paper dolls we used to make for you when you were little. Do you remember them?"

"I do," Amethyst said with a smile. "You used to sit on the counter while we were baking something and play with paper dolls for the longest time. You'd color clothes on them and give them names. Don't you remember, dear?"

"I remember."

Amaryllis continued. "When they were cut out, we sewed the backs to the fronts, leaving a hole for stuffing. Then we put in some ivy for fidelity, a bay leaf, and marjoram."

"I always like to add some basil," her sister added. "I like spice in a relationship."

"Then we put in some rose petals, lavender, and orris root to make the love sweet and true."

"Then we finished sewing the poppets shut."

"Sister lit two pink candles for true love and we put them on the altar," Amaryllis said, her voice full of remembered excitement. "As we spoke the magic words, we moved the candles closer and closer until they were touching. Then we lit a white candle for protection and to ensure that your love would be pure.''

"That was pretty much it,'' Amethyst said with a nod. "We opened the circle and let the candles burn themselves out.''

"You see? It's not so different from other spells you saw us cast when you were a child.''

Rhiannon didn't know what to say. She had often seen her aunts and cousins casting circles when she visited, but she hadn't thought much about it. That was their religion, and it had little effect on her other than to strike her as a peaceful and beautiful way to worship. Now it seemed her that her aunts might have known what they were doing.

Shadow Dancer jumped in her lap and settled down as if he were prepared to spend the winter there. Rhiannon petted him automatically. "How does the spell work? Those are only kitchen herbs and ordinary flowers.''

"It just does,'' Amethyst said. "It always has. Of course, we had to experiment to get the proportions just right. Your grandmother taught us, but she never measured anything. We soon got the formula right, though.''

"I certainly do like your young man,'' Amaryllis said. "He reminds me a bit of Papa. Doesn't he remind you, sister?''

"Yes, he does a bit. But I believe Mr. Dawson laughs more. Papa had a sternness about him.''

Rhiannon pushed the cat from her lap. He jumped back up and settled down again. "I don't know what to think. I just wish I had never made that silly bet. Is there a way to undo the spell?''

"Whyever would you want to do that?'' both sisters exclaimed.

"Don't you like your young man?" Amaryllis asked, her brow crinkled with concern. "He seems so nice."

"I like Chad a great deal. But you shouldn't have cast a spell on him. If it worked—and I'm not saying that I believe it did—it's not fair."

"But he's your soul mate," Amethyst explained patiently. "He's your intended."

"I do wish we had met ours," Amaryllis said with a sigh. "Don't you, sister?"

"I do, but we've been happy," Amethyst said. "I don't see how we could have been happier."

Rhiannon again pushed the cat away. "Please, let's talk about this spell and Chad. Shadow Dancer, go sit on someone else for a change!" she said sternly to the cat. He only blinked at her.

"There's no use in telling him that," Amethyst said with a laugh. "He's chosen you. He's your familiar now."

"He's drawn to your inherent magic, you see," Amaryllis added. "You'll be so happy together."

"I don't know that I'm going to marry Chad," Rhiannon objected.

"I meant the cat."

"Has Mr. Dawson proposed?" Amethyst asked eagerly. "So soon!"

"Yes, I mean, no. You're confusing me." She frowned at the cat. "I don't want or need a familiar. Go away." She thought the idea of having a familiar sounded as phony as casting a spell.

"It's no use. Once he chooses a person, he stays with her. He's not at all fickle."

"Once he chose us, he's stayed with us ever since."

Amaryllis bobbed her head up and down. "We will miss him."

"Perhaps we could get a kitten," Amethyst suggested. "Not a special one like Shadow Dancer, of course, but one as a pet."

"I suppose we could. We never had an ordinary pet. It might be fun."

"I can't take this cat back to Longview with me," Rhiannon objected. "In the first place, my apartment building doesn't allow pets, and in the second, you're attached to him."

"He's not ours any longer. Are you certain you want to return to Longview?"

"Of course. I live there. Remember?"

"At least Rhiannon is starting to ask questions about the Craft," Amaryllis said comfortingly to her sister. "If she leaves, she will come back more often."

"I never suggested that I would be staying here permanently. I've always said that I have to go back. I have commitments. Plans."

"Yes, dear, we remember." Amethyst patted her niece's arm. "Don't you worry. Everything will work out just the way it's supposed to."

Rhiannon sighed and let Shadow Dancer curl into her lap again. It was wonderfully peaceful in Cypress and she loved being at Hallowmoon. Shadow Dancer purring in her lap gave her a feeling of belonging that surpassed what she'd felt for her old way of life. She was no longer so interested in going on the expedition to the Nile and digging up ancient civilizations. And then there was Chad. "I haven't made a decision about staying. Or going."

The phone rang and she glanced at it. "That's Chad. Will you tell him to come on out?"

Amaryllis picked up the phone and said, "Mr. Dawson, Rhiannon says you're to come on out." She hung up without questioning who was on the end.

Rhiannon stroked the cat. "I could stay, I suppose. It's not as if I have people waiting for me in Longview. I wouldn't be running into Rick here."

Amethyst smiled and winked at her sister. "You think about it, dear. I'm sure you'll make the right decision."

"It's like the phone call," Amaryllis said. "You've always had a way of *knowing*. And things have always moved about you. I've seen it frequently since you've come here."

"It's only a coincidence," Rhiannon said quickly.

"She sounds a bit like her father when she does that, doesn't she?" Amethyst said. "I do miss him, for all his stubbornness."

"He was like a son to us," Amaryllis replied, her voice touched with sadness. "On Samhain we must contact him and see how he's doing in Summerland."

Rhiannon wasn't at all sure she wanted to try to contact her father from the beyond, even though she did miss him a great deal. Her aunts had always maintained that the line dividing the living and the dead was at its most flexible point on Halloween. It was the time when Wiccans could most easily commune with those who had gone on before them.

"We have so much to teach you," Amethyst was saying. "You should have been learning all this from childhood. Now you'll have a great deal to remember all at once."

"Fortunately we have kept a good Book of Shadows.

Everything is written down in it in case you forget anything after we're gone.''

"You're not going to die for a long time yet," Rhiannon protested. "Both of you are in good health."

"I expect you're right," Amaryllis said placatingly. "But someday we'll go to Summerland just as everyone does. I only wanted to reassure you that you have a reference to rely on when the time comes."

"I don't know that I'll follow your ways." Rhiannon stood and dumped the cat unceremoniously on the floor. "I'm not making any guarantees."

"It's up to you. We would never force anyone to walk our path. That would be harmful to them and it's against the one primary law."

" 'And none be harmed,' " Amaryllis added, in case she had forgotten. "We can't ever harm anyone. That would be wrong."

"I have to think. When Chad comes, will you tell him I'll be on the bridge?"

"Of course, dear."

Rhiannon left the house, Shadow Dancer at her feet. There were so many decisions to make, and it disturbed her a bit to see which way she was leaning. A core part of her wanted to assure her aunts that she would stay at Hallowmoon and look after the welfare of their beloved town and carry on the family tradition. An even larger part of her didn't want to leave Chad, no matter how unreasonable it was for her to have fallen in love so quickly. It would be so easy, so comfortable, to marry him and do as her aunts hoped. But the logical part of her said she should return to Longview.

She shook her head. She couldn't allow herself to

think magic was real. Not even the magic of falling in love.

At the bridge she leaned on the railing and gazed into the lazy water. Recent rain had swollen the stream, and she could see fish swimming in the golden depths. Not all of them were the sort local to Louisiana.

"You look as if you're pondering the fate of the universe," a voice said from behind her.

She turned to smile at Chad. "I feel as if I am. I'm glad to see you."

"I'm curious about my phone call." He glanced back at the house, which could be glimpsed through the tall trees. "When your aunt answered, she didn't say hello or even wait to see if she was delivering your message to the right person. What if I had been someone else?"

Rhiannon looked away. "Then I guess I'd be having this conversation with a plumber or plastic siding salesman." She drew in a deep breath. He might as well know the worst about her. "I frequently know who is calling before I answer the phone."

"So do I, but you had no reason to know I was calling at that time or that I was asking if I could see you."

"I just knew."

"More of your family voodoo?" he asked with a smile.

"It's not voodoo. I keep telling you that. It's entirely different."

"Hey, don't get upset. I was only teasing. Were you serious?"

"It rained last night," she said, changing the subject. "We've needed rain."

He looked over the rail, then leaned closer. "Are

those . . . Why are there goldfish in your stream? Am I seeing things?''

''My aunts put them there. They feel sorry for them in pet shops so they buy them and set them free in the streams or ponds. You'd be surprised how big some of them grow to be.''

He seemed to be puzzling over this eccentricity.

''Chad, I'm considering staying in Cypress. My aunts need me.''

His face lit up in a smile. ''That's the best news I've heard all day!'' Then he sobered. ''Why do they need you? They seem healthy enough. Is that why they drew up their wills?''

''No, it's a little more complicated than that. They want me to take care of Cypress for them when they're gone, and they need me here to teach me how to do it.''

''You lost me on that one.''

''I know. It's complicated.''

''So you are staying?''

''Maybe. Right now I'm leaning that way.''

He took her in his arms. ''You don't know how I've dreaded you leaving. I was afraid that's what you were going to say.''

''Would you really follow me if I left?''

''Yes. I don't understand how it happened so fast, but I love you and I'm not going to lose you.''

''I'm afraid of what's happening to us,'' she said reluctantly as she rested her cheek on his chest and held him tight. ''It's that spell they cast. I asked some questions, and they really did cast one.''

He was silent for a moment. ''Rhiannon, I know your aunts are a little on the kooky side, but I don't believe in spells. Are you saying that you do?''

"Of course not! Maybe," she amended. "I don't know. They were pretty convincing."

"I can't believe in that. There's no such thing as witches or whatever they think they are."

She pulled away and looked back at the water. "You're wrong."

"Look," he turned her to face him, "it doesn't matter. All that is important is that I love you and you love me. Marry me, Rhiannon, and we can sort it all out later."

Happiness leaped in her heart and she opened her mouth to say yes when she noticed Shadow Dancer sitting on the bridge railing and watching her intently.

"I love you," he said earnestly. "I love the way you laugh and how you make a tiny little frown when you're thinking and how you move and how you kiss. I particularly love the way you kiss." He smiled down at her and drew her closer. "Will you marry me?"

"I don't know. I have to think about it."

"You what? You don't know?" He frowned and loosened his embrace. "I didn't expect you to say that. Aren't you sure about our love for each other?"

"I'm absolutely certain we feel as if we're in love. That's not the question. I'm just not sure it's the real thing and not something my aunts conjured up."

"Come on, Rhiannon. That's nonsense." He dropped his arms to his sides and frowned at her. "It's all well and good to wonder how it happened so quickly, but it's crazy to think we're under some sort of spell. That sort of idea is as wacky as . . ." He stopped in time.

"As my aunts? That's what you were going to say." She frowned up at him. "That's a rotten thing to say!"

"I didn't mean it that way. I like your aunts. But if they think they can make me or anyone else fall in love against their will, that's nonsense. It doesn't work that way. It never has and it never will.''

"I'm not so sure about that," she retorted.

"And while we're on the subject, what did you mean about having to take care of Cypress?"

"There's no way I'm going to explain that to you. Especially not in the middle of an argument!" She stopped. "We *are* having an argument, aren't we?"

"We wouldn't be if you were talking sense."

"Maybe the spell is starting to wear off on you. It sure sounds like it!"

"No, I'm just saying what I should have said the first time you brought this up. I don't believe in witchcraft and I'm tired of hearing about it."

"Are you! And now you're going to dictate what I'm to think and say around you? In that case, I'm certainly not going to marry you. I don't even want to be around you!" She turned to stalk off the bridge.

He caught her arm. "Stop. Don't go. I'm sorry."

She frowned at him. "I don't believe you."

"Look," he said as he pulled her closer, "everyone fights from time to time if they have an opinion. I wouldn't trust a relationship that ran smoothly all the time. Either one of the two wouldn't be sharing their real feelings or one of them would be redundant."

"It's that basil Aunt Amethyst put in the poppet. She added too much spice."

"Rhiannon!"

She stepped into his arms and hugged him. "I don't want to argue with you. I want everything to go smoothly, the way it has so far."

"Lawyers are known for arguing. It can't always be smooth sailing."

She opened her eyes. Shadow Dancer had moved closer, until they were almost on an eye level. He was purring loudly. "Let's walk," she said as she turned away from the cat.

Arm in arm, they went deeper into the woods.

"Witchcraft aside," she said, "how do you feel about psychics?"

"I think ESP exists, but I've never seen proof of it. Maybe I just want to believe in it."

"Would you be upset if, say, I was psychic?"

"No, that would be great. I wouldn't have to call to say I'm going to be late coming home from work." He looked down at her. "Are you serious?"

"I'm afraid so."

He thought for a while. "I could handle that. Is that really how you knew it was me on the phone?"

She nodded. "And sometimes things move around me. Things that shouldn't move, like chairs and boxes."

"Show me." He pointed at a rock. "Move that without touching it."

"I can't control it that way. It just happens. I can't make it start or stop."

He made no comment. They walked farther down the path.

"I know you don't believe me, but if you're going to love me, you have to know what I'm really like. Rick couldn't handle it. I think that's one reason he stopped seeing me."

"You explained all this to him the way you're explaining it to me? Maybe you scared him away."

"No, he observed it firsthand. We dated for several months before we became engaged. The engagement lasted over a year."

"Why so long?"

"I don't know. The time never felt right for us to be married."

"Maybe your subconscious was trying to tell you something."

"I wish it had picked a less painful way. I was really hurt when he broke our engagement and started dating someone else."

"Are you still hurting for him?"

"No," she said with a shake of her head. "That stopped before I came here, really. I just hadn't examined my feelings about him until you came into the picture. I'm over Rick."

"Are you afraid the love you feel for me might be the rebound sort?"

"I wish it was that simple. No, it feels real, I'm afraid."

"Good. I'm glad to hear that."

They reached the meadow. Without deciding that it would be, the meadow had become their special place.

"Soon it will be too cold to come here so often," he commented as they sat on the grass in the sun.

"I like the cold. We can wear coats." She pushed up the sleeves of her bulky sweater. "I'm glad it didn't rain so much the ground is wet." She looked across the clearing. "Look. Over there."

"It's a deer," he said in a low voice. "I saw one here the other day. Why aren't they afraid of us?"

"My aunts feed them. They're almost pets. I think during hunting season the neighboring deer come onto our land. No hunting is allowed here. The deer seem to know that."

"No poachers?"

366

"No. My aunts wouldn't allow that."

"You sound as if their not allowing it would make it impossible for a hunter to come on their land. Poachers can be persistent."

"Not here." She watched the deer grazing. From time to time it lifted its head and gazed in their direction, but it seemed more curious than wary. "He's beautiful, isn't he? Look at the size of his antlers. He's hidden here for a long time." She looked at Chad. "You don't hunt, do you?"

"No. I don't even own a gun."

"Good. That's important to me."

He leaned closer and kissed her. "I love you," he murmured as he nuzzled her ear.

"Exactly as I am?"

"I love you," he repeated.

Rhiannon kissed him and lay back in the grass. She was aware that he hadn't answered her, but she put aside the nagging doubt. She loved him, and at the moment that was enough.

Chad stretched his length next to hers and drew her half under him. Braced on his elbow, he gazed into her eyes. "Your eyes are the color of the sky," he said in wonderment. "I've never seen eyes so blue."

"How did I ever find you?" she whispered. "Perhaps I never would have. When I visit, I don't often go into town except to run errands for my aunts. To think, we might never have met."

"I would have found you. Something would have called me to you. Can't you feel it, Rhiannon? We were meant to be together."

"Do you really believe that?" she asked breathlessly.

"I do. Can you doubt it?"

Lynda Trent

She shook her head, and the grasses rustled beneath her hair. "I have no doubts. Not at this moment."

His lips met hers and she closed her eyes. Warmth soared through her, taking away the chill of the day. She wrapped her arms around his neck and returned the kiss with ardor. Her lips opened eagerly beneath his and her tongue met his, promising more.

Chad ran his hand beneath her sweater and up her satin skin to cup her breast. Rhiannon felt the warmth of his palm and as his fingers explored, she gasped with pleasure. Her bra was sheer lace and was easily pulled aside. Then his skin was against hers and her heart beat faster.

His fingers teased her nipple, bringing it to aching fullness. Rhiannon moved beneath him, offering more of herself, moving in tantalizing rhythm, her hips against his.

She turned her head and saw Shadow Dancer watching raptly. She raised up and said, "Go to the house. Now."

The cat turned and trotted away.

Chad watched him go. "How did you do that?"

"He obeys me now." She pulled him back down to her and kissed him into forgetfulness.

Chapter Five

"Chad, I want you to do something for me," Rhiannon said. "I want you to convince me that the love we feel for each other is real and not something conjured up by my aunts."

Chad frowned at her across the table. The restaurant wasn't crowded, but he glanced around to be certain no one could overhear their conversation. "I wish you'd stop thinking that. How am I supposed to convince you?"

"I don't know." She looked miserable as she poked at her salad with her fork. "I've thought and thought and I can't come up with a way."

"You're making yourself unhappy for no reason. Why are you doing this?"

"Because I want to really love you," she said earnestly. "I want to be positive that you love me. Otherwise, I can't marry you."

"That's crazy," he hissed under his breath. "I've tried to be understanding and patient, but you're taking this too far. There's no such thing as witches and spells and hexes. That's nonsense."

"I would have said the same thing not too long ago," she said, her eyes beseeching him to understand. "Since I've been here this time, I've realized I was wrong. My aunts have been explaining it to me and it all makes sense. Haven't you noticed how few divorces and what little crime we have in Cypress?"

"So what? It's a sleepy little town where everyone knows just about everyone else. The same families have lived here forever and there aren't a lot of newcomers to upset the balance. There are probably hundreds of towns just like this all over the country."

"I think it's my aunts' protection and happiness spells."

He watched her in silence for a moment. "Rhiannon, I just came from court where I defended a man who lost control of his temper and drove his car through another man's winter garden. This afternoon I'm to see a woman who is filing for divorce from her husband, and it has all the appearances of being a messy case before it's over. I'm the wrong person to convince that there's no crime or divorces in Cypress."

"I didn't say there aren't any bad things happening at all. Only that our average is far below the national average. ABC filmed a documentary on the town last winter."

"I remember. People will talk about that for years." He watched her sip her tea. "I can't for the life of me understand why you're so hung up on this witchcraft stuff."

Rhiannon glanced around. "My aunts don't like for me to talk about it away from the house, but I had to see you and talk to you. I have to decide whether I'm staying here or returning to Longview. My month's rent is due soon and there's no reason to pay it if I no longer need the apartment."

"Great. Marry me and you can move into my house."

"I wish it were that simple."

"It is. All you have to do is say yes and I'll call a preacher."

She frowned. "What's the big rush? Shouldn't we get to know each other before plunging into marriage?"

"I can wait. I want you to be certain you love me enough to spend the rest of your life with me. If the divorce rate is going to drop any lower, I wouldn't want you to feel trapped."

She managed a smile. "It's not that people *can't* get divorced, it's that they don't want to."

"I see. You can come back to the office with me and explain that to Mrs. Libermann, who wants to murder Mr. Libermann or at least to bleed him dry through child support and whatever else she can get."

"I guess they weren't meant to be together. If they don't become bitter, they'll probably find someone else who is better suited to them both."

"You're pretty optimistic."

"You haven't seen how it works." She leaned nearer to say earnestly, "I have. They've been teaching me and it all makes sense. That's why I think we're under a spell. It all happened so quickly and thoroughly."

"If you keep talking like this, everyone is going to think you're as wacky as your aunts." He knew as soon as the words left his mouth that he had said the wrong thing. He tried to fix it. "What I mean is that no one with a grain of intelligence believes their lives are ruled by magic and spells. That's ridiculous."

Her blue eyes darkened with anger. "You're saying I'm ridiculous?" Her voice was level, but he could hear the undertone of warning beneath it.

"I didn't say that. Not exactly."

"You think my aunts are 'wacky'? Are you saying that everyone in Cypress holds this same opinion?"

"Don't get upset. You can't deny that they are eccentric at the very least. And that's not taking into account these alleged spells and curses."

"They don't do curses. And they only do spells that are beneficial."

"What if someone overheard you saying that? A person who doesn't love you as much as I do would think you had a screw loose."

She drew herself up straighter in her chair. "I have a screw loose?"

"Stop repeating everything I say." He was trying not to lose his temper, but she was making it difficult. "All I'm trying to get you to do is to have a reasonable conversation."

"I was under the opinion that we were. And once again you're trying to censor what I may or may not say. I'm not going to put up with that."

"I'm not doing any such thing!" He frowned at her and tossed his napkin on the table. "You're being deliberately argumentative."

She glared at him for several long seconds. Then she stood and said, "I think it would be best if we don't see each other again. Not for a while, anyway. You're obviously having second thoughts if you can label me as 'wacky' and as having a 'screw loose.' I want more understanding from a relationship.''

"Rhiannon, sit down and let's talk this out." He got to his feet and put out his hand to stop her.

She avoided his hand. "No, I don't think that's such a good idea. This is what I was afraid of. You may think you love me, but you apparently don't even like me. That means that if there was no spell, you wouldn't have fallen in love with me. That's why I'm calling it off." She turned and walked away.

Chad called after her and saw heads swivel in his direction at the disturbance. He sat back down. Cypress was as fond of gossip as any town, and he didn't want them to be the subject of conjecture for weeks to come.

Rhiannon drove back to Hallowmoon as tears rolled down her cheeks. She had finally seen what she had dreaded. Chad didn't like her underneath it all. He wasn't really in love with her. Therefore, it wouldn't last. She might love him forever, but she knew from experience that wasn't enough.

Instead of going into the house, she parked in the rear and headed straight for the meadow. She wasn't entirely sure how to undo what her aunts had done, but she fully intended to give it her best shot.

When she reached the meadow, she paused and thought back to those starlit nights in her childhood when she had come here with her aunts and cousins. She thought she remembered what they had done, but she hadn't been paying all that much attention at the time. Giggling with her cousins had seemed more interesting then.

She picked up a stick and went to the stone circle where fires had been lit. She had no matches, so she would have to do without one. Pointing the stick at the ground, she traced an imaginary circle in a clockwise motion around the stones, beginning in the east. Then, one by one, she called the protectors from each of the four corners to pay heed to her and to watch over her. In the center of the circle, she raised the stick high and evoked the guidance and protection of Spirit. Spirit was the fifth point of the star.

Rhiannon knelt in the circle, facing east. Calling forth the words she had heard as a child, she stated exactly what she wanted to have done. Methodically she undid the love spell cast by her aunts. Taking two small stones from the fire pit, she named one "Chad" and one "Rhiannon," then threw one in one direction and one in the other.

Far in the distance she heard thunder and looked up to see clouds were moving in. Soon it would rain. Thunder growled again. Rhiannon stood and, using the same stick, walked around the perimeter of the circle, thanking each of the guardians for protecting her and for doing her bidding. She declared the circle dissolved.

A finger of lightning sizzled toward the distant trees. Thunder tumbled hard on its heel. Rhiannon left the meadow and jogged toward the house.

"There you are, dear," Amethyst said as she scooted her tiny feet across the waxed floor. "I told sister I heard your car drive up, but when you didn't come in, we were worried."

"I'm fine," she lied. She wanted to go to her room and cry her eyes out. "I've been to the meadow."

Amaryllis came into the room in time to hear her. "To the meadow? That's nice. What were you doing there?"

"I was undoing the spell you put on me."

Both aunts' mouths fell open. They were identical in their expression of shock. "You did what?" Amaryllis asked in trepidation.

"I got rid of the spell." Rhiannon didn't meet their eyes. "I have reason to think Chad wouldn't have fallen in love with me if he hadn't been bewitched, and I don't want that."

"What exactly did you do?" Amethyst asked. Her voice quavered in her concern.

"I cast a circle the way I've seen you do so often and I commanded that your spell be dissolved."

"I don't think she can do that," Amethyst said to her sister. "Can she do that?"

"I don't know." Amaryllis frowned at Rhiannon. "You didn't take our poppets, did you?"

"No. I have no idea where they are and frankly, it never occurred to me. I used two rocks. I named one for me and the other for Chad, then I threw them in opposite directions."

Both aunts gave an involuntary squeal. "No, no!" Amaryllis said in horror. "You didn't really do that!"

"It's the dark of the moon," Amethyst protested. "That's the time when we cast our strongest spells to get rid of something."

"I didn't know that. I guess I picked the right time by accident." Rhiannon tried to act as if she didn't care what she had done, but her aunts' behavior was causing her to be more and more worried. "Why are you looking at me like that?"

"Why, because you broke the cardinal law. You've harmed someone with a spell!" Amaryllis stared at her. "After all we've taught you!"

"Who have I harmed? All I did was undo what you had done."

"We never cast a spell to bind you to anyone in particular," Amethyst protested. "We've told you that on several occasions. That would be against all we believe in. You've sent away your intended, your soul mate! You've done a terrible thing!"

Amaryllis gripped her sister's hands. "Do you think we can undo it? Samhain is only two weeks away, and you know how strong our magic is then. And there will be a full moon this year.

Maybe we can cancel her spell."

"We don't dare try. That would be controlling toward her, and that's against the law." Both sisters turned and stared at Rhiannon.

"I did something wrong, huh," she said uneasily. "Did I mess up big time for sure?"

"I'm afraid so," Amethyst said with a sigh. Amaryllis could only nod.

When he went to the office the next day, Chad was greeted with the unwelcome news that he was to go to New Orleans to represent a case the law office was handling. No one else was free to go, and Chad had worked closely on the case from the beginning so he was to go alone. Although he tried to call Rhiannon, her phone seemed to be off the hook. He decided to try again in a day or two and give her more time to cool off.

He drove to the hotel the secretary had booked for him and checked in. Soon he was busy reacquainting himself with the twists and turns of the case.

The next day was spent in court and that evening he had paperwork to prepare for the next day's session. The following day was spent in almost the same pattern. So was the next, and several days went by before he remembered that Rhiannon had no idea where he was.

He dialed her number instead of going down to eat breakfast and listened to the phone ring repeatedly. Either no one was at home or they weren't answering. With a frown, he dialed it again. He was virtually positive the aunts never left Hallowmoon for any length of time and they practically never left together. Someone was always home. They had told him so when they asked him to call about their wills.

No one answered and he called the operator to ask if the number was working correctly. No trouble had been reported. He hung up. If he hurried, he could grab coffee before heading for the courthouse.

When he reached the courthouse, he learned his case had been delayed for two days. He intended to appraise the law firm of what was going on and return to Cypress, but they had other work for him to do while he was in New Orleans. Chad told the desk clerk at the hotel that he would be staying indefinitely.

Rhiannon was miserable. For over a week Chad hadn't called or come by the house or tried to contact her in any way. Her aunts, who had calmly weathered all her teenage rebellion and childhood pranks without turning a hair, were still put out with her. Although they were far too genteel to actually argue with her, their silence and pained looks spoke volumes. Rhiannon knew she had far overstepped the bounds this time. If there was one thing her aunts took seriously, it was their religion, and she had broken the primary rule.

Rhiannon went back to the meadow. A strong cold

front had blown through and the air was cutting against her face and hands. Dampness rose from the earth and the stone circle looked wet. The grasses were plastered to the ground from a recent rain. The meadow no longer looked soft.

Knowing her task was impossible, Rhiannon walked the outer rim of the meadow, looking for the two rocks she had thrown that day. Neither of them were anywhere to be found. Shadow Dancer had followed her, as he always did, and he sat on the stone circle waiting for her to give up the search. His golden eyes held as much censor as her aunts' these days.

Rhiannon gave up and came to stand by him. "I don't know how to reverse what I did," she said as much to herself as to the cat. She bent to stroke his fur. "I don't remember exactly what I said. Too bad you weren't here at the time." She sighed. Too late she had come to realize she believed as her aunts did, probably always had believed deep within her heart.

"Well, I have to try," she said. She found a stick and called up the circle again. It was a magical place, even on this damp and unfriendly day. The circle created a place that was neither of one world or the other, yet of both. She went from east to south around the circle, calling up the guardians once more.

She tried everything she knew how to do, but she had no idea if it worked or not. Shadow Dancer stared at her as if he had never seen such a botching of a ceremony in his life. Perhaps, she thought, he hadn't. When she was too exhausted to do any more, she released the guardians, opened the circle, and went back to the house.

* * *

Chad finally ended the case that should have taken three days and had stretched out into a week and a half. He packed and tried to call Rhiannon again. As it was every night, the phone either rang endlessly or he could hear only static on the line. He had reported the problem to the phone company, but so far he was still unable to get through.

Weighted down with luggage, Chad checked out of the hotel and went to the parking garage. All four of his tires were flat. For a moment he stood there staring at the car. Then he remembered how heavy his bags were and went back to the hotel lobby.

A garage agreed to repair the tires, but when the serviceman arrived, none of their stock fit Chad's car. "How can this be?" he demanded. "It's a standard size tire."

"I know," the man said with a shake of his head. "That's the problem. We're had a sale on and all our tires have been picked over. We only have the odd sizes left. I can get some from Baton Rouge."

Chad glanced at his watch. "How long will it take?"

"Not long. I can do it tomorrow."

"Tomorrow!" He tried to control his anger. "I have to get home today. I'll call someone else."

The man scratched his head. "Tell you what. I'll send my boy over to find some if you'll deal with me. I'll make you a good price on them tires."

"Okay. But I'm in a hurry."

By midafternoon the tires were on the car. Chad paid the man and got in to start the engine. He turned the key. Nothing happened.

"Sounds like them tires weren't but half your problem," the man said in his laconic drawl. "I don't believe your car is going to start."

Chad refrained from saying what was on his mind. He got out and lifted the hood. Everything seemed to be in order. It just wouldn't start.

"I could haul it over to the shop and have a look at it," the man said. "I can get right on it first thing in the morning. Noon at the latest."

Chad groaned and went back to check into the hotel again.

Days had gone by since Rhiannon had tried to reverse the spell. Chad hadn't called and she hadn't been able to find him. When he hadn't responded in a day's time, she had started looking for him. His home phone was dead and the office line was always busy. She had driven by his office and his house but couldn't find him. His car was gone, but she couldn't believe he would have left town without telling her he was going. She knew for a fact he had plans with friends during this time. If she had known their names, she would have called them.

One night, feeling like a teenager sneaking out for a late date, she slipped away and drove to his house after her aunts were asleep for the night. His house was dark and his car, as always, was gone. She parked in his drive and rang his doorbell repeatedly, but no one was home. She wasn't sure what she would have said to explain her being there if he had opened the door, but she knew she had to find him.

Halloween morning she sat in the cabin watching flames dance in the hearth as Shadow Dancer lay in her lap. "I miss him," she whispered to the cat. "I never knew I could miss anyone so much. I did wrong to cast that first spell. My aunts were right. It was a harmful thing to do. If Chad really loved me, I may have destroyed that forever.''

The wood popped and golden sparks went spiraling up the chimney. Shadow Dancer purred.

"I was so wrong. I love him, Shadow Dancer. I truly do. I know now it was no spell—certainly not on my part. If it was one on his . . . well, I guess that's over now.'' She smoothed the animal's black fur. "No, I know it wasn't. My aunts would never have done that. Not and be as upset with me as they are over what I did to him. Chad really is my soul mate. Have I lost him forever?'' This was Samhain and, due to the decision she had made, it should have been the happiest day of her life. Yet all she could think of was how much she missed Chad.

Shadow Dancer looked up at her and blinked lazily.

"I miss him so much. I want him back,'' she whispered as she watched the fire.

The cat jumped from her lap and trotted over to the door.

With a sigh, Rhiannon got up and opened it. ''You're deserting me, too? I don't blame you.'' She closed the door against the cold and went back to the worktable, where she was trying to craft a wood sprite. In her present frame of mind, her talent seemed to have gone from her. She had never been so lonely in her entire life.

That night Chad drove into Cypress with the relief of a man reaching Paradise. Not only had the garage in New Orleans had to replace his ignition switch, but all the spark plugs as well. It had taken them not one but three days to find all that was wrong and repair it. Chad wasn't at all certain that the man hadn't been feeding him a line of bull in order to fatten the check, but he had been at the man's mercy once the car was on the lift.

"At least I'm home now," he said as he parked in his familiar drive. "God, it's great to be home!" He wondered, as he did constantly, what Rhiannon was doing. After him not calling for two weeks, she could be back in Longview for all he knew.

He went to the door, and a black shadow moved to greet him. He bent and picked up the cat. "Shadow Dancer? What on earth are you doing here?"

The cat purred and blinked, then meowed plaintively.

Chad took the cat in the house and dialed Rhiannon's number. As usual, it didn't work. He replayed his answering machine, but she hadn't left a message. That didn't make him feel any better. Maybe she had meant it when she said she never wanted to see him again.

"What do you think I should do?" he asked the cat.

Shadow Dancer walked to the door and sat facing it, waiting for Chad to open it for him.

"I'll drive you home. That's as good an excuse as any, and her aunts must be frantic with worry over you." He put the cat under his arm and went back out to the car. All the way to Hallowmoon, Shadow Dancer sat regally on the seat, only glancing up at the street lights from time to time and otherwise staring straight ahead.

"I'm not going to give up," he told the cat. "Even if she won't see me or talk to me on the phone, I'm going to find some way to get through to her. I love her and I won't give her up. Not over some silly reason like an argument." He frowned at the night as he drove. "It wasn't even a necessary argument. It's not as if our life-styles aren't compatible. We can work this out. We love each other too much not to make a go of it.''

The cat meowed.

When they reached the house, Chad saw the aunts were having a party. Several cars were parked in the drive and along the grassy area in front. He almost drove away again rather than arrive where he wasn't invited. Then he remembered how dear the cat was to the elderly sisters. He parked and went up the front steps.

Amaryllis opened the door and her wrinkles became smiles. ''Why, it's Mr. Dawson! Look, sister, look who's here!''

Amethyst scurried over to the door and reached out to pat his arm. ''How nice to see you. Tonight of all nights!''

Chad thought for a minute. ''Is tonight Halloween?''

''Yes, of course it is.'' Amethyst gestured behind her, where a number of people were laughing and talking. ''We're having a family get-together. You're more than welcome.''

Chad looked over their heads at the others. They were all younger than the sisters, though some not by much. Most of them bore a strong resemblance to Rhiannon, but he didn't see her among them. ''Is Rhiannon here?''

''Why, of course. She's decided to live here,'' Amaryllis said. She leaned toward him as if to share happy news. ''She's dedicating herself tonight.''

''What?''

''She's becoming one of us. Blessed be,'' Amethyst explained. ''She's in the meadow right now.''

''The meadow? At this time of night?''

''It's where we always dedicate ourselves,'' Amaryllis said, as if that were obvious. ''Because she's a solitary witch and not with a coven, she will dedicate herself alone.''

Chad frowned. ''I have to tell you something. I don't understand your religion and I'm pretty sure I never will. However, I have no problem with you believing it, since it seems to be harmless.''

'' 'And it harm none,' '' Amethyst supplied the words. ''Yes.''

''I love Rhiannon and I want to marry her. Will you object if I don't follow the family creed? Before you answer, I have to tell you that I intend to marry her with or without your blessing.''

The sisters laughed together. ''Of course we don't object. Why, Rhiannon's own father wasn't Wiccan. We loved him just as much as if he had been. You go straight to Rhiannon and tell her we give our blessings,'' Amaryllis said.

''Hurry now. You've been gone too long and she's worried about you,'' Amethyst added. ''Go. Take Shadow Dancer with you.''

''The cat? But why . . .''

''Just go.'' Amethyst was still laughing as she shut the door.

Chad stared at the door for a minute, then looked down at the cat, who was regarding him thoughtfully. ''Come on. Let's see if she will have me.'' He put the cat under one arm and headed around the house.

The path wasn't hard to find or to follow. A full moon was high in the sky and its silvery blue light made walking easy. The woods were hushed except for the occasional call of night birds and the rustle of creatures in the underbrush. Chad thought about what the aunts had said as he walked along. Rhiannon was dedicating herself that night. To his surprise, that didn't bother him in the least. There had always been something about Rhiannon that was out of the ordinary.

He saw her in the meadow and stopped to watch. Her face was filled with peace as she held a silver dagger up to the moonlight. Her lips were moving, but he couldn't hear the words. She had lit a fire in the stone circle, and it gave a golden glow to the scene that accentuated the blue of the moonlight. She wore a black dress that flowed about her, not touching her body anywhere except where the breeze molded it to her form. Although he couldn't see through it, he instinctively knew she was wearing nothing under it.

As he watched, she moved around the fire in a circle, pausing at four points to raise the athame high and murmur what he knew was a prayer. Then she bent to put out the fire.

Chad stepped into the moonlight and she turned to look at him, though he had made no noise at all. For a long moment they only gazed at each other. "Your aunts said you'd be here," he said at last.

She straightened. "Why are you here?"

"I had to see you."

Pain crossed her face. "I'm sorry, Chad. I must have inadvertently bewitched you again. I should never have said anything in front of that cat. If you don't want to be here, I release you."

"I'm not leaving. Not ever." He crossed the meadow and gave her the cat. "I don't understand, but that's okay. Your aunts said you're dedicating yourself tonight. I assume that means you'll become Wiccan?"

"I already have. I just finished." She raised her chin. "It's what I've always been, really. Most of my family are Wiccan. I've always been happiest when I follow their ways. I've decided to stay here at Hallowmoon and learn from my aunts.''

"Good.''

"Good?'' she asked warily.

"I love you, Rhiannon. I've had time to do a lot of thinking while I was stuck in New Orleans.''

"You were in New Orleans?''

"I'll tell you all about it in a minute. The important thing is that I love you exactly as you are. I don't want to change you.''

"Are you sure? I know this is a great deal to accept.''

"I know, and I'll probably never choose that way for myself. Can you handle that?''

"Of course. I love you exactly as you are.''

"I'm beginning to think there's more to it than I previously thought. After all, things have happened that I can't explain. All I know is that I had to find you.''

"You couldn't have come at a better time.'' She looked up at the moon and smiled. "You can meet all my family at once.'' She laughed at the hesitation on his face. "Don't worry. They never eat lawyers alive.''

"Oh, I almost forgot. I brought you something.'' He reached into his coat pocket and brought out a small box. "I found this in New Orleans and I knew it was perfect for you.''

Rhiannon opened the box and caught her breath. Carefully, she took out a tiny crystal butterfly. Even in the moonlight its facets caught the light and glimmered. Her eyes met his and he saw wonder and love mixed in equal parts. "It's perfect,'' she murmured. "You don't know how perfect. Will you marry me, Chad? I love you so much!''

"You took the words right out of my mouth." He stepped closer and took her into his arms.

Back at the house, Amaryllis sat in front of her crystal ball and gazed into the depths.

"Well?" Amethyst prodded impatiently.

Amaryllis smiled up at her expectant audience. "It's all working out beautifully. He said yes!"

The cousins exchanged smiles, and several laughed in their pleasure at knowing Rhiannon would be happy. "What a perfect night for a proposal," one said.

"And on the night of her dedication," said another. "It couldn't be better. I can't wait to meet him."

Amaryllis picked up the crystal ball and the black velvet cloth it rested upon and put them carefully back on the curio shelf. "Act natural, everyone. We have to look surprised when they tell us."

"It won't be easy," Amethyst said, "You know how I am about sentimental things like this."

By the time Rhiannon and Chad entered the house, the entire family was chatting and laughing. Rhiannon knew by the expressions on several of the faces that her news wouldn't be all that unexpected. She smiled at her aunts and they looked like elderly children caught with the cookie jar. She took Chad's hand. "We have something to tell you. We're going to be married."

As her family swirled around her, Rhiannon felt completely loved and accepted. She kept her hand securely in Chad's and reveled in the affection. Both her decisions had been the right ones.

Epilogue

"How was work today?" Rhiannon asked as Chad took off his coat and loosened his tie.

"Great. Now that I'm a partner in the firm and we have a young associate, we can work him to death instead of me." He pulled her to him and kissed her. "How did it go here?"

"Fine." She turned to hide her smile. "I was sick again this morning after you left."

"You were?" At once his voice was full of concern. "You're never sick. We've been married over a year and I've never known you to have so much as a cold. I think you should see the doctor."

"Actually, I did. I went this afternoon."

Chad tossed his coat and tie aside. Shadow Dancer curled in the middle of the coat and sat watching them. Chad put his arms around Rhiannon. "Well? What did he say? Is something wrong?"

"No," she said with a laugh. "I'm perfectly all right. That's why I didn't tell you about my appointment. I knew you'd worry all day. He said I'm perfectly healthy and that the baby will be beautiful."

For a moment Chad only looked at her. Then her words sunk in. "A baby?" he exclaimed as a big smile lit his face. "You're sure? The doctor is positive?"

She nodded, unable to contain her happiness any longer. "I'm due around the spring equinox. Mid-March," she added.

"Is it a boy or a girl?" Chad asked. "No, that's silly. You can't know that yet. Do you know?"

She laughed. "I have no idea. I don't care which it is as long as it looks like you."

"No, I want all our children to look like you. A baby! That's great! Do your aunts know?"

"Of course not. I wanted you to be the first to hear the news. You don't know how many times this afternoon I almost drove to your office just so I could tell you." She hugged him exuberantly.

"I'll paint the back bedroom for a nursery. We can start this weekend." He whirled her around. "We're going to have a baby!"

The doorbell caught them in a kiss. "Who can that be?" he asked as he straightened.

"I'm not expecting anyone." Rhiannon went to the door and opened it. Her aunts trotted into the room, smiling and nodding to them both.

"We're so happy for you," Amaryllis said as she handed Rhiannon a quart jar filled with an amber liquid. "This is the tea I gave your mother when we learned she was expecting you. Be sure and drink it every morning and you won't be sick anymore."

Amethyst went to Chad and patted his arm, as if she were particularly proud of him for his accomplishment. "She and the baby are going to be just fine. Don't you worry a single minute. All the women in our family have babies easily."

"I'm not worried. What's in the tea?" He was eyeing it suspiciously. "I don't know if Rhiannon should be drinking it."

"It's just an herbal concoction." Amaryllis smiled at him as if she thought it was cute of him to be concerned. "All it will do is sooth her nausea."

"The baby will be beautiful!" Amethyst said enthusiastically. "Simply beautiful!"

"And talented," Amaryllis put in. "She's going to be so much like you, Rhiannon. It will be just like having you as a baby again. Sister, remember how precocious Rhiannon was? She was the smartest baby I've ever seen!"

Chad smiled at the three women. "You seem pretty sure it will be a girl. Maybe it's a boy."

"Oh, no, dear," Amethyst said confidently. "It's a girl for certain."

"We think you should name her Brigid after our great-grandmother." To Chad she said, "She's practically a legend in our family."

"We want to name our own baby," he said firmly.

"I know," Rhiannon said as she went to him, "but do you like the name Brigid?"

"I like it very much, but that's not the point."

Rhiannon put her arms around his waist and smiled at her aunts. "We want to name her ourselves, but we'll keep that name in mind." She winked at them and her smile broadened. She had always been fond of that name, too.

Amaryllis winked back as Amethyst did the same. "We understand, dear. You should name the baby whatever you see fit."

"We'll be going now," Amethyst said as they moved toward the door. "You'll be out to Hallowmoon for supper tomorrow, won't you? Cousin Daisy and Cousin Milly are coming down from Shreveport."

"I remember. We'll be there."

Rhiannon saw her aunts out and shut the door. "Now, Chad, they mean well."

"I thought you said you didn't tell them about the baby."

"I didn't. Aunt Amaryllis must have been using her crystal ball again. They've probably known for days."

"We're going to name our own baby," he cautioned her. "I saw that wink."

"Certainly we are. But I really do like Brigid. Don't you?"

He frowned and shoved his hands into his pockets. "Yes, but I want us to name our own baby."

"We have plenty of time to think about a name."

"And it could be a boy."

She put her arms around him. "Of course it could. Or the next one could be."

He sighed, but he was smiling. "I don't know if I'll ever get used to your family. If I didn't love them so well, they would drive me crazy."

"I know," she said placatingly.

He put his arms around her. "A little girl. I've always wanted a little girl."

"A little girl with a great big Gift." Rhiannon rested

her head on his chest. ''My aunts aren't the only ones who have intuition. I think your life is going to be very interesting in a few years.''

Chad groaned, but he was smiling happily.

Shadow Dancer jumped off the couch to weave around their legs. He was looking particularly smug.

Three captivating stories of love in another time, another place.

MADELINE BAKER
"Heart of the Hunter"

A Lakota warrior must defy the boundaries of life itself to claim the spirited beauty he has sought through time.

ANNE AVERY
"Dream Seeker"

On faraway planets, a pilot and a dreamer learn that passion can bridge the heavens, no matter how vast the distance from one heart to another.

KATHLEEN MORGAN
"The Last Gatekeeper"

To save her world, a dazzling temptress must use her powers of enchantment to open a stellar portal—and the heart of a virile but reluctant warrior.

___51974-7 *Enchanted Crossings* (three unforgettable love stories in one volume) $4.99 US/ $5.99 CAN

Surrender to the fantasy...

Indulge yourself in these sensual love stories written by four of today's hottest romance authors!

CONNIE BENNETT, "Masquerade": When shy, unassuming Charlotte Nolan wins a masquerade cruise, she has no idea that looks can be so deceiving—or that her wildest romantic fantasies are about to come true.

THEA DEVINE, "Admit Desire": Nick's brother is getting married—to the woman who left him at the altar two years before. And when Nick sees them together, he realizes he wants Francesca more than ever. But little does he know that she, too, will do anything to have him in her life again.

EVELYN ROGERS, "The Gold Digger": Susan Ballinger is determined to marry for money. She doesn't believe in love at first sight—until she meets Sonny, a golden boy who takes her to soaring heights of pleasure—and gives her so much more in the bargain.

OLIVIA RUPPRECHT, "A Quiver of Sighs": Valerie Smith is a lonely writer with an active imagination. But she's missing one thing: experience. Then she meets Jake Larson, a handsome editor who takes her writing—and her body—to places beyond her wildest dreams.

___4289-4 $5.50 US/$6.50 CAN

Dorchester Publishing Co., Inc.
P.O. Box 6640
Wayne, PA 19087-8640

Please add $1.75 for shipping and handling for the first book and $.50 for each book thereafter. NY, NYC, and PA residents, please add appropriate sales tax. No cash, stamps, or C.O.D.s. All orders shipped within 6 weeks via postal service book rate. Canadian orders require $2.00 extra postage and must be paid in U.S. dollars through a U.S. banking facility.

Name_____
Address_____
City_____State_____Zip_____
I have enclosed $_____ in payment for the checked book(s).
Payment <u>must</u> accompany all orders. ❏ Please send a free catalog.